ACCUSED

Ehron Lee attempted a smile, but Abigail's expression
was cold and rigid. He was familiar with her odd
moods, but this was a look that registered pure
contempt.

"Murderer," she said, her voice barely a whisper
though heavy with intent.

Then her pitch rose as she spewed venom.

"Low-down filthy murderer! You never was no good,
Ehron Lee Burrows. I saw it right from the start. You
fooled everyone else but you could never fool me . . ."

Ehron Lee recoiled at the accusation. He tried to
speak. "Abigail, what are you say—"

She didn't let him finish. "I know the truth. You
enjoyed killin', gettin' blood on your hands. The war
was good for yuh, Ehron Lee, wasn't it? 'Cause it made
yuh what you really are: a killer and a criminal."

BLACK RANSOM

STONE WALLACE

BERKLEY BOOKS, NEW YORK

THE BERKLEY PUBLISHING GROUP
Published by the Penguin Group
Penguin Group (USA)
375 Hudson Street, New York, New York 10014

USA • Canada • UK • Ireland • Australia • New Zealand • India • South Africa • China

penguin.com

A Penguin Random House Company

BLACK RANSOM

A Berkley Book / published by arrangement with the author

Copyright © 2014 by Stone Wallace.

For information, address: The Berkley Publishing Group,
a division of Penguin Group (USA) LLC,
375 Hudson Street, New York, New York 10014.

ISBN: 978-0-425-26534-5

PUBLISHING HISTORY
Berkley mass-market edition / January 2014

PRINTED IN THE UNITED STATES OF AMERICA

10 9 8 7 6 5 4 3 2 1

Cover illustration by Robert Hunt © James Daniels/Shutterstock.
Cover design by Diane Kolsky.
Interior text design by Kelly Lipovich.

For my agent Louise Fury:
With admiration, respect, and my deepest gratitude.
So glad to have you in my corner!

PROLOGUE

THE SIMPLE DEMAND of the note, scrawled almost illegibly on a scrap of paper, could well have been written in blood:

A life for a life

And once the pounding in his chest settled and his head cleared sufficiently, he understood the meaning of the message. He didn't know who had sent it, for in his line of work there were many who could be responsible. It was understood that many men hated him, and many felt they owed him a debt. He might never discover this person's identity, but that was not as important to him as the five words scribbled in black ink on the paper.

For what the note presented him was a bargain. If the demand was ignored, it promised to be at a bitter cost.

A life was at stake. An innocent life—one dear to him, though he realized now, with shame and regret, that he had never before really considered her in that regard.

And likely, she looked upon him much the same. They

had been little more than strangers to each other for so many years. He was the one to blame, not her. How could she be responsible? He was the one who through indifference and deliberate neglect had put the distance between them.

Yet now her life depended on his making a decision too terrible to contemplate.

Sitting next to the glass-shaded table lamp, where the soft yellow glow provided the only light in the darkened parlor, he found himself unable to release the note from his grip; he was clinging to it with a strange desperation—lowering the paper in his unsteady fingers, then drawing it back to his eyes, repeatedly, vainly trying to search out more.

A clue that was not there.

A trace of hope that was not offered.

Finally he sat back in his chair, exhaled a rattled breath, and fumbled for the snifter of brandy that rested next to him on the table, beside the ornate decanter from which it had been poured. Overwhelmed with despair and crippled by a feeling of hopelessness, he unconsciously clenched his fist, slowly crumpling the note. This reflexive gesture startled him, and he hurried to unfold the wrinkled paper, in his haste spilling his drink onto his lap.

He sat up with a start, oblivious to his action, conscious only of the result, the warm wetness that pooled at his crotch and streamed down his left thigh. His narrow face tightened with a suppressed rage, though not directed at the spilled drink. He was filled with a mixture of emotions: anger, stress, worry, dread. None of which he could seem to control.

And in a sudden, impulsive move, he gave vent by tossing the empty snifter into the stone fireplace set against the far wall, listening with grim satisfaction as it shattered into dozens of tiny shards.

For a man who prided himself on possessing a calm and reasonable temperament, this was an uncharacteristic aggression. But perhaps it was necessary as it provided a brief release from the tension that consumed him, the myriad of emotions that had coalesced into a whole.

A release . . . but it relieved neither his anxiety . . . nor his guilt.

Guilt? How often he had passed judgment on those so pronounced. And now he was the accused. A judgment and sentence had been thrust upon him.

Worse from his standpoint was the sudden eruption of tears that now clouded his eyes; another emotion far removed from his character as he had disciplined himself to remain impassive in all situations, under all circumstances.

He was distracted from his thoughts when he became aware of a slow shuffle of footsteps from the next room. Descending . . .

The shattering glass had awakened his wife. He listened as she walked down the stairs, her steps slow and labored. She'd been ill; her heart was weak. Because of this, he hadn't told her about the note and its demand. Fearing the consequences, he could *not* tell her the truth.

Yet soon, inevitably, she would know. One way or another, the reality of the situation would reach her.

In a day, perhaps a week if the intention was to prolong his uncertainty or the girl's fate, another message would be delivered, how and by whom he would not know. But surely it would come, this time detailing what he was expected to do . . . where the "ransom" was to be paid.

And then—he would have to decide which course to take. The note made it clear: He had just the two choices.

A life for a life

If he wanted to save the girl, his daughter, from death . . . he would have to exchange his life for hers.

Unbeknownst to one, a note had been sent to another, though days earlier and some miles away. This message had been more bluntly delivered, found early one morning knifed to the door of his house. The wording, the terrible demand, was the same:

A life for a life

He, too, was a man who had made many enemies through his professional duties. Again, there could be any number of suspects.

The recipient of this paper responded with a somewhat different attitude. He likewise felt the fear and apprehension at the wording's intent, but because of who he was, the station of authority he held, he was also indignant at the threat, which he regarded as a blatant contempt for a position that demanded respect.

A respect he believed he had earned through uncompromising conduct and a strict adherence to his duty.

He stared at the simple wording with creased eyes, and then he crumpled the note and tossed it aside, cursing under his breath. He went over to the cabinet, opened a bottle of whiskey, and drank several straight mouthfuls. He felt the liquor trickle down the side of his chin and wiped it away with an angry flourish. He was a man given to action and reaction. Not one to necessarily choose what might be the wiser course. Not even when the life of someone dear to him was threatened.

There was no need to make a difficult decision where he was concerned.

He had a suspicion of who might be responsible. In fact, the more he thought about it, the more certain he became.

He could use that knowledge to his advantage, and by that means, he would have an edge in freeing his wife from her abductor.

He was prepared to do whatever must be done.

But he would not give in to the demand.

Two identical notes were delivered because two men shared a connection.

Neither had yet to recognize that their "bond," the key to this mystery, had begun five years earlier . . .

ONE

IT HAD BEEN a long but satisfying trip, and as Ehron Lee Burrows prepared to bed down for the night next to the warmth of the campfire built in a rock-settled clearing near the gently flowing currents of a creek, he felt relaxed and ready for shut-eye. But sleep didn't come as easy as he had hoped and he figured, rightly, that it was due to anticipation. He was impatient to get back to his wife, Melinda, and share with her the good news. Yet eager as he was, he realized that he had to try and get some rest if he planned to wake at sunup to complete the last leg of the four-day ride back to his sister-in-law's house, where he and his wife, with child, had been staying.

Ehron Lee once more tried to get comfortable. He shifted in his bedroll and turned onto his side . . . when the soft rhythm of snoring he was hearing suddenly erupted into a deep, rumbling snort, emanating from his traveling companion, his brother-in-law, Winston Maguire. At first irritated by the intrusion, Ehron Lee couldn't help but shake his head and smile as he watched Winston's mouth twitch as if in involuntary acknowledgment of the sound. Ehron

Lee had appreciated having him come along—both to have someone to talk to during the long ride and also to help assess the value of the property he had planned to purchase, as a present for his wife.

Times hadn't been easy for the couple. When they married, Melinda was just a girl of seventeen. Sheltered and somewhat naïve, but pretty and possessed of a gentle sweetness, she was someone with whom Ehron Lee fell deeply in love. Hardly had they begun their life together when Ehron Lee was called up to fight in the War Between the States, serving in the Union army. After the war ended, Ehron Lee, who had fought with distinction and through many brave battlefield actions had attained the rank of lieutenant, returned home only to find that his family's fortunes had been tragically lost. It had always been Ehron Lee's intention to work and build on his father's property in Kansas, providing a fine and stable home for Melinda and the children they hoped to be blessed with. But trekking back to Lawrence after the Confederates had suffered a bloody defeat at Sayler's Creek Ehron Lee was devastated to discover that bloodshed had also erupted two years previously in his hometown. Properties vast and small had been pillaged; menfolk and even children mercilessly killed and women violated. Ehron Lee learned that among these casualties, his father's estate had been looted, burned, and reduced to rubble by the butchering guerrilla force under the command of Colonel William Clarke Quantrill. Miraculously, Ehron Lee's father hadn't been killed, though many of the men who worked for him and who rushed to defend the property had been slaughtered. Perhaps those who died were the fortunate ones. The horror of what had transpired during those morning hours proved too much for Ehron Lee's gentle father, who promptly suffered a paralyzing stroke and would be forced to live out his years in a state of absolute incomprehension in a hospital for the insane.

If Ehron Lee was grateful for one thing, it was that Melinda had not been present at the time of the raid. Although she had briefly stayed with Ehron Lee's father after her husband went off to fight, she eventually acceded to the demand of her sister that she come live with her and her husband at their small-acreage farm in the southern Arizona town of Brackett.

And it was there that Ehron Lee, too, found himself following his horrible discovery. While Ehron Lee got along well with Winston and less well but cordially with his sister-in-law, Abigail, he was a proud man and yearned to provide Melinda with a house of their own. For the year that he lived with his in-laws, he not only helped out with labor around the farm but also worked hard at a variety of jobs to earn enough money to build a stake with which he could purchase property and build a home for Melinda and the baby she was soon to deliver.

His in-laws were basically good folk, but after a while Ehron Lee had discovered qualities in the pair not entirely to his liking. His sister-in-law had a tendency to moodiness, frequently shifting into periods of sullen behavior while Winston was an indolent sort with a fondness for a bit too much corn whiskey—though it never made him contentious; in fact, he became relaxed and good-natured, as otherwise he had a somewhat nervous disposition. But it was an environment in which Ehron Lee did not particularly favor to raise his child. Between these peculiarities and his determined desire not to further wear out their welcome, Ehron Lee decided it was time for him and Melinda to move on.

Luck smiled upon him when he learned of good acreage going for sale at a price he could just afford. The land even included a small ramshackle house. That was when he and Winston rode out together to meet the seller and survey the property. Both Ehron Lee and Winston, who was normally a wary man, were impressed with the fellow and took him to be an honest sort. It was evident that the land would need some work and the house itself required extensive repairs— extra rooms would have to be added since the seller had lived there alone and had no need to expand—but overall it looked good at the cost. And, better from Ehron Lee's standpoint, the soil looked adequate for planting and the crops sure to grow from the field would not only feed his family but should also put a little welcome money in his pocket.

By now brimming with excitement as he once more reviewed the successful outcome of their trip, relishing their good fortune, Ehron Lee was wide awake as he lay by the campfire, hands clasped behind his head, smiling broadly as he stared up into the night. He couldn't wait to tell Melinda about the deal he had made. Prudently, he hadn't told her the true reason for this trip, merely explaining that he and Winston were off to spend a little "man" time together. As with most women, Melinda would express a hesitancy to have her husband invest the money he had worked so hard for in uncertain property, even though Ehron Lee had reminded her many times that with a child on the way and, God willing, more to follow, they had to build their own life and not rely on the generosity of her family.

While he experienced a twinge of guilt about withholding this transaction from her, he felt certain that Melinda would not be unhappy with his purchase.

He was shaken from his pleasant thoughts by another of brother-in-law Winston's shattering snorts. When Ehron Lee turned to look at him, he noticed that Winston had wakened himself with the sound he had just expelled.

Winston took a moment to focus and to collect his thoughts.

"You heard that?" he said, acting surprised.

Ehron Lee nodded and smiled. "As did half the territory, I reckon."

"What're you doin' still awake?" Winston groggily asked his companion as he scratched his fingers through his mop of curly blond hair.

"Can't sleep," Ehron Lee replied with a sigh.

Winston was a heavy man, well over two hundred pounds, the layers of fat resulting partly from an improper diet but mainly owing to his excessive alcohol intake, both of which contributed to health concerns. He propped himself up on an elbow.

"After ridin' for most of the day, you can't sleep?" he

said. "Woulda figgered you'd be plumb tuckered out." He emitted an exaggerated yawn. "I sure as hell am."

"Yeah," Ehron Lee said. "Tired enough, but I got too many things rushin' through my head."

Winston smiled and maneuvered his ample bulk into a sitting position. "Yeah, well . . . guess I can 'preciate that. Thinkin' 'bout your purchase, I reckon?"

Ehron Lee nodded.

"Mighty fine little piece of property you got yourself," Winston said. "Sure to make Melinda happy."

Ehron Lee gave an absent nod. "That's what I'm hopin'." His mood suddenly became restless. "Hell, shoulda rode straight through. Coulda been back in time for breakfast."

"Early supper'll have to do," Winston said calmly with a grin.

Ehron Lee relaxed and smiled self-consciously. "Reckon I'm too anxious."

"Reckon," Winston agreed.

Winston then heaved a sigh, pulled himself with some effort from his bedroll, and lumbered over to his horse. He reached inside his saddlebag and pulled out what looked to Ehron Lee to be a small bottle. Familiar with his brother-in-law's habits, Ehron Lee didn't have to guess its contents.

"You're gonna need some shut-eye with the ride we got ahead of us, and I got just the thing," Winston said as he sat next to Ehron Lee, settling himself against a large rock. "A coupla slugs of this here corn whiskey and yuh'll feel right sleepy in no time."

Though not normally a drinking man, Ehron Lee sat up, accepted the bottle, and pulled a good swallow. He grimaced at the burning taste and handed it back over to Winston. Winston lifted the bottle in a salute and guzzled back twice as much as Ehron Lee had, though his own reaction was a satisfied exhale of breath.

"Good for what ails yuh," Winston remarked expansively as he started to pass the bottle back toward Ehron Lee, who declined with a shake of his head.

It didn't take long for Ehron Lee to feel the relaxing effects of the whiskey. Although he doubted that it would aid his sleep, it did make him less anxious.

The liquor also helped to protect his his body against the chill of the night, providing a comforting warmth. Gazing up into a vast sky filled with stars, smudges of shadowy, purple-edged clouds, and a large, low September moon and listening to the soothing sounds of the water as it coursed through the creek, Ehron Lee grew strangely reflective, which generally was not his nature as he was a taciturn man rarely given to expressing his innermost thoughts. But suddenly he was in the mood to talk, to share what he was feeling with his brother-in-law.

"Strange how things turn out," he began, at first speaking as if to himself.

Winston looked at him, the expression on his jowly, red-blotched face uncomprehending.

"Strange?" he echoed as he withdrew a half-smoked cigar from his breast pocket and struck a match against the edge of a rock to light it. "How d'yuh mean?"

Ehron Lee's gaze continued to reach far off into the night. All was still and quiet except for the crackling of the camp-fire and the flow of the creek.

"Just got to thinkin' 'bout the war," he said, his voice mellow and introspective. "Rememberin' back to the fightin'. Things that I saw. Men dyin' all around me, and me never knowin' day to day if I might be next. Most of the time doubtin' if . . . if I'd ever get back to Melinda. Yeah, sometimes thinkin' that way—'specially on those long nights 'fore we'd be goin' into battle, when everyone was quiet with their own thoughts, I'd write notes I prayed would never have to be delivered to her . . . Havin' those doubts gnawin' away at me . . . more times than not, I was sure I'd go crazy. Saw enough men that did." He paused, and then he lightened a bit. "Guess what I'm sayin' is, back then I never coulda believed things woulda worked out like they have."

"You earned some good comin' to yuh," Winston said as he puffed on his cigar.

Winston spoke those words with sincerity, appreciating Ehron Lee's need to express his thoughts. His brother-in-law had never really spoken about the war after he'd returned and moved in with him and Abigail, certainly had never discussed specific events. He'd also never talked about finding his home in ruins and the tragedy that had befallen his father. Winston understood and, out of respect, never badgered him with questions, like some folks were apt to do. But he wasn't ignorant of the horrors Ehron Lee and others like him had experienced. News was reported daily and Winston kept abreast of it all, though he tried his damndest to keep the discouraging updates from Melinda, especially the reports where the Union army suffered a defeat on the battlefield, experiencing heavy casualties—perhaps Ehron Lee among them.

Owing to his poor health and obesity, Winston was exempt from military duty, and because of that, he figured Ehron Lee would never expect someone who had not participated in the war to understand what he had been through, which likely was the reason he'd never said much. That . . . and more understandably not wanting to upset his wife with tragic tales of having to kill men and the times when he himself had come close to death. Those were experiences Ehron Lee elected to keep to himself.

Winston was correct in his assumption. There were many things about the war that Ehron Lee didn't want to discuss— or that he even wanted to remember. But he knew those memories would never abandon him. The still-vivid details often haunted his dreams, pulling him from sleep in a cold sweat, a silent scream lodged in his throat. There were the faces of the men and especially the boys he'd been forced to kill on the battlefield. Faces that once had been defined by individual features but now over time seemed almost to blend into a whole. The horrified and pleading expressions of his own mortally wounded comrades, those for whom he could do no more than try to provide comfort in their last agonizing moments of life. The helpless screams that came both from their injuries and the realization that they were dying. Nor could he forget those times when he was forced to assist in battlefield surgery: extracting bullets and even helping with the crude amputation of limbs while under heavy fire.

How could any man erase such images from his thoughts? While he tried to forget, he understood they would be stamped on his brain until the day he died.

He didn't fear death, and neither did he fear the prospect of hell. To his mind, he'd already been there.

The one truth, the one fact that Ehron Lee could never deny, was that the war had forever changed him. He was thankful that he hadn't become bitter or mean-mad like other soldiers he had served beside, those who could not reconcile defeat after all they had suffered and whose disillusionment had followed them into civilian life. But where once Ehron Lee had been a God-fearing pacifist, he now became determined to fight to hold on to what was his. He didn't resent this change in attitude. Indeed he embraced it as necessary to properly care and provide for his family in a country still rebuilding after four years of strife.

Winston took another swallow from the bottle of whiskey and once more handed it over to Ehron Lee, who considered before accepting the bottle and taking a short drink. Again he wore a sour face as the liquor burned a trail down his throat.

"You know what else I used to ponder?" Ehron Lee went on, wiping whiskey residue from his lips. "I wondered if Melinda would even be waitin' for me if I got back. Though she ain't never said so, hadda be hard on her, not knowin' any more'n I did. Each day maybe waitin' to hear if . . ." His voice drifted off and he sat quietly for a moment.

Winston puffed patiently on his cigar.

"Wondered a lot about that," Ehron Lee resumed with a deep sigh. "Girl so young, just married, facin' the prospect of bein' alone. A widow. Or maybe seein' me comin' back half a man. That's why when I came home and saw that she was the same gal I'd left behind . . . that nothin' had changed, I made myself a promise that, no matter what, I was gonna build a good life for her."

Winston said, "Well, Ehron Lee, I've knowed Melinda longer'n you . . . and I can tell yuh, you have given her a fine life. She's as happy as I ever seen her."

Ehron Lee appreciated hearing Winston tell him that, and he responded by giving his brother-in-law an affectionate clap on the shoulder. At the same time his introspective mood lifted. He'd spoken his thoughts and felt better for it. He folded his arms behind his neck, leaned back against the graying stump of a dead tree, and suddenly looked to Winston as contented as he had ever seen him.

"Yep, she's a right fine gal, Ehron Lee," Winston acknowledged. He was finished with his cigar and flicked it into the campfire.

Ehron Lee breathed out, smiled, and nodded.

"Can see yuh someday buildin' a nice ranch on that land," Winston rhapsodized. "Maybe raisin' some cattle . . ."

Ehron Lee gave his head a slow but deliberate shake. "Ain't thinkin' *that* ambitious, Winston," he replied. "Just a nice quiet farm to work on."

Winston regarded his brother-in-law with a puzzled expression before he said, "Can't rightly picture you makin' a career outta bein' a sodbuster."

Ehron Lee smiled at him. "And I can't think of any life more appealin'. Reckon I got you to thank for that."

Winston gave him a questioning look.

"Gettin' me to do most of the chores 'round the farm, yuh lazy bastard," Ehron Lee clarified with a teasing half grin. "Found I kinda took to workin' on the land."

Winston didn't take offense at the remark. He knew it to be true. He considered for a moment, shrugged to himself, then raised the bottle in another salute and drank what was left. He threw the bottle off into the darkness. They both heard it land with a soft thump somewhere in the distance.

The campfire was burning low. Ehron Lee rose and scooped up some of the dry deadwood they'd been picking up along the trail. He stepped over to the fire, lowered to his haunches, and slowly and methodically tossed the pieces of wood into the flames, watching as the fire sparked and popped, and feeling the caressing warmth against his face.

Walking back over to Winston, Ehron Lee sighed as he massaged the back of his wrist over his growth of beard. "First thing I'm gonna do when I get back is shave off these whiskers . . . then settle myself in a long bath."

"A bath!" Winston exclaimed, as he was a man not particularly concerned about his own cleanliness. "Yuh talk like you been away a month."

"Feels like it," Ehron Lee said, his thoughts focused on how much he missed his wife.

"Well, I'll tell yuh," Winston said. "You think 'bout your bath and I'll content myself with the fine meal the gals'll have prepared for us." He rolled his hand over his massive belly in anticipation.

"S'pose you've been thinkin' of nothin' else?" Ehron Lee teased him.

"You suppose right," Winston admitted freely.

Ehron Lee said, "Well, what say I help yuh get your mind off your appetite? How 'bout some music?"

Winston was a simple man not possessed of many abilities. But he did have one talent—he could play the mouth organ—and it was a skill appreciated by Ehron Lee.

"Sure," Winston agreed. He reached into his breast pocket and withdrew the instrument. "Anythin' particular?"

Ehron Lee's mouth curved in a slow smile and he gave him a wink. "Think you know."

Winston nodded and he readied his lips with some puckering and then blew out the chords of a gentle harmony. Ehron Lee instantly recognized the tune: "Barbara Allen," a particular favorite of his and Melinda's. The song they had danced to at their wedding. Hearing the song now, he felt momentarily wistful but, in a way, that much nearer to his wife.

He gently sang the opening lyrics: "In Scarlet Town, where I was born, there was a fair maid dwellin', made every youth cry well-a-day, her name was Barbara Allen." He softly hummed along with the rest of the song while his thoughts took him back to a specific time not so very long ago . . .

He recalled the day when he was working alone in the field, enjoying the warmth of the midafternoon summer sunshine and even the clean, honest sweat from his labor. Melinda had joined Winston and Abigail when they rode into town to pick up some groceries and a few supplies from the mercantile. Ehron Lee remembered there was something else, too: a strange little mystery that Melinda had been trying to keep secret from him. A surprise she promised to reveal once she came back from town. In the days before, he'd occasionally catch her throwing him a sly, sideways glance and then quickly turning away when he met her eye. He suspected Winston and Abigail had been let in on her secret but likewise were close-mouthed.

He had almost finished his work that afternoon, leading the mule-drawn plow across the small stretch of soil, when he heard a familiar call, traveling at him on the still prairie air. He hastened to turn at the sound.

She came running through the field toward him, excitedly calling his name, arms outstretched in anticipation of an embrace. The moment would always stay with Ehron Lee, for framed forever in time was the vision of Melinda rushing through the tall grass and between the cottonwoods that bordered the field—her long honey-colored hair tied in a ribbon but flowing out behind her as she ran, fair-complexioned skin, the soft pink rosiness of her cheeks, sensitive puckered lips, and cornflower blue eyes so bright and lively he swore he could see them clearly from where he stood.

Ehron Lee's heart beat a little faster, as it always seemed to do when he was in her presence. He dropped the reins, drew a breath, and started toward her, whipping off the battered old hat he was wearing and wiping the perspiration from his brow with the back of his hand.

When Melinda reached him, she threw her arms around his shoulders, embracing him tightly while she kissed him full on the mouth. Ehron Lee immediately responded by encircling her petite waist with his strong arms. He just barely repressed himself from expressing his foremost thought: *My God, you're beautiful.*

"Can't say I disapprove of the greeting," he said once their lips parted. "But that's some hello, considerin' you've only been gone for a coupla hours."

Melinda gazed up at him, her eyes smiling as brightly as the curvature on her lips. Still, it took a while for her to speak what was on her mind. What she seemed so excited about. Ehron Lee was patient, though inwardly he was bursting at the seams to hear what she had to say.

Finally she said, "I been wantin' to tell you for the longest time but just hadda be sure."

Now Ehron Lee looked a little perplexed. A bit concerned, in fact.

Melinda inhaled a deep breath that she released with emphasis.

"Went to see the doctor," she said. "He told me . . . well, he said it ain't just gonna be the two of us much longer."

Ehron Lee felt momentarily numb as he wasn't sure he was hearing correctly. Maybe, he reckoned, he'd been out in the sun too long. His expression went comically blank. He began to wipe the palms of his hands against his jeans in an unconscious gesture.

Gradually what his wife was telling him began to sink in, though he was unsure of what to say.

He fumbled with his words and his hands made a vague gesture. "Why, you—you ain't even showin' yet. Shouldn't there be . . . I mean, shouldn't your belly . . ."

Melinda giggled at his awkwardness. "It's still early."

Ehron Lee coughed self-consciously. He felt a little foolish at his naïveté.

"Guess I ain't had much experience with babies and all," he tried to explain.

"Well, don't you worry none, *Daddy*," Melinda said as

she tenderly kissed his cheek. "You'll be gettin' plenty of practice."

"Reckon," was all Ehron Lee could manage.

But then, suddenly overwhelmed, he stepped back, planted his closed fists firmly against his hips, breathed out heavily, and exclaimed, "Damn, you're just too young to be a ma!"

Catching Melinda's quick look of surprise, he grinned at her reassuringly.

Relieved that he was just being playful, Melinda sighed as she gazed into her husband's eyes.

"Just tell me you're happy, Ehron Lee, that's all I want to hear," she urged sweetly.

Ehron Lee took his wife into his arms and pulled her close. "Happy? How could I feel otherwise?"

They kissed again, a lingering, passionate kiss that solidified the love between them and the love both would soon share with their child. Then, with their arms wrapped tightly around each other, Ehron Lee and Melinda walked through the gold-spilled sunshine across the field back toward the house, preparing for yet another new beginning in their life together . . .

Winston finished playing the song. He glanced over at his brother-in-law and saw him sitting with a faraway look on his face. Winston nodded knowingly and put the mouth organ back into his shirt pocket. Both men settled into silence, gazing up into the sky, each relaxing with his thoughts on this peaceful night. From somewhere off in the distance they heard a lone coyote bark.

There was a brief moment of unnatural stillness, followed by a sudden agitation of the two horses tethered near the edge of their camp—and then a quick rustling from somewhere in the surrounding brush. Before Ehron Lee or Winston could fully comprehend what was happening—or react to it—two men emerged from behind them, moving swiftly to either side of the pair. One was brandishing a Henry .44

rifle, the other an eight-gauge shotgun, both leveled in their direction.

Though Ehron Lee briefly considered the move, there was no point in attempting to reach for the holstered Colt revolver, which was lying close to where he was sitting. He would never have had a chance.

The two men who had come upon them were dirty and unshaven. Big men—muscular, not fat. Even without them brandishing weapons, their appearance suggested trouble. Both wore wide-brimmed Stetsons that shadowed much of their faces.

The man holding the Henry was dressed in dusty, well-worn buckskins, looking as if he'd spent several months roughing it in the wilderness. He was the first to speak.

"Whyn't yuh toss your gun belt over this way—slow and easy," he said.

Ehron Lee looked hard at the man, saw the intent in his eyes, and did as instructed, trying to keep the trembling from his fingers. He felt both apprehensive and angered.

"Where's yours?" Buckskins asked Winston.

Winston jerked his head over to where his horse was standing. His gun belt was slung over his saddle, next to his saddlebag.

Buckskins nodded. "That's fine. We can jus' leave it there."

"We don't want no trouble," Winston said in as steady a voice as he could manage.

"Don't plan to give yuh none—if'n you cooperate," Buckskins said as he flung Ehron Lee's gun belt over his shoulder. "Just wanta trade off our horses. Yeah, and those two of yours'll do jus' fine." He spoke to his companion. "Todd, bring our ponies 'round. I'll keep an eye on these . . . gentlemen."

The man named Todd chuckled from his throat then walked off until he was consumed whole in the darkness, though his heavy footfalls echoed behind him. Buckskins moved in to face both Ehron Lee and Winston.

"You got nothin' to worry 'bout," he said. "We're givin' yuh a fair exchange."

Neither Ehron Lee nor Winston spoke. Instead they looked at each other warily.

Soon Todd came back into the light of the campfire leading two unsaddled, though sturdy-looking bay stallions.

"Can't see nothin' wrong with your animals," Winston said weakly, not hiding his nervousness very well.

"Ain't," Buckskins agreed. "Jus' been ridin' 'em for a spell. Need some rest and waterin' . . . and we just ain't got the time."

Buckskins walked carefully over to where his partner was standing, all the while keeping his rifle trained on the two men.

"You fellas play it smart and stay put for a bit, huh?"

The two men untied then mounted the big sorrels belonging to Ehron Lee and Winston and prepared to ride off.

"Wait," Ehron Lee called. "What about our saddlebags?"

Buckskins wore a crooked grin. "Don't think so," he said, adding a mocking "Adios" before he whooped and whipped the horse into a run, followed by the same maneuver from his partner.

Ehron Lee and Winston slowly got to their feet, but it was too dark to watch where the men were riding. Not that it would have done them any good.

After a few moments Winston walked over to one of the bay stallions and patted its flank.

He exhaled a relieved sigh. "My rump ain't gonna 'preciate ridin' bareback, but least they didn't leave us stranded."

"Yeah. But you know they was up to no good."

"No doubt 'bout that," Winston said with a rock of his head. "But that ain't none of our concern—least for now. Once we get back to town, we can notify the law and let them try to figger it out."

"I'm for startin' back now," Ehron Lee said definitely. "Not much chance of us gettin' any shut-eye. And the quicker we report this, the less distance those two hombres will be able to make."

"S'pose so," Winston said, though his tone was hesitant. "'Course you know we'll be ridin' unarmed?"

Ehron Lee responded with a slight grin. "You think anything more can happen to us?"

Winston scratched the stubble under his flabby chin and said thoughtfully, "Maybe that's what I don't wanta find out."

They extinguished the fire and tied up their bedrolls. In about a half hour the two men had broken camp and were riding through the night with the brightness of the silver dollar moon to guide them. It was a clear, flat trail dotted with clusters of plant life indigenous to the region, but still it was unfamiliar territory so they rode at a cautious pace. Both wore heavy ponchos that they'd brought along in anticipation of the cold autumn nights. In place of the saddles that had been taken along with their horses, the men resorted to compromise and sat atop folded blankets, which they'd tossed over the stallions' coarse backs. Even though Winston was generously padded on the behind, the ride was uncomfortable for both men.

The animals rode well, smooth and easy, giving further rise to their curiosity over the "trade." But the truth was, both Ehron Lee and Winston suspected the answer, and while neither man spoke it, they had little doubt the mounts they were riding had been stolen.

To break the uncomfortable silence that came from this realization, Winston said to his companion, "How much money did yuh have in your saddlebag?"

"'Bout twenty dollars. You?"

Winston grinned. "I just came along for the ride. Kept my cash at home."

"What about liquor?" Ehron Lee asked with a smirk.

"You could use a snort?"

"Just askin'."

"Reckon I was thinkin' ahead," Winston chortled. "What I had was what we drunk."

"Yeah, sure got lucky there," Ehron Lee remarked sardonically.

It was as dawn was approaching, announcing the start of the new day with a bronze glow peeking then steadily rising on the horizon, cresting the distant mountain peaks and splashing the first rays of sunshine over the eastern landscape, that the two men noticed what appeared to be shadowed riders cresting a hill—and after holding their position for only few moments, beginning a slow but steady advance toward them.

"See 'em?" Ehron Lee asked cautiously.

Winston lifted the brim of his straw hat. He raised a hand to his brow and squinted against the brightness of the breaking dawn.

"Uh-huh. Looks to be 'bout eight or ten of 'em."

"Injuns?"

"Can't tell. Don't think so. But ridin' our way for sure."

"Let's hope they'll just ride on past."

Winston straightened himself on the horse. He patted his extended belly. "Mebbe. But I don't like what my gut is tellin' me."

The group of riders continued forward, not veering off as the two men had hoped. Luckily they weren't hostile Apaches, known to ride this territory, though ongoing military maneuvers had pretty much kept their aggressions at bay, but cowboys, though they didn't look any too friendly either. Once they got near enough, part of the group separated into two columns and formed a loose half circle around Ehron Lee and Winston. The lead riders held their positions in front and, with their revolvers drawn but not aimed, gestured for the two men to halt their horses.

They had no choice but to obey, and they reined in their mounts, coming to a smooth stop, though Winston's stallion seemed anxious and stamped its foreleg against the ground.

Even though he was uncertain at the intrusion, Ehron

Lee tried to speak confidently. "Mornin'. Anything we can do for you fellas?" he said.

"Supposin' you let us ask the questions," came the curt reply.

Both men immediately took note that no one in this group appeared to be wearing a badge. If they weren't lawmen, had they lucked into another run-in with a bunch of desperados?

"Name's Bert Stradd and these here are my boys," the man who was obviously in charge said. Ehron Lee couldn't help recognizing that both in appearance and authority, he, too, had likely been in the military.

With that, Stradd flipped open the side flap of his unbuttoned gray duster and revealed a tin star.

"Deputy sheriff, Cullen County," he said.

The knowledge that Bert Stradd was a lawman did little to lessen the pair's apprehension. With a group of men this large, this looked to be serious business.

Stradd's own gun wasn't drawn since he was well protected by his men. Instead his gloved hands rested easily on the pommel of his saddle.

He continued. "Some of these fellas work for Elmer Bryant; the rest of us are his friends. We're what you might call an unofficial posse."

"What's that got to do with us?" Ehron Lee asked casually, though with his brow furrowed.

"Those are Elmer's horses you're ridin'," Stradd said straightly. Then he spoke over his shoulder. "Ain't that so, Ed?"

A man who looked like an old wrangler returned, "Would recognize Mr. Bryant's stallions anywhere."

Stradd smiled an unfriendly smile. "Y'see, Ed here would know. He's been Elmer's ranch foreman for goin' on ten years. Knows Elmer's stock sure as the back of his hand."

"Sure do," Ed said in a drawl. "And Mr. Bryant's stallions ain't like none others bred in this county."

Winston spoke up. "Whoa, now hold on, mister. We know these horses is stolen. We got ours taken from us last night and got left with these two. Where they come from, we ain't got no idea."

Stradd's steely gaze shifted from Winston to Ehron Lee.

"That's the truth," Ehron Lee concurred. "We was campin' out on our way back from doin' some business when two fellas came up on us and said they wanted to trade their horses for ours. Since they were armed, we wasn't about to argue."

Stradd squinted suspiciously. "Business, huh?"

One of the riders cut in. "Business nothin'. These two look like a coupla saddle tramps to me." He punctuated his remark by spitting tobacco juice out the side of his mouth onto the ground.

"Was lookin' at buyin' some property," Ehron Lee said simply.

Stradd was silent though it was clear he was assimilating each word spoken, each gesture made by the pair.

"Which I did," Ehron Lee added.

"Notice neither of yuh is heeled," Stradd observed with a tilt of his head.

"Hardly," Ehron Lee said. "Grabbed our side arms along with our horses. As you can see, took our saddles, too."

Stradd kept his eyes on the pair for several moments, as if assessing them, and then he glanced over his shoulder at the men behind him. Their expressions were set and mean. They looked as though they were ready to pull out the ropes to string the two up.

Fortunately, the man called Bert Stradd looked to have some reason about him. He focused his attention back on Ehron Lee. "Bought some land, you say? And you're ridin' in from the west . . ."

"That's right," Ehron Lee said immediately. "And you're comin' from the east, where I assume this thievery took place. Well, let me ask yuh: Why'd we be comin' back in the direction of where you say we stole the horses from?"

Stradd's eyes narrowed and his words came strong, laced with a suggestion of offense at what was perceived as Ehron Lee's challenge.

"Remember, we're askin' the questions here," he said. "Anyhow, you tell me. All I know from where I'm sittin' is that those are Elmer Bryant's horses. And you're ridin' 'em. Ain't sayin' your story *might* not be true . . ." He paused and then exhaled a breath. "You got some proof of that land you say you bought?"

For an instant Ehron Lee looked hopeful . . . until he remembered.

"Bill of sale was in the saddlebag of my horse," he muttered.

One of the posse sputtered out a laugh that sounded more like a cackle. "Well, ain't that all-to-hell convenient."

Ehron Lee looked straight at the man and spoke with utter conviction. "We ain't lyin', mister."

"What 'bout the fella who sold you this land?" Stradd said. "Can he vouch for yuh?"

"Could. Can give you his name," Ehron Lee offered. "Albert Patterson. But first time we met him was at the farm, a deal set up through an acquaintance of his who heard I was lookin' to buy some property. *His* name was Mike somethin'. Can't recall. Didn't really matter at the time."

"Where could one find this Patterson?" Stradd asked.

Ehron Lee lowered his eyes and sighed heavily. "That was a coupla days ago. Said he was movin' on after the sale. Seemed to be in a hurry to close the deal. Didn't say where he was headed. Don't know how to reach him."

"As I said, ain't that just all-to-hell convenient."

Stradd said to his men, "Any of you ever hear of an Albert Patterson?"

There was a mumbling among the posse that indicated no one knew of him.

By now the sun had almost cleared the mountain-tipped horizon. The skies were clear, and as they reached across the pastoral vista, it promised to be a beautiful autumn day. Winston took note of this and was just hoping he'd be around to see the end of it. As it stood at the moment, things didn't look so good.

Bert Stradd confirmed Winston's uncertainty when he

gave his head a slow, almost regretful shake. He raised the brim of his Stetson over his brow and said, "Can't say you got me convinced. As for neither of you havin' weapons, well, that's a mite suspicious, too, ridin' unarmed in these parts."

"I told you, our guns were taken," Ehron Lee said, nearing exasperation.

"Some of the fellas who work for Elmer but who got there a little late said they never saw a gun pulled anyhow. The old man was jumped and just got beat pretty bad. By a big fella, they say." Stradd regarded Winston appraisingly. "You look like you're purty powerful."

Ehron Lee looked askance at his brother-in-law, who was starting to appear very nervous. That troubled Ehron Lee. These cowboys were eagerly waiting for *any* sign they could interpret as guilt.

Ehron Lee tried to smooth away the tension. "Sure, Winston here's a big man, but he ain't hardly got the energy to roll outta bed, much less beat someone. 'Sides, that ain't his nature."

Stradd said, "Wouldn't take much energy to beat Elmer. The man's old, not to mention sick and feeble. What's more, he's near blind. Yeah, even if Elmer came around, he could never say for sure who jumped him. Reckon that's a mite bit of good luck for yuh."

"Yeah, good luck if we was guilty, which we ain't," Ehron Lee declared.

Winston swallowed back the bile he felt rising sourly in his throat, and when he spoke, his voice sounded desperate.

"We ain't no horse thieves, mister, and we sure ain't beat up no old man," he protested. "Both of us got families. I—I got a wife. Ehron Lee here, his wife—"

One of the posse interrupted with a sneer, "Don't matter a good goddamn to me if'n you got families, wives . . . grandmothers. Lotsa your type do. Things have been rough since the war ended, and I seen a lot of decent folk go bad 'cause of the way things are. Don't know either of you and sure as hell can't see no reason why you two should be any different."

Ehron Lee was able to maintain a fair demeanor of calm, but it was getting increasingly difficult for Winston, whose nerves looked about to give.

"At least give us a chance to prove ourselves," Winston said, his voice high and nearly a shout. "That's only fair, ain't it?"

"And how d'yuh suggest we do that?" one of the posse said casually.

"Get after them real thieves," Winston blurted out. "They ain't got that much of a head start. They—they was headin' west, last we saw."

"Ain't much to ask," Ehron Lee added.

Stradd said, "Or you could be tryin' to stall us. Send us off on a wild-goose chase while you two conveniently head off yonder. Don't think so. As I told yuh, we're all friends of Elmer, and as it looks now, there's a good chance he ain't gonna recover from that beatin' he got. Would be more to our likin' to string you both up right now and leave yuh to the buzzards." He paused for effect, then he exhaled a breath. "But count yourselves lucky we ain't no vigilantes. We'll let the court deal with yuh. 'Course you ain't got much of a case. But that's 'bout as fair as you're gonna get from us."

Winston was perspiring fiercely, an anxious fat man's sweat that dripped down his face in rivulets, as if he'd just dunked his head in a bucket of water, and his breathing came more rapidly and in a wheeze. His chest was heaving erratically. Ehron Lee was growing ever more concerned as he feared that Winston might just suffer a heart attack and drop dead on the spot.

Ehron Lee understood that things looked bad. They were riding stolen horses, and he had no proof of his land purchase. But the fact that they weren't guilty of any wrongdoing and would be able to plead their case before a judge offered them some hope. At least they wouldn't be mob-lynched, the victims of frontier justice, which had been Ehron Lee's first worry.

Winston slipped into a panic. He shouted, "I ain't guilty of nothin' and damned if I'm gonna swing for it!"

And in a quick, sudden action, he slapped a meaty hand against the flank of his horse, startling the animal into a desperate run.

Ehron Lee shot up ramrod straight. "Winston, you damn fool!" he cried.

Winston didn't get far. He never had a chance, and had he been thinking rationally, he would have realized that his attempt was plain suicide. One of the posse members calmly half turned on his saddle, and with his six-shooter drawn, he fired a single bullet, hitting Winston square in the back, the impact throwing him sideways from the horse. Ehron Lee heard Winston groan and watched helplessly as his brother-in-law struggled to lift himself to his knees before collapsing face first onto the ground. He didn't move.

Two of the men quickly broke away from the group, galloping off on their mares to retrieve the stallion, which had been spooked by the gunshot.

The eager young buck who had fired the shot blew away the drifting smoke from the barrel of his revolver, fancy-twirled it before reholstering, and said matter-of-factly, "Man claimin' to be innocent don't try to run off like that."

Bert Stradd simply turned toward Ehron Lee, who looked dumbstruck, and said in a self-satisfied manner, "Your friend made a bad move. Well, he ain't got no worries now. But don't look too good for you, pardner."

Two

MADAM ROSINA'S BORDELLO in the town of Justice, a quiet, peaceful community situated in a lush green parcel of valley nestled in the rolling foothills of Cullen County, boasted an impressive clientele, the most prominent of whom was Charles Hugh Harrison, circuit judge, who always made it a point to avail himself of the pleasures these premises offered whenever he presided over a judicial matter in town.

Of course, since Judge Harrison was regarded as a pillar of decency and respectability, his character beyond reproach, he planned each visit prudently, exercising caution to maintain secrecy, arriving under cover of nightfall, per a prearranged appointment forwarded by a coded telegram. He was allowed a back entrance separated from the rest of the house, which provided a stairway leading to a comfortable upstairs room where he could indulge his pleasures in privacy.

Naturally Judge Harrison paid for these special privileges, fees somewhat steeper than those of less conspicuous customers. But for a person of his reputation, he understood and accepted this as a necessary precaution.

Judge Harrison was a fastidious middle-aged man of

slim, short stature whose gaunt features were dominated by a sharply arched nose, atop which he perched gold-rimmed spectacles that enlarged his small, beady eyes. His stern demeanor befitted his profession but stood at odds with his mischievous personal enjoyments. Married for many years and father to a teenage daughter, Harrison maintained little romantic inclination toward his wife—a woman whom he rarely saw with so much of his life now spent traveling to dirt water towns throughout the southern regions of the state. Likewise, he'd had little time to spend with his daughter, Evaline, a girl he'd barely watched grow through her adolescent years. Financially he'd provided both with a fair degree of stability, but his frequent and lengthy absences had left an emotional void between him and his family.

Harrison would convince himself that his weeks and oftentimes months away performing his judicial duties were the reason he utilized the services of prostitutes. Such an argument would help assuage whatever guilt might begin to gnaw at his conscience. But, in truth, Harrison possessed little guilt, permitting himself neither self-reproach nor remorse for his actions. He simply preferred the company of such women. They satisfied him in a way a more intimate relationship could not. Perhaps because of the nature of his work, he needed to maintain emotional detachment even in his private life. He had the natural urges of most men toward women, responding as they satisfied his physical needs, though it was another quirk in his character that he was loath to reciprocate.

And as long as he could pay, and pay well, his "requirements" were always accommodated. Whores cooperated with his demands, no matter how strange they might be.

Judge Harrison had ridden into Justice just before sunset. He checked into the town's one hotel, The Jubilee, which was filled to capacity but had a room already reserved for him. After unpacking his luggage, he allowed himself a bath, followed by a light supper in the hotel dining room. The trial for which he had come to town was scheduled to begin the following day, and adhering to his usual pattern, Harrison was eager to enjoy a night of relaxation at his preferred pleasure palace before assuming his "professional" title as "His Honor" at ten o'clock the next morning.

Judge Harrison would be presiding over the trial of a man accused of horse theft and attempted murder: an ex–Union soldier named Ehron Lee Burrows. Harrison had been wired all the details of the crime, and it looked to be a simple trial. Harrison dispensed justice by following the letter of the law, and there appeared to be little defense for the accused, outside of a probable plea for leniency from his attorney. But when he reviewed the evidence offered, Harrison saw no reason to grant such a request. Horse thievery in itself was a hanging offense; a vicious assault upon a helpless old man only compounded the seriousness of the crime. Much to his satisfaction, Judge Harrison could not see the trial lasting beyond a day.

But that would be dealt with tomorrow. He had other less sordid duties to pursue this night.

With Justice observing peace and quiet at this late hour, town activity was now confined to the saloon, where men played cards or just socialized over drinks. Harrison quietly exited out the back of the hotel and walked casually through the empty streets, ostensibly on a nightly constitutional but, in fact, making his way to the bordello. The bordello was a well-maintained, wood-framed, two-story house that prior to its present status had a respectable heritage. Ironically the house had been owned by a man called Justice, for whom the town was named. Percival Justice had founded the town after spending most of his life at sea and acquiring a substantial fortune in the shipping industry. The town never quite achieved the level of expansion Percival had hoped for during the years he settled there, and following his death, with most of his funds tied up in businesses that turned only a meager profit, and with no heirs to whom he could leave his estate, his house, perhaps his one worthwhile asset, was purchased by Rosina Perez, a Mexican madam of some wealth, who saw her own enterprising way of expanding her profits. She succeeded quite admirably, as her establishment was clean and comfortable, and tastefully decorated. The girls who worked for her were both professional in their duties (most had come with Rosina when she emigrated from Mexico) and proper in their care and hygiene. And most important, Rosina operated her business with respect to discretion. Her reputation was such that customers were known to come from all parts of the territory to partake of the pleasures of her establishment.

The house was situated just outside town, within walking distance but far enough from official boundaries not to be considered a part of Justice itself. The services provided by the bordello were accepted but not acknowledged by the town officials.

A narrow, willow-bordered pathway provided entry to the grounds, the dense overhang offering suitable protection of anonymity for nocturnal visitors to the house.

Judge Harrison's arrival was expected and so the back door was unlocked for him. He climbed the stairs to his room, where he checked his pocket watch and saw that he was about fifteen minutes early for his appointment, which was how he preferred it. He never wanted his "companion" to be waiting for him. He was a man of meticulous routine, and this extended even to his pleasures. Arriving early allowed him time for a drink (a bottle of champagne was always set on the nightstand) and to prepare himself by spraying the room, and his person, liberally with imported perfume.

Almost as an afterthought, he removed the wedding band from his finger and placed it in the pocket of his trousers.

When his companion for the night announced her presence with a knock at the door, punctually at the appointed time, which pleased the judge, Harrison, already undressed and clad only in his robe, crossed the room and opened the door. The girl standing outside the room was Mexican: dark eyes and tanned skin, with long raven hair that she wore loose around her shoulders. Through his spectacles Harrison gazed at the girl appraisingly and, finding her suitable to his discriminating taste, invited her inside, not with words but with a mere nod of his head.

Truth be told, the girl, Angelique (or "Angel," as she was known to her customers), was not as impressed with Judge Harrison as he was with her. She was a fairly new addition to Madam Rosina's stable, having been encouraged away from a border town cantina, where she was performing the same duties under less favorable conditions and little pay. Naturally she hadn't been told who tonight's customer was, but his austere, almost hawk-like look, complemented by a neatly trimmed goatee that made the middle-aged man look old enough to be her grandfather, coupled with a somewhat intimidating bearing, suggested someone of importance whom, she detected, held her in low esteem. He exuded a chilly arrogance.

Not that his opinion mattered. Angelique had no illusions about herself or what she did for a living. She was a whore and she knew it.

This was her first appointment with Charles Harrison, and she didn't know what to expect. Judging by his appearance, Angelique would have guessed his occupation as undertaker. While withholding his identity (as was always the case), Madam Rosina had called him a "gentleman of suitable character," but Angelique had had turns with other so-called "respectables," and she usually found that while they may have been upstanding citizens in their professional life, under the sheets it was quite a different matter.

Money was always the incentive, however, and Madam Rosina was generous in sharing her profits with her girls. Therefore, Angelique accepted the glass of champagne her client silently offered her as a preliminary overture. There would be very little conversation, and when Angelique was about to introduce herself as Angel, Harrison raised his hand to silence her. He neither wanted nor needed to know who she was. He kept such arrangements impersonal, no intimacies.

This was not particularly uncommon to Angelique—though quite often her customers provided false names to allow for at least the facade of personal connection.

After a single glass of champagne, Harrison disrobed, and buck-naked, exposing a most unappealing physique, he proceeded into bed, with Angelique likewise expected to follow. Consuming the rest of her champagne quickly to hopefully hasten the effects, the girl stepped behind a decorative partition and began removing her outer garments, uncertain if not uneasy at the prospect of what was to come, but readying herself to do her "professional" best to please the customer . . .

Judge Harrison's night of pleasure at the bordello proved all that he could have hoped for. The few words he did speak were brief whispered instructions of what he expected from the girl, and while a few of his requests were somewhat peculiar, Angelique was seasoned and complied without complaint. But it had all been prelude. When the moment came, Harrison was quick on the draw, releasing but one pull on the trigger. By the time he drifted off to sleep, an exhausted Angelique had admirably fulfilled some of his fantasies.

For Angelique, the experience was far from memorable. Of course, her personal pleasure in the affair was barely a consideration. For her, the night wasn't as exciting as it was painful. The old man seemed to have to struggle to achieve his own puny "thrill" and often he would squeeze Angelique's forearms with a strong grip while in the midst of prompting stimulation. Angelique was certain she would end up with some bruising, but this wasn't entirely new to her. She would simply file these *souvenirs* away under "hazards of the trade."

Still and all, Harrison was impressed with the little señorita Rosina had provided, and beyond paying her fee, which he left in a sealed envelope on the night table, he also supplied a generous gratuity, which Rosina would *not* share with the girl.

Judge Charles Hugh Harrison returned to his hotel room before dawn feeling fully satisfied and ready to get down to the day's business.

Ehron Lee Burrows had spent almost two weeks sitting in the town jail awaiting the arrival of the circuit judge. Shortly after his jailing, Ehron Lee was notified by the sheriff, Buck Leighton, that his wife, Melinda, together with her sister, Abigail, would be arriving by stagecoach later in the week to visit him. Although he desperately missed his wife, Ehron

Lee didn't want Melinda, just months from delivering the baby, to see him locked behind bars, a possible candidate for hanging. He urged the sheriff not to let her in. Sheriff Leighton wasn't about to grant him that request; he was of no mind to deal with a determined female. He bluntly told Ehron Lee that there was no way he would keep her out if she insisted on seeing him.

What Ehron Lee couldn't know was that Melinda would not be the problem. His sister-in-law, Abigail, was so distraught over the death of her husband that her already fragile personality had become even more unstable.

Yet when she first came inside the jailhouse, following after Melinda, she appeared calm and composed. She sat herself next to the sheriff's desk and let Melinda have her time with Ehron Lee. She was quiet and didn't react to the pain-wracked voice and the tears that streamed from her sister's eyes as Melinda clung desperately to her husband's hands when they reached outside the bars of the cell.

They didn't speak for long; neither knew what to say to comfort the other. Ehron Lee struggled to give her reassurance, but he could only tell her what he knew for certain— and that could not include his prospects for the future.

"I'm innocent, honey, you gotta believe me," he said. "And they shot Winston only 'cause he got scairt and tried to run off."

Ehron Lee couldn't tell if she'd even heard him. Her features reflected a strain he'd never seen on her before, aging her beyond her tender years. She seemed to have trouble accepting any of what he was saying. It was almost as if she were struggling to find a safe place in denial.

He tried to lighten the mood. He placed the flat of his hand against his wife's slightly bulging tummy. "Baby's doin' just fine," he said with a smile. "You gotta take care of yourself, honey, for the little one."

But at the mention of the baby, Melinda's emotions became so overwhelming and painful for Ehron Lee to watch that he finally motioned for Sheriff Leighton to escort her from the jail. Surprisingly, she didn't resist; she understood how difficult this was for her husband. Ehron Lee was grateful she had made the decision to leave without protest.

He had barely collected himself before Abigail calmly rose from her chair and walked over to his cell.

Ehron Lee attempted a smile, but Abigail's expression was cold and rigid. He was familiar with her odd moods, but this was a look of pure contempt.

"Murderer," she said, her voice barely a whisper though heavy with intent.

Then her pitch rose as she spewed venom.

"Low-down filthy murderer! You never was no good, Ehron Lee Burrows. I saw it right from the start. You fooled everyone else, but you could never fool me . . ."

Ehron Lee recoiled at the accusation. He tried to speak. "Abigail, what are you say—"

She didn't let him finish. "I know the truth. You enjoyed killin', gettin' blood on your hands. The war was good for yuh, Ehron Lee, wasn't it? 'Cause it made yuh what you really are: a killer and a criminal."

Her body trembled in a barely repressed fury. Ehron Lee just stood there, stunned into silence, unable to respond, scarcely believing any of what he was hearing. It was as if Abigail had become another person, someone hostile and vindictive.

Her thinking was not rational, and as she continued to rant, it was clear that she held Ehron Lee responsible for what had happened to Winston, her emotionally charged accusations doing nothing to assist Ehron Lee's claim of innocence in the eyes of the sheriff, who had rushed back into the office upon hearing her outburst.

Buck Leighton urged Abigail from the office, though she continued to shout her accusations until she was outside on the boardwalk. Buck attempted to quiet her, then when she calmed after a few moments, he came back inside, closing and locking the office door behind him.

"I didn't see your wife outside, Burrows," he said. "Don't think she heard any of what was goin' on."

"She—she don't know what she's sayin', Sheriff," Ehron

Lee said numbly. "She's still upset by what happened to Winston."

"Can you blame her?" Buck said flatly.

Ehron Lee's eyes sparked defensively.

"I ain't guilty of no wrongdoin', Sheriff," he protested. "Those men that *are* responsible are still out there."

"You claim you saw those men, Burrows, yet you never gave me much to work with, other than they were both big men, one dressed in buckskins, and that the other fella's name was Tom or Todd or who knows what," Buck reminded. "'Round these parts, don't exactly make either stand out."

"It was dark, and their faces were pretty much covered," Ehron Lee replied wearily, repeating what he'd said countless times before. "Can't tell yuh more than what I saw or what I heard."

Buck said nothing. He just observed Ehron Lee with a narrow-eyed, considering expression.

Buck Leighton and Ehron Lee were roughly the same age, though the sheriff looked considerably older. His skin was lined, and traces of gray had begun to appear in his curly black hair as well as in his eyebrows. Though it wasn't his place to make character judgments of his prisoners, Buck thought Ehron Lee to be a decent sort, and the few times they did speak, the exchanges were pleasant, if brief. Not that he could be called upon to give an honest assessment of his character. It was also known to Buck that Ehron Lee had fought in the war, and the sheriff had seen enough through his job to understand how the stress and carnage of battle could change a man—and not for the better. Many of those he'd had to arrest, as a lawman in various counties, for both minor and more serious offenses were men who, before the war, had been peaceful, honest citizens. But their wartime experiences had released some dark side of their nature that never before had been given rein. So with that in mind, he couldn't take lightly those accusations thrown at Ehron Lee by his sister-in-law, though he, too, had to admit she was somewhat of a queer, unsettled sort.

Buck felt definite compassion for Ehron Lee's wife,

though. Although he was unmarried, he understood how difficult it must be for her, how she would defend her man, even under such damning circumstances. That aside, as each day passed, he began to disapprove of Melinda Burrows coming around the jailhouse so often, given her delicate condition and how upset she got during each visit. In truth, he simply wanted the trial over, so that, for her sake, some conclusion would be reached.

The morning of the trial, Buck brought Ehron Lee some breakfast. Ehron Lee moved wearily off his bunk and stepped just as slowly toward the bars of his cell. He took one look at the greasy concoction of eggs, ham, and a buttered biscuit and instantly determined that he had neither the stomach nor the inclination to eat. He'd had little interest in food since the day he was arrested, merely picking at the meals provided, leaving most on the tray. His loss of appetite was made evident by how his clothes had started to hang loosely on his frame.

The sheriff had also brought along some coffee. Ehron Lee accepted the beverage, reaching for the tin cup through the bars of the cell. The coffee was cold and strong, and he consumed only a mouthful before handing it back to Buck.

He said little that morning, his thoughts focused on what the day ahead would bring. It was difficult for him to feel optimistic about the outcome. Out of spite, his sister-in-law had taken to bad-mouthing him all over town, her accusations blackening his character and surely prejudicing the citizens.

To add to his doubts, Ehron Lee wasn't much encouraged by his lawyer. Addison Telborough had been court-appointed since Ehron Lee had no funds to speak of, and he appeared to have prepared his case in a perfunctory manner. Maybe it was because of his downcast mood, but to Ehron Lee it seemed as if Mr. Telborough was just a little too persistent in reminding him during their visits that he didn't have much of a defense. Maybe he was trying to brace his client for the probable outcome . . . or perhaps he was simply preparing to justify his own lack of success when the verdict was delivered.

In any case, Ehron Lee truthfully couldn't fault him; he knew his chances at acquittal looked slim. He also understood that he really had only one hope, and that was finding Albert Patterson, the man from whom he'd bought the property and who could at least provide some credibility to Ehron Lee's claim. Unfortunately, despite Telborough's assurances that this search was being undertaken, Ehron Lee felt distinctly that no effort was being put into trying to locate the man.

Adding to Ehron Lee's discouragement was the knowledge that the county prosecutor was a man with a large number of convictions to his credit. He wasn't from Justice and would be riding into town from the big city to provide his service to the people.

Still holding the tray of food that Ehron Lee had refused, Sheriff Leighton said, "Well, since you ain't up to eatin', might as well make yourself presentable for the trial."

Accompanied by Deputy Bert Stradd, the man responsible for his capture, Ehron Lee was taken in handcuffs to the livery stable, where the manacles were removed and he was allowed to bathe in a trough filled with fresh water. Outside of a few basin washes done in his cell, this was the closest Ehron Lee had come to cleaning himself since before his arrest. He had to bathe quickly. By the time he finally emerged from the trough, the water was quite filthy, but he felt at least a little refreshed.

Escorted back to the jail, Ehron Lee was permitted a shave and hair trim by the town barber, and then he was given a fresh change of clothes to wear for the trial.

Ehron Lee hoped that Melinda wouldn't be present, though he knew that would not be the case. She'd attend the trial—most likely in the company of Abigail, which only made matters worse. Abigail had made no secret of the fact that he would get no support from her. But what troubled Ehron Lee more was the thought that maybe she was working at turning Melinda against him. Abigail was the older of the two, and Ehron Lee had seen firsthand during the time they had lived with her and Winston the strong influence Abigail had over her sister. She had practically raised Melinda after their mother died, taking on a maternal role of nurturing and disciplining, which the immature Melinda accepted. That pattern of obedience followed Melinda into adulthood. Even as a grown woman, Melinda was diffident when she was with her sister, always cautious not to do or say anything that might displease her.

But she *had* displeased Abigail once, and that was when she chose Ehron Lee as her husband.

Ehron Lee never knew for certain that Abigail had opposed the marriage, though if she had, it was the one time she'd failed in her attempt to bend the will of her sister. It was enough that Ehron Lee always felt Abigail disapproved of him. She was cordial with him, polite, but Ehron Lee suspected that was mainly because of the friendship he had shared with Winston. Now that Winston was dead, and with Abigail holding Ehron Lee responsible, there was no reason for her to pretend any longer. She'd revealed her true feelings, emotions that she had probably kept bottled up for some time.

No, not even for Melinda's sake—or perhaps to her thinking, it was *for* Melinda's sake—would she put in a good word for him.

She wanted to see Ehron Lee pay the penalty for her husband's death.

The trial of Ehron Lee Burrows provided some much-needed diversion for the town of Justice, where nothing much by way of excitement was known to happen. The saloon was closed for business and would serve as a makeshift courtroom, since no such "official" building existed in the town. Customer tables were moved aside from the center of the room, and rows of chairs were already lined up for the spectators. A desk had been brought in from the back office and placed at the front of the long mahogany bar, to serve as the judge's bench. By nine thirty, the place was already packed with curious citizens, many of whom were unable to find seats and who were standing against the walls. Most of the people were from town, but a smattering came from other parts of the county. It seemed as if everyone knew the old farmer Elmer Bryant—or they were simply looking for an entertaining way to spend their day.

Ehron Lee even recognized some folks from in and around his own town of Brackett, perhaps summoned by the court to provide a character statement. If intended to aid in his defense, Ehron Lee didn't see that offering a hell of a lot of support. He didn't have much to do with the people of his community. He was seen as a quiet man who pretty much kept to himself. Content to do his work at any of the odd jobs he held in town, then at day's end to hurry home to his wife, not one to socialize with the locals.

Ehron Lee was seated with his lawyer, discussing a few last-minute items with him while trying to ignore the murmurs and comments of the crowd, most of whom for either justice or amusement seemed eager for a guilty verdict.

Ehron Lee deliberately kept his focus straight ahead, on where the judge would be seated, not wanting to know if Melinda was in the crowd. He could feel her presence but did not want to confirm it. He decided that when it came time for him to take the stand, he would keep his eyes averted from the crowd. It would be painful for him to look into Melinda's face. It would be even worse to meet Abigail's condemning stare.

Judge Harrison entered the saloon from the back room exactly as the grandfather clock standing next to the bar signaled ten o'clock. He looked properly stern and solemn, official in his somber black suit, befitting an undertaker, starched white shirt, and string tie, neither his appearance nor his demeanor betraying his previous night's escapades.

A hush descended over the room and everyone rose. The judge took his seat. One of the townsmen stood next to the desk and faced the crowd.

"Court is in session," he stated. "Judge Charles Hugh Harrison presidin'."

The judge addressed the assembled. "Be seated."

Those who had chairs sat. The others remained standing.

Judge Harrison glanced over the papers set before him. He cleared his throat, frowned, and formally read the charges.

"Ehron Lee Burrows, you're accused of horse theft and assault with murderous intent." At that, the judge further creased the furrows in his forehead and turned to the townsman.

"By the way, what is the present condition of Mr. Bryant?" he asked.

"Oh, he's still unconscious, Judge," the man replied. "Ain't doin' well at all. Doc still ain't sure if'n he'll make it."

Judge Harrison nodded, then proceeded, looking directly at the accused and his counsel.

"Burrows, how do you plead?"

Ehron Lee's lawyer stood up and answered on Ehron Lee's behalf, "My client pleads not guilty, Your Honor."

The judge squinted through his spectacles and again cleared his throat. "As I understand, Mr. Telborough, you'll be presenting your case for the defense first. Very well, you may call your first witness."

Addison Telborough looked down at Ehron Lee. He was to be the *only* witness called for the defense: the accused himself. As Ehron Lee rose and tried to keep his gait steady walking to the witness chair, he already felt the case was lost.

It would be his word alone against Bert Stradd, the sheriff's deputy, and the other men who rode in the posse, along with the witnesses at the ranch who saw—as much as they were able—the attack on Elmer Bryant. Those men could not in truth identify him . . . but under the circumstances, that offered little promise. They were a hard-bitten bunch not as interested in legal formalities as in their own brand of justice. They wanted someone to pay for the crime, and innocent or not, Ehron Lee had enough evidence against him to be looked upon as guilty.

Through the silence that followed his swearing in and

that preceded his lawyer's questioning, Ehron Lee heard sobbing and knew where it was coming from. Try as he might, he couldn't keep his eyes from Melinda, who was seated next to Abigail near the back of the room. She looked especially prim and pretty, attired in a light blue cotton dress and matching bonnet, items he'd never seen her wear before, which led him to assume she'd purchased them specifically for the trial. He felt both bitter and heartbroken.

He'd always promised to buy her a new dress but had saved his earnings to purchase the property he now had doubts they would ever enjoy. The first new dress Melinda had owned in a long while was bought by her, not for pleasure, but so she could look presentable at her husband's trial.

Then Ehron Lee caught the smug look on Abigail's face, unsympathetic and oblivious to her sister's emotions.

Addison Telborough began his questioning. Ehron Lee provided answers but was so aware of Melinda and what she was going through that he spoke his words weakly, with little conviction. His voice was so low that more than once Judge Harrison had to insist he speak louder.

Ehron Lee's testimony concluded in less than ten minutes. The prosecutor, also looking smug, didn't even bother to cross-examine him. Ehron Lee had told his story exactly as it had happened, but a fleeting look at the impassive faces of both the spectators and the jury told him they were not convinced. As he walked back to his seat, he was unaware that he had begun to massage his fingers around his throat, an unconscious gesture that was perceived by some as his acceptance of the outcome.

Before he sat himself back in his chair, he glanced over at Melinda, who was trembling and in tears, a kerchief pressed against her mouth. Perhaps she also interpreted a message in his gesture. Ehron Lee tried to comfort her with a weak smile, which was all he could manage—and was relieved when he saw her abruptly stand up and walk from the saloon before the prosecution could present its case.

Abigail watched her go, her expression vacant. She did not join her.

She stayed in her seat and displayed no reaction as her husband Winston's character came into question. What had been provided through statements given by members of his community was that he was shiftless, irresponsible, and not particularly bright. It was not too difficult for these citizens to believe that he could have been swayed into stealing some fine horses—perhaps to make some quick, extra money since his laziness and fondness for alcohol precluded there being much earnings from his farming.

And of course, his rash attempt at escape only seemed to confirm his guilt.

Witnesses then marched forward as called by the prosecutor. Each man, including Bert Stradd, delivered his testimony in complete confidence—except for one telling fact that Addison Telborough took advantage of during his cross-examination:

No one could *conclusively* identify Ehron Lee Burrows as one of the two perpetrators.

There was evidence against Ehron Lee: the stolen horses he and Winston had been caught riding, the foolhardy escape attempt by his brother-in-law . . . but sufficient reasonable doubt had been established by his lawyer. The horses *could* have been stolen by others and traded off with Ehron Lee and Winston's mounts. Addison Telborough brought up the fact that just a few days before the arrest a mercantile in the town of Shalett over in the next county had been robbed by two burly men who had gotten away. Also, Winston's attempt at evading arrest *could* simply have been the result of the nervous man's panic.

Still, the final verdict rested with the jury, and the looks on their faces offered no assurance. They reached their decision swiftly, after only a few minutes of mumbling among themselves. They quieted and settled back into their chairs, indicating they were ready.

Judge Harrison asked officially, "Has the jury reached a verdict?"

The foreman, a rough-looking cowboy who seemed to have about as much compassion for the accused as he'd have for an Apache, stood up, clasping a battered Stetson in both hands.

"That we have, Judge."

"The prisoner will rise," Judge Harrison instructed.

Ehron Lee's temples throbbed. He pulled himself to his feet and stood next to his lawyer. He made himself look directly at the twelve men, none of whom owed him anything, but many of whom were, at the least, acquaintances of Elmer Bryant.

The foreman's eyes met Ehron Lee's gaze only for an instant, though with a telling glint.

"We find this here fella guilty of the charges," he said.

Ehron Lee's expression was blank. His face registered no emotion but his complexion was ashen. Addison Telborough likewise had an empty look, though he reached over and laid a comforting hand upon Ehron Lee's arm.

There was a moment of excited babble among the spectators. Judge Harrison pounded the gavel and called for order.

Everyone hushed with anticipation as he prepared to pass sentence.

The judge hitched his spectacles against the narrow bridge of his nose. Then he leaned slightly forward and, with his elbows resting on the desk, made a steeple of his fingers, assuming a proper posture for what was to come.

"Ehron Lee Burrows, you have been found guilty of horse theft and attempted murder during the commission of the crime." The judge paused and the expression on his face became thoughtful. "Under normal circumstances, my judgment would be clear." He paused again. "However, in listening to the facts of this case, despite the verdict, I see there does exist some possibility of doubt as to your guilt. Not a lot, mind you, but enough for me not to sentence you to the most severe punishment it is my right by law to impose. It is therefore the judgment of this court that you be sentenced to five years of hard labor at the penal institution at Rockmound. Sentence to be carried out immediately."

The reaction of the spectators was immediate, and expected.

Many leapt to their feet objecting to the sentence. They felt they had been cheated out of proper justice. They wanted to see Ehron Lee hanged.

Judge Harrison rapped his gavel several times to restore order, and when the ruckus subsided, he announced, "Court is adjourned. Bar will open once these tables and chairs get put back proper."

The shouts of objection quickly changed to hoots and cheers. Men scrambled to put the saloon back in order.

Judge Harrison disappeared into the saloon office to prepare the papers to deliver to the sheriff, which would be forwarded along with the prisoner to Rockmound.

A momentary relief washed over Ehron Lee with the realization that his life would be spared. He wished with all his heart that he could rush out, collect Melinda in his arms, and tell her that he would be coming back. Five years was not a long time. He'd been separated from her for nearly as long during the war, and that was much worse, where each day he never knew if it might be his last, lost to her forever, a casualty of battle.

But he'd be alive these next five years, without the same worry of dying . . . and while it would hurt enormously being apart from her, at least prison set aside days when she could visit him. When, for however briefly, he could see her. Talk to her. Perhaps even touch her.

But slowly his relief started to fade as the bitter reality set in, the five years they were taking from an innocent man. He hadn't done anything to deserve that punishment. Nor should he ever have been arrested. He'd never stolen from any man. He'd never harmed another soul except in battle, where it was expected of him, following the rule of war, where it was kill or be killed.

All he could truly be accused of was trying to provide a better life for his wife and . . . his family.

The baby, almost forgotten by him during this ordeal. The child he would not get to know during those first years of its life. He would not be there when Melinda delivered the baby. He would never experience the joy of holding his newborn son or daughter in his arms. This realization deeply saddened him.

Then almost as quickly his sorrow transformed into cold dread as it became clear to him where he would be serving his sentence: Rockmound Prison. It had two other names, which legend had it were fitting to its environment: Cartridge Hill—so given because of the number of prisoners who were shot to death while trying to escape—or more popularly, Hell's Doorway. He'd heard horrible stories about that place, mostly told in whispers, as if even the mere mention of the prison's name might bring forth a plague of evil.

The doorway to hell, where the daily routine hardly varied. Prisoners were locked in leg irons, fed meager, miserable meals. Hard labor was *exactly* what it suggested. Days in the quarry spent crushing rocks into sand under the relentless heat of the searing sun. Trigger-happy guards who would rather shoot an escaping convict than break a sweat bringing him back to his cell. The prisoners were treated worse than dogs and life was held cheaply. If the term "living death" could be defined, it would be by those who served time at Rockmound.

Men had survived their terms at Hell's Doorway, but often all that remained was a broken shell of a human being.

Contemplating the potential horror that awaited him at Rockmound, a reminder of what he'd learned about the inhumane conditions at Andersonville, Ehron Lee suddenly thought that if not for the hope of eventually being reunited with his beloved Melinda, of someday being a father to his child, it might have been a more merciful sentence if the judge had just ordered him to be hanged.

Ehron Lee suffered another sharp jolt back to reality when he turned his head and saw Abigail wading toward him through the crowd. When she got close enough to his face, her expression twisted into a snarl.

"Five years. Yuh think you got off easy, Ehron Lee, but mark my words. I promise you here and now that Melinda won't be waiting for yuh when you get out. I'll do everything in my power during that time to convince her to leave you.

I'll take her and the baby away where she'll be able to start a new life. A life free of your tarnish. She won't be there and neither will the child . . . *if* you get out. But as far as I'm concerned, Ehron Lee, I hope you rot."

Abigail spoke with such cruel emphasis that Ehron Lee was thankful Sheriff Leighton was standing next to him; otherwise he was sure he would have gone for her throat and throttled her. He only wished that he had the opportunity to speak with Melinda, to warn her of her sister's intentions and to urge her not to listen to anything she might say.

But he was powerless. Soon he would be distanced from Melinda—locked in a prison cell, and Abigail would regain the complete control over her sister that she'd had up until the time Melinda met and married Ehron Lee. A control which she still tried to enforce during the period the couple lived with her and Winston. Ehron Lee understood how easy it would be for her now. With Melinda weak and vulnerable, Abigail's influence would be absolute.

"C'mon, Burrows," Buck Leighton said woodenly, no emotion, no expression, doing his job. "Gotta take yuh back to the jail 'til the wagon arrives."

Ehron Lee looked bewildered. "Melinda," he muttered numbly. Then with more emphasis: "Can't I say good-bye to my wife?"

Buck gave his head a slow, regretful shake. "Don't advise it, Burrows. We gotta get yuh ready. Don't think you want your woman to be watchin' that. 'Sides, you don't got a whole lotta time."

Back at the jailhouse, Ehron Lee understood why the sheriff had discouraged him from seeing his wife. She would have watched the humiliating process of him being locked in shackles, a mandatory precaution for "condemned men" to prevent any attempt at escape along the trail.

He would be the sole occupant of the prisoner wagon. He was about to begin his long journey to Hell's Doorway, accompanied by the driver and a shotgun-carrying guard.

He was locked inside the transport compartment: a cell on wheels, which was a primitive enclosure, surrounded by metal walls with two narrow windows, barred with rows of sturdy but weathered metal slats. Ehron Lee felt like a caged animal, and would feel even more like one as the wagon started its deliberately slow ride down the main street, where he was gawked at by citizens, as if he were some wild beast on exhibit. Many who had been at the trial were now sufficiently drunk to step from the saloon and shout cruel comments. He was further humiliated when some of the unruly boys of the town picked up chunks of hardened mud from the street and tossed them at the windows, jeering and taunting the prisoner.

Ehron Lee didn't even try to see if Melinda was among the onlookers. It would have been too much to bear.

And for Melinda to see him now would be too much for her.

But suddenly she was there, rushing through the crowd toward the wagon.

She walked with quick strides to keep pace with the rolling wheels. She reached out and pressed her hand against the bars, tightly, desperately, as the prisoner wagon rolled down the street.

Ehron Lee fought back his tears, though Melinda's were flowing freely.

"Ehron Lee," she said with a tremor in her voice, "this isn't right. It isn't fair. . . . Why couldn't they see that?"

"You just stay strong, Melinda. I'll be back," he assured her staunchly, mustering as much conviction in his voice as he was able. "Just remember that. Trust me. I'll be back."

He pressed his own hand against the bars, curling his fingers through the opening to touch her hand, but they connected only for an instant . . .

And then Abigail was behind Melinda, taking her by her slender shoulders and pulling her away from the wagon, her eyes shooting daggers at Ehron Lee, at the same time confirming her promise. She didn't say anything.

She didn't have to.

The look of triumph was etched into her expression.

THREE

THE RIDE TO Rockmound Prison would take four days, weather and trail conditions permitting, the prisoner wagon traveling north across the coarse flatlands and requiring navigation through the rock-strewn trails of a narrow canyon passage that was bordered by large walls of sandstone. The trail also bordered Navajo country, and though the threat of an uprising had successfully been thwarted with many of the tribe rounded up and sent on the Long Walk to Fort Sumner, there was always the chance they might run into renegades still at large and known to occasionally scout these parts, thus the other reason for the shotgun guard's presence. There were occasional rest stops, where the driver and his riding companion would take a break to water the horses and to stretch their legs, but this was a privilege not extended to Ehron Lee. That was given only when Ehron Lee *urgently* expressed the need to relieve himself, which wasn't often because he was given only minimal water and was mostly dehydrated. The midday sun was especially oppressive and Ehron Lee's thirst was constant.

The driver and shotgun guard were resentful. Although

no special privilege was ever given to any prisoner they transported, they took out their specific displeasure of this trip on Ehron Lee. Per their contracts, both were paid "by the head" and on a typical run from other parts of the territory, they carted no less than six prisoners to Rockmound. Cullen County posed another problem. Outside of Ehron Lee's conviction, as of late there had been no crimes in the county serious enough to warrant "hard labor" incarceration at Rockmound. The judge's order stated that Ehron Lee's sentence could not officially begin until he was delivered to the prison, and it would not do for Ehron Lee to sit out time in the town jail while waiting, perhaps for months, for a sufficient roundup of county felons.

Thus the long and potentially dangerous ride they were undertaking guaranteed the two men only minimal pay. This sat well with neither, and their sadistic comments and actions directed toward their "passenger" were their way of showing it.

Biscuits were the only food provided to Ehron Lee, tossed at him through the bars when the wagon was stopped, like he was a dog expected to fetch. The biscuits were dry and hard and tasteless, but he ate them if only to keep up his strength. It seemed to him that the journey was a way of preparing him for what he was soon to endure at the prison.

A form of medieval conditioning.

And in that it succeeded. His resentment grew until long before he reached the gates of Rockmound, Ehron Lee Burrows had already become a changed man. Years of bloody combat in the Civil War had not affected him as severely or as rapidly as these last weeks, where he had become the victim of injustice in Justice.

They had condemned an innocent man to a corner of purgatory, their unfair judgment not only taking away his freedom, but threatening to take from him the only person he had ever truly loved . . . along with a child he conceivably might not ever see. Their judgment had left his bride at the mercy of a vindictive sister.

Indeed, he could physically feel the hatred well up inside him, like an advancing and virulent disease. But rather than fighting it, Ehron Lee determined he could benefit from that hate. It might just be the tool he'd need to survive the next five years at Hell's Doorway.

A man named George Watson was superintendent of the prison. A bald, darkly tanned, beetle-browed individual who sported a thick mustache, which crawled down both sides of his face, Watson was an intimidating presence with an undeniable military bearing, though in fact he had never served in the army. He was a former lawyer turned prosecutor whose enmity for felons ran deep. As a young, idealistic defense attorney, he'd used his ambitious legal tactics to free an alleged murderer named Billy Burkett, who was later found to be guilty of the crime, but only after he and his gang had slaughtered a young pioneer family, including three children. While some of the gang were subsequently apprehended and hanged, Burkett himself had never been caught, and it continued to trouble Watson's conscience as he contemplated the further carnage that might result from his own fancy courtroom maneuverings. From that point onward, Watson relentlessly focused his skills on punishing, not protecting, accused felons. He was proud of his many convictions that had sent criminals to the gallows. No murderer who had ever been prosecuted by him had escaped the noose.

It was his impressive record and his determination to see lawbreakers properly punished that had earned him his appointment at Rockmound Prison. It was a job he relished.

As was his custom, Superintendent Watson was standing out on the grounds to meet the new inmate when the wagon finally rolled into the forbidding walls of the prison. The driver handed Watson the necessary papers and then brought Ehron Lee from the back of the wagon. His shackles were removed and tossed back into the wagon to await the next unfortunate prisoner to be transported to Hell's Doorway.

Ehron Lee's muscles were stiff and sore from spending so much time in a crouched or sitting position. He was achy and bruised from being jostled about on the rough canyon trails. It was difficult for him to obey Watson's order to stand erect, though with effort he did manage to straighten his posture in the man's presence. Adding to his discomfort, Ehron Lee was exhausted from the intense, near-claustrophobic heat he had been forced to endure during the long ride. He was lightheaded and nearly faint from dehydration. Only his defiance kept him from collapsing.

The driver and the guard were invited inside the superintendent's quarters for some refreshments before starting on the long ride back, but the driver declined for both of them. The prison gave him the willies, and he was eager to be away from there. He knew he'd be returning soon enough with more human cargo.

Sucking on the long, thin stem of a pipe, Watson looked Ehron Lee over with a trained, critical eye, determining what type of prisoner he would be. He prided himself on his ability to instantly reach into a man's soul; it had come from years of practice dealing with criminals. And once he spoke, Watson made it clear to Ehron Lee that the conditions the new prisoner was about to experience would not be pleasant regardless of his attitude—for on introduction he referred to the prison not by its official title, but by one of its feared nicknames:

"Burrows, welcome to Cartridge Hill," he said, forming the words around his pipe.

He elaborated—with emphasis, "Reckon you know why we call it that. But in case you don't . . ." He pivoted and pointed to all four corners of the surrounding walls. Armed prison guards patrolled the catwalks, keeping a vigilant eye on activities both inside and beyond the compound.

"That's all they do all day, every day, them and those that relieve 'em," Watson said, a note of pride in his voice. "Just stand up there waitin' for a prisoner to make a break. They get mighty antsy doin' the same thing over and over, so when they see somethin' amiss . . . well, they take full advantage of the diversion. And just so you should be knowin', each of 'em is a crack shot. Target practice is pretty much their sole recreation. You'll see a lot of guns 'round here, Burrows. When you work, when you eat. Even during break period. Chances are within a coupla weeks you'll even be seein' guns in your dreams."

Ehron Lee listened but did not acknowledge. He doubted he'd be allowed to speak in any case, unless he was asked a direct question. He hoped he wouldn't be. He didn't think he'd be able to offer much of a reply beyond a rasp; his mouth was dry and his throat was parched.

Flanked by two uniformed guards, Ehron Lee followed Superintendent Watson as he started across the sandy grounds. Watson continued speaking while they walked, though they were not words Ehron Lee particularly cared to hear.

"Wasn't sure at first where we'd put you, Burrows. Sometimes we get so crowded here we've had to fit four to a cell. But some room was made for you yesterday; three men tried to break out. Two were killed. The third . . . well, let's just say you won't be meetin' him right away. So you'll be bunkin' with just one other for the time being. 'Round here that's considered a luxury."

Superintendent Watson took another sweeping look around the compound. He wore a satisfied expression as he surveyed his "kingdom."

"Understand you were a soldier," he said crisply. "Lieutenant in the Union army. Impressive, but holds no merit here. The only uniform we recognize here is the one you'll be issued and won't have no fancy hardware pinned to it. You must know something 'bout discipline, though. Well, that's fine because it won't take long for you to discover that discipline and obedience are two qualities we insist upon here."

Ehron Lee noted the strange yet telling smile offered him by the superintendent.

"Mr. Brady, you'll take charge of the prisoner," Watson then said, turning to one of his men, who was chewing aggressively on a wad of tobacco. He was a barrel-chested man with sparse, close-cropped hair. The white glare of the sun reflected noticeably off his pink scalp.

The man named Brady expectorated a brown stream of juice, half saluted, and said, "Yessir," before giving Ehron Lee a nudge with his rifle barrel to get him moving.

Watson broke away from the men and headed toward his office. Ehron Lee, prodded forward by Mr. Brady, was directed toward another building.

Before Ehron Lee would be taken back to the superintendent to officially be read the rules of Rockmound, he first had to exchange his clothing for prison issue. He couldn't truly be considered a convict until he was dressed as one. There was no consideration of proper fit; Ehron Lee was of medium size and thin, so he was thrown a bundle in approximation of his height and weight.

Once he was outfitted in his gray, black-striped uniform, Ehron Lee was escorted by Mr. Brady to the superintendent's office, where Watson flipped through the papers prepared by the court.

A look of familiarity crossed his stern features as he came to an item recorded on one page, and he lifted his close-set, piercing eyes toward Ehron Lee.

"I see here you served under Henry Halleck at Corinth," Watson said, phrasing his words in a way that did not encourage an answer. Nor did he elaborate the reason for his comment.

In any case, it was quickly dismissed as Ehron Lee stood silently and motionlessly for twenty minutes while Watson slowly and precisely explained the rules and regulations of daily prison life. Ehron Lee listened without really hearing. What did catch his attention was a photograph sitting off to the side of the superintendent's desk. It was of a youngish woman, dark-haired, attractive, whom Ehron Lee imagined was the superintendent's daughter. Although there was hardly a resemblance between the woman encased in the ornate silver-edged frame and his wife, Ehron Lee felt a twinge of hurt, as the photograph was a reminder of Melinda.

Watson concluded his briefing with: "It's after six and you missed tonight's supper. Y'might as well go direct to your cell. Breakfast is at five a.m. Workday starts at six." He focused his attention on some other paperwork laid out on his desk and added curtly, "Dismissed, Burrows."

Ehron Lee was taken to another building. There were three such enclosures, each situated on the north, east, and west sides of the compound. Each was a long, rectangular, one-level structure comprised of large chunks of granite with rows of about twenty evenly spaced barred windows all facing south, but opening upon a view that extended no farther than the high walls of the prison. Each block was supervised by a captain. Mr. Brady was the captain in charge of the block that Ehron Lee would be occupying.

The interior was dark and depressing. The cells were separated into sections of four units, with each unit walled off from the next. A heavy wooden door with a sliding bolt lock on the outside provided entry to each. A guard was responsible for supervising each of these units. There was a narrow corridor running lengthwise between the entrance to the block and the cells, and on the width of wall between the first two cells was a wooden peg on which hung a large ring holding four oversized metal keys, positioned so that the ring was far out of reach from either of the two cells.

The cell itself was small and cramped, measuring eight feet by seven feet, and an unpleasant odor permeated the air. There were three bunks fastened to the walls by chains, two on one side and one on the other. If as the superintendent said there was occasion to fit four men into a cell, one would have to sleep on the floor.

Once Mr. Brady turned the key, locking the new arrival inside the cell, Ehron Lee noticed his cell mate, lying on the top bunk, on his side facing the wall. He was lying very still, didn't even seem to be breathing. Maybe he was asleep, maybe not. Ehron Lee was in no rush to get acquainted and so just sat himself on the bunk against the opposite wall.

After a while the man spoke.

"You don't gotta mouse around. I ain't sleepin'."

Slowly, he shifted his body and turned to face Ehron Lee. At first his face was partially shadowed, but it soon came full into the fading light of day.

Ehron Lee's first glimpse of the man almost caused his breath to catch in his throat.

He had witnessed all manner of terrible sights during the war: mutilation, disfigurement. After a while, if only to maintain his sanity, he'd become immune to most. But the face looking at him now truly chilled him.

It didn't even resemble a face, really, but rather, a ghastly mask.

The flesh was as white as a freshly laundered sheet. The only coloring evident was a long, brownish-red scar that stretched from the far corner of the right eye down to the upper lip. The eye drooped, veered outward, and had a twitch, suggesting that it had just escaped being permanently put out. A black bowler rested atop the head, under which long white hair, almost translucent, flowed straight and stringy over the shoulders and halfway down the back.

Gradually the man sat himself upright, his short legs dangling over the side of his bunk. He didn't say anything for a long while, just observed his new cell mate intently, boring into him with pale, lifeless eyes.

Ehron Lee tried not to appear ill at ease, and he kept shifting his eyes so they would not be drawn particularly to the disfiguring scar. The wound was deep and evidently had never properly healed. Perhaps because of the prominent scar and affected eye, the man's face seemed sort of lopsided.

His odd appearance made it difficult to determine his age: maybe late teens, early twenties. Whether he was, in fact, a younger man or if it was due to his strange condition, there was no suggestion of whiskers or facial hair; outside of the scar, his skin was smooth and shadowless.

Physically, he had a thin, weak build that suggested he could be bested in any fight. Yet despite his apparent frailty, he exuded a malevolent presence.

Finally, one side of his mouth started to widen in a

strange semblance of a smile. The injury to his upper lip had clearly caused some nerve damage as the other half of his mouth seemed almost immobile, making his attempt at a smile appear more cruel and cynical than friendly.

It was the same when he spoke. Only half the mouth moved, though his words were easily understood and came quickly. His voice held the trace of an accent that suggested he wasn't bred in the West.

"The name's Milo. Woodrow Milo. Don't bother shakin' hands. I don't like for people to touch me."

That was fine with Ehron Lee. He had no intention of extending his hand.

"You can call me Woody," he then added. "No need for formality where we are, huh?"

Before Ehron Lee could consider introducing himself, Woody began conversing, expressing himself in an odd manner.

"If I'da gone along with them others, you coulda had this room all to yourself," he said. "Thought about it. Mighta done it, too, only I don't fancy bein' dead or missin' a meal. Ain't no fancy dinin', for sure, but best you're gonna get." He asked eagerly, "Tell me, did yuh get supper?"

Ehron Lee got the impression he was being toyed with. If this Woody was wise to the prison routine, he'd know damn well he had arrived too late for the evening meal.

Ehron Lee just gave him a sullen look and shook his head "no" to the question. It was still difficult for him to talk, even if he was so inclined; his throat was so dry he felt as if he'd been swallowing sand.

Woody gave his head a vigorous nod. "Yeah, they'll do that to yuh. Keep yuh hungry at first, get yuh weak so's yuh can't put up no fuss."

Ehron Lee stayed silent.

Woody got an impatient look to him, waiting for his cell mate to say something in return. The talk didn't come.

"Guess you ain't never seen no one like me before, huh?" Woody then said, almost boastfully. "Was born this way. Ain't so bad. 'Cause of it, I can't do no work outdoors. Gotta keep outta the sun." He pointed a long, slender finger at Ehron Lee's sunburned face. "Yeah, I'd end up lookin' like you. Only worse. So's they keep me busy inside doin' cleanup and all. Rather be moppin' floors than bustin' rocks. No, it ain't so bad at all."

Ehron Lee nodded absently. He was in no mood for conversation, and this guy was a talker.

Woody spoke rapidly. "Yeah, so's I was tellin' yuh 'bout them other guys, the ones that used to share this cell. Yeah, two of 'em are dead. Guards never even gave 'em a chance. Shot 'em like they was rabbits. The third guy, and the worst of the bunch 'cause he did this to me . . ." At that, Woody traced a finger straight down the length of his scar. "Yeah, well, the guards fired a coupla shots into him, hurt him pretty bad, though they coulda killed him just as easy. Wish they woulda. But they're settin' him as an example to the rest of us and they ain't gonna make it easy on him. Once he's patched up, they'll throw him into the punishment pit. If the pit don't kill him, he'll be comin' back. Name's Ward Crawford. Well, I don't like him and he don't like me. He's mean and he's trouble. Watch out for him when he gets out. Yeah, got him mad 'bout somethin' and he pulls out this blade and tries to cut off my face. Right here in this cell. Woulda done it, too, if the guards didn't hear my yellin' and get here in time. That got him his first stay in the pit. Was madder'n hell at me when he got out. Funny thing is, the guards told him some things 'bout me, stuff I'd done, and then he kinda backed off. We still hate each other, but we don't cause trouble with one another. Heh-heh, ain't to no one's benefit, don't yuh know. One of us will be dead and the other will wish he was. The superintendent don't condone no murder in his prison, 'less it's done by the guards. Can't say how he'll be with you, though. Crawford, I mean. When he gets in the mood, he's meaner than a rattlesnake. Y'know, venom and all." He leaned forward conspiratorially on his bunk and spoke in a whisper, though with a wild gleam in his unaffected eye. "'Tween us, I ain't forgot what he done to me."

It was rambling talk, though Ehron Lee's wandering

attention halted abruptly at that last remark. Woody didn't have to elaborate; just the inflection in his voice and look in his eye made his intention clear, and Ehron Lee shivered inwardly with the realization that the deformed little prisoner was perfectly capable of carrying out his subtle threat. His first impression of his cell mate was accurate, with one disturbing addition: Woody Milo was likely insane.

Ehron Lee directed his focus away from Woody's distorted though intense gaze. That was when he noticed a bucket and ladle against the back wall.

"Drinkin' water," Woody said, settling back on his bunk. "Help yourself."

Ehron Lee was wary. There could be something else inside that bucket.

Woody took note of Ehron Lee's hesitance. "I ain't lyin' to yuh. Drink from the bucket myself. They fill it every morning."

Ehron Lee couldn't afford to be doubtful; his thirst was overwhelming. And while it was an unappetizing thought to be sharing the same water as his cell mate, he walked over, lifted the ladle, and took a tentative sip. It was warm but tasted all right.

"Go ahead . . . just don't drink it all," Woody said.

It was sage advice. Drinking too much too fast on an empty stomach could have unpleasant consequences. Ehron Lee drank slowly and just enough to satisfy him.

Woody said, "Might not always feed us, if'n we don't follow the rules, but each day we get a fresh bucket of water." He halted, waiting for Ehron Lee to consume his second ladleful. Then he added slyly, "'Course I prefer to wash in it."

He waited for Ehron Lee's reaction, which was immediate.

Ehron Lee spit out what he hadn't yet swallowed all over the floor. Woody's face took on a vacuous, almost uncomprehending expression, and then he started laughing, flopping back onto his bunk, pounding his hands and kicking his feet like a little kid who'd pulled a nasty prank as his laughter grew to a near-hysterical pitch.

Ehron Lee tensed, and impulsively, he started to move

toward Woody, prepared to send a fist into his bleached, twisted face. But he managed to restrain himself. If he started any trouble, especially on his first day, that would be noted and could make things rough for him. He'd learned from Superintendent Watson during his orientation that prisoners were allowed visiting privileges—once a month, depending on behavior. Ehron Lee couldn't risk losing that. But it instantly became clear that he would need to call upon all his discipline to maintain self-control, which he feared wouldn't be easy with the brutal conditions of the prison and a lunatic for a cell mate.

He desperately needed that first visit to talk with Melinda, warn her about what her sister planned on doing, and hopefully convince her not to be swayed by any of her lies and accusations. As it was, it tormented him when he considered how much damage Abigail could cause in just those thirty days.

Ehron Lee settled back on his bunk and let himself calm down, trying to shut out Woody's crazed laughter from his ears. He gazed upward out the small side window with the bars deeply embedded in granite, and saw that dusk was settling.

These were only his first hours at Hell's Doorway, and already he wondered how he would survive the next five years.

And the type of man he'd become if he did.

FOUR

SHERIFF BUCK LEIGHTON had kept a concerned eye on
Melinda Burrows during the days she and her sister, Abigail,
remained in town following the trial. It went beyond his
official duties, but he felt he owed it to her as he had begun
to look critically at the evidence surrounding Ehron Lee
Burrows's conviction.

Sitting in the saloon courtroom that morning listening to
Ehron Lee's lawyer, Addison Telborough, argue his client's
case, Buck started to observe that there might be some truth
to Ehron Lee's story. Afterward he'd met privately with the
attorney to review the details of the case, and convinced there
was sufficient reason to pursue the matter, he decided to do
some follow-up work on his own.

One thing he felt he should do was have a talk with
Melinda Burrows to tell her of his intentions, as well as find
out more about the kind of man Ehron Lee was from the
person who knew him best.

Late one morning Buck went to see her at the hotel to ask
her to lunch. Curious over the sheriff's invitation, she agreed.

Buck noticed how she was still confused and distressed over all that had happened. He hoped to provide her with a few words of encouragement.

Buck was relieved to see that Abigail had gone out for a while. He wanted to speak to Melinda without interference. What he had to say, he knew distinctly Abigail would not appreciate.

Instead of chancing to run into Abigail by walking along the streets to one of the town restaurants, Buck suggested the hotel coffee shop, which was fine with Melinda. They took a table not far from the big curtained window that overlooked the main street, the early afternoon sunshine spilling through the light fabric into the dining room, providing a welcoming bright touch to their conversation.

Both took a perfunctory look at the menu, but neither felt much like eating. Instead Buck drank strong coffee while Melinda sipped on a cup of tea.

The sheriff immediately got to the point.

"Think you understand I can't be makin' you no guarantees, Mrs. Burrows," he said. "A lot of time has passed and no tellin' where those men are now. It's a sure bet they're outta the territory. But I've notified other counties nearby askin' that they keep alert to any pair of strangers who might be passin' through. Reckon the biggest problem we got is that we don't have a good description of them two. None from that store they're said to have robbed in Shalett, nor from Elmer Bryant's boys. And, of course, your husband couldn't offer me nothin', outside of the fact that one of 'em was wearin' buckskins, and that ain't no definite identification. Like I said, no one got a clean enough look at 'em."

Melinda spoke quietly but hopefully. "But *you*, Sheriff, *you* believe Ehron Lee is innocent?"

Buck sighed. He reached for his coffee cup and held it to his lips. He had formed an opinion but decided it best to maintain professional objectivity.

"Really ain't for me to say," he said carefully. "Court found him guilty, but the judge himself showed he had reservations. And with the lack of hard evidence presented at the trial, plus a conversation I had with Mr. Telborough, I surely do feel there's sufficient room for doubt."

He refrained from adding another pertinent point: that no innocent man should be subjected to the tortures at Rockmound Prison.

Buck edged away from the topic.

"If you don't mind my askin', what are your plans?" he gently asked her.

"Thought I'd stay around town for a week or so; then, if my request is approved, I'll take the stage up to Allensfield. From there it's only a half-day ride to . . ." Melinda's voice trailed off.

Buck understood and waited patiently for her to continue.

Melinda smiled a trifle self-consciously and went on. "Mr. Telborough explained what has to be done. As it looks, I probably will only be making the one visit—least for a while, 'til after the baby comes." She smiled wanly. "Won't be in no condition to be doin' much traveling. Not right away."

Buck acknowledged her comment with a nod.

There was something else the sheriff felt he should say, but he was unsure if he should voice it, as it really was none of his affair. He debated momentarily before deciding to proceed.

"Mrs. Burrows—" he started to say.

"Please, Sheriff," the girl interjected with a pleasant parting of her lips. "I'd like it if you would call me Melinda."

Buck's craggy face likewise softened in a smile.

"Melinda." He paused for a moment, trying to figure on the best way to broach the subject. It was a sensitive matter.

Finally he just spoke his piece. "Mrs.—I mean Melinda, your sister said some pretty strong things ag'in your husband. She made it plain she ain't feelin' too kindly toward him."

Melinda lowered her eyes and placed both hands delicately around her teacup.

Buck spoke quickly. "If you'd rather for me not to be bringin' this up . . ."

Melinda drew a breath, then she sighed. She didn't directly answer his question. Instead she spoke her own words.

"Abigail . . . she's always cared for me. Protected me. Ever since we were children. After our folks died, it was Abigail who raised me. You see, there's quite a big difference in our age. She was already a teenager when I was born. So she took on that responsibility even though she really didn't have to. There were relatives who could have taken me in, but Abigail made the decision to look after me herself. She took care of me even after she married Winston." She paused to take a breath. "I know she's said some hurtful things, but—she's dealing with her own loss. She and Winston didn't always get along . . . she sometimes spoke harsh words toward him, but I know in her own way she loved him. This hasn't been easy on her, any more than it's been for me."

Buck scratched the back of his neck as he tentatively pushed on. "From what I've heard—and again, stop me if it ain't none of my business—she wants to take you away. Reckon under the circumstances she . . . might be wantin' you to leave your husband."

Melinda's lips pursed and her color started to redden. As Buck expected, the conversation was becoming difficult for her.

Melinda held herself back from expressing her displeasure at what the sheriff was saying. She didn't see how this should in any way concern him—or how especially it would be of any assistance in his trying to help her husband.

Buck took note of her troubled expression and hastened to clarify. "Reckon what I'm sayin' is now's the time your husband is gonna be needin' you. Rockmound is a tough place. I'll do whatever I can to set this right, if Ehron Lee is truly innocent. But he'll be needin' to know you're there for him, too."

Melinda felt a little easier. The sheriff had made clear his point, and Melinda now could both understand and appreciate his concern.

"Thank you, Sheriff," she said mildly.

He was relieved. "And why don't you make that Buck?" he told her.

"Buck?"

"Shortened from Buckley," Buck explained. "Think you can understand why I prefer Buck."

Melinda smiled at his remark and nodded.

She took a liking to the sheriff. Like her husband, he was a good man. She sensed that he had a genuine interest and wanted to help. She didn't question his reasons, saw nothing peculiar or suspicious in them, other than his wanting to set things right.

Buck encouraged Melinda to tell him everything she could about her husband, and in her telling, he detected nothing in Ehron Lee's character to suggest that he was a dishonest man. That was an opinion he himself had formed based on his own time spent with the man. It was his conclusion that Ehron Lee had been the victim of a series of unfortunate circumstances. But for which he—and his wife—were paying a terrible price.

Melinda deserved her husband back . . . and the baby she was carrying needed a father.

Three days later Buck received a message from the sheriff in Terrell County. Two men, one said to be clad in buckskins, had attempted to rob the general store. Buck's initial optimism faded once he learned that both men had been shot dead in the ensuing gunfight with the town law. Equally discouraging was the fact that the horses the two men had been riding were blue roans, not sorrels, which indicated that if they were the pair guilty of the crime for which Ehron Lee had been convicted, they may, prior to their failed robbery attempt, once again have traded off or stolen their mounts. Finally, they weren't carrying the saddlebag in which Ehron Lee's strongest proof of innocence—his bill of sale—might have been found. Buck conjectured that those probably had been discarded along some back trail, if not altogether destroyed to further cover the outlaws' tracks.

With the pair riddled with bullets, their corpses now laid out in the undertaking parlor, and buckskin clothing the only link to verify Ehron Lee's story—hardly compelling evidence—Buck knew he'd met defeat with his most promising lead.

Buck sat at his desk looking at the report for a long while before finally giving in to his frustration and crumpling the paper into a ball and tossing it aside.

Another bit of potential good luck had fallen by the wayside when Buck learned that Elmer Bryant had finally regained consciousness after his beating. Buck had ridden to the old man's place to find out if he could describe the two men who had attacked him, hoping that there might be enough discrepancy in his description to further remove the stain of guilt from Ehron Lee and Winston Maguire. But while Elmer had survived his injuries, Buck quickly discovered that the old man was not right in the head and retained no memory of what had happened to him.

There remained only one faint hope to free Ehron Lee, and that was in locating Albert Patterson, the man from whom Ehron Lee claimed to have purchased the land.

But with no lead to go on, with the likelihood of Patterson being virtually anywhere in the country, Buck could not see that effort bringing him or Ehron Lee much luck.

With a heavy heart he knew he had to break this news to Melinda. He held himself responsible because he had encouraged her to hold out some measure of hope. Now it looked almost certain that all hope had run out.

He returned to the hotel, where, to his surprise, he found Melinda and Abigail packing, not for Allensfield, but for their trip back to Brackett and the farm. He couldn't have known that earlier Melinda had argued with her sister that she wanted to see her husband before she headed back home, have at least that one visit with him, but Abigail was adamant that she return with her, her reasoning being that with Melinda expecting her baby, she'd need Abigail to care for her—and Abigail made it clear that she herself had no intention of visiting a prison. She added with perhaps exaggerated emotion that she was having enough trouble dealing with the memories of all that had happened. However, to pacify her sister, Abigail said that after the baby was born and Melinda was strong enough, then she could think about visiting her husband. Abigail sweetened her compromise by offering to look after the baby at that time.

Abigail, as usual, was firm in her decision and soon had Melinda convinced that what she was saying was for the best—though Melinda insisted she had to at least write to Ehron Lee to explain the situation so that he would understand the reason for her not coming and not worry. Abigail assured her that Ehron Lee would understand . . . and she even offered to post the letter for her.

Being the naïve, trusting girl that she was, the type of person she had grown up to be, Melinda accepted and appreciated her sister's offer. She stayed up a good part of the night composing exactly what she wanted to tell her husband—expressing in tender words her assurances and especially her love and belief in him.

After the letter was written, Melinda sealed it in an envelope and handed it to Abigail.

Of course, her sister had no intention of seeing the letter reach its destination. Much later, when Abigail was alone, she secretly opened the envelope, read the letter with disgust, and destroyed it. She was satisfied that Melinda would never learn of her subterfuge. After all, she reasoned, no one could really be sure of what happened to letters delivered to a distant and forbidding prison like Rockmound.

When Buck Leighton entered the hotel room later that day, Abigail greeted him coolly with a curt "Sheriff" before ignoring his presence entirely. Melinda looked timid and slightly ashamed. She knew what he would be thinking after their conversation of the other day. Buck did give her a knowing look, but he refrained from commenting. It wasn't his place. Yet his gut feeling told him that once Melinda left town with her sister, Abigail would exercise her considerable influence over the girl and Melinda would not be making *any* trips to Rockmound to visit her husband. With that knowledge, he felt there was no point in sharing with her the discouraging news he had received from the sheriff in Terrell County.

Instead he tipped his hat, wished them both a pleasant trip, and expressed the hope that Melinda would stay in touch.

Melinda said she would, but Buck caught the quick, hard glance Abigail leveled at her sister. A look that only Buck noticed, which indicated that if Abigail had her way, Melinda would have no further dealings with the town of Justice—or with her husband.

FIVE

JUDGE CHARLES HUGH Harrison finished up his business in Justice and, after capping this latest assignment with his customary glass of saloon brandy, returned by stagecoach to his quaint country home some fifty miles north of the town in a place called Bolton, for what he hoped would only be a brief stopover. Since his judicial duties were frequent, overseeing trials and settling disputes in small Arizona towns and communities, his visits home usually never exceeded a couple of weeks. During that time he mostly kept to himself, immersing himself in virtual solitude, avoiding lengthy talks with his wife, particularly about personal matters. Dinner table conversations with his wife and daughter tended to be brief and perfunctory. When it came time to retire for the night, which was always at an early hour when he was at home, and always after he had sequestered himself in the parlor for some post-dinner reading, he and his wife slept in separate bedrooms. He could conveniently justify this arrangement because of her ill health.

He spent most of his daytime hours tending his vegetable and flower gardens, not because he particularly enjoyed dirtying his hands in the soil, but because it provided him with an excuse for time alone. Early each morning he would awaken before his wife and daughter, eat a quick breakfast he would prepare himself, then dress in faded and dirty dungarees, don a battered straw hat to protect his balding head from the sun, and step out into the yard to focus on nothing but the task at hand.

Although she was ill, Harrison's wife, like most women, yearned at times for some show of affection, a romantic word or gesture, but the judge was a man incapable of expressing tender feelings. His wife would have to settle for the occasional pat on the hand or peck on the cheek—and even those moments were infrequent. Gradually she had grown accustomed to Harrison's determined avoidance of sentimentality, just as she accepted without question his constant need for privacy.

However, she was less accepting when it came to her husband's relationship with their daughter, Evaline. Since Harrison was often absent and spent so little time with Evaline, his wife felt he should take better advantage of those periods when he was home. As she would gently try to explain during rare moments of intimate conversation, their daughter was growing up and needed the guidance and wisdom of her father.

More to placate his wife, Harrison did attempt to establish a semblance of a relationship, but he found it difficult to exhibit paternal interest in his child. Even simple communication with her seemed beyond his grasp. His "relationships" with younger girls had been of an entirely different nature. He valued them solely for one purpose. He neither understood nor cared about their needs. And this thoughtlessness extended even toward his daughter.

On a deeper level, though it naturally was never expressed, Harrison inwardly resented Evaline for it had been his wish to have a son, which would never be, as Evaline's had been a difficult birth and the doctor had frankly warned the judge that an attempt at another child could prove fatal for his wife.

Nevertheless, Harrison took it for granted that, as her

father, he loved her, though, as with his wife, it was never expressed through words or displayed by outward shows of affection. If he'd ever given it thought, he would not remember even having ever kissed her. Evaline, like her mother, had come to accept that reserve as simply his nature—perhaps an extension of his professional persona. She could not imagine there being any difference between the man she saw as her "father" and Judge Charles Harrison.

Where Evaline had difficulty was in how he failed to acknowledge her accomplishments, which she was always eager to share with him. Since she saw him so seldom, Evaline sought his approval and felt a deep yet silent disappointment when such was not forthcoming. Harrison rarely if ever expressed pride in the high grades she worked hard to achieve in school, primarily to please him, or showed enthusiasm for her musical talents, particularly in piano, where she had received recognition in church recitals. Before she became sick and was more physically able, her mother had been the one to nurture her gifts and shower her with praise. Where she encouraged Evaline's talents, her father responded to what he considered "frivolities" in a dismissive manner that was hurtful to his daughter.

As such, a gap existed between Harrison and his daughter. Harrison never considered this a troubling proposition. As a man firmly set in his ways, he accepted his domestic situation as the way things should be, ignorant to the pain his uncaring attitude caused Evaline—or his wife, for that matter.

Besides, he contented himself with the knowledge that soon he would be summoned to preside over another court case . . . and partake in the pleasures of another bordello.

SIX

IN THE DAYS, then weeks, that followed, Ehron Lee Bur-rows struggled to keep the vow he had made to himself. Against the endless strain of long, arduous, sun-baked labor, busting rocks and clearing gravel-laden trails in the quarry while locked in painful leg irons, the taunting and outright cruelty of the guards, meager meals most often consisting of rotten potatoes and stale, maggoty crackers, and the tension that came from being confined with his cell mate, whose unbalanced moods were apt to swiftly change from childlike amiability to potential menace, Ehron Lee maintained good behavior and obeyed the prison rules. He never complained about the exhausting work and accepted any order given to him without argument.

During his roughest moments, only two things gave him the strength to keep going. One was the discipline he had observed in the army; the other, of course, was his determination to see his wife. He discovered that he could endure most anything by keeping the image of Melinda's sweet face imprinted on his consciousness. Then, despite the grueling days and the distance that separated them, Ehron Lee would feel she was beside him and he could continue to hold out hope.

He was certain his fortitude would be further strengthened come visiting day when he could see her and talk with her . . .

But as the assigned day approached, Ehron Lee started to grow concerned. He hadn't received word from the superintendent that Melinda's visit had been confirmed—or approved. If she had sent a letter of her intention to the prison, Ehron Lee hadn't been told. He asked to speak directly to Superintendent Watson about whether he had been notified of her arrival, only to have the guards bluntly refuse his request. He was informed that the superintendent would speak with prisoners only when *he* wanted to see them, and generally that was when a punishment was in order. Rarely was a prisoner granted an audience at his own request. Ehron Lee's only contact with Rockmound authority was through the guards, and they had proven themselves a cruel, unsympathetic lot. *If* confirmation of a visit was received, *if* permission was granted, the guards themselves would notify the prisoner. And since many of them offset their own boredom by finding ways to torment the men, often this information was withheld until the last minute, giving the prisoner virtually no time to prepare for the visit. They would meet with their loved ones fresh off their work detail, dirty, sweaty, and often so heat-exhausted they were barely able to contribute to or comprehend any conversation.

Ehron Lee didn't know if this was what the Rockmound guards were planning to do with him, but a feeling of apprehension had begun to grip at his gut. His greatest dread was that perhaps Melinda would not be coming. All manner of troubling thoughts flooded his brain: Had she taken ill, had something happened to the baby . . . or had Abigail succeeded in working her poison on her?

Late on the Friday night before visiting day a full moon passed a shaft of light into the cell, casting a lengthening shadow of the barred window across the floor.

A bitter, mocking reminder to Ehron Lee, who was

unable to sleep and was restlessly pacing the small cell, eight strides from barred window to cell door.

Woody Milo was watching him from his bunk. He was on his side, propped up on an elbow, quietly amused at his cell mate's dilemma.

"Don't hold your breath," Woody finally said, speaking in a quick, hushed tone. "Don't get many visitors out here. Too far to travel, and it's unsafe country, too. Never know when them Injuns might decide to stir up trouble. From what I hear, them that got left behind after the roundup have been keepin' themselves scarce, but you never know with a redskin. Yeah, takes a real special lady to chance that risk. And I ain't seen many of those."

Ehron Lee stopped pacing. He turned to Woody and shot him a hard look.

Woody threw up his hands in a defensive gesture. "Ain't sayin' nothin' in particular. Just been here a lot longer and seen how things are."

"She'll be here," Ehron Lee muttered with forced confidence. He had to convince himself that she would.

Woody stretched out on his bunk. "If'n I was you, I wouldn't be lettin' myself in for a disappointment," he said.

Ehron Lee was on edge, his nerves taut with an uncertainty that threatened to overwhelm him. This was one time he couldn't let Woody antagonize him because he couldn't be sure of himself, how he'd have the potential to react. Ehron Lee's behavior had been exemplary, but tonight he feared it wouldn't take much for him to become aggressive and lose those privileges he believed he had earned—if Woody didn't shut up.

He stepped over to Woody's bunk and fastened him with a cold stare. "I don't want no trouble with you, Milo," he said firmly. "So take this as friendly advice. Keep yourself outta my concerns."

Woody emitted a quick laugh. "Right now we ain't got no one but each other."

Ehron Lee regarded him with a skeptical look. "What's that supposed to mean?"

"Fact is, I'm the only friend you got in this place," Woody said brightly.

Ehron Lee brushed aside the remark with a dismissive wave of his hand and started to turn away. That was when Woody leaped down from the bunk and positioned himself directly in front of Ehron Lee, the nearest physically he had yet got to his cell mate. Too close to suit Ehron Lee.

"You think I'm jokin'?" Woody said, looking up into the taller man's face, one eye direct, the other tilted eerily downward and focused slightly to the side. "You forget that I don't do no work outdoors. I clean out the cells. Maybe a coupla times a week they take me over to the superintendent's office. Do cleanin' there, too. Sometimes—I see things. 'Course I'm careful . . . but I've taken a gander at some of the stuff that comes in." His voice took on a sly edge. "Interestin' stuff . . . like names that are on the monthly visitor list."

Ehron Lee's face was rigid, his expression grim.

"What're yuh sayin'?" he said slowly.

Woody lifted a shoulder. "Reckon what you don't wanta hear. Your wife's name ain't on that list."

The immediacy of the words impacted like a sharp puncture, deflating the hope that Ehron Lee had worked so hard to hold on to.

Ehron Lee's fists clenched reflexively. His first urge was to grab Woody by his skinny shoulders and slam him against the wall.

And then he steadied himself, collected his thoughts. He remembered who the source of this so-called information was. The twisted little punk who had been trying to rile him off and on since the day he arrived at Rockmound. Was this something else he'd cooked up for his own amusement?

"You better know what you're talkin' about," Ehron Lee said darkly, his body still poised aggressively.

Woody's blood quickened and he suddenly seemed like a scared child, sensing that Ehron Lee was ready to do him harm.

He started to stammer. "Y-You ain't g-gonna hit me, are yuh? I—I told yuh, I d-don't like for no one to t-touch me."

"You opened the door on this, Milo," Ehron Lee said with deliberate emphasis. "You finish what you started . . . and you best have somethin' to back your words."

"C-can't tell yuh no m-more than I d-did," Woody said anxiously, the stutter in his voice becoming more pronounced. "I t-told yuh: I saw the list. D-Didn't see no one n-named 'Burrows' on it. List ain't g-got that m-many names I wouldn'ta noticed."

Sensing Ehron Lee's mood shifting, Woody started to step back, toward the bars of the cell.

Ehron Lee's features contorted in thought; though, in fact, he stubbornly refused to accept what Woody was telling him.

"You're lyin'," he said thickly.

Woody shrugged his shoulders weakly. "W-Why would I?"

"If what you're sayin' is so, why wasn't I told?" he demanded. "The superintendent hadda know I was expectin' to see Melinda."

Woody shrugged, his eyes darting about the cell nervously. "W-Why would they t-tell yuh she ain't c-comin'? Havin' visitors is a p-privilege, n-not an obligation. Th-They d-don't owe you nothin'."

Ehron Lee's face paled and his legs felt strangely weak. He swallowed so hard that the bobbing in his throat was noticed by his cell mate. Ehron Lee lowered himself onto his bunk. Woody stayed pressed against the bars for a few moments, then, trusting Ehron Lee wouldn't make a grab at him, he gradually inched his way over to the opposite bunk and carefully sat himself down. His breathing was labored but he gradually regained his composure.

"'C-Course, it's likely the superintendent hisself mighta refused your missus permission," Woody said, losing his stammer as he calmed. "Seen it happen before."

Ehron Lee tried to absorb what Woody was suggesting. But it couldn't be right. It didn't make sense. He'd played by all the rules. He was owed this visit from Melinda. And suddenly he knew that if Milo was lying to him, making a cruel joke at his expense, he'd strangle him dead right there in the cell.

Ehron Lee looked back at Woody. "He'd have no call. I ain't caused no trouble. I've put up with every bit of stinkin' dirt they've handed me. There ain't no reason for them not to allow her to see me."

Woody dared to speak boldly. "You're in prison, Ehron Lee. To Watson and them others, you're just another convict. You ain't worth spit, far as they're concerned. They don't need no reason for anything they do."

Ehron Lee was too engrossed in his shuffle of thoughts to take offense at Woody's remark, as truthful as it might be.

His eyes narrowed until they became like slits. His mouth started to tremble.

"I coulda waited the month," he muttered to himself. "I could eat all the garbage they fed me for a month, knowin' that I'd be seein' my wife. That's all the reward I asked for . . . and I sweat blood for it!" His voice rose in pitch as a bottled rage uncorked and forced its way to the surface. "That's how it is, huh? Yeah . . . yeah, we'll see."

Ehron Lee thundered over to the door of the cell, widening his arms and gripping the bars tightly, whitening his knuckles, and began yelling for the guards. He was demanding to speak to the superintendent. Soon the outer door opened and a beefy, mean-faced guard stomped into the cell block. For extra emphasis he was waving his truncheon aggressively.

He spoke harshly, with a thick Irish brogue. "Stop that shoutin', or I'll be comin' in there to give yuh somethin' to really be yellin' 'bout."

Ehron Lee's indignation was so pronounced he was beyond being intimidated by this big bag of wind.

"Tell Watson I wanta see him," he said heatedly.

"And you can go to hell," the guard returned. He spit toward the cell.

Ehron Lee was wild-eyed. "You tell *Superintendent* Watson that if he don't agree to see me . . . and in five minutes . . . I'll rip this goddamn cell apart!"

"And as I'll be tellin' yuh, you can go straight to hell." The guard spit again and stomped out of the cell block.

Woody was both alarmed and amazed. Until this moment he'd seen Ehron Lee put up with the miserable conditions and rough treatment and never once let go of his temper. That clearly was about to change, and it looked to have frightening consequences.

"Take it easy, Ehron Lee," he said in a pacifying tone. "He gets them other guards in here and it ain't gonna be pleasant for either of us. Maybe—maybe things'll be different next month."

But Ehron Lee wasn't hearing. All reasoning had left him. Everything he'd kept locked within him during the past month was readying to be unleashed.

"There ain't gonna be no next month!" he erupted with such venom that Woody scrambled to the back of the bunk, pressing himself tightly against the wall, hunching his slight body and hugging his knees with both arms.

Ehron Lee's face swelled red as the blood surged into his head.

He yelled with vehemence through the bars. "Don't think I got the nerve, do yuh, you sowbellied son of an Irish pig!"

Ehron Lee began shouting, cursing. He had become more than irrational; he was in an unbridled fury. He turned to his bunk, grabbed the thin, ratty mattress with both hands, and flung it to the floor, kicking it over and over until the flimsy fabric ripped apart under the repeated impact and feathers began scattering throughout the cell. Then he stalked over to the back wall, grabbed the water bucket, and tossed it forcefully against the bars of the cell, water splashing out everywhere into the corridor.

It didn't take long for the ruckus to bring three burly guards hurrying into the cell block, one of whom was the Irishman. Ehron Lee met them defiantly, challenging them to come inside the cell. He was on his feet, eyes glazed and bulging, brandishing the water bucket as a weapon, ready to fight all of them if they dared to step a foot inside. The Irishman wore a grim smile as he pulled the big key ring off the side of the outer wall and jammed the appropriate key into the lock. The other two guards had their truncheons at the ready, likewise smiling at the prospect of beating an unruly prisoner into submission. Woody squirmed on his bunk. He was trembling, both from fear and, admittedly, excitement.

Once the cell door was opened, the guards rushed inside. Ehron Lee swung the water bucket at the first man in, the Irishman, slamming it into his jaw and knocking him back into the two guards who were following behind. With all three momentarily thrown off balance in the cramped confines of the cell, Ehron Lee tried to scramble past but was grabbed at the ankle before he could reach the door. He attempted to kick himself free, but the hand gripping him held fast and tightly, allowing the other two guards time to regain themselves and start swinging at Ehron Lee with their truncheons, delivering a battery of blows to his head, back, and shoulders. Ehron Lee desperately tried to protect himself by hunching his shoulders and covering his head, crossing his arms tightly over his skull, but he was soon overwhelmed. Woody was alternately laughing and crying as he watched the savage beating go on for almost a full minute.

Finally Ehron Lee's battered body went limp and two of the guards dragged him moaning from the cell. The third guard stayed behind and glared at the cowering Woody.

His breathing came hard as he said, scowling, "Besides bein' an ugly sonofabitch, you're one sneaky weasel, Milo. I find out you were somehow behind this . . . and things ain't gonna go much better for you." He brandished his blood-stained club in Woody's direction for emphasis.

Submerged in sweltering heat, surrounded by filth and the stink of rot and decay, suffering paroxysms of pain from his injuries, while his rage intensified; his mind slipping out of control.

Pulled semiconscious from his cell, Ehron Lee had been tossed directly into one of two deep "punishment" holes dug into the grounds in back of the compound, each of which was known by the prisoners as "the pit." Ehron Lee had lain there for several days, floating in and out of consciousness, mercifully unaware of the physical anguish that would be there to assail him once he revived: an intense, crippling pain that coursed throughout most of his body.

But in a strange way, he appreciated the suffering. It gave him a perverse strength. It contributed to the burning hatred that he now recognized was becoming a permanent part of his character.

When he first came to, he could barely lift his arms or maneuver any part of his body without enduring the most intense agony. Each movement he attempted was tentative, so mostly he held his pain-wracked body still, scarcely daring even to breathe. He didn't think any bones had been broken, though his shoulders and upper torso were covered in bruises. His eyes were puffy and his face was swollen and caked with dried blood.

As time passed, he wondered if he'd been confined to this stinking pit to rot.

To rot.

He recalled the words of his sister-in-law, Abigail, spoken to him after his sentencing and now reaching him like a distant echo: *"I hope you rot."*

Maybe she'd gotten her wish. And she'd likely gotten her other wish, too, for it was only with faint hope that Ehron Lee believed he'd ever see his beloved Melinda again.

He was overwhelmed with rage, but it was a helpless emotion. In his more rational periods he simply wanted to die, for he saw no purpose in living anymore.

It was perpetually dark where he was. The pit was truly a pit. During the daytime hours he might catch slivers of light filtering through the cracks between the pieces of heavy wood planking covering the narrow ceiling shaft about ten feet above him, but they provided little relief from the oppressive gloom. The quiet that surrounded him was nearly deafening. He was far enough away from any activity in the compound not to detect sound or motion. He existed in virtual isolation.

No one came to check on him. Not Superintendent Watson, nor the doctor, nor any of the guards. If they had, they would have to be lowered into the hole since the ceiling shaft was the only access to this unique form of imprisonment. But he wasn't totally forgotten. He was fed twice a day. His meal, a basket containing stale bread and a small jug of water, was passed down the shaft to him on a rope.

One evening there was a rare thunderstorm, and as the heavy rain poured relentlessly throughout the night, it seeped through the cracks of the planking into the pit, soon creating a pool on the earth floor. Ehron Lee was chilled by the dampness and he huddled tightly against a corner of the mud wall, trying vainly to keep himself warm and dry.

Miraculously, he survived that night without becoming ill.

Perhaps it was an approach of madness. But he took his survival as a sign.

A strange message that he had a purpose to fulfill. An unexpected destiny.

And so the days passed. Slowly Ehron Lee's body healed . . . but not his mind.

Sitting in his endless solitude, with nothing else to occupy his thoughts, he created images in his brain, disturbing but to him all too real mental pictures of Abigail hastening Melinda onto a stagecoach, heading to some unknown, faraway destination. He could hear clearly his sister-in-law's urgent words:

"Come now, Melinda, let's hurry. You know this is for the best. Ehron Lee never was no good for you."

Together they would ride off to raise *his* child—alone. Abigail would never forfeit her control over Melinda to another man.

The most troubling part was that he could see Melinda weakening and eventually surrendering to Abigail's obstinacy. As he thought about it, he and Melinda had barely had a life together. First, the long separation because of the war, and now his imprisonment. She was still a young girl with a whole lifetime open to her. He asked himself outright: Why would she stick by him any longer? And even if she waited for him to be released, what type of life could he offer her and his child, branded as an ex-convict? What work would be open to him to support his family? Melinda would most likely have to find a job. She'd have both a husband and a child to look after. How fair would that be to her?

How could she not finally give in to her sister's influence?

Obsessed by these thoughts, day by day having them run over and over in his brain like a mad rodent scurrying in an endless circle, Ehron Lee's mental faculties had become as brittle as dry kindling. Yet in an odd way he realized that he had never before thought with such clarity.

He determined that *someone* had to be held accountable for the unjust fate that had befallen him. It was the only way to make things right. Of course, nothing could ever really be put right—it was too late for that. But he was owed a debt and he intended to collect.

During the war he'd witnessed man's brutality. He saw it again when he returned home to Kansas and discovered Quantrill and his band's savage handiwork. The destruction of his father's property and the destruction done to his father's mind. Still, even during those darkest days, he never surrendered hope—not with the pure and devoted love of Melinda to sustain him, and the joy of them furthering that love in the giving of a new life. The picture he'd always envisioned: a family sharing a lifetime of togetherness.

Yet circumstances determined that it could never be. The simple happiness he sought would be denied him because he'd been wrongly accused of a crime and made to suffer a brutal penalty. *That* was the real crime, and for such a crime, there had to be justice.

An eye for an eye, the Good Book said.

For whatsoever as a man soweth, that shall he also reap.

Ehron Lee vividly remembered those words he had heard

as a boy, delivered by a minister hell-bent on preaching fire and brimstone. They had terrified him.

But now he saw a new truth in them. A truth he could use to satisfy his own purpose.

Perhaps not in the way the Good Book intended, but that no longer mattered to him. Ehron Lee Burrows could now admit he had an overwhelming resentment toward God—that Almighty Power by whom he had been abandoned. Who had allowed his wife to be taken from him and now permitted him to suffer in a living hell.

He'd been condemned not only to the walls of a prison, but also to the erosion of his soul. For he sought retribution. A justice of his own making.

Vengeance is mine.

Yes, he could pervert those words to justify what needed to be done.

Perhaps God would grant mercy and forgiveness to the perpetrators of this tragedy. But Ehron Lee would not.

And as his bitterness continued to fester, Ehron Lee held two men responsible. Two men who in their individual capacities were the architects of his damnation.

Both stood for the law and order that had condemned him.

Ehron Lee Burrows—a man who only wanted to live his life rightly.

Ehron Lee Burrows—the victim of a travesty of justice.

Maybe he couldn't take back what was his.

But somehow, someway, he could even the score.

And he swore that no matter what happened to him, regardless of whatever further cruelty they might inflict upon him, he would live to see that day of reckoning.

SEVEN

CONFINED TO A near-midnight world of claustrophobic blackness and the deafening sounds of silence, with no knowledge of the passage of day or night, Ehron Lee could not know how long he had been kept buried alive in the pit. But the day finally came when the guards arrived to set him free.

It was going on noon. The hottest period of the day, with the temperature nearing a hundred degrees.

He was lying stretched out on his back when they lifted the planking and gazed down at him, considering, with little concern, whether he was dead or alive, as he was unresponsive to their shouts. Finally one of the guards went to fetch a bucket of water from the well. When he returned, he dumped the contents directly onto Ehron Lee's face, startling him back to consciousness.

The guards laughed with cruel humor as his eyes widened in surprise and he sputtered water from his mouth.

By that time, Ehron Lee was half out of his mind. His brain alternated between hallucination and harsh reality. He was only vaguely aware of the noose-like rope being thrown down to him through the open shaft along with the shouted instructions to loop the rope under his armpits . . . then his being lifted from the darkness and thrust into the blinding daylight. The guards pulled off the rope and welcomed him back by tossing him onto the ground like the trash they considered him to be. His eyes couldn't adjust to the sudden assault of sunlight, and he frantically covered his face with his arms while he writhed about in the dirt.

One of the guards kicked him to his feet and roughly led him back to the cell block, taunting him with such remarks as how he smelled worse than a skunk. Encrusted in weeks of filth as Ehron Lee was, this was not an entirely inaccurate observation.

The cell door was unlocked with the big set of keys and Ehron Lee was shoved inside, landing sprawled onto the hardness of the floor, where he lay without moving as the guard relocked the door and departed the block with a sneer.

The outer door slammed shut, its echo reverberating throughout the cell block. Then silence, followed by the muttering of voices.

One was gruff and gravelly and unfamiliar to Ehron Lee.

"One of these days I'm gonna make a grab for those keys," it said.

The second voice Ehron Lee recognized but could not immediately place. It was higher-pitched and there was a slight edginess to the tone.

"You tried somethin' like that before and they gave yuh two more years."

"Yeah, and you can shut your mouth, Whitey," the gruff voice snapped.

Ehron Lee felt himself being pulled to his feet by his shoulders—not roughly, not gently. As his eyes regained their focus, he looked into the raw, rough features of the man whose voice he did not recognize. The face was sallow-complected with slate gray eyes topped by a mop of greasy black hair.

The man's thin lips were chapped and twisted in a cynical half-smile.

"Ehron Lee Burrows," he said affably. "Heard all 'bout yuh from Whitey here. Name's Ward Crawford."

Ehron Lee was too disoriented to place any significance to the name. Ward gave a slight, understanding nod and helped seat Ehron Lee onto his bunk.

"Fact is, I can respect any man who's gone through what we did," Ward said. "Sure ain't no picnic."

The physical effects of Ehron Lee's confinement were evident. He was malnourished and had lost a lot of weight. His previously ill-fitting prison uniform was hanging even more loosely from his body. His face was thin and had a grayish pallor. The cords in his narrow neck stood out. Congealed blood still scabbed his skin under his disheveled growth of beard, and his eyes were pouched and red-rimmed.

"You look like hell and yuh ain't gonna feel like talkin' for a spell, I know," Ward said to him. "Thing is, they'll only give yuh 'nuff time to get your strength back before settin' yuh back to work. 'Less you *are* dead, they don't put up with any deadweight 'round here."

Ehron Lee collapsed back onto the mattress and immediately fell into an exhausted sleep. When he awoke later, it was to the refreshing pressure of cool moisture being applied to his face. He blearily opened his eyes and suppressed a shudder at the face leaning over him. Slowly he became aware that it wasn't some hellish gargoyle that had followed him from the pit, but his cell mate, Woody Milo, wiping his face with a wet piece of cloth. Ehron Lee shifted his eyes and saw that Woody's other hand held a razor.

"You slept for alla yesterday," Woody said gently. Noticing Ehron Lee's stare focused on the razor, he added, "They trust me *not* to cut your throat, or mine for that matter."

Ehron Lee regained enough of his senses to tense at the remark.

Woody grinned out the one side of his mouth. "You don't gotta worry. Another one of my chores 'round here. Taught me a trade I'll never get to use on the outside." He dipped the cloth, stained a sickly brownish color with dried blood, into a bucket near his feet to rewet it.

Ehron Lee relaxed. He coughed to clear a buildup of phlegm from his throat.

"Hope that ain't our drinkin' water?" he half joked, uttering his words in a feeble voice.

Woody shook his head.

"Uh-uh. Got 'em to bring in another bucket. Nice of 'em, huh?" he said with sarcasm.

Ehron Lee tried to rock his head in acknowledgment but it still ached.

"How long did they keep me . . . *there*?" he asked.

"I'm in for life, I don't count days anymore," Woody answered stiffly. "But I'd say they kept yuh there for 'bout two weeks. That's 'bout as long as a man can take it, and some don't even make it that long. Yeah, the guards hate it when they gotta climb down into the pit and pull out a dead one. Stinks somethin' awful." He stood up and added, "They wanta put yuh back into work detail in the next coupla days. They do that . . . and likely you'll die."

Ehron Lee grimaced. Though weak and still in sufficient pain, he spoke his words with grit and purpose.

"Ain't figgerin' on dyin' . . . yet," he said.

Once more he drifted off to sleep. When he next awoke, it was getting dark in the cell. The barred window began to get gray; night was approaching. He struggled to sit himself upright on the bunk. Woody was seated across from him. Then Ehron Lee noticed Ward Crawford standing by the window, gazing morosely outside into the compound.

Ward slowly turned his head toward Ehron Lee and grinned through straight and even but tobacco-stained teeth.

"Whitey's been takin' real good care of you," he said archly, jerking a thumb at Woody.

Woody's shoulders and arms tensed as his fingers flexed, and he said with muted emphasis, "Don't like for you to be callin' me that."

Ward's mouth curled in a thin, amused smile.

"That's what yuh are, ain't it?" he said with mock innocence.

Ward walked over to Ehron Lee's bunk and lifted a foot onto the metal base.

"Whitey's okay," he said. "A pretty tough hombre, in fact. S'pose he told you how I gave him that scar."

Woody's hand reflexively touched the wound on his face and his features twisted into a grimace.

Ehron Lee saw no point in answering.

"Messed yuh up pretty bad," Ward said to Ehron Lee. "Guards look for any reason to blow off steam. You gave 'em plenty. From what I heard, you came purty close to bustin' one's jaw." Here he mocked an Irish accent: "Sergeant Liam O'Brien. Yeah, he's a skunk, one of the worst 'round this cesspool. Watson likes 'em mean and O'Brien purty much tops the list. Lemme tell yuh, this place is fulla bad characters, but ain't one got nothin' on George Watson and his band of cutthroats."

Ehron Lee bit down on his bottom lip but remained quiet.

"Still kinda stiff from my own time underground," Ward said as he flexed and rolled his broad shoulders, then winced at a sudden, sharp pain. "Not to mention a coupla bullet holes." He smiled. "'Fact, we was probably neighbors for a time. Sure, nursed me back to health so they could toss me in the pit. 'Course, 'cause they added time to my sentence, they only gave me a week down there." His smile became a smirk. "'Sides, I just tried to bust out, not bust the fat face of no guard."

"Shoulda killed him," Ehron Lee muttered scornfully through clenched teeth. "Yeah, and Watson, too . . . if I coulda got to him."

"Whitey here told me 'bout that," Ward went on. "'Bout him refusin' a visit from your old lady—"

Ehron Lee's eyes flashed angrily at Ward, silencing him.

Ward understood. His words weren't tactful, and he had offended his cell mate. He raised his hand in an apologetic gesture. A big hand thick with calluses.

"Yeah, I mean your *wife*," he corrected deliberately. He sat himself on the bunk next to Ehron Lee and spoke in a low voice. "Reckon you know now how our superintendent operates. He makes all the decisions 'round here, and if you know what's good for yuh, you don't ever question 'em.

'Course them rules don't apply to him. His woman's come 'round. Gets kinda hurtful for the fellas here when they have to see that."

"Watson's got a wife?" Ehron Lee asked with interest.

"Sure," Ward drawled. "Him and his missus got a house in Allensfield. 'Cause Watson don't get home much, on occasion she rides out here to the prison. Not often since Watson don't want none of us vermin to be gawkin' at her . . . but maybe once every coupla months. Lock themselves in Watson's office and enjoy some 'private time,' if'n yuh get my meanin'. Leastwise, that's what we all figger. And I'll tell yuh, she's a fine-lookin' lady. Watson might not spend much time with her, but he surely provides well."

"Saw a photograph in Watson's office," Ehron Lee said, remembering. "Thought it might be his daughter."

"Hell no!" Ward exclaimed. "That's his wife. Reckon he likes 'em young."

Ward noticed the flush of resentment start to spread across Ehron Lee's features.

He said, "Lemme tell yuh, the only guys with nothin' to lose in this place are those that don't got wives or families. Like me . . . and Whitey."

"I got folks," Woody protested, then hesitated. "Somewhere."

"Yeah, I know. They took one look at you and skeedaddled," Ward said caustically, speaking out the side of his mouth.

Woody huffed and looked offended. Ward grinned at him.

"Just havin' some fun with yuh, kid," he said good-naturedly.

"Just wish you'd knock it off once in a while," Woody said sulkingly. "And stop callin' me Whitey all the time."

Ward shrugged indifferently. "Whitey. Woody. Just names. Mean nothin'. Ain't *who* you are but *what* you are that matters, kid."

"And I ain't no kid, neither," Woody snapped at him.

Ward gave him a deep look. There was a hint of respect in his voice when he said, "Yeah, I know you ain't."

The momentary tension passed. Ward turned his attention back to Ehron Lee.

"Jokin' aside, don't take this guy lightly," he said, tilting his head toward Woody. "Maybe if I'd known more, I wouldn'ta carved up his face. Y'see, Whitey's a killer. Sure, went on a rampage and gunned down some parishioners as they was walkin' outta church one Sunday. Some little hick community down south—"

Woody interjected gravely, "They didn't want me to come inside. Kinda made it clear I was like somethin' sprung from the Devil."

Ehron Lee spoke again. His voice dripped bitterness. "Church. Religion. Never brought no one any good."

Ward regarded him, curiously amused.

"Lose your faith, Burrows?" he asked. He answered the question himself. "Ain't surprised. Not many believers in this corner of 'paradise.'"

Ehron Lee didn't say anything, though both of his cell mates noticed how the muscles in his face grew taut.

"Well, I got my own figgerin'," Ward said expansively. "When my time comes, I aim to either be shakin' hands with the Devil or spittin' in God's eye."

Woody spoke up. "I ain't sayin' I don't believe in God. It's people that I ain't got much use for. Hell, even here I can't go eat in the mess hall with the other prisoners 'cause they say lookin' at me spoils their appetite. It's all right if I clean up after 'em. But I gotta eat all my meals in here. Alone."

Ward ignored his cell mate's grievance and returned to the initial conversation. "Well, the only reason they didn't hang him is 'cause he's just a kid . . . and he's got that condition. People got superstitious. Thought if they strung him up, it'd bring 'em bad luck. Whitey might not like the way he looks, but it sure enough saved his skin."

"Yeah, but I'll be locked in here for the rest of my life," Woody said scornfully.

"What's your sin?" Ehron Lee asked Ward in a neutral tone.

Ward grinned and chuckled. He lowered his head and gave it a slight shake.

"Ward Crawford's as crooked as a three-legged dog," Woody muttered idly.

Ward guffawed. "Still not as crooked as your face, white boy."

Woody's features tensed but he didn't otherwise respond to the insult.

"Hell, what ain't I in here for? Little bit of everything, I reckon." Ward became strangely silent, and when he next spoke, both the expression on his face and the tone of his voice were solemn.

"Sentenced me to twenty years. Been here goin' on eight months. Killed a man durin' a bank holdup. Deputy marshal, in fact. The papers even gave me a fancy handle: Two-trigger Crawford."

"That's 'cause Crawford had two guns drawn when he shot the man," Woody offered briskly.

Ehron Lee had heard the name "Two-trigger Crawford" but refrained from acknowledging his familiarity with it.

Ward continued, speaking in the same subdued tone, "Woulda been hanged, only the man's widow pleaded with the judge to send me here. Said it'd be a more suitable punishment, rather than a quick death by rope. The sheriff sided with her. So . . . the judge did me this here favor. Yeah, I'm thirty-two now, will be past fifty by the time I get out. Y'know, Burrows, here's how I figger it: Steal my money and I can always get more. Steal my woman, I can always find another. But steal my time . . . you've taken away a piece of my life that I can't never get back. Twenty years they gave me. Twenty years for twenty stinkin' minutes."

"They wasn't gonna pin a medal on yuh," Woody remarked. "You killed a man."

Ward walked over to the cell door and spit through the bars into the corridor.

"Some peckerwood lawman," he said dismissively.

"And don't forget the two more years they just gave yuh for tryin' to bust out," Woody cheerfully reminded him.

Ward scowled.

"Took time away from me, too . . . and more," Ehron Lee said ruefully. Then he got a curious look to him.

"Twenty years . . . for killin' a deputy?" he said to Ward. "Figger if they wasn't gonna hang yuh, they'd give yuh life."

Ward spoke with cold contempt. "Twenty years in *here*, amigo—or as Whitey just obliged, twenty-two. That *is* a lifetime. Twenty years'll suck the soul right outta yuh. Least that's how they look at it."

He walked over to the barred windows and peered out-side. "No one's servin' life in Rockmound . . . 'ceptin' Whitey. And that's only 'cause they don't wanta set no one like him free on the citizens. Yeah, he'll be here 'til one day they find him dead in his cell."

Ward glanced up at the big full moon. Its brightness against the clear sky cast a whitish light across his face.

He pondered. "Five and twenty-two 'tween us. That's more'n a quarter century of wasted good livin'."

Ehron Lee nodded glumly.

Ward turned from the window. He was quiet for a moment while his eyes started to squint and a mean look darkened his features.

"Judge Harrison," Ward said, darkly pensive. "Charles Hugh Harrison."

Ehron Lee's eyes sparked at hearing the name. "Harrison?"

Ward nodded. "Circuit judge. The one that did me this 'favor.'"

Ehron Lee found the comment amusing in an ironic way, and a smile formed on his lips.

Ward noticed the odd look on his cell mate, and his fea-tures tensed.

"Somethin' funny?" he asked humorlessly.

Ehron Lee shook his head, his own expression thoughtful.

"No. But it looks as if Judge Harrison did us both that favor," he said.

* * *

"You ever kill a man, Burrows?" Ward asked Ehron Lee one night after the men were marched back to their cells after supper.

Ehron Lee was taken aback by the bluntness of the question. He didn't respond.

"Guess what I'm askin' yuh, is that the reason you've joined our little party?" Ward clarified.

Ehron Lee took his time answering. "Ain't what I'm in here for," he finally said. "But as to killin' a man . . . done my share."

Ward half smiled. "Cold-blooded—or did yuh kill 'em lawful?"

"Both, I reckon. In the war," Ehron Lee responded straightly.

"Yeah?" Ward chuckled. "Yeah, well, a spell in a Santa Fe jail spared me that 'honor.'"

The cell fell into silence. Ward rose and hopped up onto his own bunk.

Out the corner of his eye, Ehron Lee caught a sudden, brisk movement. He turned his head and looked full at a large rat that had scurried into the cell.

Woody saw it, too, and hastened into a hunching position on his lower bunk. He looked petrified and started to make odd squealing sounds.

"What's the matter, Whitey?" Ward asked casually.

"Rat," Ehron Lee answered for him.

Woody started stuttering. "I—I h-hate those th-things. G-Get it out-outta here."

Ward chuckled. "Better kill it and hide it, else it's sure to end up in tomorrow's supper."

Witnessing Woody's utter terror at the rodent, Ehron Lee started to move off the bunk to deal with it. The rat tensed, seemed unsure of which way to go, and finally scurried from the cell as fast as it had come, returning to its burrow elsewhere in the block.

"Must be as hungry as we are," Ward said.

"C-Could never be h-hungry enough to—to eat one of th-those th-things," Woody stammered.

"Dunno, Whitey," Ward said. "You'd be surprised at what a man'll do if he has to."

"N-Never be that h-hungry," Woody repeated.

Ward said to Ehron Lee, "Ever eat rat, Burrows? When you was in the war? Heard that was considered quite the delicacy at Vicksburg."

"Wasn't at Vicksburg," was all Ehron Lee said.

It took a while for Woody to calm himself. "L-Let's just stop talkin' about rats, huh?"

After a few moments Ehron Lee asked mutedly, "Anybody ever break outta here?"

Ward smirked. "I'm the wrong fella to ask."

Woody piped up, the stutter gone from his voice. "It's been done."

Ehron Lee's eyes rose and shifted toward him. His expression urged Woody to continue.

"Only one time that I know of," Woody said, licking the dryness from his lips. "Coupla guys made it. And it weren't done from inside. No way in hell you can get through them walls."

"So how'd they do it?" Ehron Lee asked.

Ward rolled onto his side, facing away from the granite wall. His own interest was piqued. He'd heard the story but never knew the details.

Woody tentatively stood up between the two bunks so that both men could see him, but kept watchful for the rat's return.

"On work detail," he said. "Got lucky and overpowered a coupla the guards then made a run for it. Don't know how they managed it, but got clean away. S'pose there's lotsa places to hide yourself out there, if'n you can get through the canyon into the hills. Prison can't afford to send out that many men after yuh, so that's another thing they had on their side. Musta been damn tough, though, runnin' off and doin' all that tricky climbin' with those irons locked 'round their legs. But by God, they did it."

Ward snorted. "What's damn tough is believin' that story."

"Oh, it's true all right, I know it," Woody said. "And 'course Navajos are also supposed to be on the prowl somewhere out in them hills. But they got by 'em, too. They was damn lucky. I'll tell yuh, 'tween the two, I'd rather meet back up with the guards. Probably'd kill yuh dead, but least I'd be keepin' my scalp."

Woody removed his omnipresent black bowler and ran a hand smoothly through his full head of white hair.

Ward was wryly amused at the ignorance of his cell mate.

"Typical Easterner, don't know nothin' 'bout the West, 'ceptin' what yuh read in dime novels," he said disparagingly. "Sure, mighty fine Apache or Kiowa trophy your scalp would make. But with the Navajo, hell, they think that kind of barberin' is barbaric. Fact, if'n yuh wanta know the truth, probably more Navajos have been scalped by white men than the other way 'round."

Woody looked offended at Ward's belittlement of him, and he brooded for a bit.

"So what happened to these fellas?" Ehron Lee asked impatiently.

After he was done sulking, Woody carried on with what he was saying. "From what I hear, the law caught up with 'em later. Had nothin' to do with their escape. They was both shot stirrin' up trouble in some cathouse. Guess they got too carried away celebratin' their freedom."

Ward shifted onto his back and clasped his hands behind his head. "Yeah, ain't that always the way," he said with a slight chuckle.

"Reckon so," Ehron Lee added.

EIGHT

IN THE WEEKS that followed, the transformation that first had begun to occur in Ehron Lee Burrows on his ride to the prison intensified as he descended deeper into the turmoil that surrounded him and the tension that came from within.

He still did the work assigned him, laboring long hours in the quarry, followed the orders barked at him by the guards, did not disobey or challenge the rules dictated by authority. As he discovered, there was no percentage in being rebellious. He'd tried it once and it nearly killed him.

Perhaps no one would even notice the change in Ehron Lee because it was not externalized; not made manifest through defiant attitude or belligerent behavior. Ominous in its subtlety, it was purposely kept dormant. But it existed deep within his soul, and each day it was acknowledged and nurtured by Ehron Lee.

Where once he had a conscience, now he didn't give a damn.

The thought of escaping from this hellhole was never far from his mind. While on backbreaking work detail, he would entertain himself by trying to figure out ways to make a clean break. It didn't take him long to discover, however, that any such attempt would be plain suicide. The odds seemed too great. The two prisoners who had successfully pulled it off had just been lucky, as simple as that.

Still, late into the evening in the privacy of their cell, Ehron Lee and Ward would occasionally speak in whispered conversation and amuse themselves by trying to come up with ways to escape. Woody would sit cross-legged on his bunk and listen but not contribute. Invariably every scheme discussed would hit a dead end with at least one potential flaw that would surely earn them an eager guard's bullet.

One night after yet another idea had been rejected owing to the risk involved, Woody stretched out on his bunk and said irritably, "All this talk don't do me no good no how. I told you fellas before, any break's gotta be made from outside. Only way it can be done. And that means it's gotta happen during work detail."

Ward sucked a tooth and said, "We already figgered that."

Woody elucidated his point. "Which means it's gotta be done during daylight hours. Hell, I spend any time outside in the sun and I'll roast like a side of pork."

"Yeah, reckon not much chance for you," Ward said. He eyed Woody speculatively, then added, "At the same time, out of all of us, you got the least to lose."

Ehron Lee turned over onto his side and stared at the shadowy form of Ward propped up on an elbow on the upper bunk.

"What're yuh gettin' at?" he asked.

Ward replied, "It's a long haul we're lookin' at, 'specially for me, but someday, Burrows, you and me got a chance to get outta here. Whitey, on the other hand, ain't got no chance." He spoke directly to Woody. "Sorry, kid, but you know as well as me the only way you're gonna leave here is when they cart yuh out in a box."

Woody was quiet, brooding at the truth of Ward's comment.

Ehron Lee exhaled. "Still don't see your point."

Ward contemplated briefly, and then he thought better of what he was going to say.

"Forget it," he said. "Just thinkin'." Then he rolled over on his bunk to face the wall.

After a moment Ward's deep voice once more rose from the darkness. It had a peculiar tone and sounded as if he was talking to no one in particular.

"Haven't figgered out how, but if it could get done once, there's gotta be a way it can be done ag'in."

Another month passed. A month that seemed like a year, with the days endlessly blurring into one another. The visiting day assigned for that month came and went, and for Ehron Lee there was no word from Melinda. No letter was delivered, nor a message from the superintendent's office, which would have been brought to him by a guard, *maybe*, if Melinda had requested and been permitted a visit.

Finally, after six months of stubbornly observing obedient behavior, Ehron Lee requested and received permission to send a letter to his wife. He understood that the letter would first be scrutinized by the superintendent before it would be delivered so Ehron Lee kept his message free of embellishments. He merely asked how Melinda was doing and asked about the baby, surely to have been born by now. He hoped that the special closeness they had shared would enable her to decipher his true intent between the lines.

Two months passed without a reply. Ehron Lee was discouraged but not necessarily surprised. What he did question was whether Superintendent Watson had indeed sent out the letter . . . or if Abigail had intercepted it. Both were likely possibilities. He felt in his heart, or at least he attempted to convince himself, that if Melinda had received his letter, she would have responded. Whatever else, she at least owed him news about his child.

He knew it would be useless to try and find out if the superintendent had prevented the delivery of the letter. If he dared to question, he would likely be regarded as insubordinate and made to suffer a punishment, the severity of which depended on the whim of George Watson. He was wise to the routine of the prison by now.

Because he was powerless in his situation, Ehron Lee had no recourse but to enforce the most difficult decision he'd ever had to make and push all thoughts of Melinda from his brain. She could not exist to him anymore. Where once he relied on her image and his memories of her to keep him sane and motivated to survive this hell, now these remembrances inflicted a pain so deep, so intense, he feared it would drive him mad. He was already a little mad, which he recognized.

He knew without question that he was a changed man when after he made up his mind to forget about Melinda and the baby he would never know, he tried to allow himself the luxury of a final emotional farewell, to once and for all free himself of his feelings. But the tears wouldn't come. He no longer possessed the ability to express such feelings—not even to himself. Not even in a rare moment of solitude.

Malice had replaced tenderness in his thoughts. Nurturing that emotion of hate was about the only thing still left to Ehron Lee Burrows's control.

Early one evening after returning from another hard day's labor at the quarry, muscles pained and aching but more accustomed to pick and shovel work, Ehron Lee was halted in his walk to the supper hall and told to report directly to Superintendent Watson. He was puzzled and not a little concerned. All sorts of thoughts rushed through his brain as he and an accompanying guard walked through the compound toward the office. It was known among the prisoners that unless it was an extraordinary circumstance, Watson sent for a man only when he was to be reprimanded or punished for breaking a rule or some other misconduct. In that regard, at least, Ehron Lee believed his conscience was clean. He'd done nothing to upset the routine.

He even considered that it might be hopeful news.

Perhaps the two men responsible for the crime of which he had been accused had been captured, and confessed. But the idea of becoming a free man so overwhelmed him that he could not entertain that possibility for long. The more likely disappointment would be too great to bear.

It seemed a long walk, like what a condemned man would experience being led to the gallows. Prisoners marching in to supper watched curiously. Ehron Lee was ushered inside Superintendent Watson's office, where, per prison protocol, he stood absolutely still, completely quiet. Watson would do the talking, and if he wanted the prisoner to speak, he would invite it.

For the moment, Watson's bald, bullet head was bowed as he was responding to some correspondence on his desk. While Ehron Lee waited to be addressed, he stole another glance at the photograph of Watson's wife, wondering how a man like him had ever earned the affections of such an attractive lady.

Had he allowed himself to think of Melinda, he would have found it difficult not to surrender to bitterness and envy.

With his head still lowered, Watson finally spoke. "Burrows, I received a letter today," he said, his tone blunt and professional.

Ehron Lee waited for him to continue.

Watson slowly lifted his eyes toward him. They were empty and gave no hint of the news to come.

"It came from your sister-in-law, a Mrs. Maguire," he continued. "Sorry to have to tell you it's bad news. Concerns your wife."

Ehron Lee struggled to keep his body from tensing. He made his face display no emotion at what he was about to hear.

Watson leaned back in his swivel chair and folded his arms across his chest. His eyes locked directly on Ehron Lee.

"Burrows, your wife died," he said.

There was no trace of compassion in the superintendent's voice, nor did any look of sympathy appear on his features. He was merely delivering the information, as was his responsibility, speaking matter-of-factly.

Ehron Lee didn't react, other than a slight tightening of his lips. He would not allow himself to outwardly express the rush of pain that consumed him. Although he could feel his insides collapsing, he maintained a rigid demeanor. He could almost sense Watson searching him for a sign of what he could interpret as weakness. A vulnerability that would heighten Watson's own sense of power.

Ehron Lee would not give him the satisfaction.

"How?" he merely asked.

"According to what your sister-in-law says, apparently she got a fever."

"Did she say anything about the baby?" he asked stiffly.

Watson shook his head and frowned. "There was no mention of any child, Burrows."

Ehron Lee remained impassive, and stood silent, appearing callous and indifferent at receiving such unfortunate news, while in truth, for each agonizing moment, he was forced to call upon all his inner strength to repress his despair.

Watson then edged the upper portion of his body across his big desk to pass Ehron Lee the letter, but Ehron Lee didn't budge. He held his ground and maintained his icy composure.

Melinda was dead. The news was a shock. The sudden, unexpectedness of learning it had hit him with devastating impact. But Ehron Lee slowly recovered. He had already accepted that she was dead, to him at least. The letter confirming it was merely a formality that he didn't need to read—or hold on to.

Watson studied him for several seconds. Then with a quizzical, somewhat disappointed look at Ehron Lee's attitude, his resolute refusal to express even a hint of emotion, he coldly dismissed his prisoner.

Wordlessly, Ehron Lee turned and walked from the office. As he crossed the compound back to the cell block, his gait became stronger, each step he took more determined.

Ehron Lee was back on regular work detail, putting in long hours of hard and monotonous labor. Occasionally he'd see

Superintendent Watson sitting atop his sterling steed on a ridge overlooking the quarry, silently observing the prisoners, like an emperor lording over his conquests.

Each time the sweat-bathed Ehron Lee spotted Watson, clean and impeccable in his uniform, he couldn't keep from glowering at the man. If Watson noticed his harsh stares, he never reacted. He was confident in his position of authority. He was surrounded by armed guards who would die to protect him.

If Ehron Lee was ever given his chance, he'd gladly kill as many of that scum as it took to get to Superintendent George Watson. He'd never before thought of himself as a murderer, but if it came to that, he did have an advantage. Because of the war, he'd been trained to kill, and though it was something he at one time had been reluctant to acknowledge, and was not an accomplishment of which he was proud, he had been skilled at it. He'd killed countless men in battle, many in face-to-face confrontations, yet he had emerged from the war without so much as a flesh wound.

He hadn't hated those soldiers he had been forced to kill. They, like him, were simply following orders, doing everything in their power to stay alive under terrible conditions.

But Ehron Lee hated George Watson. He hated him with the same venom he felt for the one other person responsible for casting him into this quagmire of filth and despair.

Two men who were living safe in their comforts, never realizing that while they were enjoying their freedom, embracing their families, Ehron Lee had committed himself to survival; driving his body and what remained of his soul onward day after day with only one purpose in mind.

He hadn't been rotting, but *plotting*.

Neither man could imagine the plan of retribution formulating inside the brain of Ehron Lee.

He had lost a wife. He would never know his child.

Superintendent Watson had a wife.

Judge Harrison had a child.

NINE

THE FIVE YEARS passed, and against what seemed insurmountable odds, Ehron Lee survived his imprisonment at Rockmound. Perhaps in some respects he was more dead than alive, but he *had* lived through his half-decade term. Physically he would recover from the bouts of abuse thrust upon him by the sadistic guards and those injuries incurred from his long years of labor.

Mentally and emotionally, though, he possessed deeper wounds, scars that would never heal.

His cell mates were men of sinister character, individuals whom a man of Ehron Lee's former gentle nature would never have acknowledged let alone form a friendship with. But under their shared circumstances, they had become his closest companions. While he would never express it, Ehron Lee could inwardly admit that the strange physically and psychologically afflicted Woody Milo and, particularly, the brutish Ward Crawford had helped him to endure those terrible years.

He could go further. They had become his blood brothers.

Throughout that period he never spoke of his wife, and neither was a mention made of her by either Ward or Woody.

Ward was as eager for Ehron Lee's release as was his cell mate himself. Five years of being locked up together had given the two men time to come up with a plan. What had begun as idle conversation to pass the time had gradually developed into a plan of some promise. Ward scolded himself for taking so long to come up with an idea that had been so simple, so obvious. He and Ehron Lee had been thinking much too broadly, and elaborately, for him to finally realize that the answer had been in their sight all along.

It was risky, uncertain, but Ward had thought out the details carefully . . . and besides, the way he figured it, whether the plan met with success or failure, he had nothing to lose. He didn't intend to leave Rockmound an old, beaten man.

Through grit and determination, he had managed to survive the first long years of his sentence.

There was no way he would serve out the years remaining—no matter what the cost.

The plan's success depended mostly on Ehron Lee. He would take much of the risk, and if all went well, Ward would return the favor. But Ward did not really look upon it as a favor, as he shared the same hatred and sought the same personal vengeance against the two men of power and distinction:

Judge Charles Hugh Harrison and Prison Superintendent George Watson.

Ehron Lee recognized that he would need a partner for what he was aiming to do, and while he admittedly wasn't sure whether he could altogether trust Ward, the man possessed those hardened, fearless qualities that would be useful in such an undertaking.

But before any such plan could be put into effect, there remained one obstacle: Ward first had to break out of Rockmound.

On a Friday midafternoon, Ehron Lee said good-bye to his cell mates. He shook hands with Ward and silently confirmed his commitment with a direct look into his eyes and a slight nod.

To Woody, he merely said "Adios" and wished him well. Woody seemed to be holding back his emotions at watching Ehron Lee depart. Even though his relationship with Ward had improved over the years and had become more teasing than contentious, Woody would rather it have been Ward who was leaving the prison that afternoon.

He knew nothing about the escape his cell mates had plotted. He could never be in on it, and once the plan took on serious overtones, Ward suggested to Ehron Lee that they keep their conversations private and confidential, speaking only when allowed during work detail and when they were alone in the cell, when Woody was elsewhere doing his chores.

As Ward sensibly explained it, "Wouldn't take much to break Whitey and get him to talkin'."

Ehron Lee left the gates of the prison, riding on the back of an open horse-drawn wagon heading toward the town of Allensfield, which was as far as the driver would take him. Once he arrived, he took part of the meager funds he had earned for his five years of labor and bought himself some durable ranch-style clothing at the local haberdashery. With merely a passing interest, he made a subtle inquiry about George Watson, mentioning to the tailor that he'd had a past acquaintanceship with the man and had heard he was the superintendent at Rockmound. As the conversation progressed, Ehron Lee discovered where the house was. The house was mainly occupied by Watson's wife, Janette. This was information he filed away for later.

He then purchased a stagecoach ticket to Colbert City. Ward Crawford had "friends" who had a hideout near there, and Ehron Lee was told by his cell mate where to find them and to introduce himself as a friend of his.

At first, Ehron Lee had been doubtful.

"You sure they're still there?" he'd asked. "That was over five years ago. Don't wanta go trekkin' on a wild goose chase."

"Don't worry 'bout findin' 'em," Ward assured him.

"That's where they set up housekeepin'. Hideout's as secure as gold so that's where they always ride back to. And if they ain't around . . . if they're off somewhere gettin' into mischief, there's always someone who is there." He didn't elaborate, just tossed Ehron Lee a wink. "Guarantee it."

As Ward told it, these men owed him a favor. They had got lucky and managed to shoot themselves free of capture following the bank holdup for which Ward was arrested, and during which the deputy marshal had been killed. Even with a promise of leniency, Ward stuck to the "outlaw code" and had refused to name his accomplices.

Ward felt confident he could count on them.

Yet when this aspect of the plan was discussed between them some months before, Ehron Lee wasn't as certain. He told Ward frankly, "I've given up trustin' people. Even those you'd swear would never betray yuh."

Ward merely smiled at his cynicism.

"Maybe," he said. "The difference is these boys know that if they don't come through for me, I might suddenly decide to spill my guts. And if they start showin' some doubt, Burrows, don't forget to remind 'em of that."

And when Ehron Lee met the bunch at a small ranch many miles south of Colbert City, he initially encountered resistance and *did* have to remind them of the debt Ward was owed.

Jess Colfax and Randy Boggs were two of the meanest-looking hombres Ehron Lee had ever encountered. The third, Brad Riley, was a youngster who had a clean-scrubbed, boyish face, which he tried to mature by screwing up his features into a perpetual mean expression. They were living with and were cared for by a girl named Cora, who was Brad Riley's sister and who, Ehron Lee quickly determined, had been romantically involved with Ward Crawford. Cora was attractive yet had a tough, hard-bitten edge about her, sporting a short tomboyish hairstyle and dressed in a checked flannel work shirt and loose-fitting faded blue jeans. Ehron

Lee had no difficulty recognizing that she was the type of gal Ward would be drawn to. She was more cordial to Ehron Lee than any of the men were and instantly peppered him with questions about how Ward was getting along.

Ehron Lee could comprehend the concern and maybe even love that Cora had for Ward, but at the same time he was puzzled about their relationship, as during the five years they had spent together in prison, sharing almost everything with each other, Ward had never once mentioned the girl.

Yet maybe indirectly he had, when he'd told Ehron Lee that he'd always find *someone* at the ranch.

The "ranch," such as it was, was little more than a cabin and a small spread of property, virtually hidden in the foothills of an ominous dark-crested rocky mountain range known as Brimstone Canyon, a desolate area west of Border Pass through which few travelers dared venture. It was rumored that the Chiricahua roamed the southern region of these mountains.

From Hell's Doorway to Brimstone Canyon. Ehron Lee chuckled inwardly as he considered the irony. Yeah, he contemplated, there was no question his path was set.

To the casual observer who might come upon the cabin, it would look to be unoccupied and neglected. A hermit, perhaps a prospector, was said to have built the cabin and settled there. Outside of very rare trips into Colbert City to purchase supplies, no one saw the man or even knew who he was. One day he simply vanished—either by choice or misadventure—leaving behind no possessions by which to establish his identity. All that remained inside the cabin were some sparse, crudely constructed furnishings, most likely crafted by the hermit himself.

The prevailing theory among the locals—and the reason this area was rarely ventured into—was that one day Chiricahua braves had come scouting down from the hills and discovered the hermit and captured him. Either that, or the old man himself had foolishly ventured too far into Chiricahua territory. His ultimate fate would remain a mystery, but given the Chiricahua's hatred for the white man and their unique methods of torture, various stories of what had happened to the hermit—becoming ever more gruesome in repeated tellings—became popular talk around saloons in the county.

The cabin provided two sleeping quarters, each supplied with a bed that suggested at some point the old hermit may have had a partner. One of the rooms was now occupied by the girl, Cora, while the three men had to work out their own sleeping arrangements in the other room.

The trio of outlaws didn't seem to do much more than drink whiskey and play cards. They'd been laying low since their last robbery some weeks before, which they'd pulled off in a neighboring county, and appeared to be growing restless with their idleness. Ehron Lee didn't like to be in their company and he sensed they weren't too sure about him either. These men were seasoned outlaws, and despite his having been hardened by his five years at Rockmound, Ehron Lee was not as yet a criminal—no matter what the court judged. Without knowing his history, the men could detect that when it came to their line of work, Ehron Lee was a tenderfoot.

Savagely slapping cards onto the table as they played their hands, the men cast periodic and furtive glances at Ehron Lee, trying to figure what part he had in the scheme their former partner Ward was proposing. They also weren't too keen on the threat Ehron Lee had relayed from their old compadre.

Taking a slug of whiskey, Jess Colfax said gutturally, "Reckon you and Crawford got to be pretty close partnered together in that cell."

"Close enough," Ehron Lee responded. He would not allow himself to be intimidated by the tight-eyed looks leveled at him.

"Don't rightly know if I approve of Ward's methods," Randy Boggs said sourly. "Sounds sorta like blackmail."

"Just callin' in a favor," Ehron Lee explained.

"Don't call tryin' to get us killed no favor, fella," Jess said.

Cora was standing at the counter with her back turned

to the men, preparing the deer meat for their supper. She'd been listening to the talk without saying a word. But suddenly she spun around to face the table, pressing closed fists against her waist, and she spoke impatiently.

"He coulda got himself hanged protectin' you boys. Don't forget, it was *me* that sat in that courthouse every day. I heard what went on. They tried to talk him into makin' a deal that coulda got him off easy—if'n he'd name you boys. But he wouldn't betray you. He kept his mouth shut."

Her brother, Brad, exhaled slowly.

"He wasn't hanged, Cora," he said.

"Maybe not. But you gonna say he knew that at the time?" Cora returned. "And even if he didn't get no rope, look where he's hadda spend them last years: Hell's Doorway."

"Hell's Doorway for him maybe," Brad said with a smirk. "For us tryin' to get him outta there, it's more like that other name they call it: Cartridge Hill." He swiftly formed his hand into a gun and fired off pretend shots at his tablemates. "Bang, bang."

The men chuckled uneasily.

"Well, from where I see it, Ward Crawford's got more guts than you three combined," Cora stated with emphasis.

Her comment silenced the men, though each wore an ill-tempered expression.

"Aw, forget what Cora says," Jess said, tossing his cards onto the table and getting up from his chair. "Fact is, we ain't got no choice but to help Crawford."

Brad spoke with some hesitation. "Yuh really think he'd turn us in?"

"Let's just say I ain't keen on gamblin' with the stakes so high," Jess replied, deadpan. "And for us it could mean the rope. Sure, they got Ward, but the law can't be too pleased we got away all this time."

Brad gave a thoughtful nod. "Reckon. Plus there are them other jobs we've pulled since then. Yeah, could definitely be a swingin' in our future if Ward talks."

Randy gently laid down his cards and started to build a cigarette. "Never worried myself 'bout Ward turnin' on us."

"If it makes you fellas feel any better, callin' in this debt wasn't what he wanted to do," Ehron Lee said. "If'n there was any other way for him to get out, he'd'a first gone that route."

"And you got the plan," Jess said, a note of doubt in his voice.

Ehron Lee gave his head a slow nod. "Had plenty of time to come up with ideas. Most wouldn't work. But this is one plan where we might have a chance. And it was Ward who came up with it."

"Good ol' Ward," Randy drawled.

"Fifty-fifty odds?" Brad said. "Or are we talkin' somewhat less?"

Ehron Lee merely responded with a slight smile.

"And tell us ag'in how *you* come into this?" Brad next asked with a suspicious edge.

"I know the layout. Know the routine," Ehron Lee answered patiently.

Brad's lips pressed into a thin, grim smile.

"And d'yuh also know 'bout the Indians that's s'posed to be scoutin' them hills?" he said archly.

"Ain't been no Indian trouble," Ehron Lee said assuredly. "Ain't seen none in the five years I been there."

"We been livin' with the prospect of trouble from the Chiricahua all the time we been hidin' out here, and I ain't seen a-one of them red-bellies," Jess said with an unconcerned shrug.

Randy lighted his smoke with a match against his boot heel, and with the cigarette slanted from the corner of his mouth, he began to drum the fingers of his left hand against the tabletop.

"Them mountain Chiricahuas they talk 'bout is just a legend," he said confidently in a slow drawl. "But reckon it's a legend that's served us well. Keeps anyone from gettin' inquisitive and crossin' Border Pass."

Jess tried to sound optimistic. "Well, we just been layin' 'round here since our last job. Maybe we could use a little excitement."

"I'm all for some excitement," Brad said. "But sounds like there's more risk."

"You boys take chances every time you ride out to rob a bank," Cora curtly reminded them.

"Yeah, but we *know* that kind of risk," Brad said with a sardonic grin.

"What happens after?" Jess asked Ehron Lee. "That is, if we pull it off."

"Likely we separate. You go your way, we go ours."

"Y'mean *you* separate, amigo," Brad said. "We ain't goin' nowhere."

Ehron Lee cast a quick glance over at Cora and noticed the flicker of disappointment that crept across her features.

"You and Ward teamin' up?" Jess said.

Ehron Lee was reluctant to answer. But he finally said, "We got some plans."

"Simple," Randy said with a derisive shrug.

"One other thing I forgot to mention," Ehron Lee added casually.

All eyes turned to him, daggering Ehron Lee with their curiosity, and still maintaining suspicion.

He said, "We're gonna need some spendin' money. 'Course that's kinda owed to Ward, as well, don't yuh reckon?"

"You're talkin' a lotta years, pal. We spent that money long ago," Brad uttered, smiling caustically out the side of his mouth.

It was Cora who voiced her opinion, and not too timidly.

"You boys scored not long ago and I ain't seen much of that money bein' spread 'round," she said.

Brad's temper flared.

"Shut up, Cora!" he snapped at his sister.

Cora wasn't intimidated by her brother's tough guy attitude and she spoke with disdain. "*You* shut up, Brad. You all lived pretty well offa the money that Ward done time for. If you can't come up with a coupla hundred dollars now . . . well, all I can say is, I ain't never seen a bunch no lower than you three."

Ehron Lee remained silent, but he was impressed. Cora was proving to be a valuable ally.

"We can stake him," Jess said blankly. "We'll put in from each of our shares."

In just the short time he had been among them, Ehron Lee had formed definite opinions about these men. It appeared that it was Jess Colfax who had the final say. Randy was quiet and seemingly complacent. Brad could be the one to worry about as he was the youngest and seemed to be a complainer, possibly reckless as well. The type who felt the need to prove himself.

After they ate supper, the men sat around the table sharing corn whiskey that they swigged from a jug. Ehron Lee declined; he wanted to keep his head clear. Instead he got up from the table and went over to the stove to pour himself some leftover coffee. It had cooled, and Cora offered to heat it for him, but Ehron Lee said he didn't mind his coffee cold. It was inky black and strong tasting and Ehron Lee added three heaping spoonfuls of sugar to mellow its bitterness. He'd noticed how Cora regarded him with a look that he interpreted as pleasant approval when he refused to partake of the corn whiskey. He understood. In Cora's environment it was rare and perhaps refreshing to see a man not guzzle back alcohol.

Ehron Lee was a little concerned about the way the others were drinking; he didn't know their personalities when drunk, and wasn't eager to find out. But he knew it wasn't his place to comment and just hoped there would be no trouble. He sensed these men possessed volatile temperaments.

Cora sat in a rocker in the next room, knitting. Ehron Lee thought it a rather odd display of domesticity given the girl's rough-grained character.

While Cora sat quietly, not offering any of her own thoughts or opinions to the matter being discussed, she listened attentively as Ehron Lee outlined the plan that he and Ward had worked out. Using cigarette stubs and broken matchsticks, he had laid out a primitive map of the prisoner work site to illustrate an approximation of where the eight supervising guards were stationed.

By the time Ehron Lee was through, the outlaw trio had looks on their faces that suggested less apprehension at the plan.

"Can see it workin'," Randy offered as he rolled a fresh cigarette.

"Shoot and scatter," was Jess's comment.

Brad sighed. "Well, so long as we can get away without gettin' shot, shouldn't be no one who can tie us in with this. Reckon we can thank Ward for that. For keepin' his mouth shut 'bout us."

Ehron Lee nodded. "It's gonna be a few days' ride. Probably smart if we throw in an extra day to rest up. Wanta hit the grounds shortly after sunup. Countin' on the guards not bein' too alert at that hour."

"You said they're pretty good with their rifles?" Brad said grimly.

Ehron Lee nodded again. "That's why we gotta hit fast." He twirled his index finger around the cigarette butts he'd laid out in a curve design. "We circle 'round the canyon from the north with long-ranges and we should have the advantage. They all keep themselves in the open."

"Like shootin' targets," Jess said.

It was a hot night with an uncommon humidity that had developed following a late afternoon rain and that had lingered into the night. It permeated the air inside the cabin, and Ehron Lee had trouble sleeping. The hour was almost midnight and he was wide awake. He had lain out in a bedroll on the floor in the front room listening to the cacophony of snores and snorts that went on in the room where the three outlaws slept.

Realizing he was fighting a losing battle, he finally decided to get up and step outdoors, hoping a walk in the night air might aid him in getting some shut-eye. It seemed a trifle cooler outside, and as Ehron Lee started to walk around the small property, breathing easily and feeling the sweat start to evaporate from his body, he realized of a sudden that he was a free man. It was odd but the fact really hadn't occurred to him until this moment. Perhaps prison had become too much a way of life; maybe part of him believed that his leaving Rockmound was only a temporary reprieve.

But he *was* free. Of course it wasn't the freedom he had envisioned and desperately sought those five years ago. He had hoped for a much different outcome. He certainly had never expected to become the person he now was: hardened, vindictive, devoid of most of the feelings he once had possessed. He had survived both the bloody carnage of the war and the brutality and cruel conditions of Hell's Doorway but realized he had paid a bitter price.

Ehron Lee leaned himself against the straight fence that bordered the south side of the property, behind which stood the weathered old railings forming a circular corral where stood four quarter horses, and as he stared out at the shadowed and serrated mountain peaks of Brimstone Canyon reaching skyward beyond the horizon, he contemplated all that was to come. He had a lot going through his brain, but he remained firm in his determination. He couldn't turn back from what was ahead even if at that very moment Melinda appeared and came rushing into his arms. The damage had been done and it was irreparable.

Yet he knew he couldn't do it alone, and that was why he agreed to help Ward Crawford. He needed a man beside him who carried the same hatred that consumed him. The same determined thirst for revenge. Ehron Lee's conviction strengthened once he'd recognized that he and Ward Crawford shared a strange bond in their past and perhaps had been brought together at Rockmound specifically for that reason.

He was deep in thought when soft footfalls approaching from behind snapped him back to awareness. He turned around and saw Cora walking toward him. She was wearing a cotton robe, which she had open over her nightgown, and looked as feminine as Ehron Lee had yet seen her.

The night was dark and inked with clouds, but the moon was bright. Cora walked to where her face caught a splash of moonlight. The subtle glow seemed to soften features that earlier had looked both weather-worn and strained.

Because she'd been living with three outlaws, Ehron Lee could well understand why she appeared older than what likely were her years.

She smiled at him. "Those boys' snorin' is shakin' the whole house."

Ehron Lee smiled back tentatively.

"So hot, can't see how no one can get any sleep," she added, stepping a bit closer to Ehron Lee and resting her arm against a fence post. "Then I reckon those boys drank 'nuff to put out the lights on a horse."

Ehron Lee held his smile and lowered his head a bit. He could tell that she was trying to make conversation. He wasn't much in the mood for talk and was hoping to have a few moments of solitude, but Cora had been friendly to him and he wasn't about to respond to her kindness with rudeness.

Still, he wasn't sure of what to say. It had been a long time since he'd last spoken to a woman. And the words he'd said to that girl had been tender and exclusive.

"Must be kinda different for yuh, livin' with three—"

Before he could finish, Cora cut in. "Outlaws?"

"Was gonna say 'men,'" Ehron Lee clarified.

Cora allowed herself a smile and gave her head a mild shake. "No, not particularly. Lived with men all my life. After my ma died, was just my pa and Brad. Then after Pa died and Brad ran off with his bunch—Ward and Jess and there used to be some others—well, I just up and trailed after 'em. Reckon that's why I don't exactly come across like a girl should."

"Wouldn't say that," Ehron Lee offered kindly.

Cora appeared slightly embarrassed by his comment.

"Aw, I don't know much 'bout all that," she said, kicking her toes in the dirt. "Dolls and frilly things. Don't think I ever smelled no perfume . . . or even put on a fancy dress."

"Well, you look just fine to me," Ehron Lee told her.

Cora sighed. "But I'd be tellin' yuh that I sure miss Ward. All these years it's gotten awful lonesome without him. Can hardly believe it's been so long since I last seen him."

Ehron Lee was silent. He inherently felt that Cora wanted him to tell her if Ward had talked about her, perhaps expressed some feelings, or just that he missed her.

None of which Ehron Lee could truthfully say that Ward had so much as hinted at.

Cora spoke pensively, and it was as though she were speaking to herself. "Reckon knowin' the type of man Ward Crawford is, he wouldn't say too much 'bout me."

"Didn't have much time to talk . . . 'bout personal matters," Ehron Lee said gently, attempting to smooth over her disappointment.

Cora sighed again, a heavier exhale of breath. "Six years in that place. Maybe he forgot." She paused then spoke with emphasis. "I hope he makes it. Hope he gets out and gets clean away." She paused, then looked directly at Ehron Lee. "Can you be tellin' me where you two will be ridin'?"

Ehron Lee lowered his eyes and shook his head. "Can't."

Cora eyed him skeptically. "Can't?"

Ehron Lee breathed out. "Truth is . . . I don't know. Ward's been workin' that out."

Cora nodded and said resignedly, "Not surprised. Ward was always a man who had to follow his own path. Reckon the one thing I do know is that if he ain't in jail, in time he'll end up dead. He ain't ever gonna ride honest."

"Guess you also know that what we're plannin' ain't gonna be safe for none of us, including your brother," Ehron Lee said.

Cora's attitude perplexed him.

"Brad's been ridin' into a bullet ever since the day he hooked up with Jess and them others," she said dispassionately.

Ehron Lee regarded her curiously.

Cora looked straight back at him, meeting Ehron Lee's puzzled stare with eyes that had become cold and intense.

"I come to accept that outcome a long time ago," she said harshly. Then her attitude softened and she looked almost apologetic. "He ain't nothin' like Jess or Randy. He pretends to be of their type and I know he's got bad blood, but the real truth is that he just ain't never growed up. Can't be no good end for someone like that."

"Guess what I can't figger is why you stay, if'n yuh know that."

Cora shrugged and said neutrally, "What else is there for me? I don't know no other life. Never had any schoolin' . . . and Pa never gave me much thought. He worked some . . . and drank more. Didn't do much fatherin' with Brad neither—which is why he took to the life he has."

Ehron Lee nodded his head sympathetically, but he had no words with which to respond, other than, "There's a lot of sadness in this world."

Now it was Cora's turn to eye him inquisitively.

"You've seen some, I imagine," she said.

Ehron Lee's features tightened almost involuntarily. He realized too late that he shouldn't have said what he did. He didn't want to pursue the topic.

"Some," was all he said. His tone wasn't exactly rude or brusque but possessed enough abrupt inflection to hopefully discourage Cora from questioning further.

Cora understood. She could see by Ehron Lee's expression that whatever had happened in his past pained him and was not anything he wanted to discuss.

They stood quietly for a few moments, listening to indistinct, far-off sounds that seemed to emanate from somewhere deep in Brimstone Canyon.

"Hear that at night sometimes and wonder if it might be them Indians," Cora said, considering.

Ehron Lee was likewise curious, but that was a consideration he wasn't about to acknowledge.

"Wouldn't be concernin' myself," Ehron Lee said with a reassuring smile. "Like that fella Randy said, probably just a legend."

Cora nodded, not altogether convinced. But as with the

eventual fate of her brother, the inevitable end of the trail
for Ward and the others, and even the uncertainty of her
own future, the prospect of the Chiricahua living on the
other side of the canyon was something she simply had come
to accept.

"Maybe we should head back inside," Ehron Lee then
suggested.

Cora nodded again, and the two walked in silence back
to the cabin.

Two days later the men were ready. They were equipped
with four long-range Winchester '66 repeater rifles and, for
extra measure, holstered Colt Army revolvers. Each of the
outlaws had his own horse. Ehron Lee, however, had arrived
at the cabin on foot after hiking many miles to the location
from the nearest stage depot outside Colbert City, following
the specific directions Ward had mapped out for him since
it was remote property and difficult to find. He was given
Cora's horse to ride, which seemed to be a sturdy, strong,
and reliable animal. Cora did not object even though this
would leave her pretty much bound to the house and property until her men returned.

The men prepared to ride out at dawn. Cora joined them
at the corral to see them off. It looked to be a gray, overcast
day, and the gloom was reflected in Cora's mood that morning. She awoke with a bad feeling. She felt with certainty
that not all of the men would be riding back to the ranch.

The men, though, were eager to hit the trail. They were
a bunch that craved excitement, and they had been inactive
for too long. Danger was part of their trade, and each had
come to regard this latest adventure not merely as a payback
to Ward Crawford, but as a new challenge.

Despite her expression of resignation to Ehron Lee
regarding what she perceived as the ultimate fate of her
brother, Cora stayed by Brad as he saddled and readied his
horse that morning. Ehron Lee and the others noticed her
display of concern, and Jess began to tease Brad. Cora was

offended by his remarks, but Brad just looked angry and was brusque with his sister, acting tough for the benefit of his compadres and dismissing her attention.

Cora waved them off, and Jess, Randy, and Brad whooped their horses into a gallop, riding off fast and furious. Ehron Lee stayed behind only for a moment, sharing a silent expression with Cora before tipping the brim of his Stetson in a gentlemanly fashion and following after the others.

Cora stayed put until they were gone from her sight and the dust raised up from their horses had long settled.

Then she walked back into the cabin, sat herself on the rocker, and did something she could never remember doing before.

She wept.

TEN

DURING THE FIVE years that Ehron Lee Burrows had been locked away at Rockmound, Buck Leighton had been appointed to the post of United States marshal after his efforts had successfully led to the capture of a murderous gang of outlaws who had waylaid a stagecoach just outside Justice, killed the driver along with two of the passengers, and seriously wounded the shotgun rider. Buck and a small posse had soon tracked down the criminals; they cornered them in the valley and arrested the bunch without a shot being fired. His deputy, Bert Stradd, likewise involved in the apprehension of the outlaw band, was rewarded by assuming the duties of sheriff of Justice.

Truth be told, Stradd was offended at what he regarded as a token promotion. From his standpoint, he looked upon it as a *demotion* compared to what Buck had been handed. He might have worked under Buck Leighton as his deputy, but in his mind he considered himself a far better lawman than the sheriff.

Inevitably Bert grew resentful, and his bitterness led to frequent visits to the saloon, where he could boast about his accomplishments to patrons, who quickly became bored with his repeated and ever more expansive versions of exploits that lost all basis in truth. Soon fiction overtook fact, and Bert Stradd was no longer regarded seriously by the citizenry. With his pride wounded, Stradd resigned as town sheriff, and both he and his tall tales drifted away into a well-deserved obscurity.

As time passed, Buck Leighton had finally surrendered his efforts to find evidence that would free Ehron Lee, and as his new responsibilities consumed him, he soon forgot about the man he'd believed had been falsely convicted.

One day while Buck was in the town of Brackett on business, he happened to stop into Chamberlain's Emporium to purchase a few items and noticed a girl browsing the merchandise whom he vaguely recognized but could not quite place. The curious way the girl looked back at him also suggested a distant memory on her part. Finally Buck walked directly over to her and it suddenly dawned on him who she was.

"Mrs. Burrows?" he said. "Melinda Burrows?"

Melinda studied him only for an instant before her lips parted in a slight smile.

"Sheriff Leighton?" she responded.

Buck removed his Stetson and extended his hand in greeting.

"If I ain't mistaken, thought the two of us decided to forgo the formalities," he said.

Melinda accepted his handshake warmly. "Well, yes . . . but that was a long time ago."

Buck furrowed his brow thoughtfully. "'Bout five years."

Melinda's expression became downcast, and she gave a hasty nod.

Buck didn't want to renew their acquaintanceship on a bleak memory, especially as he recognized that their meeting could not help but to be an unpleasant reminder. Instead his face lifted in a grin.

"You're lookin' fine—Melinda," he said.

And she did look well. Although she had matured during the time since Buck had last seen her, her face still retained a fresh youthfulness that belied some undoubtedly difficult years. Only a slight premature creasing around the eyes reflected the sorrow she had carried with her through this time.

She moistened her lips. "As are you, Sheriff."

"Buck, remember?" he corrected. "But actually I—I ain't a town sheriff anymore. Got myself promoted." He said this matter-of-factly, without boasting.

"Yes. Come to think of it, I did read about that in the newspaper," she acknowledged. "Federal marshal. Quite an honor. But from what the paper said, you earned it."

"My one moment of glory," Buck said jokingly. His tone got a little more serious. "Truth is, just got lucky."

"Well . . . I'm sure you're doin' a fine job."

"Thank yuh, ma'am," Buck said appreciatively. "Actually, though, been pretty quiet duty so far."

A heavyset, wide-bottomed female customer excused herself as she attempted to squeeze between them in the narrow aisle, maneuvering her girth between shelves cluttered with dry goods and knickknacks. Buck stepped out into the intersecting corridor to make room for her and tipped his hat in acknowledgment of her appreciative smile.

Melinda stepped out after him. She failed to respond to Buck's subtly amused expression as he watched the woman waddle down another aisle.

"And—how have you been keepin'?" Buck asked the girl, keeping his tone casual as he was aware that it could be a delicate question.

Melinda's eyes flickered before she replied, "I've—been well."

It became clear to Buck that he and especially Melinda were trying hard not to step into conversational territory that both understood would be difficult *not* to discuss. But the emporium was not the place to talk. Buck decided to invite her for a cup of coffee. Her acceptance or refusal of his offer would tell Buck whether she was open to conversing.

"I think that would be nice," she answered.

"One of the last times we spoke was in a coffee shop," Buck said to Melinda as he pulled out her chair at a corner table in the little Brackett restaurant.

"I remember," she said.

Buck rested his Stetson on the wall peg behind their table and sat across from her.

"Reckon we got us some catchin' up to do."

Melinda nodded agreeably, if a trifle tentatively.

"S'pose I should start by askin' 'bout your baby," Buck said.

"Not a baby anymore." Melinda smiled, though her tone seemed to be guarded. "Almost five."

"Boy?"

Melinda nodded. "Named him Charlie. Was a name—we'd both decided on."

"Right fine name. Kinda thought it might be a son," Buck said pleasantly. "Assume he keeps yuh busy?"

"He can be a handful at times. But he's a good boy."

Buck cleared his throat. "And your sister?"

Melinda's face took on a pained look.

"Abigail—she took sick about three years ago," she said dolefully.

Melinda didn't elaborate, and it wasn't necessary. Buck understood.

"I'm sorry to hear it," he said compassionately. He waited a moment before he went on. "If you don't mind my askin', how're you and the little fella gettin' along?"

Melinda's voice held a forced optimism. "We're doing all right. Abigail left us some money, and we have the house."

There followed an awkward silence, which thankfully was broken by the arrival of their waiter. Buck decided he wanted an early dinner and asked for a steak with a side order of fried potatoes and greens. He insisted that Melinda join him in a meal but all she chose was tea with honey and a hot buttered biscuit.

After the waiter left their table, the silence between Buck and Melinda resumed. They sat quietly, occasionally glancing at each other with strained smiles, until the waiter returned with Melinda's order. He placed the plate with the biscuit before her and poured the tea into her cup from a silver pot. He told Buck he'd be back shortly with his dinner, then returned to the kitchen.

Finally Buck sighed. He looked directly across the table at Melinda and said gently yet firmly, "Whyn't we both just speak what we know's on our mind?"

Melinda delicately spooned the honey into her tea, keeping her lashes lowered.

"I don't really know what to say," she said. "I suppose I've had to put that aside." There was a lengthy pause before she went on, "He never wrote. Never answered any of my letters. I'd hoped he would understand that I wouldn't be able to visit until after the baby was born, but maybe he didn't see it that way . . . maybe . . ." Her voice receded.

Lines of concern embedded themselves in Buck's features.

"Did yuh ever consider that maybe he never got those letters?" he ventured cautiously.

Melinda raised her eyes to him.

"Why wouldn't he?" she said, mildly agitated at the insinuation. "And even if that was so, why didn't *he* ever write?"

"Maybe he did," Buck said softly.

Melinda prepared to take a sip of her tea. But she halted, and gingerly lowered the cup back onto the saucer. The light blue of her eyes seemed to deepen and her gaze was penetrating.

"What are you sayin'?" she asked warily.

Buck chose his words carefully. "I didn't know your husband well. But I did know how he felt 'bout you. Leavin' you was even harder than his havin' to do time for somethin' it ain't likely he did. I think I can say that if there was any way for him to do so, he woulda gotten letters off to you."

Melinda blinked twice. "Are you suggesting that . . . the *prison* wouldn't let him write me?"

Buck shifted in his chair, leaning forward. "Possible. Also possible that he did write and the letters never made it to you. Maybe . . . someone got to 'em first."

"Someone got to them?" Melinda echoed, scarcely believing she was hearing correctly. "But who? And why would someone . . ."

Buck had a definite suspicion "who," but if he voiced what he was thinking—that it was sister Abigail who somehow had prevented those letters from being delivered to Melinda—and possibly had never posted those written by Melinda—he was sure to offend the girl.

"Ain't sayin' that's what happened, just offerin' a maybe," Buck told her.

Melinda looked thoughtful—and troubled.

"And maybe . . . you're thinkin' Abigail," she then said.

Buck said nothing. But to Melinda it was a telling silence.

"I—I gave her those letters to post," Melinda uttered numbly. "She always insisted on doing that for me, because of me havin' to spend so much time with the baby. I appreciated her always offering to make that trip into town . . . but I never thought . . ." She focused her stare directly on Buck. "That's what you're thinkin', too, ain't it?"

"All I can say is that there ain't no rule ag'in prisoners receivin' or sendin' out mail," Buck said. "Lessun if they're bein' punished."

"Ehron Lee wouldn't cause no trouble," Melinda said with certainty.

Buck took note how this was the first time in their talk that she had referred to her husband by name.

"No, don't seem the type," he agreed.

"Then if'n what you're sayin' is so, I been wrong 'bout him . . ." Almost against her will Melinda's mouth formed the words she found difficult to say: "And I been wrong 'bout Abigail, too."

"'Tween us, can't see it no other way," Buck said. "'Specially with how she felt 'bout him."

Melinda's eyes began to glimmer with a faint misting of tears.

"I—I can't imagine what he's been thinking all these years," she lamented. "I remember you tellin' me that he'd be needing me . . . and I wasn't there for him."

"You can't go blamin' yourself, Melinda," Buck assured her.

Melinda spoke with self-reproach. "How can't I? You're right, I knew how Abigail felt about Ehron Lee. I know how she blamed him for what happened to Winston . . . how she said such awful things . . . and with no letters comin' from him, I—I started to believe what she was saying all that time was true."

Buck tried to ease her guilt, and her grief.

"Abigail had her own hurt," he said.

"I know," Melinda said deliberately. "But she had no call to use her hurt to take away my happiness."

"No. No, she didn't," Buck acknowledged solemnly.

Melinda's voice was becoming emotional. "Ehron Lee was the finest man who ever lived, and she never would look at him that way. She resented him right from the start. But she was my sister and I wouldn't allow myself to think badly of her."

Buck thought it might be best if they leave. He no longer had much of an appetite, and Melinda looked both upset and restless. He could have told her more; perhaps he should have. He knew the date of Ehron Lee's release from Rockmound was nearing. Actually, he was a little surprised that Melinda herself had not mentioned it.

Perhaps she forgot—or chose to forget. Regardless of what she now knew, maybe she had made the decision simply to move on with her life and put each memory of a painful past behind her. A decision she would keep.

If that was the case, and Buck suspected that it might be, he could understand. He wouldn't remind her and possibly compound her hurt.

The waiter brought over his meal just as they prepared

to leave. Buck shook his head and pulled out some money to pay the perplexed server, leaving him some extra silver for his trouble.

By the time they stepped outside, Melinda had regained her composure and now looked a little guilty and apologetic.

"We should have stayed," she said. "You didn't have your supper."

"That's all right," Buck assured her. "Can eat later."

Buck walked with her along the boardwalk to where her buggy was parked. He helped her in and then she turned to him.

"Why don't you ride back with me to my place?" she suggested. "Ain't far and I can fix you something to eat."

"Ain't necessary," Buck said.

"It's no trouble."

Buck appreciated the invitation but wasn't sure if he should accept. He was feeling that his presence was keeping a memory alive that Melinda shouldn't have to deal with.

Melinda noted his hesitance and determined the likely reason for it.

"'Sides," she added warmly, "I'd like you to meet my son."

Buck looked momentarily puzzled. He didn't see the boy anywhere around, wondered why he wasn't with his mother.

Melinda read into what he was thinking and explained, "I have a neighbor, a nice Mexican woman, who comes by on occasion to look after Charlie when I come into town to do errands."

Buck suddenly decided it wouldn't seem right if he refused her offer. And Melinda was genuine in extending it. It wasn't mere politeness.

He gave an appreciative nod. "All right, Melinda. And thank you. I'll follow you out on my mare."

The meal Melinda fixed for him wasn't the steak and potatoes he'd earlier had a hankering for—rather, a plate of beans and some biscuits she'd had left over from breakfast, which she'd warmed atop the woodstove. But Buck enjoyed his supper and ate heartily, wolfing down two helpings with the gusto of a ranch hand on a cattle drive. After he was finished, Melinda eyed him suspiciously.

"Thought you said you wasn't hungry."

Buck looked a little self-conscious, but he recovered swiftly.

"Well . . . wasn't," he replied. "But been a long time since I et home cookin'. Most of my eatin' comes in restaurants."

Melinda maintained her sly look as she brought the small pot of beans to the table to refill his plate. Buck considered, then he raised his hand to halt her.

"Temptin'," he said. He patted his belly. "But I think two plates'll suffice."

He glanced across the table at little Charlie, who was still eating and eyeing the stranger warily. Buck gave him a wink and the boy frowned and went back to concentrating on his food.

Buck couldn't recall much about the way Ehron Lee looked, but he could see a resemblance between Charlie and his mother. He was an attractive child, though quiet, shy . . . and unsure of the stranger sitting across from him.

Buck smiled at the boy and accepted a refill of coffee from Melinda.

"Why don't yuh set yourself, Melinda?" he said.

"Should clean up the dishes before I get Charlie off to bed," she replied.

"Tell yuh what. Join me in a cup of coffee and I'll lend a hand with the cleanup," Buck offered.

"No, I couldn't ask that," Melinda objected. "You're a guest."

"You ain't askin'. I'm offerin'," Buck said pleasantly.

Melinda considered only briefly before she gave an appreciative nod. "That's awful kind of you."

"Least I can do after yuh takin' the trouble to fix me this fine supper."

"Wasn't nothin' special. Just beans and biscuits."

A smile gradually worked its way across Melinda's face, and to Buck, it appeared the most genuine smile he had yet seen on her. He was about to comment on how nice she looked with a happy expression, then decided it might not be appropriate.

As Melinda went to pour herself a cup of coffee, Buck looked back over at Charlie, who was staring at him intently, curiously, but who instantly focused his attention back on his supper once he was noticed.

Buck chuckled and said to Melinda, "Fine boy, but he does have a mite suspicious nature."

"He doesn't get to see a lot of people," Melinda confessed meekly.

Buck attempted to put her at ease. "Well, reckon workin' 'round this place keeps yuh right busy."

"Does," Melinda said, exhaling a breath. "Abigail did most of the chores, then we hired a fella but turned out he did more sleepin' than work. But it's got to the point where I'm thinkin' ag'in 'bout taking on some extra help. That is, if I can find someone dependable."

"If'n you'd like, I can put out a word," Buck offered.

"I—I'd 'preciate that," Melinda said gratefully.

"Well, gonna be a few years 'fore this here fella can lend a hand," Buck said, tossing a glance at Charlie.

Melinda's face took on an odd look. "Ain't sure how much longer I'll be keepin' this place. Reckon I might only give it another few months."

Buck suddenly understood. Without her having to elaborate or Buck having to ask, Melinda was saying that she would wait to see if Ehron Lee came back after his sentence was served. She obviously *did* know that his release would be soon. Whether this was something she'd had in mind from the first or a decision she'd just made based on the talk she and Buck had earlier, Buck couldn't be certain. But their initial conversation prompted Buck to believe that it was most likely she'd had a change of heart, now with the realization of her sister's probable deception.

He took a sip of his coffee. "Wonderin' why maybe you didn't think of movin' sooner."

Melinda sighed. "Abigail wanted to, but not 'til after the

baby was born. By then I hadn't heard from Ehron Lee and . . . I figured he didn't want to be a part of my life anymore. I was ready to go along with Abigail . . . then she got sick."

"If'n yuh don't mind my askin', how long has your sister been gone?" Buck asked gently.

"Been almost two years," Melinda said.

"And you decided just to stay put?"

Melinda nodded. "And reckon you now know why."

"I do."

"Guess I always held on to that fragment of hope that Ehron Lee might decide to come back," Melinda admitted unashamedly.

"And still do?" Buck ventured.

Melinda's silence pretty much answered his question.

Buck truthfully wasn't sure how he felt about that decision. He had little doubt that if Ehron Lee did return to his family, he would be a changed man. He saw men who had survived Rockmound, and he could not remember one who was not damaged by the experience—and many were men who had already been hardened by life: criminals, outlaws, and murderers. Despite having served in the war, Ehron Lee, from what Buck could remember, was by nature a man of gentle persuasion—the type of person to be most affected by his years in prison.

What also troubled Buck was Ehron Lee's long separation from Melinda, his not having heard from her during the time he was locked away. How would he interpret that? Might he feel he'd been abandoned by his wife? If so, that did not suggest the promise of a happy reunion. If he did return home, it could be as a man consumed by hatred and bitterness, presenting the potential for an unpleasant, perhaps even threatening, environment for Melinda and their young son.

Buck never spoke his concerns. But he did quietly make up his mind that he would keep a careful watch on Melinda and Charlie.

But first he'd wire the prison through Allensfield and find out what he could about Ehron Lee. He wanted to know the exact date of his release. How his behavior had been during the last five years. Most important, he wanted to know from the superintendent the type of man who soon would be set free on society.

And then Buck planned to keep track of his steps.

ELEVEN

EHRON LEE WAS long gone from Rockmound by the time Buck Leighton's wire reached the superintendent. In fact, just two days after the message arrived on Watson's desk, Ehron Lee and his three companions were seated atop their mounts along a narrow rocky trail in the protection of cover between the high walls of the box canyon, waiting for the day's labor to begin at the prison work site. It was just before dawn, and within the hour, men would be marched from their cells, fed a meager breakfast, and transported inside caged wagons to the location where they would bust rocks, pick and dig through stone and gravel, and clear the way for a mountainside passage until their sunburned, blistered, and exhausted bodies would be shuffled back into the wagons and returned to the prison come dusk.

Ehron Lee suppressed a shudder, recalling the miserable memories of not long ago when he was among those men. He harbored a hope that in the confusion that was to follow, Ward Crawford would not be the only one to escape. In his five years Ehron Lee had formed a strange brotherhood with those likewise tortured souls. No matter what their crimes, in his view not one deserved to be subjected to the mistreatment and outright brutality that were part of the daily routine at Hell's Doorway.

All four of the waiting men were clad in dusters, had the brims of their Stetsons pulled low, and each wore a kerchief 'round his neck, which, when the moment came, would be drawn up to conceal the lower portion of his face.

The Winchesters, loaded to capacity with .44-caliber rimfire rounds, rested in each of the dusty scabbards, at the ready.

"Yuh sure Ward knows this is the day we're comin'?" Jess Colfax asked Ehron Lee.

"Knew it was to be this week, dependin' on you boys," Ehron Lee answered, steadying the reins on his horse with his free hand. "If it weren't this week, he'd a-knowed we wasn't comin'."

"Yeah, imagine he wouldn't take too kindly to that," Brad Riley commented wryly.

"Kinda too bad we can't all stop for a drink after this is done," Randy Boggs remarked. "Been a long time since we last saw ol' Ward."

"Just remember, we scatter and make separate ways back to the ranch," Jess reminded Randy and Brad, his manner dead serious. "Always the chance they might catch one of us, but no way they'll get us all."

Brad shifted on his saddle. "Comfortin' thought," he said.

Jess swallowed some water from his canteen, wiping away the residue from his lips with a sweep of his hand.

"Y'know somethin', Burrows?" he said to Ehron Lee. "Ain't never killed no one in cold blood, but it don't bother me a bit shootin' down these peckers. Reckon I feel a sorta kinship with them prisoners. Really troubles me to hear how they was treated."

Ehron Lee nodded approvingly. "Was hopin' yuh'd feel that way."

Jess's eyes scouted out Randy and Brad.

"Think we all do," Jess said.

Ehron Lee took a quick study of each of his companions.

Jess and Randy looked calm and confident. Only Brad had him concerned. Though the morning was cool, Ehron Lee noticed that Brad was continually mopping beads of perspiration, either real or imaginary, from his brow. He didn't seem quite the hard guy he pretended to be.

The four men sat in preparedness for another twenty minutes before they could hear the faint rumble of the two prison wagons as they rode over the rough and rocky terrain leading to the quarry. Ehron Lee recalled that daily ride and how the drivers would laugh and push the horses to go faster, deliberately choosing the roughest trail so that the men crowded tightly together inside the "cages" were jostled and tumbled about for almost the entire length of the trip, their stomachs heaving from the unsteady motion, coupled with the rotten breakfast they'd consumed.

Yet Ehron Lee was grateful for these memories as they quickened his blood and intensified his fury. Like Jess Colfax, he had no hesitation about killing these swine. Each one deserved a bullet for the stinking cruelty they had inflicted upon both him and the other prisoners.

Given what soon was to come, Ehron Lee was quite calm. To his way of thinking, it would be little different from charges he had made in the army.

The men could hear the barked commands of the guards, ordering the leg-ironed prisoners to get out of the wagons. Ehron Lee edged his horse out slightly toward the clearing, hidden in deep shadow between two looming boulders, from where he could safely peer out to gauge the activity and to see if he could spot Ward among the like-dressed inmates. That was difficult; it would have to be Ward who would notice them when they rode in, and react accordingly.

Ehron Lee knew that work wouldn't begin until the lead guard blew on the whistle. By that point each of the eight guards would be in his assigned position. Four of the guards would be standing watch high on vantage points known collectively as "the overlook." The remaining four would be supervising, out among the prisoners, two on horseback, the other two on foot. Ehron Lee understood that because they would be directly with the work crew, those four would be the most difficult targets. The plan was that he and Jess would concentrate on those men on the ground while Randy and Brad would take aim on the guards standing perched on the rocky ledges.

When the moment came for the charge, there would be no turning back.

Ward Crawford had been ready for his liberation since the week began. Today it was Wednesday. As he clambered down from the prison wagon with the others, he held great anticipation. He felt in his gut that this would be the day and his senses were keenly alert. He knew he would have to act quickly and surely once his men rode in and the shooting started. There should be enough commotion to allow him at least a few moments to make a break toward one of the horses before any of the guards took notice. Those who weren't killed instantly would be too busy trying to save their own hides.

He wasn't kidding himself that there was still a heavy risk involved, but Ward had always been a gambler and favored playing the long odds.

Shuffling in leg irons alongside the other convicts toward the work areas assigned for the day, Ward was handed his tool, a shovel with which to scoop up crushed rock and gravel, by a guard ever watchful and prepared for a sudden, impulsive move by a desperate convict, who then stepped back to a safe distance with his rifle re-aimed. Once the men were all properly positioned, a signal was given to another guard.

The whistle indicating the start of the workday sounded, echoing through the quarry.

Hardly had the first sledgehammer and shovel been lifted . . . when the charge began and pandemonium ensued.

Four masked riders suddenly appeared, racing forward from the mouth of the canyon, accompanied by a barrage of gunfire.

Well-placed bullets from the long-range Winchesters instantly blasted two of the guards from their high perches, both bodies tensing at the impact of lead before tumbling to the ground.

Ehron Lee and Jess Colfax rode fast into the quarry, discharging their rifles at the two mounted guards who presented the easiest targets. They, too, died fast. By this time, the remaining guards, those two still on the overlook and the two men at ground level, had recovered from the surprise attack and were firing their rifles at the marauders. The prisoners, unsure of what was happening, dropped their tools and scrambled for cover. Ward Crawford, though, was close enough to one of the guards to swing his heavy shovel at his head, connecting with powerful impact, and hearing the man's neck break. He then moved as quickly as his leg irons would allow toward Ehron Lee, who rushed on horseback toward him. Ehron Lee slid his Winchester back into the scabbard and extended his hand, using all his strength to pull Ward up onto the horse, though because of the restriction of his leg irons, Ward was forced to sit sidesaddle, his legs draped over the horse's flank. To keep himself steady as the horse bucked and jerked amid the panic and the gunfire, he wrapped his left arm tightly around Ehron Lee's waist.

Jess fired off a rifle shot that blasted a hole through the skull of the last standing work site guard, though the two remaining on the overlook had dropped flat, and from prone positions were firing repeated rounds at the outlaws.

There was so much shooting that the quarry soon was heavy with the acrid smell of gun smoke.

"No chance of gettin' 'em now," Ward shouted to Ehron Lee. "Let's just get the hell outta here!"

Jess and Randy were already following that direction, riding fast toward the safety of the canyon walls. But before Brad could start after them, his horse was hit in the neck by a rifle bullet and he was thrown to the ground. The animal dropped heavily to its side, neighing and kicking out its last breath as Brad tried to avoid the bullets that ricocheted around him and crawled along the ground before regaining his footing. He started to run but another long-range shot rang out, tearing into his side. He struggled on for a few steps before collapsing to his knees. His whimpering turned into a desperate cry.

"Ward! Help me!" he pleaded.

Ward glanced at the boy before using his free hand to grab Ehron Lee's revolver from its holster.

"He's done for," he said, and then he took quick aim and shot Brad between the eyes. Brad's expression registered neither shock nor disbelief; he just looked numb as he died instantly. His body stiffened and Brad dropped face-first into the stony rubble.

As Ehron Lee whipped the horse toward the protection of the canyon, Ward said, loud enough to be heard, "Hated to do that. But if them guards had got to him and he talked . . ."

Ehron Lee didn't need to hear an explanation. He understood; it was a practical, not bloodthirsty decision. Yet where once he would have risked his life to save the man—where many times he had done just that, braving enemy fire to rescue a fallen comrade during the war—now he was indifferent. If any compassion still existed within his soul, it was encased in cast iron. Survival was his objective.

All he said in response was, "Just hold on tight. You ain't sittin' too firm and we gotta ride far and fast."

"Just hightail it, amigo, I ain't lettin' go!" Ward shouted to him.

Protected by a blanket of cover as clouds of gun smoke and gray dust rose behind them, Ehron Lee raised himself in the stirrups and wheeled his horse, then he whipped the animal into a dead run. Shots were still being fired, but by now the pair were out of range, Ehron Lee skillfully navigating the sharp turn into the canyon trail . . . and onto freedom.

They rode through the canyon, veering south and not slowing until they were deep in the hills, miles away from the prison and, at least for the time being, free of pursuit. For the last bit of travel Ehron Lee slowed the horse, surely exhausted from the run and bearing two men, to a canter. Ehron Lee further eased the horse to a slow trot as he scouted the area. He finally reined the horse to a halt in a tree-shaded area by a little stream where the animal could water and rest for a spell. He and Ward could also use a breather.

"Brought along a change of clothes in the pack roll," Ehron Lee told his companion as they dismounted. "But can't do much 'til we get those leg irons offa you."

Ward hastened to join the horse at the stream. He lay on his stomach by the slow-running currents, slurping up mouthfuls of the cool, clean water. After his thirst was quenched, he dunked his head whole into the stream then splashed handfuls of water over his face and rubbed some along the back of his neck to wash away the dirt from the quarry.

"We can ride into Allensfield tonight," he finally said to Ehron Lee. "There's gotta be a locksmith there who can get off these cuffs. But in the meantime, let's make my movements a little easier." He gestured toward Ehron Lee's Colt Army revolver.

Ehron Lee handed him the gun, only for a quick instant hesitating in the suspicion Ward might decide to swing around and use the weapon on him.

Ward gave Ehron Lee a look that suggested he knew what he'd been thinking. Then he pressed the barrel firmly against the chain link nearest to the left cuff, tensing the chain by widening his legs as far as they would separate . . . and he pulled the trigger.

The chain link blew apart as the report of the gunshot reverberated through the hills.

He repeated the procedure to the right side of his leg. Another echoing explosion as the length of chain blew off from the iron cuff and dropped into the grass. Ward picked up the section of jangling metal, regarded it for an instant with an expression of disgust, and tossed it hard into the stream.

"Now I can get outta this stinkin' prison uniform," he then said with a half smile.

Ehron Lee wore a concerned look as his eyes darted about the site. He worried that the gunfire might have alerted their pursuers to their position.

"Don't get yourself into a tizzy 'bout anyone hearin' that shot," Ward said to him. "I guarantee you they ain't even started lookin' for us yet. What's more, Whitey was right: 'Til they can get a posse together, they ain't got a chance in hell of findin' us no time soon."

Ward took the clothing from the pack roll and went off into the bush to change. He folded his prison wear into a tight bundle and buried it deep within the thick foliage. When he walked back out, he was wearing a black flannel shirt and brown trousers, along with a pair of old loose-fitting boots, which he just barely managed to slide over the leg cuffs—and brandishing the six-shooter that also had been included in the package, courtesy of his friends. He set himself against a tree and looked relaxed as he indulged himself to some comfort and soaked in the abundance of nature surrounding him.

"Never realized how different the morning air feels," he said contentedly. "Or how it tastes. You ever taste the air, Burrows? Don't taste quite the same when you're sweatin' in it all day."

Ehron Lee walked over to the horse and gently led it away from the stream. The animal was thirsty after its long ride, and Ehron Lee didn't want it to drink too much too quick.

"Hungry?" Ehron Lee asked. "Et most of the grub on the trail with the others, but got some jerked beef in the saddlebag."

"It'll do. Et the so-called breakfast," Ward said with a cynical intonation.

Ward checked over his gun. He opened the cylinder and saw that all six chambers had been cartridge fed.

"Reckon Jess and Randy are on their way back to the ranch," he said, snapping the cylinder closed. "Well, we'll be seein' 'em soon."

Ehron Lee whipped Ward a questioning look.

"Sure," Ward drawled, amused at his companion's expression. "Where d'yuh think we're headed?"

Ehron Lee stepped over to Ward and sat next to him on the grass. Ward grinned, though he kept his focus on the distant mountain crests.

"You been there, Burrows," he said. "It's a perfect hide-out. Couldn't find no better place. 'Sides, don't hurt to have some extra hands for what we're plannin'."

"That include Cora?" Ehron Lee asked subtly.

Ward's expression hardly altered at the mention of her name.

"Cora," Ward said dryly. "Hell, ain't thought 'bout her for a long time. So she *is* still with the boys, huh?"

Ehron Lee nodded. "You know she was, Ward. Yuh said someone would be waitin' at the cabin, and I reckon you was meanin' her."

"Yeah, guess I was," Ward said with a self-conscious grin.

"She kinda shamed the others into givin' us some cash," Ehron Lee added. "'Bout six hundred dollars."

"She's a right handy gal," Ward said. He pondered. "Could be useful, too."

"Reckon she could be," Ehron Lee agreed. Then he jerked his head toward the quarter horse.

"And just so's you should be knowin', that's Cora's pony we're ridin'," he said further.

"Well, I'm mighty obliged to her for the loan of her mule," Ward said.

Ehron Lee squinted. "Ain't hardly a mule."

Ward didn't reply. Ehron Lee shrugged, accepting Ward's term as just one of the man's peculiarities.

Ehron Lee plucked a long string of grass and slid it between his teeth.

He said, "Y'know, in all the time that we was together, you never said nothin' 'bout yuh havin' a girl."

"Didn't I?" Ward exclaimed with mock surprise.

Ehron Lee saw through his feigned ignorance.

Ward smirked and eyed his companion sideways. "Reason for that. Never considered Cora my girl."

"From what I gathered, ain't quite the way she saw it."

"Get to know her some, amigo?" Ward asked leisurely, without any real interest.

"Some," Ehron Lee replied, just as casually.

"I ain't sayin' we didn't have some good times together," Ward said, straightening his posture against the tree. "But it never went no further than that. Hell, with the kinda life I been leadin', I wasn't gonna burden no woman . . . that is, if I was ever gonna let myself get tempted. Which I wouldn't."

"Seems to me she woulda stuck by yuh no matter what," Ehron Lee commented, a tinge of repressed hurt evident in his words.

Ward detected the slight change in inflection in his companion, and understood. He shifted the topic.

"We'll rest up for another hour or so," he said, pulling back his arms and stretching, displaying solid muscle under the tight fabric of the shirt. "There's s'posed to be a hill trail into Allensfield. No need to rush. Best if we ride into town come nightfall."

"Think it's safe to head there so soon?" Ehron Lee asked with some doubt.

"'Less I'm missin' my guess, last place they'll look for us, Burrows," Ward said with assurance. "Once they get enough men together, they'll start by combin' these hills. Wouldn't think us fools 'nuff to go ridin' into town. 'Sides, I gotta get these damn irons offa my legs . . ." He winked. "And we both got us some business in Allensfield."

Ehron Lee looked at him.

"We gotta act fast," Ward told him. "Can't overstay. We stick to carryin' through with our plan, we grab Watson's wife tonight."

TWELVE

EHRON LEE AND Ward proceeded toward Allensfield after darkness had descended upon the town. Once they neared the town limits, Ward dismounted and walked alongside Ehron Lee as he slowly rode the horse forward. Maintaining caution, they chose to avoid the main street and instead traveled along the dust through the back routes. Allensfield was a small town and quiet at this hour. It prided itself on being a Christian community and didn't offer a saloon or other forms of "entertainment"—anyone so inclined would have to travel about seven miles west to the somewhat rowdier town of Jasper. And many of the churchgoing, God-fearing folks of Allensfield did just that—often.

"Know this town. Fulla Bible thumpers, righteous hypocrites," Ward remarked disdainfully.

"No different from other places I been," Ehron Lee muttered in agreement.

A drink would have gone down good for both men, but there wasn't time as they had other priorities.

"Got a lawman in town, so we best keep on guard," Ward advised as they moved through the shadows of the alley toward the locksmith shop. "Likely he's joined the hunt, but yuh can't never be too careful."

The locksmith was an elderly widower who also lived on the premises, setting up cooking and sleeping arrangements in the back of his shop. The establishment was closed and so Ward banged on the rear door, which was the entrance to the man's living quarters, while Ehron Lee stood watch for any passersby.

When the old man finally opened the door, he found himself staring into the barrel of a gun.

"Open up, pops," Ward said to him, grinning.

The old man hastily obliged. Ward and Ehron Lee pushed their way inside and followed him into the kitchen, where he had been preparing a pot of stew for his supper.

"Anyone else here?" Ward asked brusquely.

The proprietor could scarcely get out a nervous "No."

"Fine," Ward said. He turned to Ehron Lee. "Keep him covered while he works his magic."

Ward placed his own gun into his holster then removed his boots and rolled up the legs of his trousers, revealing the iron cuffed around both ankles.

"You got exactly five minutes to get 'em off," he instructed.

"F-Five?" the old man stammered. "D-Don't know if—"

"I'll be countin'," Ward told him steadily. Just to make sure his point was not misinterpreted, he swiveled toward Ehron Lee and said with an almost indifferent attitude, "Yeah, don't think I killed a man since noontime."

Removing the cuffs took a bit longer than the allotted time, owing to the locksmith's unsteady hands. Ward, still covered by Ehron Lee, then tied and gagged the old man and locked him inside a closet in the main room. Ward figured that should keep him until morning, by which time they'd be far from town.

Before leaving, Ward spotted a large knife sitting on the counter. He wore an enigmatic smile as he grabbed the knife to take with him.

"What's that for?" Ehron Lee asked.

"You got the note?" Ward said.

"Both of 'em," Ehron Lee replied with a nod of his head. "Had 'em in my pocket for over a week."

Ward hefted the knife, admiring the blade. "Well, this is just a little somethin' extra. To show Watson we mean business."

Ward also lifted a kerosene lantern from the table. "Better take this along, as well, so's we can see where we're goin' in this godawful dark."

The men quietly stepped out the rear door, back into almost pitch blackness.

"Gotta get me a horse," Ward said in a whisper to his partner. "And gotta do it quietly. Can't afford to start up no ruckus."

"Good chance we'll find one at the superintendent's house," Ehron Lee said, speaking hushed as well. "His missus always rides out in a buggy."

A slow smile crept across Ward's lips as he gave an approving nod. "Yeah, that's right."

Ehron Lee remembered the directions he had been given by the Allensfield tailor after he'd first come to town following his release from Rockmound, when he'd inquired about Superintendent George Watson. That would be their next stop . . . and the first part of their plan.

Ward climbed up behind Ehron Lee on the horse, and once again they used the back routes as much as possible to get to the house, which, fortunately for them, was on the outskirts of town.

The two-story wood-framed house equipped with a wide front patio stood alone on a small, fenced-in plot of land about a quarter mile from the main road leading into Allensfield. The house would have been difficult to find but for a light coming from one of the upstairs front windows.

"The missus must be gettin' ready for bed," Ward said. "Shame we have to disturb her."

"Any chance Watson might be home?" Ehron Lee said.

Although Ward kept it to himself, his initial thought, spurred on by Ehron Lee's question, was a vision of Watson being the one to answer that door. Ward could then enjoy the opportunity to release every ounce of hatred and hostility he'd chewed up and digested during his years at Rockmound with one swift plunge of the blade of his knife into the sonofabitch's gut. But *no*, he determined, it wouldn't stop there. That blade had a lot of tearing to do . . . and would go on with its work long after Watson was dead.

The answer that Ward gave Ehron Lee, however, was less violent, more to the point.

"Wouldn't be pleasant for him if'n he was," he replied. "But doubtful that he is. He's gotta deal with what happened at the prison today. That's why we gotta get this done quick tonight. Never get a better opportunity."

There was an open path next to the fenced enclosure that led to a small barn in back, which the men assumed housed the horse and buggy the superintendent's wife used for her trips to the prison.

"Whyn't you ready the horse, Burrows," Ward suggested. "I'll tend to the missus. And hand me one of them notes you wrote."

After Ehron Lee passed him the paper, he went toward the barn, keeping the lantern upraised to guide him through the dark. Ward made his way up the walkway to the front porch of the house. He walked up the steps slowly, quietly, preparing himself for what he was going to say. He knew the words, just had to present them convincingly.

He knocked on the door, scuffed his boot heel against the hardwood, and waited.

After several minutes he heard hurried footsteps approaching from within. Then the door opened a crack, and Ward finally saw close up the face that for many years he had only seen from afar and in a photograph in the superintendent's office. The funny thing was the woman looked older than Ward imagined she had to be. But there was no question that she was a lady prim and respectable.

He spoke to her in a kindly voice. "Mrs. Watson?"

"Yes," the woman, Janette Watson, said uncertainly. She responded to this caller from behind the door.

"Mrs. Watson, I apologize for the lateness. My name's Runyon, Joe Runyon. I was sent out from Rockmound by your husband," Ward went on, delivering his words with as much sincerity as he could fake. "There was some trouble at the prison today."

"Trouble? W-What sort of trouble?" Janette Watson said, anxiety starting to creep into her voice. She obviously hadn't heard about the breakout that morning, which was to their advantage.

"Well, your husband asked me to send for you, ma'am," Ward said, bowing his head. "There was an escape today. Don't want to frighten you, but Superintendent Watson is a-feared these prisoners that broke out might be somewhere in this vicinity. Might even . . . well, might even be headed your way. They're a right mean bunch and . . . Anyways, he'd like it if you could be with him 'til these men are apprehended."

Janette looked only momentarily doubtful.

"You say you're from Rockmound?"

"Yes, ma'am. Started there only recently. Do some relief work for the guards. Just came in to start my shift when your husband asked me to ride out and fetch yuh. He was quite insistent."

Janette stood quietly, studying the stranger's features from behind the protection of the partially opened door, trying to determine if she could trust what he was saying.

Ward spoke up. "Just followin' the superintendent's orders."

She hesitated briefly but soon her expression shifted into one of acceptance. She was concerned and Ward had convinced her. She opened the door all the way and told him to come and wait inside while she went upstairs to get dressed, as she had been preparing for bed and was clad in her night robe.

When she came back downstairs, now attired in a patterned pale blue housedress and wool sweater, and walked with Ward to the open door, she noticed Ehron Lee out front on the pathway—sitting on her horse. This puzzled the woman and she turned to face Ward.

But before she could utter a word, she froze. All the sincerity was gone from the face of the man who called himself "Joe Runyon." In its place was a cold, dreadful mask, the thin lips widened into a malevolent grin. The face of Ward Crawford—prison escapee, vengeful outlaw.

Janette Watson felt her legs weaken as she stared at the gun he had drawn on her.

Her voice faltered. "W-What do you want?"

"Just step outside, Mrs. Watson," Ward told her smoothly. "Don't wanta have to hurt you, so you'd do best to stay quiet and cooperate."

Janette had no choice but to obey. Followed by Ward, she walked out onto the porch, her steps measured and tentative. Ehron Lee was silent but gestured for her to climb up behind him on the horse.

Ward closed the door behind them. Then he pulled out the folded paper from his trousers pocket and added his personal touch: withdrawing the knife he had taken from the Allensfield locksmith and thrusting the sharp-edged blade through the note, pinning it solidly into the door.

Janette spun around abruptly at hearing the blunt impact.

Ward responded to her apprehension with a cold, chilling smile and urged her forward toward Ehron Lee. Then he mounted the other horse.

Turning to his companion, Ward said, "Simple as pie, huh? When it comes to their man, women is so trustin'."

Thirteen

"'FRAID I HAVE some troubling news, Melinda. Think it best if I speak with you inside," Buck Leighton said to the girl as he stood outside the doorway of her trim, modest country house.

Melinda's expression instantly took on a look of concern and she invited Buck in. They took a seat inside the parlor. Before Buck could speak what was on his mind, Melinda started to rise from her chair and offered him coffee, which he refused with a wave of his hand.

Melinda seated herself, and Buck spoke to the point.

"Heard from the superintendent at Rockmound," he said, fiddling with the brim of his hat. "Some years back a letter was sent to the prison, written by your sister, informing Ehron Lee that . . . well, that you had died."

It took a moment for Buck's words to register with her, but when they did, Melinda looked dumbfounded. Her lips moved but nothing came out.

"I confess I debated tellin' yuh this, Melinda," Buck admitted. "But I figger you got a right to know."

Faint words finally fumbled from Melinda's mouth. "I can't . . . no, she—she . . ."

Buck could understand Melinda's incredulity, but he'd had a totally different reaction upon learning of this. He wasn't a man to be disrespectful to the dead, but he saw Abigail Maguire as a right hateful person. From what he both knew about Abigail and had also experienced back at the jail when Ehron Lee was his prisoner, Buck recognized that this type of cruel tactic was not beyond her capability.

He gazed out the window into the yard, where little Charlie was playing. He exhaled a soft sigh.

"She said nothin' in the letter 'bout the boy," he said.

Melinda was nervously massaging her hands. She looked down at the whitening of her knuckles and unclasped her hands.

"Hearin' this . . . it explains everything, don't it?" she murmured.

"Yeah . . . 'pears to."

Melinda grimaced. "But to think that she . . . that Abigail would do something so awful."

"Hard thing to accept," Buck acknowledged.

"Even knowin' it's true, don't know if I *can* accept it," Melinda said stubbornly, struggling to comprehend her sister's betrayal.

"Would you be mindin' if I was to ask you somethin' . . . rather personal?" Buck said.

Melinda didn't respond either way so Buck just pressed forward.

"Are you a Christian person?"

Melinda's expression became baffled, then she looked a little wary.

"Why do you ask?" she said tentatively.

"I'll be tellin' yuh," Buck said, waiting for her answer.

Melinda's face went thoughtful, as though she had to search deep within herself for what to say.

"Wasn't raised in no church," she said. "Ehron Lee and me . . . we didn't go to services. Never had much opportunity with Ehron Lee doin' most of the work 'round my sister's place. Do know that he felt strongly 'bout God. Always made a point of prayin' 'fore supper, even speakin' a word sometimes 'fore he'd go outdoors. Talked 'bout havin' read the Bible. Reckon bein' in the army does that to a soul." She sighed in considering. "Don't really know what I feel." She cast him another suspicious glance. "Why'd you be askin'?"

Buck waited for a few seconds before he said more. When he did reply, it was with a shrug. "Maybe no reason specifically. But . . . maybe it might help some with what I'm gonna tell yuh."

Melinda cocked her head, expectantly if apprehensively.

"Ehron Lee got his release from Rockmound," Buck told her outright.

Melinda's eyes focused sharply on him.

"When?" she asked anxiously.

Buck couldn't determine by her tone if she was excited by the news or possibly distressed. He could appreciate either emotion.

"Little over two weeks ago," he said.

Melinda considered before she lowered her head. There was a strangeness to her voice when she said, "And he won't be comin' back. No reason to now."

Buck said nothing.

"Where d'yuh suppose he went?" she asked rhetorically. After a hesitation she answered the question herself. "Nowhere really for him to go. Guess he'll just head somewhere and try to start a new life for himself. Maybe even if he'd never gotten that letter from Abigail, that's what he woulda done. Too ashamed to come back because of what they did to him. What they made him." She spoke with some anger. "But it's so unfair. Him never knowin' the truth. Never . . . gettin' the chance to know his son."

Buck felt her anguish. He understood because he had his own guilt. He thought that maybe he could have done more . . . though the reality was there simply wasn't anything else he could have done to help her husband.

"I think he woulda come back, Melinda," Buck said

gently. He spoke against what he truly felt—or wanted to see happen, but Melinda needed to hear these words.

Melinda's eyes started to tear.

"And yuh can't say 'never,' Melinda," Buck added encouragingly. "Anything can happen at any time." He took a breath. "Hell, look how after so many years you and me just bumped into one another."

Melinda gave him a weak smile accompanied by a faint nod. She appreciated Buck's comforting words though she felt in her heart, with a painful, regretful certainty, that she would never see her husband again.

Her beloved sister had made sure of that.

She thought about the question Buck had asked her. About her Christian beliefs. Although he didn't make clear why he had asked the question, Melinda realized that for her there was no simple answer.

For a while she'd hoped that Abigail's soul would rest in peace. But now she thought different. Until her own dying day, Melinda would never forgive her.

FOURTEEN

CORA RILEY HEARD the hoofbeats of the horses, distant at first then steadily nearing the cabin, and fearing it might be unwelcome visitors, she hastened to rouse Jess Colfax and Randy Boggs from their corn whiskey–induced slumber.

Both men scrambled out of their bedrolls and instantly went for their revolvers.

"Douse that light," Jess ordered Cora, who promptly extinguished the flame inside the lantern, plunging the house into darkness.

Jess and Randy inched toward the window in the kitchen, glancing outside into the night while they waited for the approaching riders to come into closer view.

No one uttered a sound; even their anxious breathing was muted.

The hoofbeats slowed as the two horses moved deeper onto the property. Jess squinted but was still unable to make out the identities of the riders; all he could see were three shadowed forms, two riding together on the same horse.

"What the . . ." he started to say.

Then—his mouth broadened in a grin.

"Well, I'll be a sonofabitch!" he bellowed. "It's Ward Crawford."

Cora hurried forward to peer through the window. In seconds she, too, was smiling widely.

Only the laconic Randy seemed unimpressed.

"Likely come lookin' for another favor," he said in his customary drawl.

"Burrows is with him . . . and so's some woman, looks like," Jess observed.

Cora's expression turned hard and suspicious. "Who d'yuh s'pose *she* is?"

"Whyn't yuh let 'em in and find out," Jess said, turning to her with a smirk.

Cora's jealousy wasn't well hidden. She narrowed her eyes at Jess. "That's what I intend to do." She walked with determined strides into the main room and opened the door.

Ward ambled inside first. He greeted Cora expansively, with a big hug, lifting her off the floor and twirling her. Still uncertain about the female he'd brought along, Cora responded to his display of exuberance with reserve. Ward hardly noticed.

Janette Watson followed, prodded on by Ehron Lee. Cora eyed the woman icily—until she noticed the look of cold fear reflected on her features.

"This here is Mrs. Watson," Ward said to the group. "She's come a long way and she's tired and I reckon a mite hungry. In fact, we all could use a bite, so Cora, why don't you rustle us up some grub?"

Cora's gaze remained braced on Janette.

Ward could detect Cora's uncertainty over their hostage. It amused him. He asked her again to fix them something to eat and then he'd explain the situation. Cora muttered that they'd already eaten supper but that she could fry them some eggs. Ward said if she scrambled his, that would be fine.

Ehron Lee and Ward sat at the table and wolfed down their meal, washing it down with some coffee Cora had brewed. Janette refused to eat and sat still and quiet in a chair in the main room. Her pose was stiff, she continued to wear the face of apprehension, but she hadn't uttered a sound.

She had already figured that she was to be a hostage, but why—and for what reason—she hadn't been told. Therefore she listened intently as Ward and Ehron Lee spelled out what they were planning to the others seated around the table.

"I think us bustin' yuh outta Rockmound paid yuh back in full," Randy said after hearing what Ehron Lee and Ward had to say. "Cora's little brother died helpin' us do it."

Ward deliberately ignored the comment about Brad being killed. He also avoided returning the look that Cora gave him.

"This ain't no part of any debt still owed," he said. "Just somethin' you might wanta come in on."

"Could be interestin', if there was some cash involved," Jess put in. He leaned forward, planting his forearms on the table. "Just what is the payoff?"

"Ain't one," Ehron Lee spoke up.

Jess and Randy glanced at each other.

"So what're you gettin' out of it?" Randy wanted to know.

Ehron Lee smiled slowly. "Call it 'satisfaction.'"

"Damn poor reward if'n yuh ask me," Randy said miserably.

Ward looked over at Janette. He told Cora to take her into the bedroom and to stay with her. He didn't want Janette to hear the rest. If she knew the outcome of what they were planning, she might attempt something foolish. It was best if she was kept in the dark until the moment of decision.

Cora didn't look pleased but she wasn't about to cross Ward. With a swift jerk of her head, Cora gestured Janette into the bedroom in which she slept, then she followed her inside and shut the door.

Ehron Lee lowered his voice and outlined the rest of the plan to Jess and Randy.

Randy, whom Ehron Lee had pictured as an agreeable, easygoing type, was suddenly adamant that he wanted no part of their scheme. Jess was less resistant but likewise had

his doubts. As he told them, he couldn't see any reward for
his participation.

"Two women kept hostage," he said, considering. "You're
gonna bring a heap o' trouble on all of us."

"Not likely," Ward said. "Watson and the judge are gonna
know if they try anything funny, like reportin' to the law,
they ain't ever gonna see their two ladies ag'in."

"So if this judge and the other one show . . . and you kill
'em like you're plannin', what 'bout them girls?" Jess questioned. He hooked his thumb toward the bedroom. "That one
in there has had a good look at each of us, 'specially you and
Burrows."

Ehron Lee frowned. "Ain't decided on that yet."

"Well, you better make a decision," Jess said. "'Cause
you let 'em ride away afterward and you know right where
they'll be headed. Every lawman in the state'll be after yuh.
Hell, after *us*."

Ward leaned back, tilting the front legs of his chair off
the floor and balancing himself. "He's got a point."

"Damn right," Jess said bluntly.

Randy stood up from the table. "You can decide whatever
yuh want, but count me out. My neck ain't quite in a
noose yet."

As Randy started to walk away Ward glanced at him over
his shoulder and said, "You do what you have to, Randy.
But this is where we'll be bringin' 'em, so you might do best
to ride outta here."

Randy looked disgusted. He gazed flatly at Jess.

"And you?" he asked.

Jess's eyes went from Ward to Ehron Lee.

"Don't care much for judges or lawmen," he said simply.

Randy gave a hasty nod. "All right. I'll pack up my gear
and ride out in the morning."

He walked into the other bedroom and shut the door
behind him.

Ward sat looking at that closed door for a while, as if
pondering. Finally he said, "If I didn't know I could trust
Randy, think I'd put a bullet into him 'fore sunup."

"Trust nothin'," Jess commented. "Whether he cares to admit it or not, his neck is already deep in a noose."

With the guarantee from the others that there were no hard feelings, Randy Boggs rode off early the next morning. He didn't say where he was headed and no one asked. It was part of an unspoken agreement among the outlaws that once any of them decided to part company with the others, his ultimate whereabouts would not be known to them. It was a precaution to prevent one from informing on his partners. If he did not know, he could not say, no matter how much pressure might be put on him.

Seated around the table having breakfast, Ehron Lee, Ward, and Jess discussed the next phase of the plan.

While doing his time at Rockmound, Ward had learned from questioning other convicts that Judge Harrison's family lived north, in the town of Bolton. That was another fair distance to travel, about a day-and-a-half ride straight through. It wouldn't be wise for Ehron Lee—and certainly not Ward—to attempt it alone. Jess couldn't be considered since he was a brutish-looking individual whose presence would immediately arouse suspicion among the townspeople.

Ward suddenly lifted his eyes from the table. "Cora could probably do it."

The response from the others was slow in coming.

Finally Jess shook his head and stifled a laugh. "She's got a hard 'nuff time dealin' with there bein' one fee-male here. She sure as hell ain't gonna go out of her way to bring in another."

Ward regarded Jess with a flat stare. Maybe Jess had a point but he hadn't come up with a better suggestion.

Jess looked away from Ward's cold eyes and tried to ease the tension. "That's 'bout three days' travel, at least. And Cora might be tough but she ain't no man. Can't see her havin' an easy time of it, keepin' that girl behaved on the ride back."

Ward was silent, his eyes still leveled on Jess. Then he shifted his focus to Ehron Lee.

"Still think it should be Cora," Ward said. "But someone should go along."

"I'll ride with her," Ehron Lee offered.

"Think that's smart?" Ward asked him.

Ehron Lee responded with a sardonic smile. "Sure. I'm a free man."

Ward nodded. "Okay. Figger Jess and me can watch things here."

"Be mighty sad if the two of yuh couldn't hold on to the reins of a lone woman," Ehron Lee remarked.

His "humor" wasn't appreciated by the others and went unacknowledged.

"Still gotta talk Cora into goin' along with it," Jess reminded them.

"Yeah, well . . . you let me handle that," Ward said, unconcerned.

Cora wasn't easy to convince. She shared the same objections as Randy Boggs. She thought it was a crazy scheme. Risky, and with no reward to justify that risk. But what might override her doubts was the strong affection she had for Ward, and he eventually hoped to persuade her by taking her outside for a walk and expressing his own feelings for her, tender emotions that he was forced to exaggerate. Ward was a smooth talker and knew how to manipulate a gal like Cora, who may have possessed a rawhide exterior but inwardly was romantic and impressionable.

"Know none of this makes sense to you, Cora. But can't go on to any kind of life without first gettin' back at 'em for what they done," Ward explained to her. "Burrows and I been carryin' 'round a burnin' hatred for a long time. Gotta snuff out that fire they put into us."

Cora listened sympathetically, tried to let her feelings for Ward overcome her objections.

"I think it's wrong, Ward," she argued. "Just plain wrong."

Ward shrugged his shoulders meekly. "Mebbe. Probably. But wouldn't be the first wrong move I ever made."

Cora's eyes drifted down to the dirt at her feet that she had unconsciously shuffled into a small mound, and she shook her head emphatically.

"You knew when yuh hooked up with us, none of us was chasin' an honest life," Ward reminded her.

After a bit, with her head still lowered, Cora acknowledged his words with a slow nod.

"And though you been there to take care of us, we ain't never come right out and asked yuh for a favor," Ward added in a more serious tone.

Cora finally surrendered. As she knew she would.

She spoke softly, uncertainly. "What do you want me to do?"

"Not askin' much." Ward shrugged. "Just spend time 'round the town and check out the situation. See what you can learn 'bout Judge Harrison's daughter."

Cora wrinkled her forehead. "How d'yuh suggest I do that?"

"Shouldn't be hard. Bolton's a small town. Can't be too much of a secret, her comin's and goin's. From what I hear, she's Harrison's only kid."

"I know Bolton," Cora said with a tilt of her head. "Grew up on a farm not far from there."

Ward nodded. "Well, that's fine. Just pretend to be goin' 'bout your business. Maybe do some shoppin', stop to have tea in a restaurant. Get yourself known a little, just don't make yourself too suspicious. Try to find out what yuh can and let Burrows know."

"And then what?" Cora asked carefully.

Ward tilted back his Stetson and scratched the side of his head. "Well . . . when the time is right, Burrows will step in, and the two of you bring her back here."

"And then . . ." Cora pressed.

Ward moved forward and laid his fingers lightly against her cheek. "That, honey, is somethin' you don't gotta be worryin' yourself over."

* * *

Ehron Lee and Cora started their ride toward Bolton just before sundown. It would be a clear evening and easy for travel. They wouldn't go far that night but counted on getting an early start in the morning that could see them into Bolton come tomorrow dusk.

They rode until after ten and camped out in a hollow off the trail, settling in the desert grasslands among a profusion of velvet mesquite trees. Ehron Lee collected dry wood to start a small fire while Cora pulled some canned beans from her pack. They'd left the cabin before having supper, intending to eat by campfire.

They ate quietly, offering only a few words to each other about nothing in particular. Ehron Lee suspected that the girl had questions, though, and after he was finished with his beans, tossing his empty can deep into the surrounding bush, he sipped the coffee Cora had brewed over the open fire and he volunteered his story. Cora listened in silence, occasionally nodding her head in sympathetic acknowledgment of all that he had endured. Yet there was no display of emotion in his telling. He could just as easily have been telling a trail story to cowhands. Cora thought that peculiar. All the same, she admired Ehron Lee's strength. By the time he was through, Cora well understood why Ehron Lee had set out on this vengeful path. Had she not spent many of her years alongside outlaws, she may have thought differently, looked upon this plan as a savage act, but living outside the law had become a way of life she understood. In an odd yet perfectly natural way, given her circumstances, it was also a lifestyle she had come to embrace.

She also respected the type of man who would choose this desperate road. It showed courage and an independence lacking in those who conformed to the rigid rules dictated by society. These men elected to live by their own rules, enforcing their individuality through any means necessary.

This respect and acceptance extended even to her brother, Brad, felled under gunfire. He died young but had chosen to live life on his own terms. When told of Brad's death, she was saddened; she grieved, but the emotion passed. She had the strength to recognize and accept that men such as Brad, Jess, and Ward were living on borrowed time. They likely realized it, too, and were determined to live each day with an unbridled passion.

"Never made a dishonest move in my life," Ehron Lee told her, idly poking at the fire with a long stick. "Whatever I now become, it was their doin'."

"Can see you was a decent sort once," Cora observed. "Most of the men I've known . . . they was bred bad."

Ehron Lee turned his face toward her, the glow of the shifting flames reflecting on his profile.

"Can't let it go, Cora," he said with emphasis, as though trying to justify to himself what was to come as much as explain it to her. "Thought I might decide ag'in doin' this once I was let out . . . but it's somethin' that's plain become a part of who I am now. Like a poison in my blood. It's what I *gotta* do."

"Ward feels the same, I know," Cora said understandingly. "He's got his own reason—that's just the kind of fella he is. How he's always been. But he ain't got nowhere near as much reason for hate as you." She hesitated before adding meekly, "Reckon, though . . . that somehow makes it worse."

Ehron Lee gazed up from the fire, and when he next spoke, there was almost a strain in his voice. "I got no urge to hurt those women. But 'fore I pay back Harrison and Superintendent George Watson, I want them two to know somethin' of the pain they caused me."

FIFTEEN

THE ROCKMOUND ESCAPE and massacre of the supervising guards at the quarry work site kept Superintendent George Watson busy for several days, and it was not until the weekend that he decided to grab a few hours of needed rest and visit his wife at their home in Allensfield.

He walked onto the porch and discovered the message knifed to the front door of his house—and upon entering the house, he found that his wife, Janette, was missing.

Once his shock, followed by outrage, subsided, he used his intelligence to consider likely culprits and concluded that his wife's kidnapping was connected with Ward Crawford's escape from Rockmound. Later, when he learned about the Allensfield locksmith being forced at gunpoint to remove iron cuffs from the legs of an intruder on the same day as the breakout, he knew for a certainty that Crawford was involved. According to the two surviving guards, there were at least four men who participated in the work site break—one dead, a picture of whose corpse was forwarded to the territorial marshal for identification—yet the locksmith had said that only two men had burst into his shop that night.

The locksmith had been frightened and his descriptions of both men had been vague. Watson was curious who the accomplice was but not as concerned for his focus was centered on Ward Crawford, as he was the key person responsible. The man he most wanted to see pay for this crime. The man he now determined he would see hanged.

He told no one in town about what had happened. He neither wanted nor believed he needed outside assistance. Since assuming his duties at Rockmound, Watson had maintained absolute control, a strict independence. He had come up with his own way of dealing with this crime.

Around noon on Sunday morning, he returned to the prison and immediately sent for Sergeant Liam O'Brien, his toughest and most trusted guard. When O'Brien arrived at the superintendent's office, Watson sat him down and confided in him, telling O'Brien about the kidnapping of his wife and the strange ransom note knifed to the door. There was no hint of panic or urgency in his voice; he spoke surprisingly calmly, though O'Brien knew Watson well enough to detect the fire burning inside him, noticed the hint of a flare in his usually icy eyes.

O'Brien recognized the signs as his ruddy complexion turned even redder from the blood that surged into his head. He was livid that such a brazen act could be committed against a man for whom he felt enormous respect and loyalty. He also felt a cold fury for the slaughter of the six men who had been his comrades.

Without the superintendent having to say so, O'Brien voiced his own suspicion that Ward Crawford was responsible for Mrs. Watson's abduction.

"And if that be the case," he added, his anger intensifying his Irish brogue, "his cell mate musta been knowin' his plan."

Watson naturally had already come to the same conclusion. He ordered that Woody Milo be brought to his office.

"That, sir, will be my utmost pleasure," O'Brien said.

A short time later O'Brien returned to the office, accompanied by an apprehensive Woody. Woody knew why he had been summoned, had expected it ever since learning of the prison break. What he couldn't understand was why Superintendent Watson was calling for him *now*, days after the escape.

The stern, intense look on Watson's face almost paralyzed Woody, whose body jerked reflexively when O'Brien slammed the office door behind them—and the three were alone.

O'Brien instantly backhanded the black bowler from Woody's head.

"You stand respectful before the superintendent," he ordered.

A dark, consuming silence engulfed the room. Watson's cold stare was fixated on Woody the whole time, while O'Brien began to beat his truncheon against the open palm of his hand, slowly and with purpose.

Woody looked about the room with a nervous cringing.

Finally Watson spoke. Despite his penetrating gaze, the tone of his voice was level and official.

"I want you to tell me all you can 'bout Ward Crawford," he began.

Woody started to squirm. He was afraid to answer as his nerves were such that he knew his words would come out in a stammer. He shrugged his shoulders innocently and stayed quiet.

"You shared a cell with him," Watson went on. "I know he told you somethin' 'bout what he was planning."

"Answer the superintendent," O'Brien growled at the prisoner.

Woody swallowed hard, and tried to get the words out. "M-Me and Crawford . . . we—we n-never talked much."

Watson slowly shook his head. O'Brien began to beat the truncheon against his hand with more emphasis. The sound seemed magnified within the quiet of the office.

"And there he be goin' with his stutter talk," O'Brien remarked.

"C-Can't tell yuh w-what I don't know," Woody argued feebly.

"You *do* know and you *will* tell, Woodrow," Watson said icily.

"Ward woulda . . . he w-woulda killed me . . . if I f-found out what he was p-plannin'." He spoke with more desperation. "Why would he t-tell me? He knows I c-could never go with him. Knows you woulda g-got me to talk."

"So he never told yuh nothin', did he?" O'Brien said very slowly. He punctuated his remark with a sharp slap of the truncheon against the hard back of a chair.

Woody started at the abrupt action. Then he swallowed again and his good eye widened in fear.

"Could do that all over your body, you whitewashed weasel," O'Brien threatened. "Give yuh some real color, if I got a mind to."

Woody turned to the superintendent with a pleading look etched into his scarred, twisted features. But Watson appeared not about to interfere.

O'Brien stepped closer to Woody, brandishing the truncheon in an aggressive fashion.

"Crawford and those who helped him get away killed six good men, all friends of mine," he said, breathing the words into Woody's face. "And they done more than that, that maybe yuh know 'bout, maybe yuh don't. But either way, you best start tellin' us what you *do* know."

Incoherent sounds started to emanate from Woody's throat. His body trembled violently, as if he were in the throes of a seizure.

"No need to get heavy-handed, O'Brien," Watson said reasonably. "Maybe Woodrow needs some time to think this out. Some quiet time alone."

Woody's brain was so addled that his first thought was that he was going to get a reprieve and be returned to the safety of his cell.

O'Brien smiled knowingly at Watson's suggestion. "Think I understand, sir."

It took a moment for Woody to comprehend, and when the realization came as to what they actually had in mind for him, he shouted *"No!"* and made an attempt to rush for the door. His panic was so great that he couldn't seem to turn the knob, his fingers fumbling frantically. O'Brien stepped over easily and grabbed him by the collar, almost lifting his slight body from the floor.

"And would yuh be thinkin' there'd be anyplace for you to run?" O'Brien said pleasantly.

Watson finally rose from behind his desk. He walked over to Woody, who was struggling feebly against Sergeant O'Brien's strong grip.

"I—I'm t-tellin' yuh the t-truth . . . I swear . . . I don't know nothin'!" Woody shrieked.

"We'll see," was all Watson said, before gesturing with a twist of his head for O'Brien to escort Woody outside to the back grounds of the prison compound.

The door to the office closed, and as Superintendent George Watson returned to his desk, he could hear Woody's agonized screams as he was dragged through the corridor and soon thrust outside into the blazing afternoon sun for his long walk to the pit.

Sixteen

THE DAY STARTED out sunny if a shade cool, but as morning neared into the noon hour, the sky became overcast and a light drizzle started to fall. The gathering clouds became even more foreboding, and Ehron Lee suggested to Cora that they'd do well to find themselves some cover as a heavy rain seemed imminent.

They pulled off the trail into a grove of cottonwoods, where the dense leafy overhang would provide some shield against the uncertain weather. Once they were settled, they threw on the ponchos they had brought along and seated themselves under one of the large trees. The air had gotten cold as the wind had picked up and had a sharp bite. Their ponchos provided some comfort against the chill, but since the fabrics weren't waterproof, the ponchos offered little protection from the rain that seeped steadily through the foliage. To compensate, both adjusted the wide brims of their Stetsons to repel the relentless pellets of water.

Attempting to keep warm, Ehron Lee and Cora found themselves huddled together. Nothing more was meant by this maneuver other than necessity, a response to the dampness and the cold. Still, they felt a little awkward with their bodies pressed so close to each other, though neither offered a comment to attempt to justify the arrangement.

It was Ehron Lee who finally spoke, and he merely offered an observation.

"This'll slow us gettin' into Bolton."

Cora nodded and shivered a little. She pushed her body even tighter against Ehron Lee, casting him a quick upward glance to see if he might object. His only reaction was a slight, understanding smile. Then, as if by reflex, he reached out his arm and wrapped it around her shoulder, drawing her yet closer. Cora did not discourage his considerate gesture.

At least that was how she believed he had intended it.

Cora, however, was feeling something a mite different. For reasons she could not quite comprehend, she was forming a strange attraction to Ehron Lee. This had come upon her so suddenly, and unexpectedly, that she found herself questioning. Was it because of the time alone she was spending with him—or that he had trusted her enough to confide in her his tragic past . . . or was she simply misinterpreting the sympathy she had for all that he had gone through? She had no ready answer and, in fact, was trying to suppress the sudden guilt that washed over her . . . a guilt over how it had shifted her affections. Ward Crawford had always been the man she harbored feelings toward. During all the years of his imprisonment, Cora had eagerly hoped he would someday return to her. She had maintained an unwavering devotion, even discouraging the advances of Jess Colfax, who more than once had attempted to fill the void left by Ward, and she never lost the expectation that Ward might choose her, if not as his bride, then as his life companion. Yet now that he was free, she saw and felt things differently.

While she recognized that Ehron Lee was not cut from the same cloth as Ward Crawford, both men shared similarities she found appealing: primarily a rugged independence, though Ehron Lee, despite possessing a heart hardened by vengeance, had not revealed the callous or brutal nature that was an inherent characteristic of Ward.

Although she hardly knew him—he was still little more than a stranger—Cora's impression of Ehron Lee was that he was a good man who had gone astray because of cruel circumstances. She had as much admitted this to him, though it had brought forth no acknowledgment. But where Ward Crawford's attentions went no further than having her along only for a good time, or calling on her when she could serve some useful purpose, always with his charm at the ready, she recognized Ehron Lee as a man capable of compassion. She saw him as someone who might truly care for her and whom she could care for in return.

Cora contemplated all this as they sat together quietly under the rainfall. Maybe she was having these feelings only because Ehron Lee had his arm around her and was holding her close, and for the first time in a long while she felt safe and protected being with someone. She had never experienced much affection in her life and perhaps she simply did not know how to correctly interpret or respond to it.

To her embarrassment, a sigh inadvertently escaped her lips (which thankfully Ehron Lee either didn't notice or simply didn't acknowledge) with the realization that soon the rain would lift and with it would probably go her fantasies. Unfounded or just plain crazy, they had provided her with a pleasant if brief interlude—and a reminder that maybe she was more of a woman than she often gave herself credit for.

But her thoughts shifted as she considered the brutal reality that lay ahead, and for the first time since she had taken up with the outlaw band, Cora could truthfully admit she was afraid. She was apprehensive not only of the circumstances of what was to come, but of how the act that Ehron Lee was planning would forever brand him as a criminal.

Ward was born under the shadow of the gallows. Ehron Lee still had a choice. It might not be too late for him to cast aside his scheme and ride on far past Bolton. He could still turn back, and it saddened Cora to see that by choice and with a soul so corrupted by hate he would likely bypass that road to redemption.

Although the rain hit hard, pelting the ground around them with a drumming rhythm, the downpour didn't last long. Soon the rain once again turned to drizzle and the clouds began to break up, allowing the warmth of sunshine to stream through.

Ehron Lee and Cora shook the water from their hats and quickly removed their wet ponchos, draping them over their horses' withers to sun-dry them as they rode on.

Ehron Lee wiped dry then mounted his leather saddle. He smiled at Cora and further cemented her dread when he said, "Might make good time yet."

Cora forced a smile in return, and she nodded. Once more he made it plain that he was committed to fulfilling his purpose.

The hour was late when they rode the trail into Bolton.

As it was when Ehron Lee and Ward Crawford rode into Allensfield, the streets of the town were empty, only for an entirely different reason. Most of its citizens had congregated at the many gaudy, false-fronted saloons that occupied the main street of Bolton. The noise and musical entertainment spilled out into the deserted night.

Both Ehron Lee and Cora were bone-tired from their long ride and decided to find a hotel. There was a decent-looking establishment along the main route called The Royal, and Cora went inside to register while Ehron Lee walked the horses a little farther to the livery stable. Although it was dark and his features were sufficiently shadowed, Ehron Lee lowered the brim of his Stetson and kept the talk short as he handed the stable owner the reins of both ponies and paid him the $5-per-week boarding fee. He wanted to stay as anonymous as possible. As a stranger in a community like Bolton, he knew he would be a likely candidate for suspicion once news of the girl's disappearance became known. Until he was needed, he'd let Cora do the scouting while he stayed inside the hotel.

He held the second note in his pocket. The ransom note to be delivered to Judge Harrison.

When Ehron Lee got back to the hotel, Cora was waiting for him, seated on the settee in the dimly lit lobby. He'd expected her to get two rooms but instead found that she had registered them as man and wife. He tried not to show any surprise, especially when he caught the curious look the bespectacled desk clerk was giving the two strangers. As he thought about it, he realized Cora had probably done a smart thing. What could look more innocent than a married couple? And wisely she had signed them in as Mr. and Mrs. Arthur Dodds.

As they started up the staircase to their room, the desk clerk called after them.

"Travelers?" he inquired.

Ehron halted and turned to the man. He started to speak but nodded instead.

"Newlyweds," Cora offered cheerfully, looping her arm around Ehron Lee's and squeezing it affectionately.

As if in an echo, the word reverberated back to Ehron Lee: *Newlyweds . . .*

The word was spoken innocently, Cora surely had meant nothing more by it than a convenient explanation, but its impact struck Ehron Lee like a thunderbolt. In an instant it evoked a spasm of memories that he'd believed he had long kept dormant. He could not permit those thoughts to resurface, and only for an instant did he acknowledge the painful reminder before he forced himself to suppress the emotion it threatened to reignite.

Fortunately, neither Cora nor the desk clerk noticed his momentary discomfort.

The desk clerk scratched his chin and furrowed his brow. "Seems sorta strange you two didn't bring along any luggage."

Ehron Lee made up his answer quickly. "That'll be comin'.

Tonight we don't wanta be thinkin' 'bout any unpackin'." He winked. "Reckon yuh might know what I mean."

The desk clerk looked only momentarily perplexed before he caught on, chuckled, and waved them on. Ehron Lee and Cora exchanged a quick glance and finished the climb up the stairs to their room. Once inside, Ehron Lee locked the door while Cora went to light the bedside table lamp. Ehron Lee then flopped himself on the bed, letting out a prolonged breath.

"Think you convinced him," Cora said.

"Maybe. But don't know how much we look like . . ." He halted, unable to say the word. "Well, what you said we was. 'Specially comin' in the way we did."

Ehron Lee had a point. His appearance suggested he'd just come off a cattle drive while Cora, wearing dirty jeans and a heavy flannel shirt, was dressed more like a ranch hand than a new bride.

"Well, we couldn't think out everything," Cora said, shrugging. Her eyes wandered around the room, which was small and plain and furnished only with a bed, bureau, and chair. "Just hope we won't have to be here too long."

"I hafta agree. Spent enough time locked in a small room," Ehron Lee stated heavily.

He started to pull himself from the bed. "Anyhow, you take the mattress. Don't mind takin' my shut-eye on the floor."

Cora spoke up, perhaps too quickly. "That ain't necessary."

Ehron Lee looked at her and gave his head a deliberate shake. "No way lettin' a lady sleep on the floor."

"Well . . . that ain't what I meant," Cora said coyly.

Ehron Lee hesitated, unsure—then he caught her drift. He looked at her blankly.

"Don't think that's rightly proper."

Cora's face flushed and her expression gave way to embarrassment, her eyes avoiding Ehron Lee's.

Ehron Lee tried to ease his own discomfort as well as what Cora now seemed to be feeling.

"Cora," he said, "you're a right fine gal. But if you're suggestin' what I think yuh might be . . . well, I—I just ain't ready to be thinkin' 'bout no other woman. Don't know if I ever could, to be honest. 'Sides, you and Ward . . ."

"Ward and me have been the same all the years I known him," Cora replied in a soft voice, barely registering above a whisper. "Oh, I hoped at one time there might be somethin' more . . . but I know I was only foolin' myself and that there can't never be."

Ehron Lee said nothing, just rocked his head in acknowledgment.

"Reckon I was wrong—and just plain stupid," Cora said with sharp self-reproach.

"Don't be gettin' angry with yourself, Cora," Ehron Lee said to her. He frowned. "Only hope *I* didn't do or say somethin' to get yuh to thinkin' . . ." He knew he hadn't— certainly not intentionally—though it went beyond him to fathom what went on in the mind of a girl like Cora.

Cora gave a vague smile. "No. Just me . . . bein' silly."

"Well," Ehron Lee said dismissively, "then let's just put all that aside and you get yourself into bed. We got us some work ahead of us."

Cora nodded sheepishly.

Over the next couple of days, Cora made her rounds throughout Bolton. First, though, she purchased a new dress— nothing fancy—so that her cowgirl wear would not make her conspicuous in a town where it was evident the female population dressed like proper ladies.

It didn't take long for Cora to gather information. She discovered that Judge Harrison was a man greatly admired by the community. While he rarely participated in the affairs of Bolton with his duties frequently taking him many miles from home, his reputation was well known, and he was respected by the citizens. There was even talk of encouraging him to run for town mayor once he retired from his judicial duties.

Cora also learned through her casual observation that Harrison's daughter, Evaline, was likewise admired by the townspeople, specifically for her musical gifts. People spoke affectionately of her and many predicted that she had a promising future as a concert pianist. This troubled Cora as she knew that kidnapping a judge's daughter was bad enough, but when the girl was as fondly regarded as Evaline Harrison, that would surely bring upon them even more trouble.

Cora returned to the hotel at the end of each day to report her progress, inwardly hoping that the more she revealed, the more it might discourage Ehron Lee from going forward with his plan. But she quickly discovered that he remained stubbornly determined, and nothing short of jail or a bullet was going to change his mind.

Another problem Cora had to deal with was the growing curiosity from the hotel desk clerk, who one day had finally questioned why he'd watch "Mrs. Dodds" leave each day and yet he never saw her "husband" wander from their room. Anticipating this question, Cora had readied a persuasive answer, explaining that "Mr. Dodds" had taken ill shortly after their arrival and needed a few days of rest in bed. The clerk seemed to accept the story, adding with squinting eyes, "That's a shame. Reckon that 'splains why the two of yuh ain't left town yet."

Cora smiled demurely and said, "Yes." Without realizing it, the clerk had provided the perfect answer to a question yet to be asked by others so inclined.

Meanwhile, Ehron Lee was growing restless and irritable being stuck inside the room. It had only been three days since their arrival but seemed much longer with the boredom weighing heavily on him. All he had to occupy his time were his thoughts and endless games of solitaire. He managed to suffer through only because of his conditioning at Rockmound. Yet his present situation was even more frustrating since he *wasn't* behind lock and key and *could* get out and walk about if he chose. There were no high walls or gun-toting guards to hold him back. This time he was a prisoner of his own decision, which under the circumstances he wouldn't be wise to challenge.

But the memory of the suffocation he too frequently felt in his cell was still fresh, and already he was becoming short-tempered and often was sharp with Cora. Although these outbursts were unintentional and brief, prompting Ehron Lee to apologize and explain that he was just venting his frustrations, Cora always felt trepidation after each eruption as it was a suggestion of a rage she hadn't wanted to accept was part of Ehron Lee's character.

She came to Ehron Lee late on the afternoon of the third day to say that she'd learned Evaline Harrison was scheduled to perform at a church social that evening. Before Ehron Lee could protest that any kind of a public gathering was the worst place to lure her away from, Cora suggested that Evaline would probably be arriving early to prepare for her recital. Ehron Lee considered. He couldn't know for sure that she'd be going early or whether the girl would be alone or accompanied, but this looked to be the best opportunity they would get. Besides, they had to make their move soon. Time was at a premium. And he knew he couldn't endure being cooped up much longer. He was eager to be free of his self-imposed imprisonment and away from Bolton.

"How far from the house to the church?" he asked.

"Not very," Cora responded. "Maybe a ten-minute walk."

Ehron Lee didn't speak, but the glint in his eyes urged her on. He was impatient to hear more.

Cora reluctantly obliged. "The church is on the other side of some woods, set apart in a field. There's a side road from town that can get to it. But from where the judge's house is, she'd most likely use the trail through the woods to go to the church."

"Any chance she might ride that trail?" Ehron Lee questioned.

Cora shook her head. "Don't reckon she would. It ain't that far a walk from the house."

"Good," Ehron Lee said, satisfied. "Wouldn't wanta have

to chase down no horse. Probably bring the whole county after us."

Just then Cora's face took on a look of concern.

"What if—she ain't alone?" she asked warily.

Before Ehron Lee could respond, at that exact moment, a shifting of light in the gloom of the curtained room cast a shadow across a portion of his face that seemed to distort his expression into a frightening, predatory image. As the shadow settled, his complexion darkened and his eyes seemed to turn black.

"Be their bad luck," he said tautly.

Cora had discerned from her years as a companion to lawbreakers that few words needed to be spoken when it came to intent. A nod, a gesture, or even a look could register just as potently as a slug fired from a Colt .44. Ehron Lee had spoken his few words—a trick of the light or perhaps a sinister intervention had done the rest. Either way Cora understood what he intended, and she barely suppressed a shudder.

Cora knew he could not afford to harm the girl. He needed her to carry out his plan. But if by chance a companion happened to be with her tonight, Ehron Lee had just made it clear that he would not be leaving behind a witness.

It was difficult for Cora not to let her apprehension surface at the sudden malevolence in Ehron Lee's attitude. He said his piece without any rise of emotion but it made no matter. He had confirmed what he was capable of . . . what he *would* do if necessary, and it frightened her. He was so determined to avenge himself on the two men responsible for his imprisonment and whom he also blamed for losing his wife and child that killing an innocent in the process seemed to be of no concern to him. It was as if in an instant he had shifted into a different person, devoid of the warmth and compassion she so much wanted to believe still existed in him. Now he was someone she did not recognize.

Someone Cora could admit she suddenly was afraid to know.

Ehron Lee pulled some folding money from his pocket.

"You settle up with the hotel," he said. "I'll follow and meet yuh at the stable in ten minutes."

Cora took the cash Ehron Lee thrust at her and nodded.

Ehron Lee then reached for an envelope on the bureau. On it was handwritten: *For Judge Harrison*.

Ehron Lee instructed her carefully. "Take this note. 'Fore yuh come to meet me, go into some store along the way and mosey 'round a bit . . . and when you're sure no one is lookin', put it somewheres. Someplace where it won't be seen right aways but where it's sure to be found. With Harrison's name on it, it's sure to get to him."

Cora had difficulty hiding her uncertainty. She felt her body stiffen, then made herself relax as best she could.

"You're really goin' to go through with this?" she said, her words more of a statement than a question.

Ehron Lee responded to her comment with quiet astonishment, then he studied Cora for a moment, and finally offered an understanding nod.

"Reckon this is just startin' to come real to you, ain't it?" he said.

Cora didn't answer. But she silently acknowledged the truth in his remark. She had lived with outlaws. She had cared for them, fed them, and tended to their wounds if need be. But she had never participated in any of their crimes. Ehron Lee was right—maybe none of this had seemed real to her, until now. Perhaps she would have run if she could, but the time had come and there could be no backing away.

Ehron Lee spoke to her straightly, his eyes fit tight into hers. "Know you gotta have some backbone, Cora. Whatever happens, I'm countin' on yuh not to let me down."

Cora answered with more conviction than she felt, "I won't."

She started to turn away, and then she stopped herself. Her eyes flashed back toward Ehron Lee, and holding her ground, she spoke what she felt she had to say; for what she was about to participate in, and the threat it posed to her as

much as Ehron Lee, she was entitled to that much—
consequences be damned.

With effort, she kept both her posture and her voice
steady. "I just want you to know one thing, Ehron Lee. I
spent a good part of my life with lawbreakers, my own
brother among 'em, and though I ain't done no more wrong
than look after 'em, I reckon my soul is still smudged. Just
want yuh to know that 'cause of that, I'll see this through,
but if'n there'd been any way to stop you . . . I surely
woulda."

She waited for Ehron Lee's reaction. She didn't know
any more what to expect from him. Perhaps it might be an
aggressive response. But he didn't move from where he was
standing. His eyes stayed on her, but the look on his face
was vacant. Finally, after tense seconds passed, his lips
curved in a thin smile and he nodded.

"I already figgered that," he said.

While Cora kept the desk clerk occupied by paying their
hotel bill, Ehron Lee quietly slipped outside. He doubted
the clerk would ever be able to give a description of him, if
it came to that—and as for Cora, it was doubtful any suspicion would fall upon her after their deed was committed.
And even if it did, that would hardly matter.

Both would be long gone from Bolton come nightfall.

Cora walked into the general store, which was about
midway between the hotel and the livery stable. She briefly
perused the merchandise and waited until the store clerk
left the cash counter to deal with a customer before she took
the envelope that contained the ransom note and, with fingers she struggled to keep steady, surreptitiously buried it
among some purchase orders sitting on the counter. She then
walked out casually and continued along the boardwalk
toward the stable.

Ehron Lee had the horses saddled and ready. The stable
owner paid them no attention as he was writing something

down in a ledger in a back office. Before they mounted, Ehron Lee gave Cora a scrutinizing look. He could perceive her reluctance even as she struggled to maintain a façade of confidence. He made no comment as he knew that was the best he would get from her.

Pacing their mounts at an easy, steady gait, they rode off through the dusty streets of town, Cora leading Ehron Lee toward where the woods opened upon the country church.

It was a good location. Cora had been correct: The path leading to the church was too narrow for any access other than by foot. But the dense brush off to the left of the trail had a deep side cutoff, which provided good cover for the pair, along with an uninhibited view. This was where they would position themselves, seated atop their horses, while they waited for Evaline Harrison to come walking toward them down that path.

SEVENTEEN

THE WHITE, BLINDING glare of the overhead sun reflected on their grisly discovery. It was a sight not unfamiliar to either man.

"Ain't gonna get anythin' outta him now, sir," Sergeant Liam O'Brien said morosely to Superintendent Watson as both men stared into the shadowy walls of the pit.

Watson was silent for a long while, his focus fastened on the body sprawled face up in the mud and the filth.

"Looks dead all right," he finally muttered. "Dead as John Wilkes Booth."

"If you'd be askin' me, I'd say he damn well got scared to death," O'Brien offered, running the palm of his hand over his white-whiskered chin.

Watson didn't acknowledge, though the sergeant had obviously reached the correct conclusion. The evidence lay beneath them.

The white, scarred face, now hideously sunburned and blistered, stared up at them from the pit, the features twisted in a rictus of horror; the good eye, though sightless and glazed, was open wide; the mouth frozen in what looked to be a mute scream. The fingers of both hands were gnarled, twisted like claws, encrusted both in blood and mud, as if he had tried in his desperation to climb his way out of the hole.

Watson drew a breath and said lowly, "Better off for him, but leaves me without an answer."

"Do yuh think he really knew anythin', Superintendent?" O'Brien queried.

Watson turned his head and looked at the sergeant without answering.

O'Brien went on, gesturing with both hands into the pit. "Well, I mean, look at the man. Never seen such a horrid look on a man's face. And desperate enough to rip his hands to shreds tryin' to pull himself free. I'd be thinkin' that if he coulda been tellin' you what you wanted to know, he'da done it."

"Doesn't really matter now, does it?" Watson said in a tone of resignation.

He turned and started back to his office. O'Brien watched him go, then called for a couple of the guards standing nearby to come and remove Woody Milo's corpse from the pit. The men walked over, reluctantly but obediently. Pulling a body from the punishment pit was a duty none of the guards, tough and hardened though they were, relished.

George Watson shut himself in his office and poured a stiff drink of whiskey from the bottle he always kept handy. Glass in hand, he dropped into the chair behind his desk and gazed absently at the amber liquor. Then he turned and stared steadily at the photograph of his wife. He didn't want to contemplate what she might be experiencing, held hostage by a vicious brute like Ward Crawford. He couldn't imagine the fear and uncertainty she was going through at the moment.

He felt no sorrow for Woody Milo, nor regret for the terrible death that he himself was responsible for—burned alive in a hellish pit, for unlike usual procedure and hoping for some quick answers from Woody, Watson had ordered that no planking be placed over the hole, exposing Woody and his skin condition to a full assault of the sun's rays.

Instead Watson was bitter. He was angry and frustrated. What he had considered his ace in the hole had died in the hole, and now he found himself with only the one recourse. He would have to wait for that second note and meet with the kidnappers of his wife . . . on whatever terms they dictated.

Yet as he tossed back the liquor with a swift twist of his hand, he remained determined that neither his pride nor his position would be completely compromised by their demand. He would not sacrifice his wife to Ward Crawford and his killer scum.

But neither would he ride blindly into a bullet.

EIGHTEEN

SHE CAME ALONG the tree-bordered walking path alone, an early star-specked twilight soon to be upon her—a young, innocent, fresh-faced pretty girl, softly humming a song that perhaps had personal meaning but was not a tune recognized by the two lying in wait. Not that it was of any importance to either. Its only significance was that it signaled the girl was coming their way.

Ehron Lee could watch her approaching from his distance, his presence protected from view by the clutter of trees, branches, and shrubbery. Cora noticed her, too, and breathed out an audible sigh as she saw the girl was by herself. Ehron Lee turned to look at Cora as he heard the sound of relief escape her lips. He didn't acknowledge the sigh, merely tilted his head to indicate that she was to follow as soon as he prompted his horse to slowly trot toward where the greenery opened upon the man-made cutout path.

Evaline Harrison halted abruptly and looked startled as the horse ridden by Ehron Lee emerged and blocked her passage. The stranger didn't speak, just smiled at the girl. Evaline returned the smile tentatively. Her eyes shifted once she saw the second horse, ridden by Cora, move free of the trees and stop behind and on the far opposite side of the stranger's mount.

Evaline tried not to let her uncertainty show, though she felt a quivering in her belly that reminded her of the queer nervousness she used to feel prior to performing a piano recital.

Still wearing a smile, Ehron Lee spoke in a kindly voice, though the words he uttered were hardly pleasant.

"I don't want you to scream or try to run. Listen to what I'm tellin' yuh and no one's gotta get hurt."

While Evaline couldn't understand what was happening, what the stranger meant by his words, she instinctively knew she was in trouble. Of a sudden her body felt weak and she was overcome with the sensation of light-headedness as the blood flow to her brain seemed to slow, noticeably paling her complexion. She became unsteady on her feet and looked as if she was about to pass out.

Cora grew concerned and was quick to express it. "She don't look well," she said with an urgency.

Ehron Lee acknowledged her concern. He swiftly slid off the saddle of his horse and took quick strides toward the girl. Evaline had already started to sway and Ehron Lee grabbed her just as her eyes fluttered shut and her body began to topple. His response to her faint wasn't gentle. He slapped her once across the face, startling her back to semiawareness, at the same time alarming Cora with his action. Evaline was conscious, though still very disoriented. Ehron Lee guided her to Cora's horse and helped her mount. Cora lended her own hand. Even though the girl was wearing a long dress, she was made to sit with her legs straddling the flank of the horse.

"You ain't gonna be much comfortable ridin' double, but you hang on," Ehron Lee instructed her, taking her arms and wrapping them around Cora's waist. Evaline's grip was weak and Ehron Lee had to use force to encourage her to hold on to Cora with more strength.

"We got a long ride, girl," he said bluntly. "It's up to you if we make it easy or hard."

Evaline looked at Ehron Lee. Her eyes expressed a sad pleading from which Ehron Lee at once had to separate himself. Because for one quick moment of rationality—of perhaps sanity—he questioned his decision, this girl's part in his scheme of revenge, but just as swiftly he made himself discard this doubt.

It was what he *had* to do. And Judge Harrison's daughter *had* to be a part of it. If Ehron Lee experienced pangs of momentary conflict, emotional doubt . . . they had to be ignored.

Unbeknownst to Ehron Lee, Cora had closely been observing the whole procedure with his handling of the judge's daughter. Perhaps her years of being among hard-bitten criminals had made her more acute to their peculiarities, if rarely their sensitivities, but she sensed definitely the turmoil that seemed to exist within Ehron Lee. She knew that what he was doing with these women was not really what he wanted to do. He had told her that he didn't want to hurt them—and Cora knew that in his heart he *didn't* want to bring them harm. Yet she also realized that Ehron Lee held on to enough corrupting hatred from the cruelty brought upon him to truly execute extreme punishment if denied the justice he felt was owed him.

Once again Cora had to concede defeat as there was no way of dealing with such a vengeful attitude. Ehron Lee and Ward had taken one woman as their hostage. Now with the kidnapping of the judge's daughter, Ehron Lee had made steadfast his intent.

But what she feared most was the uncertainty of the inevitable.

She could not guess the outcome.

NINETEEN

RANDY BOGGS RODE a long way from Brimstone Canyon, unsure of where he was going or what he would do once he got there. He had a little money in his pocket so he had no immediate concern financially, provided he didn't give in to the temptation of fast women and crooked gambling.

Randy robbed banks—may even have killed a man or two in his time—but he also could admit that he was never as ambitious or as carefree as his partners. Those fellas enjoyed the wild times and freely spent their loot on their various entertainments, while Randy was content just to quietly lay low between bank jobs. Still, earning a quick dollar or partaking of some female companionship was not the farthest thought from his mind at this time. Now that he was away from the others, he thought seriously about retiring from his outlaw ways. They'd enjoyed a long run of luck, much more than they were entitled to, he reckoned, but with Brad Riley getting killed at Hell's Doorway and now with the crazy kidnapping scheme Ward and his pal Ehron Lee had concocted, he had the gut feeling that time was running out. Randy determined he wasn't ready to invite a bullet yet; he still had some good living to do. So as he rode the countryside trail to a destination unknown, enjoying the solitude, he gradually became firm in his resolution to hang up his guns.

He considered his options and frankly was surprised that he knew of no alternate direction that satisfied him. He'd lived outside the law for most of his life and truly had never given thought to the prospect of earning an honest dollar. He supposed he could likely find work on a ranch, but did he really want to settle into a routine after years of living by his own rules? Even in his most whiskey-fueled imaginings, he couldn't envision himself working from cockcrow to sundown following somebody's orders. Just a little better than being in prison, the way he saw it.

Maybe he could put down some of the money he had on his own piece of property. Work the land himself.

Randy chuckled at the thought of himself as a farmer—clad in mud-caked denim overalls, his brow dripping sweat from under a straw hat. He might be owing to no man but neither could he see himself adhering to the self-discipline of clearing fields overgrown with weeds, and planting crops. Whatever he might decide, Randy could not see such labor in his future. He promptly canceled that option from future consideration.

He was heading north and soon came to a roadside sign informing him that he was only ten miles from the town of Brackett. He'd heard the name but had never visited the town—"professionally" or otherwise—so he could ride in without fear of being recognized by the citizens.

Randy decided he might just take a few days' rest there.

Ehron Lee and Cora kept themselves off the main roads as much as possible as they traveled with their hostage back to the cabin. This slowed their progress more than Ehron Lee would have liked, but it was a necessary course. Although the girl, Evaline, cooperated fully, never once raising a fuss, and there looked to be nothing overly suspicious about the trio as they rode along, Ehron Lee knew that should news of the abduction became known, people they encountered along the way might remember seeing the three and the direction in which they were riding. The promise of reward money could do plenty to jog the memory.

When they set up camp for the night, either Ehron Lee or Cora would keep watch over the girl. Ehron Lee remained a trifle wary when he took his shut-eye—and perhaps with reason. While Cora said or suggested nothing to give him suspicion, she fought the urge during Ehron Lee's periods of slumber just to let the girl loose and deal with the consequences herself. Evaline had not spoken at all during their journey, though when Ehron Lee slept, Cora wished she could say something to the girl, maybe offer some words of encouragement—at the same time realizing that no matter what she said or how she voiced them, they would only provide shallow comfort. Besides, if she ventured to speak, she might be overheard; she suspected that Ehron Lee slept with one eye—or ear—open. Perhaps that, too, was the reason the girl maintained her silence. When they sat together by the low campfire listening to Ehron Lee's snores, Cora would catch the girl looking at her in a way to suggest that she wanted to talk, but dared not.

Eventually, with Cora doing most of the guiding since she knew the trail better than her companion, they made their way back to the cabin nestled in the foothills of Brimstone Canyon. Once they were settled inside, they ate a quick meal and took time for rest. Evaline was put inside the bedroom with Janette Watson and made as comfortable as possible, kept under Cora's watch. Ward wanted them both out of his sight for the time being, this decision readily agreed to by both Ehron Lee and Jess. Neither wanted to look upon the faces of the two women until the time was right.

In the meantime, Ehron Lee prepared for the one final duty for Cora to perform.

He wanted her to ride into Colbert City and send off two telegrams, one addressed to Judge Charles Harrison, Bolton, the other going to George Watson, Allensfield. All that would be said in these messages was a place and a time, nothing else. The two men would understand and follow the instructions. Cora complained that sending such vague telegrams might look suspicious to the telegraph messenger. Ehron Lee asked if she was easily recognized in Colbert City. Cora said no, she'd gone there only once or twice, and not for some months. Ehron Lee told her she'd have no worries. Ward Crawford, standing nearby listening, concurred. Reluctantly, Cora agreed, though her hesitation was hard to ignore.

Later, with Jess and Cora keeping watch inside the cabin, Ehron Lee and Ward stepped outside into the night air.

They walked by the south fence and finally stopped at the outer edge of the corral, where Ward went about building himself a cigarette. Ehron Lee had noticed that since they'd arrived at the cabin, Ward was smoking almost incessantly, rolling a new cigarette before even extinguishing the one he'd been inhaling and held clamped between his teeth. He'd questioned him about that and Ward merely shrugged, explaining that, as Ehron Lee knew, obtaining tobacco at Rockmound was an earned privilege and that he had a lot of catching up to do. Although Ehron Lee didn't smoke, he understood Ward's reasoning.

Once his cigarette was burning, Ward indulged in a deep drag before turning to look at Ehron Lee.

"How was she?" Ward asked bluntly, referring to Cora.

"She came through," Ehron Lee answered.

"Know that . . . but how *was* she?" Ward repeated with emphasis.

Ehron Lee didn't answer immediately. He considered his reply as he bit down on his lower lip.

"In truth? Wasn't sure 'bout her," he finally conceded.

Ward drew another long drag. "Figgered. So you think it's smart to send her into Colbert?"

Once more Ehron Lee took his time answering.

Then with a deliberate exhale, he said, "As I think 'bout it, probably not."

Ward's face took on a disgusted look. He finished his

smoke with a final deep puff, then flicked the smoldering butt to the ground, mashing out its glow with his boot heel, tiny sparks escaping the crushing impact.

"Okay, amigo, then you're the one that's gotta do it," he said. He spoke his words as casually as if he were dusting cigarette ash from his shirtsleeve.

Ehron Lee gave a nod in agreement. He had already accepted that his being the one to send off the telegrams would be the most sensible decision.

"S'pose at this point don't really matter, does it?" he muttered.

Ward grinned and hooked a thumb at the cabin, toward a single window aglow with light. "Burrows, with us holdin' them two girls, wife and daughter of some purty important men, we gotta figger that no matter how it goes from here, we're both set for a neck-stretchin'." To take the bitter sting out of the truth of his words, he added, "But if we pull this off like we're plannin', ain't no reason we can't see ourselves maybe enjoyin' a stay in Mexico sittin' in some cantina with a coupla señoritas, washin' back bottles of tequila."

Ehron Lee allowed himself a moment to absorb what Ward was saying. Then, drawing a breath and eyeing his companion directly, he said, "Just too bad we can't count on Cora."

Ward gave him a peculiar look, but before he could say anything, Ehron Lee had turned and started back to the cabin.

Ward Crawford was not a man possessed of great human insight but he could grasp the intent behind Ehron Lee's words. His partner was saying that Cora had shown herself as too soft, and as such could not truly be trusted. Although Ward had known another tougher sort of girl those years before he had gone to prison, even he could detect a change in Cora that conceivably could pose a threat to their plan. Ehron Lee's remark served as a reminder for Ward to keep a close eye on Cora, perhaps stay watchful for any hint of suspected betrayal.

*   *   *

Since he was a free man, one not likely to risk later identification, Ehron Lee saddled a horse and rode into Colbert City. He tethered the horse to the hitching post outside the telegraph office and sauntered inside. He remained nonchalant as he wrote out the messages to be sent to the judge and the prison superintendent. Yet he eyed the telegrapher carefully as the young man scanned the vague wording and registered no reaction. Perhaps because the telegrapher was young, maybe an apprentice, he did his job perfunctorily, barely acknowledging his customer, which pleased Ehron Lee. He pulled money out of his pocket to pay him, and then stepped casually from the office.

Ehron Lee stood out on the boardwalk, feeling a sense of both relief and satisfaction.

Finally it was done: the planning, the preparation, the risks. Each procedure had fallen precisely into place.

Whatever happened now would be solely up to the two men to whom the telegrams would be delivered. They would either obey the simple directions to the letter—or ignore them. Ehron Lee felt confident both would choose to respond to the instructions. Both men stood to lose a lot by not following their individual messages to the letter.

Ehron Lee made his time in town short, climbing onto his horse and riding the miles back to the cabin.

By midweek next, Ehron Lee would be watching from a rocky overlook for Judge Harrison to arrive at the appointed location; the following day Ward Crawford would be there awaiting Superintendent George Watson.

While not explicitly expressed, it was understood that the men were to show up *alone, unarmed*. If either dared to challenge those unwritten instructions, the deal was off.

One would lose a daughter; the other, a wife.

TWENTY

RANDY BOGGS DROPPED both himself and his belongings off at a dingy Brackett hotel room and tried to remain as inconspicuous a figure as possible while he moseyed alongside the town folk. He enjoyed being out and about, savoring it as a refreshing change from long periods of isolation hidden away in a mountainside cabin. He especially could take comfort in the fact that his identity was unknown. While he was responsible for a series of bank holdups throughout the territory, he was simply part of a masked gang of outlaws who, outside of that one setback with Ward Crawford some years back, had kept themselves and their exploits in the clear.

Confident in his anonymity, as the days passed, Randy gradually began to grow more relaxed being seen regularly in town . . . at the same time, he also felt the itch of restlessness. The outlaw nature was ingrained in his character, and coupled with perhaps boredom and frequent visits to the saloons in town, this initiated a subtle frustration that started to give way to a more feverish vent.

Randy had enjoyed playing cards as a pastime with his

outlaw companions, but he had no real skill at high table stakes. During another dull afternoon, he'd wandered into the saloon and set himself up for a game of five-card stud with sharps who came across as hillbillies. However, at the last moment, one of the bunch would suddenly be dealt a high card, wiping Randy clean every time.

As the afternoon wore on and his dollars disappeared like ghost wisps in the desert, Randy's suspicions heightened, and soon he was convinced he was being cheated by his yokel tablemates. He'd been betting large in the hope of recouping his losses. He could ill afford to lose his stake, and as he watched another pile of his money slide across the table into the hands of one of the players, his desperation overtook him. He pushed back his chair and stood up suddenly, assuming an aggressive stance.

The three men seated around the table regarded him with amused expressions. They had dealt with such types before—in fact, card hustling was their family profession. And in an instant not one came across as the yokel he had pretended to be during the playing of their game.

One said, "Looks like what we got here is a poor loser."

Another remarked snidely, "More likely a poor gambler."

Randy fixed the table with a steely-eyed stare. "Ain't no way I can come up empty every hand," he said thickly.

"You callin' us cheats?" another of the players said in a challenging tone.

The customers in the saloon fell silent as their attention turned toward the far corner table and the tense situation that was developing among the cardplayers.

The second man added, "'Cause if'n you are, you'd best be prepared to back up them words. Mama wouldn't 'preciate you sayin' her boys was dishonest."

Randy's blood quickened and he felt the temptation to draw his gun. He'd drunk enough shots of whiskey—courtesy of the "generosity" of his fellow players—which, coupled with his sudden certainty over his losses, had fueled him into a volatile mood. By nature he was not an impulsive man, but he also was not the sort to be taken advantage of, and as he surveyed each of the smirking faces seated around the table, he knew that he had been played for a sucker.

Although his hand remained far removed from his holster, he didn't back down. It appeared to the spectators that the situation was at a stalemate. The choice was Randy's. Either he would have to make a move or let things lie and walk peaceably from the saloon.

The seconds that passed were punctuated by the measured and methodic ticking of the grandfather clock. For many long moments it was the only sound heard in the saloon. The barkeep kept a steady watch on the table, his hands held under the counter gripping a shotgun, which he had no hesitation about using if trouble should erupt in his establishment.

Finally Randy relented. What decided it for him was the knowledge that no matter what the outcome, he'd lose either way. Either shot dead where he stood or facing arrest for murder, which would bring with it other problems that he had hoped to avoid since riding away from his gang.

He couldn't know that his sensible decision to lower his defenses would encourage one of the cardplayers to suddenly draw on him.

Randy had half turned from the table when he heard one of the saloon girls scream. He spun back around, just in time to see the barrel of a pistol aimed straight at him. The gun fired and Randy's swift, spontaneous action caused him both to dodge the bullet and to slide out his own revolver and level it. A second shot was fired. This time the bullet hit, searing into his side. But just as reflexively, Randy pulled the trigger of his Colt and watched the man jerk backward as the single bullet tore a hole into his chest. As the man dropped stone dead to the floor, the barkeep withdrew his eight-gauge and commanded Randy and the others not to make a move. He then ordered one of his waiters to rush out and fetch the sheriff.

Numb to the pain and the blood spurting from his own injury, Randy sobered sufficiently to know that the bullet lodged in his side was soon to be the least of his worries.

* * *

Only a day or two earlier, Buck Leighton was at Rockmound Prison visiting with Superintendent George Watson. Buck had proven himself capable in dealing with murderous desperados, hence his special appointment to United States marshal. Now he had been assigned to round up those men responsible for the bloody prison shoot-out that had led to the escape of Ward Crawford. Buck decided he would need some assistance in that department and had come to Rockmound bearing the identification of the accomplice who had been killed at the quarry, who was the one link to the others who were involved. Perhaps Watson could offer more.

"Name's Brad Riley," Buck said, laying the photograph of the dead youngster across the superintendent's desk. "No arrest record but the kid was known to run around with a bad crowd."

Strangely, Watson avoided looking at the photograph. He covered it with the flat of his hand and slid it aside.

"No arrest record. How would I know who he is?" Watson said tautly.

Buck was puzzled by this coldly dismissive attitude. That is, until he studied the look of exhaustion that masked the superintendent's features; the man's face was drawn and pale, suggesting that he hadn't slept for many a night. Watson's intimidating manner was nowhere in evidence. Instead he looked like a man mired in defeat. Buck distinctly recognized that something perhaps more troubling than the prison escape was affecting George Watson's mood.

When Buck Leighton first arrived at the office, Watson didn't rise from his chair to greet him. Nor did Watson invite Buck to have a seat, and neither did Buck presume to sit at the empty chair across from the desk as he felt it was perhaps improper given his official capacity.

For the longest time Watson remained seated behind his desk, though with a gradual shift in expression that possibly suggested he was contemplating revealing something more to the marshal.

Buck stood silent, fiddling with the brim of his hat, and patiently waited for the superintendent to decide whether he indeed had something to share with him. Watson glanced up at Buck. Drumming the thumb of his left hand atop his desk, he finally slid open the top side drawer. Then he pulled out a piece of paper, which, again, he momentarily debated sharing with the lawman.

He breathed out a heavy sigh and waved the paper in his hand.

"Showing you this might cost my wife her life," he said soberly.

Buck walked 'round to the side of the desk, and Watson, after a tentative maneuver, finally pressed the paper into his hand firmly, as if wanting that physical connection while doing so. Buck unfolded the paper and read what was written:

A life for a life

He lifted his eyes toward the superintendent but said nothing.

Watson spoke, and despite his effort to maintain self-control, his voice was rattled. "It's a ransom demand. And I know it's from Crawford. She was taken right around the time he escaped from here. He was seen in Allensfield the same day. And like every other piece of scum in this prison, he hates me enough to . . . to do this." He fixed his tired stare on Buck and said heavily, "For all I know, Janette's already dead."

Buck would like to have spoken encouragingly, offer something to offset Watson's concern. But it was in his character and part of his professional duty to present his words truthfully. And in this case the best he could do was to remain objective in his opinion.

"Hard to know how a man like Crawford thinks," he said solemnly.

"If she's not dead, I know I can expect another note."

Buck gave a slow nod. "Likely."

"When he came into Allensfield that night, he was with someone." Watson exhaled with a furrowing of his brow.

"Couldn't get much of a description, but chances are whatever he's got in mind, he's not alone in this."

"There must be somethin' to go on. What 'bout Crawford's cell mates?" Buck asked. "Men spendin' all that time together, somethin' mighta been said."

Watson blinked. He wasn't about to mention Woody Milo or his fate.

He hesitated just briefly before he said, "You know one of 'em, Marshal. You wired me 'bout him: Ehron Lee Burrows."

Buck's face responded expressively. At the same time his posture straightened in a reflex.

"Burrows?" he said. "Him and Crawford shared a cell?"

"For the five years that Burrows was here," Watson told him. "But he was released just a few weeks before—"

Buck cut in gravely. "Released . . . believing that his wife was dead."

Watson looked perplexed.

Buck's own expression was dire. "I ain't sayin' nothin' for certain, got nothin' definite to go on . . . 'ceptin' a hunch."

"A hunch . . . that . . . Burrows is involved?" Watson surmised.

"The pieces fit," Buck said with a tilt of his head. "And after all he's been through, can see him holdin' a hateful grudge."

"Blames me because I kept him locked up," Watson said in a voice that was low but betrayed no sense of personal guilt or wrongdoing. "Holds me responsible for his wife never comin' out to visit."

"Can breed a powerful lot of resentment in a man," Buck said. Then he added, "Ehron Lee wasn't no criminal. Not when they brung him in here. But locking up a man with that kind of bitterness with a hard case like Ward Crawford seems a surefire bet for trouble."

Watson said thoughtfully, "He was a hard one to figure. Caused some problems in the beginning, as I recall, but seemed to straighten out. He was always hopin' to get some word from his wife. Yet when I told him 'bout the message I received, sayin' that she'd died, he didn't react anywhere near the way I thought he would. It was like . . . he didn't seem to care."

"I'm sure he cared, Superintendent," Buck offered. "Cared more than he let on."

"Marshal, this isn't the way I planned it," Watson said strongly. "But dammit, now I see I gotta play by whatever hand they deal. I think you can agree I don't have much choice."

"Seems that way," Buck said. "But since it's gonna be a risk no matter how you go about it, it'd be smart to give yourself an edge on the odds."

It took a few moments for Watson to interpret what Buck was saying. Then it became clear to him and he was doubtful, and he scrubbed the palm of his hand along his jaw and down his neck in an unconscious response to his uncertainty.

"When you next hear from 'em, I figger they'll set up a place to meet with you," Buck said. "Somewheres safe—for them. They're also gonna know you ain't 'bout to do nothin' to jeopardize your wife's safety. All I gotta know is where that meetin' place is. I'll be watchin'—alone, outta sight, and I guarantee I won't do nothin' to put your missus in danger."

Watson considered for a while longer. Then he set his eyes firmly on Buck and said without restraint, "It's my wife's life we're talkin' 'bout." He calmed himself, embarrassed by his outburst, and exhaled a resigned breath. "Don't like what you're suggestin'. But what choice do I have."

Buck shrugged and spoke his words with brutal intention. "You can always go along with whatever they want."

Watson responded with a hard, bitter look.

Buck Leighton had managed to obtain George Watson's assurance that he would be notified as soon as or if a second note was delivered. He said to wire him in Brackett, which was where Buck had decided to move forward with his hunch. He rode back to the town with the intention of once more paying a visit to Melinda Burrows. Maybe he was playing a long shot, but if Ehron Lee was involved in the abduction of Watson's wife, Buck reasoned that it had to do with Ehron Lee's misinformed belief—his ignorance of the fact that he'd been betrayed by his sister-in-law, and instead his assumption that it had been deliberate cruelty thrust upon him by the prison superintendent—that Watson had withheld his wife's correspondence from him.

It was imperative that Ehron Lee be told the truth. That he know of Abigail's cunning. That Melinda hadn't died; she'd given birth to his child, his son, and hadn't abandoned him during his years at Rockmound. If Ehron Lee could be made to see the truth, maybe George Watson's wife had a chance.

But for that to succeed, Buck would have to convince Melinda to come along with him once he heard from Superintendent Watson that a follow-up note had been delivered. It was Buck's one chance to reason with the man. Ehron Lee would need to see her, and Melinda would have to explain and be utterly sincere in her telling of what really had happened.

Yet even that presented a gamble. There would still be Ward Crawford—and possibly other bandits—to contend with. If Crawford and Ehron Lee were working in some vengeful union, Ward's participation would be for an entirely different purpose. He would have his own reason for going along, perhaps based more on primal outlaw bloodlust, completely separate from Ehron Lee's own twisted sense of justice.

Ehron Lee was not truly a criminal and perhaps could still be reasoned with; Ward Crawford was a cold-blooded killer who likely would not be taken alive.

Buck had hardly gotten off the stage in Brackett when he was informed by one of the townspeople of the saloon shooting in which a stranger to town had been wounded and arrested. Apparently the bullet injury, which at first had seemed minor, had caused more damage than originally thought and had swiftly become infected. The stranger was in and out of a delirium, locked in the town jail, and in moments of lucidity became overwhelmed with doubt that his shooting would be considered self-defense. This had set a panic in the man and he had done some talking that had seemed curious to the Brackett sheriff but which might be of value to the U.S. marshal.

Buck delayed his visit to Melinda Burrows and hurried along the boardwalk to the jailhouse. Once he went inside the office, the sheriff, a dusty old character named Pillsbury, close to retirement and eager to hang up his badge, greeted Buck curtly. He rose wearily from his chair and, walking with a pronounced limp, escorted Buck into a side corridor where the cells were situated. The sheriff commented that "business" had been slow, and of the three cells, only one was occupied. He chortled as he added, "And by a dyin' man."

Buck paid no attention to the sheriff's words or his dispassionate attitude. Not immediately. Not until he noticed in the stink-laden cell closest to the door a man lying under a blanket on the bunk, moaning and twitching and obviously in very bad shape.

Buck frowned and said with abrupt concern, "Why the hell hasn't he been looked after proper?"

"No point," the sheriff replied with a lift of his shoulder. "Ain't nothin' can be done for him. Can die here as well as anyplace."

Buck gave the sheriff a sharp, critical look.

"He been looked at by the doctor?" Buck asked roughly.

"Like I told yuh, he's dyin' . . . and he's feverish," the sheriff explained simply. "Yeah, Doc's been here. Was outta town when they brought him in, didn't get back 'til a coupla days later. By that time the fella took a turn for the worse. We cleaned him up as best we could but couldn't dig the bullet out. Infection set in. The sawbones said just to keep him quiet and comfortable. Ain't been too quiet, though. Been spoutin' off all sortsa wild talk."

"D'yuh know who he is?" Buck asked.

"Boys he was playin' cards with said he introduced himself only as Randy. You'd hafta ask him, only he ain't makin' much sense anymore. For a time he kept goin' on 'bout some fellas he used to be with. Can't figger what he meant other than he was likely workin' outside the law. Mumblin' 'bout robbin' banks . . . said somethin' 'bout some girls plannin' to be snatched."

Buck's head pivoted toward the sheriff and he eyed him questioningly.

"Girls . . . bein' snatched," he echoed.

The sheriff stiffly rubbed the back of his neck. "I dunno. Just somethin' he said along with his other ramblin's. Couldn't rightly figger anything he was sayin'."

Buck responded with urgency. He ordered the sheriff to unlock the cell, then he stepped inside and went over to the man lying on the chain-fastened bunk, dropping to a knee beside him. Buck didn't recognize the sweaty-faced stranger who called himself Randy, but he knew he had to get him to talk—to tell Buck what, if anything, he knew—in the short time remaining to him.

Again, he was playing a hunch.

Buck was impatient, and while he had rebuked the sheriff for allowing a mortally wounded man to breathe out his last moments of life confined in a jail cell, his own attitude came across as brusque and demanding.

For close to a quarter hour Buck attempted to question Randy, but his efforts yielded nothing of value. Weaving in and out of consciousness, his eyes glassy and unfocused, the man offered little beyond what had already been established by the sheriff. It was evident that he'd had an outlaw past but in his dying expressed little regret for what he'd done.

Then—just toward what seemed to be the end—a momentary awareness overtook Randy and his eyes flashed wide, seemingly alert, and he spoke with clarity, though his sentences were clipped.

"Can tell yuh," he uttered anxiously. "But if'n I do . . . yuh can't be hangin' me. Never meant to kill no one. Sonofabitch—he cheated me! Shot at me first. Was—was only defendin' myself."

Buck spoke reassuringly. After all, no matter what had happened back at the saloon, there was no way a noose would be strung around his neck now.

"No one holds yuh responsible for that," he said. "But tell me 'bout these girls you talked 'bout. The ones you said was plannin' to be snatched."

Randy was momentarily confused, then his face relaxed and he smiled; the smile widened into a grin.

"Girls," he said. "Don't know no girls . . . 'ceptin' Cora."

Buck scrunched up his face. "Cora?"

"Could always count on her. Hell, we all could."

"Tell me 'bout her," Buck urged quietly. "Tell me more 'bout Cora."

Randy said he was thirsty and asked for water, which Buck furnished for him, ladling a taste of the cool liquid into his mouth from the bucket on the floor.

"Cora," the man then went on, the grin receding to a slight smile upon his lips. "Yeah, she stuck by us. Had to . . . 'cause of her brother. He couldn't get away fast enough. Never told her . . . 'bout Ward havin' to shoot him. Had no choice. He couldn't let him talk."

Buck didn't have to guess who "Ward" was. *Ward Crawford.*

"Talk? 'Bout what?" Buck said, speaking hurriedly, with more determination. He needed answers and realized there might not be much time left. At the very least, at any second Randy could slip back into incoherence.

"The escape."

"From Rockmound?" Buck asked.

Randy nodded weakly and suddenly his expression twisted in pain. When he recovered, he spoke with another jolt of clarity.

"Fella, he came to us. Said . . . Ward wanted us . . . wanted us to repay a favor."

"What favor?"

Randy's eyes took on a faraway look.

"Don't think I gotta worry 'bout hangin'," he muttered, his voice and senses fading rapidly. "Reckon . . . I'm gonna die all on my own."

"Who was the man who came to you?" Buck pressed.

Randy didn't answer.

Buck leaned in close. "Just tell me this—nod or shake your head if you hafta. Was the man who came to you . . . was his name Ehron Lee?"

Again Randy didn't reply. But maybe it wasn't necessary that he speak his answer. Hearing the name prompted a spark of recognition, registered in his eyes. His lips began to silently form what looked to Buck to be "Ehron."

Finally Randy breathed out and lapsed into unconsciousness for what was probably the final time. Buck rose to his feet and stepped from the cell.

The sheriff was seated at his desk. His head rose and he asked neutrally, "He dead?"

Buck walked right by without acknowledging the question.

He had hoped to find out more. But what he did discover was important. Ehron Lee was involved in the Rockmound prison break . . . which meant it was almost a surefire guarantee he'd partnered with Ward Crawford in the kidnapping of Superintendent Watson's wife. What puzzled him was Randy's reference to "girls." Was there someone else who was in jeopardy?

Outside of leading the deputized posse that had captured the stagecoach desperados, Buck Leighton had had a relatively uneventful career as a lawman. Yet he'd discovered there were elements of his job that, while not fraught with danger, were oftentimes just as unpleasant.

The fact was not lost on Buck that almost every time he'd spoken with Melinda Burrows, it was to deliver grave news. What he had to tell her now was something he dreaded even more than if he'd had to notify her that her husband was dead. At least in that situation, hard as it might be, there was an end. With what was happening now, it was only the beginning . . . and worse, he would have to involve Melinda in a risky venture that did not guarantee a promising outcome. He dreaded the next few minutes as he stood on her doorstep, waiting for her to answer his knock.

When she opened the door and Melinda saw him, hat in hand, his features set and serious, she felt herself grow momentarily weak, expecting to hear the worst. But his familiar attempt at a smile gave her at least a momentary strength and she recovered sufficiently to invite Buck inside.

Once seated in the parlor, Buck got straight to the point, carefully gauging Melinda's every reaction to the words he spoke. Perhaps because she had been through this before with Buck, her face didn't express much emotion and she remained quiet until the marshal was finished with what he had to say.

As Buck expected, Melinda's first reaction was disbelief. He perfectly understood her doubt and decided not to argue his side, instead allowing Melinda the time to absorb the facts and, hopefully, reach the same conclusion as he had.

And soon, on reflection, she did.

She spoke calmly, reasonably. "With all that's happened, I reckon he could change. But to do what you're suggesting— a prison break, kidnapping some innocent woman—when he was free and could have gone on with a new life . . ."

"I think he woulda gone clean," Buck offered honestly. "But too much has gone ag'in him."

Before Melinda could again put unfair blame on herself, Buck hushed her.

"You got no reason to feel guilt, Melinda. Think clear and you'll see none of this is your fault. If anythin', without yuh knowin', you was caught in the middle."

Melinda's voice was cautious. "And yet you think I can do somethin' to help?"

"I do," Buck said firmly. "Leastwise where your husband's concerned."

Melinda rested her wrist on her knee and rubbed it repeatedly with her other hand.

"And this other . . . this Ward?" she said.

Buck took his time in answering.

"Well," he drew out. "He's a type that'll have to be handled different. The way I see it, he'll have to be gotten to first, otherwise might be no way to reason with Ehron Lee. And dealin' with Ward Crawford . . . that's my job."

Melinda went quiet. She sat considering for a while, weighing the truth in what Buck was telling her. Of course she realized he wouldn't be saying such things unless he firmly believed they were so. More important, if there was any way she could help Ehron Lee . . . she knew she would.

Finally she set her eyes directly upon Buck and nodded.

"I'll do whatever needs to be done," she said.

TWENTY-ONE

THE PROGRESSIVE ILLNESS of Judge Charles Harrison's wife, which had resulted in longer confinements to her bed, made it easier for Harrison to fabricate a reason for Evaline's sudden absence. The morning after receiving the first note, delivered to him by the shopkeeper's helper in whose store the envelope addressed to him had been found, Harrison gently, and he hoped convincingly, explained to his wife while he sat at her bedside that a telegram had arrived inviting their daughter to visit the school at which both parents had previously discussed enrolling her. She would be gone for only a few days, he assured her. He went further, telling his wife that he'd had to send her off early that morning as no other stagecoach would be leaving Bolton until later in the week. Harrison patted his wife's hand, adding encouragingly and as a reminder that it was an opportunity neither wanted Evaline to miss out on.

Although she expressed disappointment and some bewilderment at her daughter leaving without saying good-bye, Mrs. Harrison was too ill and weak not to accept her husband's story and the reason for Evaline's hasty departure.

Before Harrison could leave her room, she had drifted back off to sleep.

Throughout much of their marriage, Harrison's relationship with his wife had been built on lies and deceit. But strangely, and perhaps inexplicably, this was the first time he'd ever truly felt guilty about not being honest with her. Just as it had become apparent to him that with what was to come, he might never be able to make amends.

It was an anxious period for Harrison as he awaited the arrival of the second note. He both anticipated and dreaded its delivery. With it would come the hope that his daughter was still alive. But at that point there would be no turning back from what Harrison had decided he must do. To save Evaline, he would have to follow through with the note's demand.

His only certainty was that the outcome would be his own death.

George Watson felt only slightly more optimistic. When the telegram arrived at his office, detailing nothing more than a meeting place, a date, and an approximate time, he understood, and he wasted no time dispatching a wire to Buck Leighton in Brackett. Buck received the message through the sheriff's office and went to fetch Melinda, who had readied herself for this moment and was prepared for the journey both in attitude and attire, donning old work pants, a heavy flannel shirt, and a wide-brimmed hat to protect her against the merciless rays of the desert sun during their long ride.

She had already made arrangements with her Mexican neighbor to look after her boy, Charlie. Buck didn't rush Melinda and stood patiently as she spent some minutes with her son, gently explaining to him that she had to be away for a short while but would be back as soon as she could. The boy looked sad and Melinda had to struggle to keep the tears from her own eyes, afraid that it would further upset her son to see her cry. The Mexican woman was kind yet firm and managed to comfort Charlie, telling him in broken

English to stand straight and strong for his mother, and the boy wiped dry his watering eyes and waved meekly as he watched his mother ride off with Buck.

With the information forwarded him in Watson's wire, Buck, together with Melinda, headed out directly to the location specified in the telegram: an apparently desolate, rock-strewn area some miles from Border Pass, the exact meeting spot marked by a strange natural formation that was seen by some as a bad omen. There stood a solitary tree with gnarled and barren branches that stretched over the passageway like long, bony fingers, which was known simply as The Skeleton Tree, and was referenced in the telegram. Buck wasn't familiar with the region and had never heard of The Skeleton Tree, and at some point would need to seek out directions (as would, he assumed, George Watson), but it was his intention to arrive early to scout out a good secure spot to keep him and Melinda out of sight while still watching what was to transpire between Watson and whoever would be there to meet him. Buck still wasn't certain of how he would proceed. He understood that there were a number of variables involved, and during the ride he finally decided it would be best not to settle on any plan and to play things as they came.

The ride would take a couple of days, and there wasn't much talk between Buck and Melinda during their journey headed southwest. Both had their own thoughts, and Buck understood particularly how difficult this was for Melinda. She'd had to absorb an awful lot recently, and though he didn't voice it, he admired her all to hell. She couldn't know what they were riding into any more than he did, yet she was doing so willingly, to help both her husband and a woman she'd never met.

Yep, Buck thought, Melinda truly was a gal with some grit.

TWENTY-TWO

"WHAT DO YOU think they're going to do with us?" Evaline apprehensively asked Janette.

It was a question she had asked before—many times—seeking an answer that Janette was unable to provide.

The days leading up to the payoff of the "ransom" passed quietly at the cabin. Janette Watson and Evaline Harrison spent most of their time in the one bedroom, checked on occasionally by Cora, whose actions were carefully watched by Ehron Lee and Ward. Ehron Lee still didn't have total trust in Cora and his doubt had become shared by Ward. The bedroom was a small enclosure, and secure; there was no window or opening through which the women could attempt an escape, only the door leading out into the hall-way. There was just the one entrance and exit from the cabin itself: the main door between the kitchen and front room. During the day, at least one of the men kept watch, and the men slept in shifts throughout the night so that one was always awake. Never was Cora permitted to watch the two women alone. No reason was given to her, but none was necessary. She understood that she was not trusted.

As the older of the two hostages, Janette Watson comforted Evaline as best she could, offering vague words of encouragement though she shared the girl's uncertainty, reassuring Evaline that everything would be all right and even boldly demanding the confirmation of that assurance from Cora when she would come into the room with some food and the pitcher of water that was brought to them daily, drawn from the clear-water stream just beyond the property.

Cora knew that whatever words she might have spoken would not be convincing, and each time she would leave the room as she'd entered it, silently, without acknowledging Janette's entreaties. Then, through the closed door she would hear Evaline start to weep and would feel helpless and fight back her own tears.

She just wanted this terrible experience to be over as, day by day, she dealt with the overwhelming guilt of her own part in the ordeal these women were going through.

The men mainly sat out their wait by playing cards. Boredom and the anticipation of what was to come soon began to weigh heavily on Ehron Lee and Ward, though both managed to deal with it, a patience nurtured from their years of imprisonment. Jess Colfax, on the other hand, had neither experienced prison nor possessed the same sense of purpose as his companions, and his restlessness was more pronounced. He would have much preferred to be planning for another bank score, where at least he could see some reward for his trouble. Growing impatient and frustrated, he was drinking heavily to pass the hours and had started to complain that he was putting his neck out for no payback.

On this day his face had a flushed, fevered look and it was evident that his tolerance had been exhausted.

"Yuh coulda rode off with Randy, Jess," Ward reminded his companion, eyeing him coldly. "It was your decision to stay."

"Yeah, and maybe I shoulda thought it out more," Jess grumbled. He sloshed back more whiskey from the jug on the table. "Don't know what the hell I was thinkin'."

"Don't care if'n yuh wanta have a drink, just go careful with it," Ward advised.

Jess gave him a blank stare.

He growled, "Yuh tryin' to reform me?" then defiantly pulled back another good swallow.

"You'd be smart to find some other way to blow off steam," Ehron Lee said to him.

Jess veered his eyes toward the closed bedroom door and wore a wet, wicked smile. "Could blow off more'n that . . . with what's in the next room."

Sitting in the front room, within earshot, Cora heard him utter those words, noticed his shifting expression, and felt herself stiffen anxiously.

Ehron Lee moved to break the tension.

"Don't start gettin' none of them thoughts," he told Jess sternly.

Jess responded with a tightening of his features, then he lowered his head and mumbled drunkenly, "Tired of just sittin' 'round this stinkin' place. Tired of eatin' the same stinkin' canned grub. Tired of the same stinkin' company."

Jess slapped his cards down on the table without finishing his hand and stood up. He staggered the few feet over to the counter and leaned against its surface to steady himself. Both Ehron Lee and Ward watched him carefully. Cora, too, eyed him warily. Jess was agitated, and in such a state, mixed with alcohol, his mood could turn unpredictable.

"Whyn't you go sleep it off?" Ward suggested.

Jess spoke miserably, his words slurred. "Sleep it off, that's all yuh can say? Sleep *what* off? Got yuh outta a tough spot, Ward, and now I'm goin' loco waitin' for a payoff I ain't gonna get."

"Once this is over, you'll get a payoff, Jess," Ward said calmly.

Jess was too drunk to detect the odd inflection in Ward's voice, though Ehron Lee and Cora noticed, and instantly suspected what Ward intended. Jess merely raised his lolling head to him.

Ward explained patiently, "There's 'nuff cash here for all

of us: Burrows, Cora, you, and me to ride south. Head down to Mexico. Plenty to do there."

Jess seemed oblivious to what Ward was saying. The high-proof whiskey demolished what remained of his comprehension with the impact of an eight-gauge. He was swaying and his eyes were heavy-lidded. Finally, rocking on his feet, he made his way to the unoccupied bedroom to pass out.

There was silence in the cabin for the next several moments. Ehron Lee kept his focus on the playing cards he held in his hand. Then he slowly lifted his eyes and looked directly at Ward. Ward returned the gaze and nodded.

"He'll behave himself," he said quietly, adding, "But when this is over, there's only one payoff he'll be gettin'."

TWENTY-THREE

GEORGE WATSON HAD taken the stage from Allensfield to Colbert City. Judge Harrison did the same, though he rode in from Bolton. They arrived a day apart from each other, which was how the kidnappers had planned it.

Judge Harrison reached town first, on the morning stage. He asked directions from the fellow who ran the livery stable. Its neatly painted signage proclaimed: TRUSWELL'S LIVERY, HORSES AND BUGGIES FOR HIRE. He got directions on how to get out to Border Pass and where he could find The Skeleton Tree. The stable owner, Bob Truswell, regarded Harrison curiously; it was an odd request since the area was so desolate and rarely traveled—and though he himself didn't believe in such things, as a lifelong resident of the town, he was well acquainted with the superstition surrounding The Skeleton Tree. But it was none of his concern and he provided the information and then rented Harrison a buggy, even though he suggested to the judge that the trail was pretty rough and better traversed by a horse. Harrison merely forced a smile and said he enjoyed his comforts. He rode off, leaving Bob Truswell to scratch his head.

The following day, the afternoon stage brought forth George Watson. He had traveled a greater distance and was tired enough from the long ride to consider settling in the town overnight and starting out early the next morning. He had another long, even more difficult ride ahead of him. He knew, however, that was not a luxury he could afford. He, too, would need a way to get out to the appointed rendezvous and was directed by a citizen to Truswell's Livery to see about acquiring a horse for a few days. Once the transaction was completed, Watson asked the same directions as had Judge Harrison, leaving Bob Truswell truly puzzled. In all his years as stable manager, he couldn't recall even once being asked how to get to Border Pass and, specifically, The Skeleton Tree. Now within a day of each other, *two* queries had come his way.

"Had a fella come in yesterday askin' the same thing," Truswell said as he readied the horse the stranger had chosen.

"That so?" Watson said with muted interest. He was curious, though not inquisitive as he thought it likely might be Marshal Buck Leighton who had passed through, per their arrangement.

"Yeah, wouldn't think much 'bout it, only that just ain't a place people 'round here tend to go. 'Fact, most everyone I know stays clear of Border Pass."

"Well, I'm not from around here," Watson said brusquely. Noticing how Truswell was regarding him with suspicion, he muttered an explanation. "Gotta meet some folks there, then we'll be ridin' on."

"Strange place for a meetin'," Truswell commented.

Watson half smiled. "Reckon. But these are strange people."

Once again, realizing it was none of his affair, Truswell obliged with the directions, then ambled out onto the street to watch as George Watson rode off, heading west.

Jess Colfax had a hankering for fresh meat. Farther out toward the mountains there was plenty of wild game to be had and early the next morning he loaded shells into one of the Winchester '66 rifles and announced that he was going to bring back a buck for supper. Both Ehron Lee and Ward were agreeable to the idea. It not only might serve to offset Jess's restlessness and the threat of his deciding to act on impulse, but also would help replenish their food supply, which was running low, and neither Ward nor Ehron Lee thought it prudent to venture into Colbert City.

For today was the day of the rendezvous with Judge Charles Hugh Harrison.

While a partly sober Jess packed up some gear and headed out into the wilderness for his hunt, Ehron Lee readied himself for his ride to Border Pass and The Skeleton Tree. He'd been anticipating this moment for what seemed an eternity, yet as the time now neared, he was possessed of a strange uncertainty. The plan was to bring Harrison back to the cabin, where he would be presented to his daughter, and then have the judge decide who between them was to die. Ehron Lee had no qualms about killing Harrison—indeed, he looked forward to blasting the buzzard's soul into oblivion. But regardless of what was to happen—whatever choice the judge made—Ehron Lee knew that another, more difficult decision would have to be addressed concerning the women hostages. Both Janette Watson and Evaline Harrison could identify them; not only had their faces been seen, but Ward and Jess had both freely referred to everyone involved by name. And Ehron Lee suspected that was not simply carelessness. Whatever choice Watson and Harrison made, they would not leave the cabin alive. That debt had to be paid. It seemed to Ehron Lee that Ward intended the same fate for the two women, as well. What particularly troubled him was that he could almost appreciate such reasoning, at least where his part was concerned. Ward was a prison escapee, a fugitive, and would forever be on the run. Jess Colfax would be dead; that already had been decided. But if the women were released, he, Ehron Lee, still legally a free man, would live out the rest of his days hunted by the law.

While he recognized that he didn't have much of a life to look forward to, he didn't want to compound his misery by spending his every waking hour looking over his shoulder. Most of all, he would never allow himself to be taken back to prison.

As difficult as it might be, and though it neither could nor would be him who would settle the matter, Ehron Lee understood that there looked to be only one resolution.

Ehron Lee kept himself out of sight, concealed behind a cluster of large rocks that formed a natural raised and serrated border just a short distance from where The Skeleton Tree stood. He was eager to see Judge Harrison again—very eager. The judge was instructed to reach the meeting place by twelve noon on this day. Ehron Lee figured Harrison for a punctual man, and if he was going to show, it would be close to the appointed time. Of course there was always the vague possibility he might decide to forfeit his daughter's life and not come. But Ehron Lee thought that unlikely. The man was a buzzard . . . but he was also a father.

The sun was hot and Ehron Lee was sweating profusely. His clothing was saturated, his shirt sticky from relentless perspiration, the material clinging uncomfortably to his body. Moisture from his brow dripped into his eyes, blurring his vision, and he had to constantly brush the sweat away to keep his view unimpeded. He checked his water canteen—full when he rode out this morning, now almost empty. He hadn't counted on the day being so oppressively hot. He trickled down the last remaining drops and tossed the canteen away. Fortunately, it wasn't a long ride back to the cabin, and Ehron Lee would be glad to get back there. The intense noonday heat was a reminder of what he'd often had to endure working in the quarry at Rockmound. Most important, he had to keep up his strength. He had to stay alert, on the off chance Harrison might decide to pull a fast one. One could never be sure of how a desperate man might think.

*   *   *

Judge Harrison arrived at the destination shortly before one o'clock in the afternoon—on foot, his black coat flung over his shoulder, his white shirt stained with sweat, his flat crown hat protecting his eyes from the blinding glare of the sun. He'd discovered that Bob Truswell had been correct about attempting to navigate a buggy through the Border Pass and finally had given up the attempt. Since he had no concern about returning the buggy to town as he knew that he would not be coming back from the meeting with the kidnappers, he left it sitting back on the rocky trail. He, too, quickly became exhausted from the heat as he walked to where he expected to find The Skeleton Tree. By the time he finally came into Ehron Lee's sight, he looked almost on the verge of collapse. Ehron Lee climbed down from his position among the rocks to meet him. He carefully maneuvered his steps through the tricky levels of outcropping with his revolver drawn but not aimed. Judge Harrison stopped and looked carefully at the man. His face betrayed no hint of recognition. It seemed apparent he could not remember Ehron Lee.

"You the man that has my daughter?" the judge asked weakly.

Ehron Lee didn't answer. He, too, gave a studied gaze. Even after all these years he clearly recognized the man whose judgment had taken away his life. A man he resented even more because, with all he had suffered through, Ehron Lee would have preferred a death by hanging. He'd lived with an ongoing torture. Hard emotions quickly took hold and Ehron Lee struggled with the urge to shoot the judge dead then and there.

But he fought and controlled the impulse. Partly because what he was looking at now was not a man of power and authority—one who could dictate and damn another man's destiny—but someone stripped of his dignity. A man reduced in pride and stature in ex-convict Ehron Lee's presence.

Yet Ehron Lee was beyond feeling compassion for the judge's humbled position.

"Just tell me, is my daughter all right?" Harrison said, a slight pleading in his voice.

Again Ehron Lee failed to respond. Instead he gestured with a wave of his gun for Harrison to walk ahead of him. It was only a short distance to where Ehron Lee had left his horse, off the trail in a clearing, but Harrison had to call upon all his remaining strength, ebbing rapidly, to complete the walk.

"You ride, I'll guide," were the first words to leave Ehron Lee's mouth once they came to the horse, standing close to a wall of rocks whose overhang provided cooling shade for the animal.

Harrison obeyed, giving a nod in acknowledgment, and he struggled to mount the horse, faltering a couple of times before getting himself settled on the saddle. He waited until Ehron Lee was seated behind him, then he half turned his head and asked gently, almost kindly, "Don't suppose you have a sip of water handy?"

Ehron Lee ignored the request.

"Just ride steady," he instructed the judge.

While Judge Harrison had no specific memory of Ehron Lee, he had a different reaction when he was pushed into the cabin and was instantly greeted by the outlaw killer Ward Crawford, seated at the kitchen table, lips stretched wide in the same cocky grin he'd worn throughout the trial over which Harrison had presided six years previously.

"Ward Crawford," Harrison managed over a dry swallow, the words spoken nearly inaudible.

"Pleased yuh remember, Judge," Ward said pleasantly. "Saves me havin' to take time to reintroduce myself."

Ehron Lee closed the door to the cabin and stood behind Harrison. "Reckon his conscience only lets him recall the guilty ones," he said pointedly.

Harrison started to turn. But before he could completely

face the man standing in back of him, Ehron Lee couldn't restrain himself any longer and he hit the judge across the side of the face with a sharp backhand, knocking him off balance.

Cora looked startled. Ward chuckled and slowly started to rise from the table.

"Okay, Burrows, yuh got that outta yuh," he said.

Harrison's eyes were wide, and for the first time he looked truly frightened. He held his hand against his cheek and stepped back tentatively. As he did so, Ward stuck out his foot. Harrison's leg caught on Ward's boot heel and he tripped over backward. He recovered swiftly and attempted to scramble to his feet. Ward pressed his boot heavily onto the judge's back and held him pinned to the floor.

"P-Please," Harrison implored, his voice rising in pitch. "I—I just want to see my daughter."

Suddenly there was a sharp cry from the bedroom. It was Evaline, recognizing her father's voice.

"Daddy!"

"Evaline," Harrison called back. Before he could say anything more, Ward stepped down harder on his back, causing Harrison to gasp and then fall silent.

Evaline was shouting for her father, frantically pounding at the door until Janette Watson was heard shushing and calming her, and soon the only sounds coming from the bedroom were Evaline's gentle sobs.

Cora watched silently. She glanced down at Judge Harrison, sprawled helplessly on the floor, and was upset when she saw the tears that came into his eyes. She felt sickened but there was nothing she could do. She was as powerless as any of the hostages.

It was dusk that same day when Buck Leighton and Melinda Burrows located the spot where George Watson was to rendezvous the following noon with his wife's kidnappers. They set up a small camp far from the trail where they wouldn't be noticed by an unlikely passerby—or an early appearance from one of the kidnappers. It was a warm evening so Buck thought it wise not to start a fire. They ate their supper cold from the can and slept comfortably if fitfully under the blankets they'd brought along for their travel.

Both rose early, just after sunrise. It was an uncertain day they faced. Buck had his worries of what was ahead but maintained a calm composure for Melinda's sake. Her own trepidation was understandably apparent. After five years she would be meeting the husband who had long believed she was dead. A man changed by his experience and who now chose to live outside the law. George Watson had told Buck earlier that the only difference he'd noted in the man at his release was that he seemed to lack compassion. Watson said that he never could have guessed that Ehron Lee Burrows would become a savage criminal capable of participating in such a heinous act. Buck thought differently. He only hoped that Ehron Lee might still feel some of the love he'd once had for Melinda. It was their one chance of possibly rescuing George Watson's wife . . . and preventing the murder of Watson himself.

After eating a quick breakfast of biscuits and jerky, Buck readied himself to venture forth to The Skeleton Tree. It wasn't too far a distance from their camp, and it was understood that Melinda would stay back until Buck had an opportunity to survey the situation. There was little chance she could be exposed to potential danger with what was planned, but Buck wanted to keep her protected for as long as possible.

As he took up his position, Buck had thought out what he was going to do. His hope was that it would be Ward Crawford who would come to meet Watson. He posed the most threat and Buck's plan was to try to get the drop on him once he showed up at the rendezvous. With Watson to hold the killer at bay, Buck and Melinda would have their opportunity to try and reason with Ehron Lee. If . . . God willing that still was possible.

Jess Colfax took a final swig of the whiskey he'd brought along on his hunt and tossed the empty bottle far into the bush, venting his frustration and letting loose with a barrage of curse words. He'd stayed the night deep in the foothills of Brimstone Canyon and not only hadn't shot a buck, but had never even spotted one. This lack of luck only intensified his foul mood. He was fed up with the way things were going and decided, if he couldn't reap at least a little enjoyment from tagging along with Ward and Ehron Lee, he might as well just be on his way. What particularly angered him was that all the diversion he needed was locked behind that bedroom door. Those fellas owed him the right to some pleasure—after all, if something went wrong, he'd be just as guilty as them and would suffer the same punishment . . . even though none of this was his idea. He surely wouldn't hurt those girls, and the way he figured, even if he did, what would it matter? They were as good as dead anyway. Ward would be a damn fool to release them, and whatever else his faults, Ward Crawford couldn't be taken for a fool.

Jess packed up his gear and started his journey back to the cabin. He decided he was going to lay his cards on the table. Either he was permitted a little fun, or it was adios.

He'd had to cut his own path in since the heavily wooded hills were dense with foliage and underbrush. He followed the trail he'd made as best he could, but there wasn't much clearing. He cussed again, mumbling aloud that he might just have gone and got himself lost. To punctuate his irritation, he slammed a fist into the trunk of a tree, ripping the skin from his knuckles.

As he tore off a corner of his shirt to bandage the wound, Jess heard a shuffle in the bush and stopped what he was doing, instead shifting to his other hand and readying his Winchester. Moments later a small rabbit scampered into view. Jess instinctively took aim at the critter, then he lowered his rifle. Better not to bring anything back than walk into the cabin displaying a meager rabbit.

Jess started on his way, hoping that if he wasn't lost, he'd find himself back at the cabin before nightfall. He was mighty hungry, and even the prospect of digging his supper out of a can didn't seem so unappealing at the moment.

Whether Jess had ever been aware of it, he possessed keen intuition, and as he walked, of a sudden, he had the strange feeling he was being watched. He sensed a presence hidden somewhere among the trees, whatever or whoever was there carefully following his progress. For a moment he considered it might be that elusive buck. Or possibly a bear, though none to his knowledge had ever been seen around this region. In any case, he tightened his hold on the Winchester, raising it to the ready. He kept his ears alert for any uncommon noise, but he heard no sound other than a faint rustling of the leaves as a breeze passed through.

Everything seemed all right. Only he couldn't escape the feeling—

In an instant the silence was shattered by a sharp cry, and before Jess could determine its source, he was pounced upon. As if from out of nowhere, someone had broken free from the bush and had wrestled Jess to the ground. It took a minute for Jess to regain his senses, and when he did, he was staring into the fierce face of a bare-chested Chiricahua warrior, clearly determined to kill him. The Indian was gripping a knife poised aggressively above Jess's chest, which Jess held back by grabbing hold of the attacker's forearm with one hand, struggling to keep the blade from descending into his flesh and bone. The Indian was powerful, but Jess's survival instinct was strong and his free hand balled into a fist, which he pummeled into the Indian's jaw, knocking him free of Jess's body. The Indian lay momentarily stunned, which gave Jess time to roll over and reach for his rifle. By the time he cocked the lever and took aim, the Indian was back on his feet, looking fearful and unsure of what to do. No such doubt existed in Jess. Without hesitation, he fired off a succession of shots, blasting the Indian backward into the bush, where he lay still.

Another Chiricahua showed himself—but only briefly, for once he saw the rifle being swung in his direction, he disappeared quickly into the protection of the trees. Jess could hear his footfalls crunching against the ground and cracking small branches as he ran off. Jess only briefly considered chasing after him, but he knew how fast Indians were on their feet and decided against such a maneuver.

All was quiet.

"Sonofabitch," Jess muttered breathlessly. He took a moment to compose himself, then pulled to his feet and walked over to where the dead Chiricahua lay. He took a good look at the brown face, which was frozen in an expression of shock and surprise. The Indian looked to be a youngster, not even twenty years old. But his age didn't trouble Jess. His concern was that he'd discovered firsthand that the legend of the Chiricahau roaming Brimstone Canyon was, in fact, no legend. And in all the years they'd been hiding out at the cabin, unbeknownst to any of them, an enemy had lurked nearby.

TWENTY-FOUR

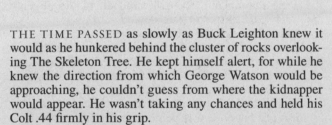

THE TIME PASSED as slowly as Buck Leighton knew it would as he hunkered behind the cluster of rocks overlooking The Skeleton Tree. He kept himself alert, for while he knew the direction from which George Watson would be approaching, he couldn't guess from where the kidnapper would appear. He wasn't taking any chances and held his Colt .44 firmly in his grip.

Finally, as the noonday sun reached and held high, reflecting a blinding white glare against the choppy rock surfaces, a sweat-drenched Buck glanced out from his vantage point as he heard the slow approach of a horse, and saw that it was George Watson, riding in from the northern trail. Buck quickly scanned the areas east and south but saw no activity. Whoever was to meet Watson had yet to show himself. Buck was a bit puzzled; he felt sure the kidnapper would have been the first to arrive, if only to make sure beforehand that Watson was following instructions and arriving alone.

Buck held his position and remained still and perfectly quiet. He wouldn't let Watson know he was there until the moment was right, which wouldn't be until the kidnapper showed.

Watson halted his horse next to The Skelton Tree, which he regarded with an unpleasant expression. He'd ridden long and far and almost nonstop throughout the preceding night, and dismounted stiffly, taking a few steps in each direction both to loosen his leg muscles and to scout the area. It registered on his face that he was as bewildered as Buck to discover that no one was there to meet him.

Although his senses were alert, Buck was so preoccupied watching Watson's movements that his defenses were down when at the last possible moment for him to react he heard a crunch of gravel behind him and felt his body instinctively tense in anticipation before he heard the deep yet smooth voice:

"Drop the gun slow and easy, amigo."

Buck's heart skipped a beat. He had no choice but to obey the faceless command. The Colt slid from his fingers onto the ground. He started to rise, slowly.

"Slow and easy," the voice commanded.

Again, Buck had no other option than to do as he was told. In the next second his earlier hopes of getting the drop on the kidnapper faded completely when he heard a more familiar voice say fearfully, "Buck, do as he says."

It was Melinda. Somehow they had both been outsmarted by the crude but obviously perceptive intelligence of—

Buck turned around.

Ward Crawford.

The outlaw, standing just behind Melinda with two guns drawn, was exhibiting his trademark grin. He was wearing an expression that seemed to suggest outright that either they were now his prisoners or the soon-to-be victims of his criminal bloodlust. He would make the call.

Ward spit out a laugh, then he bared his yellowed teeth. "Knew I couldn't trust that viper Watson."

"Melinda," Buck said with concern.

Ward's eyes sparked eagerly at the mention of the name. "Melinda? Couldn't just happen to be you're Melinda *Burrows*?"

Melinda didn't acknowledge though she felt a cold shiver rush through her at this outlaw assuming who she was. She stepped away from Ward and moved briskly toward Buck. She wrapped her arms around him and Buck reciprocated by placing his own arm around her shoulders and drawing her close.

Ward gave an amused smirk.

"So you really ain't dead," he said.

Reflexively, Melinda gave a shake of her head. Buck hadn't wanted that to be known yet, but he was too slow to halt her response.

Ward inspected the silver badge pinned to Buck's shirt. He grinned. "Mr. U.S. Marshal and the widow woman. Ain't hard to figger where this was goin'."

"Ain't what you might be thinkin'," Buck countered.

Ward's face became skeptical. Still he ignored Buck's comment and instead called out, "All right, Watson, discovered your little trick. We're comin' down, and if you're smart, you won't move a hair on your ass."

Melinda whispered to Buck, "How—how did he—"

Buck shushed her and hugged her a little more tightly.

With his pair of Colts still aimed at the two, Ward sidestepped over to the incline, where he could take a glimpse at Watson. Watson had heard the barked order and was standing in the open, arms pulled outward in surrender.

Ward looked back toward Buck and Melinda, urging them down toward the trail with a wave of his guns.

"Might be it 'splains a lot seein' you two," he said. "'Course, don't mean a damn thing to me. But you bein' Burrows's wife, gonna be mighty interestin' when he gets his chance to look at yuh." He took on a scrutinizing expression. "Thing I can't rightly tell is if you two is partners . . . or maybe a cozy twosome. Reckon we'll let Ehron Lee figger that out, huh?"

Once everyone was on the trail, Ward lifted his gun and fired an upward shot, which spooked the horse Watson had come in on and the animal bolted.

"Ain't that far to go," Ward said. "And I think a walk

might just be the thing to work off some of your . . . ambition."

Buck purposely kept himself from meeting Watson's penetrating look, almost accusing in intent. Watson had expressed his reservations about Buck getting involved. Buck had insisted, and now all of them were at the mercy of Ward Crawford.

By the time Jess Colfax reached the cabin, he was of two minds about his earlier ordeal. He could tell the others about his run-in with the Chiricahua and let them make the decision if they wanted to stay put, or he could keep his mouth shut and just ride off on his own. Either way, he wasn't going to risk losing his scalp should the Chiricahua go on the warpath after learning of the death of one of their own. Jess wasn't all that familiar with the ways of the Indian, but from what he'd heard, "blood for blood" was the Apache creed and since the Chiricahua were known to be the most blood-thirsty of that tribe, their vengeance would likely be swift and devastating. Jess also knew that it wouldn't take the Chiricahua long to track down the cabin and its occupants.

Time was the deciding factor. Jess regretted not reacting fast enough to gun down the Chiricahua that witnessed the killing and who got away. There was no doubt the Indian would report to the tribe what had happened. It could be days or perhaps even hours before the Chiricahua mounted their attack. Jess determined he would not argue the point with his companions. Ward was just crazy enough not to concern himself over the threat and likely could attempt to delay if not outright halt Jess's departure over the barrel of a gun.

Jess hesitated while mulling over these thoughts before he shrugged to himself and went inside the cabin. Ward apparently hadn't returned from Border Pass, but a man he did not recognize was in the front room, off in a far corner, gagged and tied securely by strips of rawhide to a wooden chair. Ehron Lee and Cora were seated at the kitchen table, sipping coffee. Cora wore a troubled look.

"Ward ain't back yet?" Jess asked.

"Soon," Ehron Lee replied.

Jess jerked a thumb toward the front room.

"That's *His Honor*," Ehron Lee said sardonically. "Judge Harrison."

Jess nodded vacantly. It was of no matter to him. Then he said abruptly, "Well, you can tell Ward I made up my mind to get outta here. This ain't none of my affair, and I can't see no point in sittin' this out with yuh."

Ehron Lee considered before he drew a breath.

"Reckon that's your choice, Jess," he said neutrally.

Jess's voice took on a defensive edge. "Damn right. But I reckon I got some money comin' to me."

"Yeah?"

"From our last bank job," Jess clarified.

Ehron Lee turned to Cora. "That so?"

Cora nodded and rose to her feet and said, "I'll get his share."

She went to fetch the money. The outlaws' loot was stashed in a secret location somewhere outside the cabin— the exact spot known only by Cora. It was a practical, agreed-upon decision since none of the bunch truly trusted the other. The arrangement was that Cora would serve as their "banker," doling out cash as needed and keeping track of each withdrawal so that each share would be properly accounted for.

While they waited, Ehron Lee studied Jess. Despite his efforts to appear calm, the man looked nervous, as if he was hiding something.

"No one's gonna stop yuh if'n yuh wanta go, Jess," Ehron Lee said.

"Don't expect no one will," Jess returned sharply.

Ehron Lee eased back in his chair. "Then why're yuh actin' like yuh got a rattler up your pants?"

Jess's eyes got wide and they shifted in what to Ehron Lee was a telling motion. His voice got a little shaky as he said, "Told yuh before: There ain't nothin' in this deal for me."

"That all?"

"Yeah, sure. What else would there be?"

Ehron Lee shrugged and drank some of his coffee.

Jess was coming across like a man in distress. Soon he started to pace the kitchen floor, purposely avoiding Ehron Lee's probing gaze.

Ehron Lee wasn't sure what was up, but there was no denying Jess was holding back something. He'd been gone— supposedly on a hunt—overnight, hadn't brought back any meat, or an explanation, and now was acting as if he had to make a quick getaway. Ehron Lee's suspicions mounted.

Cora came back inside the cabin holding a fistful of money. Jess stepped over quickly and grabbed the bills from her hand. It was his hope to be gone before Ward returned, but in the next instant he glanced out the kitchen window and saw three people nearing the cabin on foot, followed by Ward on horseback. Jess grumbled under his breath.

Ehron Lee noticed how Jess's attention was held by whatever was happening outside, and he got up and ambled over next to him. He, too, saw the small group approaching. At first, outside of Ward and the bald, distinctive figure of Superintendent Watson, he couldn't identify the other two being led on by Ward, although to his initial puzzlement, one looked to be a female, dressed like a man in baggy pants and wearing a wide-brimmed hat that shadowed her features but failed to disguise the long honey-colored hair that caught and reflected the sunlight. Ehron Lee directed his focus on her. It took a few seconds before recognition struck, and in that instant when he finally made the connection, it felt as if his heart had stopped.

He wiped his hand over his eyes, blinking several times. *But it couldn't be*, he tried to rationalize. What he was looking at was impossible. Melinda . . . was dead!

Yet what his eyes followed was neither a ghost nor a mirage, or even the figment of a desperate, fevered mind. Ehron Lee was looking at the flesh-and-blood vision of the girl who had been his wife. The wife he'd spent the last years trying to forget, the woman he struggled to keep buried deep within the unconscious recesses of his brain.

Still doubting that it could possibly be Melinda, Ehron Lee surrendered to an impulsive action, and he rushed to the front door. His move was so quick and so sudden that Cora was startled enough to half rise from her chair.

Jess stayed put, looking nervous. He hadn't moved fast enough. Now he would have to wait for the right opportunity; worse, he would have to tell Ward of his intention to leave. He couldn't just walk out and chance falling victim to Ward's volatile mood.

Ehron Lee found himself locked in a moment of hesitation, as if unable to summon the courage to open the door and take that first step outdoors. His brain simply could not properly process what that move would lead him to. If it truly was Melinda . . . then what? Too much time had passed, too many terrible things had happened. Ehron Lee had to accept the fact that neither he nor Melinda could recognize each other for who they had once been. To each other. To themselves.

Ehron Lee was so preoccupied with what was churning around inside his brain that he wasn't immediately aware of the gentle touch on his arm. Finally he acknowledged the fingertips lightly pressing against the fabric of his shirt and he half-turned. It was Cora, eyes cast upon him with a look of questioning concern.

"Melinda. It—it's my wife," he said dazedly.

"But you said—" Cora started to say.

Ehron Lee spoke with strained emphasis. "It's her. Gotta be her. Couldn't be mistaken."

Cora slowly slid her fingers away from Ehron Lee's arm. And then she drew in a breath and regained her own composure.

"Then you gotta go to her, Ehron Lee," she said determinedly.

Ehron Lee regarded her peculiarly.

"It's what you need to do," Cora went on. She paused, bit

down on her bottom lip, and said, "Ehron Lee, this is wrong. All of what we're doing is wrong. I—I don't know how it makes any sense, but the way I see it, your wife comin' here might be the only way to set things right, and—"

Before Cora could finish what she was saying, the door opened from the outside, and Ehron Lee surprised her by releasing his grip on the handle and stepping aside. While his thoughts were still clouded in confusion, in a moment he would have no choice but to consider Cora's words. Shortly, he would be standing face-to-face with his wife.

He made himself stand firm. His expression betrayed nothing of what he was feeling. The look on his face was inscrutable—a look he managed to maintain only through years of conditioning at Rockmound, where no matter what punishment was being meted out, one could not react to it. Cora moved away from him, taking a seat at the table, where Jess now sat, his posture stiff. Although Cora had her own thoughts, and admittedly still held feelings for Ehron Lee, she knew she could not involve herself in this "reunion" in any way.

George Watson was the first to enter. His face was stern; he presented the picture of a man not about to allow himself to be intimidated by a pack of outlaws. Ehron Lee noticed how his eyes shifted about the cabin, evidently searching for his wife, before his gaze fell upon Ehron Lee and held a brief look of vulnerability. Watson recognized his former prisoner, though the acknowledgment sparked only for a moment before it faded from Watson's features and his strict, reserved demeanor returned.

Melinda and Buck Leighton came in next. Buck had his arm protectively around the girl, but she still looked frightened and uncertain. Yet that was ignored by Ehron Lee, because she was in every way as beautiful as he remembered her. His lips moved involuntarily but no words came out. Only Cora noticed the pained look on his face.

Melinda turned her head and she saw him. In an instant her fearful expression gave way to a strange look combining hope, sympathy . . . and sorrow.

Neither spoke. Neither knew what to say. For Ehron Lee, it was the shock and surprise of standing just feet from the girl he had once loved with such passion and desire, the wife whom he had been led to believe was dead—yet was very much alive. Melinda hesitated because she now could see the truth of what her husband had become. A gentle man turned vengeful criminal, and even with Buck's earlier assurances that she was not to blame, Melinda could not altogether be eased of the guilt she felt, the part *she* had played in his terrible transformation.

The uncertainty both felt at being in each other's presence after so long and under such circumstances was palpable.

Finally Ward entered, both guns still drawn. After he was inside, he kicked the door shut behind him. He ordered Watson, Buck, and Melinda over against the far wall of the kitchen, next to the table where Cora and Jess were seated. Then Ward turned to Ehron Lee.

"Reckon you wasn't expectin' this," he said with a mischievous wink.

Ehron Lee found his voice, though his words were troubled.

"Why is *she* here?" he asked, addressing no one in particular.

"Ask the marshal," Ward replied with a nudge of his head toward Buck.

"Was my idea, Burrows," Buck stated solidly. "Wasn't her decision."

Almost with reluctance Ehron Lee brought himself to turn his eyes fully on Melinda. She met his gaze but didn't confirm or deny what Buck had said. She couldn't—or perhaps wouldn't.

Buck explained, "You had to know the truth, Burrows. Your wife never abandoned you. Just as with you believin' she was dead. All that was a lie. A lie concocted by your sister-in-law."

Ehron Lee's expression became strained.

"Abigail?" he said mutedly, still looking at Melinda.

Melinda responded as if she herself were responsible for her sister's actions. She lowered her eyes and gave a quivering nod.

"I never knew," she finally said. "She never sent the letters I wrote. If you wrote to me, I never got those letters."

George Watson spoke up. "Not a single letter from your wife ever came across my desk, Burrows. That's a fact."

"I wrote to you as often as I could, Ehron Lee," Melinda said, her eyes softening and becoming moist. "And when you didn't answer, I thought that maybe . . . maybe that was the way you wanted it."

Ehron Lee's face registered a quick look of astonishment. For seconds he remained silent.

"How—how could you ever have thought that?" he then said in a distant voice.

Ward was impatient. Plans had been made and he didn't want anything to interfere with Ehron Lee's participation, especially not sentiment. Ward had hoped that seeing his missus in the company of the marshal might heighten his partner's intent. Now with all that was being said between them, he determined her presence could pose a definite problem.

"All mighty purty," he growled. "But Burrows, we got us some business to attend to."

While Ehron Lee and his wife were exchanging their words, Buck allowed himself his first good look at their surroundings. That was when he caught sight of a man bound to a chair in the shadowy corner of the front room. It was dark where the man was sitting and a gag looked to be covering his mouth. Buck didn't immediately recognize the other "captive" as Judge Harrison.

Meanwhile, Jess Colfax seemed fidgety. Finally he stood up from the table and sidled over to Ward. Ward gave him an irritated look.

"I'm ridin' out, Ward," Jess muttered out the side of his mouth.

"Ain't gonna stay for the party?" Ward said, deadpan.

Jess wagged his head from side to side. He frowned in

thought and debated telling Ward about his encounter with the Chiricahua and what, inevitably, they could expect. But again he decided against it. Whatever happened to any of these people was not his worry. Jess's concern was only for his own safety.

Ward cocked an eye suspiciously. Jess was awkward in his manner and Ward's keen observation detected it immediately.

"Somethin' you ain't tellin' us, Jess," he said, phrasing his words as a comment rather than a question.

Jess tried to keep his voice steady. "No. I just gotta be movin' on."

Ward's dark eyes pierced into him and he hesitated a moment before he relaxed his stare. Then he nodded and shrugged.

"Well, your choice, amigo," he said, sounding casually indifferent. "No one's keepin yuh here."

Jess couldn't hide the relief that washed over him.

"Thanks, Ward," he said appreciatively.

He started to walk toward the door. His steps were swift. Rather too hurried. He spoke over his shoulder, "You don't gotta worry 'bout me sayin' nothin'. I—"

Ward fired a single shot just as Jess was opening the door, the bullet hitting the outlaw square in the back and propelling him forward with enough impact to slam the door shut with his jutting jaw. His hands scratched feebly at the wood as his body slowly slid to the floor.

"I know I don't, Jess," Ward muttered dully to the dead man.

At the gunshot Melinda screamed, twisting and burying her head in Buck's chest. Buck started to make a reflexive move toward Ward, but a grim-faced Ehron Lee leveled his own gun at the lawman and cocked the hammer.

Evaline Harrison began shouting from the bedroom, calling desperately for her father, whom she feared might have been the recipient of the bullet just fired.

Cora called back to her. "Your pa's all right. Be quiet in there."

Ward viewed each of his hostages with an expression of pure menace.

"Reckon yuh got the message," he sneered. "If I'm willin' to kill an old pal, there ain't nothin' stoppin' me from pluggin' any of you."

"And that's what you intend to do?" Buck asked boldly.

Ward grinned. "Ain't decided yet . . . 'bout some of you." He then looked directly at George Watson before he shifted his cold, cruel eyes toward Judge Harrison.

TWENTY-FIVE

BUCK AND MELINDA were prodded forward at gunpoint by Ward into the unoccupied bedroom, across from the room that held Janette Watson and Evaline Harrison. The outlaw then had Melinda manacle the marshal's wrist to the hardwood bedpost, using as a restraint Buck's own handcuffs. As with the other bedroom, the room was virtually bare, offering just a bed with blankets and a chair. No window. Just the one door, watched and guarded from the front room, ensuring that there was little chance of escape.

After Ward left the room, the two remained quiet, until Buck felt sure the outlaw was out of earshot. Still, he was cautious and kept his voice low.

"You gotta tell Ehron Lee 'bout the boy," he said to Melinda, who was seated next to him on the bed.

Melinda surprised Buck with her answer.

"Seein' the way he is, I—I don't know if I can," she replied pensively.

Buck waited for her to elaborate, though he already understood her reasoning.

Melinda noticed the way Buck was looking at her, and her voice took on a defensive edge.

"Don't you think that's what I was hoping to do?" she said. "I wanted to tell him 'bout Charlie the minute I saw him. But he's a different man now. And knowin' that he has a son . . . a boy he likely won't ever see . . . I can't see no good comin' from that."

"Or it could save the lives of these people," Buck presented solemnly.

Melinda considered his words. She comprehended what Buck was saying, but she wasn't entirely convinced. She knew better than anyone the type of man Ehron Lee was before suffering the misfortune that had befallen him: a man who had experienced violence yet was not a man *of* violence. But he had proven he was no longer of that character when he'd aimed his gun at Buck, prepared to kill him, and possibly even her, when the marshal had attempted to react to that man being shot. She feared that if she told him about their son, Ehron Lee might grow so resentful of his circumstances he might decide he had nothing to lose and become even more dangerous than his partner.

What did puzzle Melinda, though, and what she avoided mentioning to Buck, was why Ehron Lee had not asked *her* about the child. Had his brain become so twisted by hate that he no longer remembered that she had been carrying their baby—or did he simply not care?

All of these thoughts that spun around in her brain placed her in a dilemma. Would she be wise to offer him the truth that he was a father? Could she take that chance and possibly risk putting everyone in greater danger?

Buck noticed her struggle with indecision, reflected by the troubled and shifting look on her face. He finally decided to present the reality of their situation bluntly.

"Melinda, the way things look, none of us are gonna get outta this alive. The only chance we got, as I see it, is if you talk to Ehron Lee."

"Maybe . . . maybe I could," she said, biting her lower lip and speaking her words haltingly. "But Ehron Lee ain't alone in this. That other one . . . that Ward Crawford, you seen what he done. He's vicious. You heard what he said. You think he'd give me the chance to talk to Ehron Lee?"

Buck fell into a frustrated silence. He acknowledged the truth in what she said. Ward Crawford was a mean hombre and surely would do whatever was necessary to prevent Melinda and Ehron Lee from speaking together.

At the same time, Buck found himself surrendering to a moment of weakness, becoming angry with himself. He had brought Melinda into this, planning for a different outcome. But his plan had backfired because of the clever maneuvering of Ward Crawford. He felt he had failed at his job, and because of that, they all were at the outlaw's mercy.

And mercy was not something any of them could expect from a vindictive, cold-blooded killer.

Ward Crawford stood in the front room, arms akimbo, observing his two rawhide-bound captors with a hostile expression meant to threaten and intimidate. This moment had been a long time coming, and Ward relished every second. George Watson had been bound to a chair next to Judge Harrison. Harrison responded to Ward's glare with a look of trepidation. Despite his own helplessness and uncertainty of what was to come, Watson maintained a steely stare of defiance.

"Be easier to shoot you coyotes now," Ward said, speaking through clenched teeth. "But that don't hardly make up for what you're owed. No, don't hardly at all."

While Harrison was still gagged and unable to utter more than muffled sounds, Watson was permitted to speak.

"I don't make any apologies," he said grimly.

"Don't expect none," Ward acknowledged with a thin smile. "What you gotta make is a choice."

Watson gave him a determined look. "You might as well kill me now. 'Cause that's my decision."

"Mighty admirable, *Superintendent* Watson," Ward said tauntingly. "Only ain't gonna be that simple."

Watson's face did not change expression. "I figgered as much. You want to milk this dry, don't yuh? Keep this goin' for as long as you can."

Ward shrugged. "Might be the idea. Seems only fair, don't it?"

"Your own sense of justice."

"Had a taste of yours," Ward replied abruptly. "From here on in, the only justice I'll be recognizin' is my own."

"'Til the law catches up to you and you're dangling from a rope," Watson returned.

"Could be. Never really doubted that outcome," Ward admitted. "'Course ain't likely you'll be 'round to see it."

Watson's next words came impatiently, with emphasis. "You say my wife is in the next room. I want to see her."

Ward nodded, pleased to finally see some emotion rise from the superintendent; equally pleased that it was he, Ward Crawford, who now made the decisions.

"Ain't ready for that yet," he said dryly.

Ehron Lee sat at the kitchen table, his own gaze fixed on the two restrained men, though occasionally his eyes would veer toward the closed door of the bedroom where his wife was held. Cora sat across from him and noticed how his eyes wavered. She was still desperate to do something to prevent any killing. She knew she had no hope of reasoning with Ward. She could almost smell the bloodlust coming off him. The man she had once known was no more. Whatever had happened to him in prison, whatever cruelty he had suffered, had completely destroyed any of the decency that at one time existed within Ward Crawford.

But there had to be a chance, even a slim one, with Ehron Lee. Yet if he possessed any doubt over what was to come, if there was any moral struggle, he wasn't displaying it other than by the shifting of his eyes toward the bedroom. But that could be enough. It was a long shot, Cora didn't know how she could manage it, but Melinda Burrows seemed the only one who could possibly bring an end to this—and Cora also knew that could only happen if Melinda somehow convinced her husband to turn against Ward.

The problem was that every second counted. Cora had no way of knowing how long it would be until Ward tired of his cruel game and began making good on his threat.

Dusk came and the clouds drifting westward took on a purple hue as they darkened against the deepening blue of the southern skies. The autumn air grew cool as night approached. Ward felt a gnawing of restlessness and decided to step outdoors and have a cigarette. He wasn't comfortable leaving Cora alone with Ehron Lee and asked her in a casual way to come outside with him. At the same time, he didn't know if he could trust Ehron Lee not to take advantage of that opportunity to go speak with his wife. He had no doubt that if they spent even moments together, she would try to influence him—especially with that lawman in the room.

He took Ehron Lee aside to a corner.

"Burrows," he said, amiably yet sternly, "think it best if you let things be. With your missus, that is. Reckon you know why."

"I—don't want to talk to her," Ehron Lee assured him, though the strained look on his face seemed to suggest otherwise.

"We go on like we planned, like she was never here," Ward told him. "Understand? Otherwise none of what we done is worth snake spit."

Ehron Lee nodded, though he said, "You shouldn't have brought her back here."

Ward smiled crookedly. "What choice did I have?"

Ehron Lee couldn't argue. Ward was right, of course. If anyone was to blame, it was the marshal. And Ehron Lee's brain began to decipher why the marshal had made that decision. The more he thought about it, the more it angered him.

Ward saw the creeping tension overtake Ehron Lee's mood. He still held on to a little doubt about his loyalty, but he also didn't think his partner would be fool enough to risk all that they had accomplished—and jeopardize the plan—so close to reaching the climax both had long envisioned, that Ehron Lee himself had initiated.

"Okay, amigo," Ward said.

Then, with a swift jerk of his head, Ward gestured for Cora to follow him outside.

When they were out by the corral, absorbing the refreshing cool of the slight evening breeze while Ward indulged in a cigarette, Cora decided she could no longer keep her troubling feelings to herself and confronted Ward outright.

"I know you got reasons, Ward, but it ain't right what you're puttin' them people through."

Ward dragged deeply on his cigarette, tilted his head upward, and blew out a gray cloud of smoke.

"What d'yuh think me and Burrows was put through all them years?" he retorted.

"But . . . that woman, that girl, they ain't done nothin' to yuh," Cora said.

Ward looked at Cora, twisted his lips into a half smile, and shook his head. "No, but none of this coulda been done without bringin' 'em into it. You know that."

"Then get it done," Cora said forcefully. "Get done with what you gotta do and let 'em go free."

Ward regarded the orange glow on the tip of his cigarette before flicking it off to the side.

"Do that and I'll have the law chasin' me for the rest of my days." He turned his body fully toward Cora, gently lifted her chin with his fingertips, and gazed into her eyes. He added, "For the rest of *our* days."

Cora started to soften—but only for a moment. Then she averted her eyes from him. She could no longer be fooled by Ward and his attempts at charming her. His false sincerity. At one time his smooth words would have worked on her, as caressing as silk against skin. But she'd become wise to his ways and knew better now. His techniques had become obvious. Ward had revealed his true colors, and he was no more interested in sharing his life with her than he was in sparing his hostages. All he was trying to do was justify what he'd intended from the beginning. Get her to understand his reasoning and make her believe that unless he followed through completely with his plan, the two of them could never have a future. But Cora knew that future didn't include her.

She attempted to reach Ward through a different approach.

"Ehron Lee ain't gonna stand by and let you kill his wife," she said adamantly.

Ward became quiet as he pulled out his pouch of tobacco and started to build a fresh cigarette.

Cora responded harshly to his silence. "How d'yuh plan to handle that?" she demanded. "Shoot your partner, as well?"

"Don't be cornerin' me, Cora," Ward said.

Tension grew apparent by the sudden tautness shadowing Ward's features. Cora noticed the unsettling change in his expression and felt apprehensive. She was familiar with the violence in the man and knew that Ward could be pushed only so far. Still, in her desperation, she couldn't allow herself to back down completely.

Cora drew a breath and her tone softened. "I just gotta know what you're aimin' to do."

"For what matter?" he snapped.

"I seen how there ain't no trust 'mongst any of you. Ehron Lee and you'll come to odds 'fore long, and sooner than that if'n you go through with what you're plannin'."

"Burrows has got but one choice," Ward said hotly. "He either rides along with me or he's on his own."

Cora stood looking at Ward for several seconds, until she found she could no longer meet the coldness in his eyes. She understood that nothing she could say would change his mind. She had just the one option, and it was a long shot. It was also a dangerous gambit. With there being little chance of Melinda Burrows persuading Ehron Lee to stop his course of revenge while Ward was intent on keeping the two of them apart, Cora's only recourse if she was going to save the lives of these people was for her, *herself*, to try to reason with Ehron Lee.

"Always knew you had gumption, Cora," Ward said, regarding her a little more tenderly. "Always kinda admired that quality in yuh. Like a woman with some grit. But now ain't the time for any of that to be given rein. All right, let's get ourselves back indoors."

Both were inside the house when the clouds of smoke began to rise from deep within the southern cliffs of Brimstone Canyon, pressing gray against the purple cloud smudges and spreading out before dissipating along the panoramic mural.

Many years before, Chiricahua scouts had brought forth information to the tribe that miles beyond where they camped there was a cabin where some white men dwelled. Since these people did not encroach upon their sacred land where they held council and where many of their people had been buried, the Chiricahua, though warlike in nature, had let them be. A lengthy and somewhat treacherous distance separated them, and in their wisdom they recognized the consequences of such an assault to achieve so little. Yet the Chiricahua were prepared to protect their ground and had displayed their retaliation tactics when once a man had ventured too far into their territory and had been tortured and killed for his trespassing.

Now a more serious trouble had presented itself. News of the death of one of the tribe had been brought to the Chiricahua, described as an act of aggression, by the young warrior who had run a great distance on foot. Worse, the youth who had been killed was the son of one of the tribal elders. The council met briefly to discuss the matter before it was decided that the white man responsible must pay with his life for his action and retaliation must be swift and merciless. The council also judged that those who were with him, those who might dare to prevent them from seeking their justice, must not interfere or they would suffer the same fate.

TWENTY-SIX

WARD CRAWFORD WAS a cautious man. During those times when he was on the run with the law in pursuit, he had trained himself to stay awake for long hours with one finger tensed on the trigger of his Colt. Nothing much had changed. He'd formed a habit that served him well. It would come in handy on this night.

Come sunup, he would exact retribution upon Judge Harrison and Superintendent Watson. Until then, he wanted them to sweat out the night in uncertainty. By morning both would make their final decision as to which two among the four would die, and he and Ehron Lee would carry out the executions.

Ward stuffed the kerchief back into George Watson's mouth and tied the knot firmly so that the dirty fabric pressed deeply and painfully into his cheeks. The discomfort was intentional. He explained to his partner, who was watching the procedure, that he was merely taking a precaution. He stated that he wanted neither man to have the opportunity to speak before daybreak.

Ward sat himself at the far end of the kitchen table, where

he could keep watch. He wasn't about to stray too far with Melinda Burrows just several feet away in the next room. He also intended to keep awake 'til sunrise. His distrust was such that he feared if he allowed himself even a few minutes of shut-eye, Ehron Lee might use the opportunity to sneak into the bedroom to speak with his wife. Ward hadn't decided exactly what he would do in the event that should happen, but he'd come to realize in his steadily growing paranoia, hastened by Cora's questioning and the presence of Melinda Burrows, that circumstances threatened to become tenuous enough that a single misstep by Ehron Lee might edge him closer to a bullet, which would regrettably but effectively end their partnership.

As Ward sat taking periodic glances at Ehron Lee, he now debated the wisdom in his move to bring them all to the cabin. George Watson was sure enough a dead man in any case. Would it have been smarter just to have shot them all back at Border Pass? Ehron Lee would never have had to know about his wife and the marshal lying in wait. All Ward would have to tell him was that Watson had brought along a gun and Ward was forced to shoot him in self-defense. He now knew that he should have made that choice. It would have prevented the complication that Melinda Burrows's being among them possibly presented.

For the time being, all Ward could do was play his hand as the cards were dealt. Whatever might develop between now and sunrise, he intended to maintain the edge.

Ward eyed the jug of whiskey still on the table and resisted the urge to take a swig. He had a thirst but had to keep himself alert. The days had been long and he knew even a few belts would make him groggy.

Cora knew that, too. She watched Ward surreptitiously as he took this time to relax. The fatigue was evident on his features. To ward off the inroads of sleep, he constantly and deliberately swept his tobacco-stained fingers through his greasy black hair. If Cora could coax him into taking a drink, maybe two, there was little question he would soon surrender to a deep slumber. She needed only a few minutes to talk with Ehron Lee.

She reached across the table and gently pushed the jug of whiskey toward Ward. Ward watched with half interest as the jug slid across the surface, and when it was before him, he lifted pouched, tired eyes toward Cora and smiled weakly.

Cora returned the smile and gave a nudge of her head.

"Why'nt yuh go ahead," she said. "Ehron Lee and me can watch things here."

Ward looked at her dully for a few moments longer, and then he reached for the jug and started to lift it to his lips. He noticed the expectant expression Cora had on her face. And in that instant he shattered her expectations by shattering the jug against the side of the table. Ehron Lee, who sat facing the two hostages in the front room, turned suddenly. Cora's eyes widened and a lump formed in her throat.

Suddenly Ward looked *very* alert.

"'Have a drink, Ward,'" he said in a mocking voice. "'Me and Ehron Lee can watch things.'"

Ward thrust his body away from the table and withdrew his Colt from its holster in a swift, fluid movement. He aimed the revolver at Cora, held steady for an instant, then turned the black hole of the gun barrel toward his amigo, his partner-in-crime, Ehron Lee.

Ehron Lee likewise rose to his feet. He was startled by the unexpected move, but he stayed calm.

"You better watch how you're handlin' that," he cautioned.

"'Fraid my finger might slip, Burrows?" Ward returned in a taunt. "Fact is, been watchin' a lot, and I just ain't sure anymore if I can trust either of yuh."

"You're just tired," Ehron Lee said, keeping his voice level. "Been a lot for alla us. Like you said, we finish this in the morning, then we get movin'."

Ward eyed his partner skeptically. "Yuh mean nothin's changed?"

Ehron Lee appeared puzzled by the remark.

Ward clarified his point when he nudged his head toward the far bedroom, which held his partner's wife. He was sly, playing each of his moves a certain way, but his senses were attuned to even the slightest false note in Ehron Lee's manner or response.

Ehron Lee understood the gesture, and at the same time he recognized the need to pacify his partner, ease whatever doubts he had. He was careful in his reply.

"You been keepin' a level head up to now, Ward. This ain't the time to go gettin' antsy."

Ward gave a slow nod.

"Okay, Burrows, only a few hours to go," he said grimly. "Then we finish this."

Ehron Lee gave an agreeable nod, aware that Ward was carefully scrutinizing his every move.

Ward eyed him with a tight stare. "I mean we *finish* this, Burrows. 'Til then I'll be watchin' . . . and so will my pistol."

Ehron Lee nodded.

Ward motioned toward Ehron Lee's gun belt with an upward jerk of his revolver.

"And that bein' said, don't see the need for any extra gun," Ward added. "Think I'd feel a mite more trustin' if'n you'd pass me over yours."

Ehron Lee was staring into a bullet and knew he really didn't have a choice. Nor was there any point in his arguing. Handing over his gun was the last thing he wanted to do, but wordlessly, he slowly withdrew his revolver and thrust it butt-forward at Ward.

"Just takin' another precaution," Ward explained with a fierce grin.

Ehron Lee sat back in his chair. His brain racing, he found himself in a predicament, one that he had never expected to experience when he and Ward had embarked on their plan of retribution. He wanted to talk to Melinda, but he knew that even if that were possible, she would try to convince him to free the hostages, and with the situation taking the turn it had, he truthfully couldn't know if he would be able to resist her pleas. He still possessed a burning hatred toward Judge Harrison and Superintendent Watson for what he had endured at their discretion, the injustice of his conviction and imprisonment. The sadistic cruelty he had endured at Rockmound. But what had propelled him most was his belief that because of their actions he had been denied his wife. Now learning the truth, that it had been Abigail who had engineered a betrayal that not only affected him but Melinda as well, he doubted that he could bring himself to execute, or even permit the killing of, the two men.

What was worse was that innocent people would also likely die. Judging by what he now saw in Ward, he had no doubt his partner intended to kill everyone, possibly including Melinda, so that there would be no witnesses left behind. Ward was a cold killer; covering his tracks was more important to him than sparing lives. Yet he had to know that Ehron Lee would never stand by and watch him murder his wife. At that point, if there was any sense left in him, Ward Crawford had to expect there would be a showdown. Maybe he even welcomed it.

And when—*if*—it did come to that moment, Ehron Lee knew that he could turn killer.

But his Colt had been taken from him . . . he wouldn't stand a chance going up against Ward unarmed.

As the time ticked by and a tense silence engulfed the cabin, Ward fought to keep awake. He had Cora make him strong coffee, several cups of which he guzzled down as if it were fine whiskey. He kept vigilant, rarely letting his attention veer from Cora and Ehron Lee, both of whom he insisted sit with him at the table. *They* were his concern now, not his prisoners. Ward had laid Ehron Lee's gun on the table and kept a hand over it, the implication clear. He was prepared to use it if either of them tried anything funny. Cora couldn't guess what Ehron Lee was thinking, but her own thoughts were clear: She and Ehron Lee were as much Ward's prisoners as the hostages.

Ehron Lee periodically shifted his eyes toward Cora,

quick, furtive glances that she caught and interpreted. At least she hoped she was reading them correctly. The look in his eyes seemed to express to her that Ehron Lee had misgivings about what was to come, and that he needed to find some way to stop Ward before sunrise. Cora understood that if Ehron Lee was, in fact, of another mind, this change in attitude was likely due to his wife now being involved and that she was as much in danger as any of them. But no matter what the reason, regardless of her own twinges of jealousy at Melinda's presence, she was glad for it.

Ward tilted his chin upward, indicating George Watson and Judge Harrison. He returned the solemn gaze of both men.

"Look at them two," he said glumly. "Gotta wonder what's goin' through their heads, knowin' what's comin' up in just a few hours." He turned to Ehron Lee. "Sorry it won't be you what's pullin' the trigger, amigo. Reckon you are, too."

Ehron Lee simply regarded Ward with a blank expression, deliberately concealing whatever he was feeling. He wasn't sitting far from the gun that lay on the table. More than once he debated making a grab for it; Ward was tired, his eyes were heavy-lidded, and lines of fatigue showed on his face. Just maybe his reflexes would be slowed enough for Ehron Lee to snatch it from him . . .

Or just maybe Ward would shoot him dead, which meant no one had a chance.

As with the hostages, he would have to wait. Sweat out the next hours and hope for the miracle of just the right moment.

Cora's mind was working, too, and she saw what might be an opportunity. A slim chance but it was all that they had. She kept notice of Ward's exhaustion and his struggle to stay awake. Yet she knew there was no guarantee he would give in to his fatigue. In fact, it was doubtful. She'd witnessed for herself his stubbornness, even against his body's needs. When he set his mind to something, his determination was fierce, and she had never seen him as determined as he was now.

Even if he dozed, Cora feared Ward would keep one eye half open.

Cora recognized another problem. Ward Crawford was a man who lived by his instincts, and as such was never what one could call a rational man even under circumstances when his thinking was clear. With his brain fogged from fatigue and mounting suspicion, he was completely unpredictable. The slightest provocation might trigger him to act on impulse.

Her own brain worked feverishly. Ehron Lee needed to arm himself. She knew it likely would be suicide for him to make a grab for the gun lying on the table. Despite Ward's sleep-deprived appearance, it was always possible he might be feigning fatigue just to see how far they would go . . . to see if either of them might be reckless enough to attempt a move against him. He never totally trusted anyone, and Cora didn't put it past him to be much more alert than how he was coming across.

But—she knew there were other weapons kept in back outside. Hidden in a feed chest. If she could get outdoors, somehow slip a gun to Ehron Lee without Ward noticing . . .

It was a chance she decided she had to take.

"I have to go outside," she blurted out.

"Huh?" Ward said, at the same time giving his head a reviving shake.

Cora gave him a strong look and repeated, "Outside."

It took a moment for Ward to comprehend. "Out back?" Cora nodded demurely.

Ward hesitated as he regarded her skeptically.

"Well, come with me if you hafta," Cora said haughtily.

Ward's eyes slid across the table to Ehron Lee, who sat there with a look that didn't reveal anything. His expression was genuine; he had no idea what Cora was planning to do outside of the obvious.

Nor could Ward be sure she was up to anything. He had been sitting in prison during the time his outlaw companions started using the feed chest as a place to store their surplus firepower, weapons seized from their numerous raids. He knew nothing about the cache.

Still, he didn't like it. A seemingly innocent, necessary request—but his instincts made him wary.

"All right," he finally grumbled. "But make it quick."

Cora wished that Ehron Lee would again turn to look at her, but his attention was on the two hostages. She hoped that even brief eye contact between them would indicate her intention. For her plan to succeed, there had to be a silent agreement between the two. He had to be ready to accept her passing of the gun when she came back inside. The transfer had to be as smooth as silk, undetected by Ward. With Ehron Lee not knowing what she had in mind, he might not be prepared and react accordingly, thus alerting Ward that something was up.

She hesitated only seconds before rising, still hoping that Ehron Lee would shoot a glance her way. But he seemed to be preoccupied with his own thoughts, taking her request as nothing more than what it seemed.

"Well, if you're in such a hurry to go, just get it done with," Ward barked at her.

The sharpness of his voice pulled Ehron Lee away from himself and he finally cast his eyes on Cora, now lifting herself fully from her chair. She needed just that moment and she made the most of it, widening her eyes in an attempt to convey her message to Ehron Lee, hoping that he understood. But she didn't know, could not be sure, since Ehron Lee's expression betrayed nothing.

If her ruse was discovered, she and most likely Ehron Lee would be shot dead. But she realized there was every chance of that happening in any case, and so she decided to carry on with her plan. The gun would have to be concealed, however, and with her clothing consisting of jeans and a flannel shirt, there was no way she could sneak the gun in without Ward noticing. She walked over to grab her poncho off the wall peg. She tried not to be obvious as she fitted the garment over herself.

Ward was watching her . . . and so was Ehron Lee. There

looked to be the response she'd been hoping for, though subtle, in his expression. The slightest nod he passed to her confirmed it, and Cora felt a sudden surge of confidence.

"Seems like you're bundlin' yourself purty good just to mosey outside to do your business," Ward said.

His remark, which again relayed his misgivings, caught Cora off guard, but she recovered smoothly.

"Might have to walk a bit, and it's gettin' colder," she replied.

Ward hesitated before he nodded. "All right. But get it done quick and get back inside."

Cora left the cabin. Ehron Lee now believed he had figured out her real intention. He couldn't know her specific plan but suspected she had something up her sleeve and that he had to be ready for whatever that was. He decided to hopefully heighten their advantage and regain Ward's confidence by casting his own doubt upon Cora.

"Yuh trust her?" he asked Ward.

Ward's face registered a curious look.

"That ain't somethin' I expect to hear from you, Burrows," he said.

"Maybe I got more at stake than I expected," Ehron said. "Maybe 'cause of that, you got reason not to trust me . . ." He thrust a thumb toward George Watson and Judge Harrison. "But I got no love for them two."

Ward spit on the floor and said with a sneer, "It ain't them two vultures that concern me. We know what's gonna happen to them. It's them others . . . yeah, and that includes your wife, Burrows."

Ehron Lee had to speak the hardest words he'd ever had to say—and make them sound convincing.

"She was dead to me a long time ago. That aside, she's got no business bein' here."

"Yeah, well, she is," Ward said strategically.

"Yeah, she is," Ehron Lee acknowledged straightly.

Ward listened to how he spoke his words—the inflection in his voice sounded genuine. But they did little to lessen Ward's suspicions. After all, they were only words. He wasn't so numbed by sleeplessness not to recognize that what Ehron Lee said and what he really felt were not necessarily the same and possibly his words were simply a ploy to get Ward to lower his guard.

"Might be best if'n yuh prove it," Ward said cagily.

Ehron Lee suffered a sick feeling in his gut. He knew what Ward was aiming at. He understood what was expected of him. What Ward was offering was all or nothing.

Ward regarded him broodingly. "Can't be leavin' behind no witnesses, Burrows. If you're still really in with me, if'n we ride out together . . . I'll give yuh a chance."

"A chance?"

Ward's cold, hard eyes burrowed into him. "Yeah. Once I take care of these others, I'll give yuh back your gun—and save yuh one bullet."

Ehron Lee fought back a heavy swallow. "For my wife."

The thin line of a smile traced across Ward's lips. "We both know she ain't no longer your wife."

Ehron Lee didn't answer.

"'Fact, I reckon she's cozied up with that lawman in there," Ward added, veering his eyes sideways, indicating the bedroom.

Ehron Lee knew that Ward was trying to get a reaction out of him. But as tough as it might be, he wasn't going to oblige. He kept himself calm and steady. Possibly there might even be some truth to what Ward was saying; Ehron Lee noticed how the marshal had held Melinda close when they were brought into the cabin. On top of that, a lot of lost years had passed between him and his wife—Ehron Lee believing her dead, Melinda falling prey to her sister's machinations and thinking that he wanted her out of his life. Neither was to blame, of course, nor could Ehron Lee truthfully believe there could be a rekindling of the same love that once had existed between them. A cruel quirk in destiny had decided otherwise. Whether Buck Leighton was "cozying" up to Melinda really seemed unimportant now.

"So I figger you see there ain't nothin' really stoppin' yuh from what's gotta be done," Ward said.

He'd spoken his words openly and loud enough so that George Watson and Judge Harrison heard. They turned their faces to each other and shared a quick glance. Harrison's eyes were wide with fear; Watson's gaze remained steady and controlled. Both understood that not only were they to be murdered come sunup, but their wife and daughter, respectively, were to share the same fate at Ward Crawford's discretion. Perhaps both should have guessed the outcome, but when presented with the ransom, neither could afford to take the chance to search beyond the obvious. When it came to family or loved ones, emotion took precedence over reason. Although both were men hardened by the demands of their profession, each had forgone rational thinking and succumbed to sentiment. This had become especially true for Judge Harrison, a belated realization that affected him powerfully in what were to be his last hours.

Harrison was a man seized in the grip of terror so overwhelming that he was virtually numb in his comprehension. George Watson had kept himself composed enough to know there was a chance at hope. He had listened to the conversations taking place at the table. His keen eye had picked up the subtle signals between the girl Cora and former inmate Ehron Lee. He understood that this mute exchange between the two, whatever it indicated, might be their only salvation.

Meanwhile, Cora rummaged through the feed box out back of the house, going about her work quietly and stealthily. Yes, weapons were stashed there, yet she couldn't know whether any had been equipped with ammunition. The few rifles and the eight-gauge she pushed aside were of no value. She had to find a handgun, something that she could fit under her heavy poncho to smuggle inside. She struggled to keep her hands from trembling. She was rushed, knowing that she had to act quickly and working under darkness with no light to guide her, relying only on her fingers to fall upon a weapon that would be of use: a weapon that she prayed would be loaded with cartridges.

It had been too long. Ward's suspicions would grow to

where he would be sure to check her person when she came back inside. She cursed under her breath. She was unable to lay her hands upon a pistol. The boys' raids had yielded only heavier firepower . . . of absolutely no use to her.

There was no point in seeking any further. Cora heaved a breath, held back her tears, and made her way back inside the cabin, composing herself so as to appear totally natural. At the same time she would have to express in some unobtrusive manner her failure to Ehron Lee. With a sinking heart, she knew it now would have to be up to him . . . and it was clear that with Ward's doubts focused on him, Ehron Lee's position was more tenuous than her own. His risk would be greater.

Ward watched her carefully as she walked into the kitchen, his dull, tired eyes lifting and lowering. Since she had nothing to hide, Cora slid out of her poncho and tossed it aside onto a chair.

Ward checked her over again, searching. There seemed to be nothing out of place and he looked satisfied. Ehron Lee tossed a deliberately harmless glance her way. He could see immediately that she had not succeeded in whatever her plan. The expression on her face was vacant yet at the same time telling.

TWENTY-SEVEN

THE LONG NIGHT seemed to wear on endlessly. But eventually, inevitably, the first signs of a gold-tinged sunrise appeared on the eastern horizon, the tendrils of daylight stretching across the vast landscape, cresting the mountain peaks and hilly rises and finally spilling over into the valley.

Locked inside a windowless bedroom in which neither could know the hour or be aware of the approach of sunup, Buck Leighton and Melinda Burrows could only sit out their time and wait for the moment when either Ward Crawford or Ehron Lee would come to get them.

Buck had been awake throughout the night. Not only was he positioned uncomfortably, handcuffed to the bedpost, but his mind wouldn't relax. Melinda had given in to physical and emotional exhaustion and dozed periodically, resting her head on Buck's lap—only to snap awake at intervals with a sudden gasp. Buck was sympathetic to the trepidation in Melinda but still believed their one hope was for her to confess to Ehron Lee that he had a son. No one could guess the man's reaction, that was true, but even if there was the slimmest possibility that learning this truth might stimulate some compassion or reason in the man, Buck saw it as a chance worth taking.

"Won't be long now, Melinda," Buck said to her gently. He didn't want to heighten her fear, only express again the desperate nature of their situation.

"You think it's morning?" she asked tentatively.

Ward rocked his head. "Least pretty close to it."

"Had horrible dreams," Melinda confessed. "Every time I closed my eyes . . ."

Ward gave his head an understanding nod.

Melinda's eyebrows constricted and she said with a heavy exhale, "Wish there was just some way I could get those cuffs offa you."

Buck smiled wanly. "Wouldn't do no good even if yuh could. We could never get past 'em."

Melinda then redirected her focus and gazed steadily at the bedroom door, with such intent it was as if she were trying by sheer will to penetrate its sealed boundary.

"What d'yuh think they're doing in there?" she asked apprehensively.

"I figger just what us and them others are doin'. Waitin'."

"Waitin' . . . to die," Melinda breathed.

"We still have that one chance," Buck told her outright. "I know it ain't much, but seein' that the way things stand we're all gonna die anyway, I'd urge yuh to come clean with Ehron Lee—'bout your son."

Melinda's expression took on a vague look of disappointment, and when the words came, her voice was low.

"I—thought I might," she admitted. "If'n he'd come into the room tonight."

"That weren't likely. Not with Crawford watchin' over things. Last thing he wants is for you two to spend any time together."

"Then how am I supposed to—" Melinda started to say.

Buck spoke bluntly. "Only one way, as things look. You gotta just tell him. Even if it's in front of Crawford, as it'll most likely have to be."

Melinda breathed in deeply as she considered what Buck

was telling her. She had been hoping for a different outcome. She had wished that Ehron Lee would come in to speak with her at some point during the night. If they just could have spoken, maybe she could have got him on their side, convinced him to help these people. Help *himself.*

But he hadn't. Perhaps because of what Buck had suggested about Ward Crawford wanting to keep them apart . . . or what was even more disturbing to her, that Ehron Lee just didn't see the need. Either because his feelings toward her *had* changed . . . or was it his seeing her and Buck together and coming to his own conclusion?

If any of them stood even the slightest chance, Melinda knew that she would have to go along with what Buck was suggesting.

She decided: She would tell Ehron Lee about their son.

Finally she looked into Buck's eyes and nodded.

Sunlight filtered through the thin, tattered curtains in the front room. With purple-pouched eyes, Ward gazed into the muted glow. Then, revolver in hand, he pushed back in his chair and focused his attention on his two hostages. He began rolling the barrel of his gun along his forearm, slowly and repetitiously, taunting with malicious intent, grinning as he did so.

"I want them women out here," he said to Cora. "But bring 'em out one at a time." He narrowed his eyes and looked hard and mean at Judge Harrison. "Startin' with the judge's daughter."

In a futile effort, Harrison began to struggle against the rawhide that bound him to the chair. He emitted desperate if muffled sounds through the kerchief wrapped around his mouth. He understood that he was a dead man and had almost come to accept that. What he feared was that Ward Crawford was bringing out his daughter so that she could watch him be murdered.

Ehron Lee, too, thought that was Ward's intent. He spoke up. "That ain't the way to do this, Ward."

Ward slowly turned his face toward his partner, barely keeping his head from lolling. The Colt revolver pivoted with him, its aim landing lazily on Ehron Lee.

"Don't give a damn if'n yuh kill 'em," Ehron Lee went on. "But no need for the women to hafta watch while yuh do it."

Ward wore an amused expression. "What difference does it make? They'll all be together soon 'nuff."

Cora stayed put in her chair, her eyes flashing back and forth between the two men, absorbing the tension that once more permeated the room.

"I don't want either of them two to die easy," Ward said tautly.

Ehron Lee's voice was as firm as the expression he held. "Not that way."

"From where I sit, you ain't got much say," Ward said, his mouth twisted in a humorless lopsided grin.

Abruptly his expression changed. He glared at Cora, a virulent look in his eyes.

"Yuh heard what I told yuh," he said in a snarl.

Cora didn't budge. Mustering her courage, she met Ward's intimidating stare with her own look of defiance.

Ward's glare became more intense, as did the tone in his voice.

"Goin' ag'in me, Cora? Wouldn't advise it."

"If you're going to kill those men, leave the women outta it," Cora said back. "The young one . . . she's just a girl."

Ward kept his eyes steady on her, not noticing that Ehron Lee was very slowly and subtly starting to lift himself from his chair.

But Cora noticed as her eyes flickered toward him, and she knew she had to coax Ward's attention away from him.

"You was never that kinda man, Ward," she continued, speaking compassionately. "You done things yuh hadda, done a lotta wrong, too; you never made excuses for that. But I never knew you to be cruel. Maybe yuh got a right to kill them two. Yuh feel they wronged you. But neither of them women did you any harm."

Cora watched as the hardness of Ward's features began to subtly diminish as he seemed to absorb her words, and she hoped against hope that Ehron Lee could move fast enough to attempt his maneuver.

Then—Ward caught her eyes shifting, curiously, toward Ehron Lee. Instinctively his reflexes tensed, but it was too late. In the next instant he was tackled, his body flung to the hardness of the wood floor. Ehron Lee had taken advantage of that brief distraction to make the move he'd anticipated and he fought with all of his strength to overpower Ward. But for a man weakened by fatigue, Ward's own strength proved formidable. He clutched tightly at Ehron Lee's shoulders, holding his attacker back until he freed his left hand and slammed a fist into the side of Ehron Lee's face, briefly stunning him but not with enough force to knock him free from his straddle. Ehron Lee recovered swiftly and grabbed Ward's wrists, struggling to pin them against the floor. Ward then jerked his body in an upward motion and both men toppled onto their side, kicking and throwing punches as they wrestled against each other to gain the upper hand.

Ehron Lee had underestimated Ward's brutal strength, and he knew he couldn't hold him much longer.

"The gun, Cora!" he shouted.

Cora moved in as soon as she was able to try and retrieve the revolver, which had been knocked from Ward's hand and was lying close to where the men were grappling. Ward saw what she was aiming to do and tried to break free to reach for the weapon first. Ehron Lee struggled to prevent Ward from going for the other gun that still rested in his holster.

Cora took advantage of a quick, clear moment during the fight to bend over and scoop up the Colt. She held the gun firmly in her grip as she started to straighten her posture. Ward grimaced but saw his own advantage and kicked out his leg with a savage thrust, the sole of his boot connecting with Cora's chin before she could fully rise to her feet, snapping her head backward and knocking her out cold. Cora lay sprawled on the floor, arms and legs outstretched, the

Colt revolver thrown from her hand and now lying just feet from where Judge Harrison and George Watson sat in the front room. Either could have made a grab for the gun had he been able. But both were bound securely to their chairs and all they could do was stare helplessly at the weapon.

Yet no one could have counted on the commotion prompting Janette Watson to react. At first she edged carefully from the bedroom, followed by Evaline, and upon witnessing the chaotic situation, she dared a desperate move. Catching her sudden presence, Judge Harrison gestured with frantic eyes to the gun not far from his feet. Janette hurried over, seized the revolver with both hands, and cocked the hammer. The barrel was aimed directly at the tangle that was Ehron Lee and Ward. Janette's eyes were wide and determined, expressing an intent that both men could recognize.

"Get to your feet, both of you," she commanded harshly, taking careful steps backward. "And don't neither of you try anything or I swear to God Almighty I'll shoot."

Ehron Lee and Ward loosened themselves from each other's grip and complied, slowly lifting to their feet with hands steadily rising upward.

"Evaline, get the men untied," Janette next instructed. "Hurry!"

Wordlessly, Evaline hastened over to her father and started to fiddle with the rawhide knots tied in back of the chair.

Janette glanced down briefly at Cora's unconscious form and jabbed at her ribs with her shoe in an attempt to revive her. There was no response. Cora wasn't dead, she was breathing as her chest steadily rose and fell, but she could be hurt bad.

Ward wiped some blood from his face, smearing a crimson residue across his whiskered cheek. He appeared unaffected by the unexpected turn of events.

"Sure didn't see this comin'," he said with a characteristic grin.

Janette looked nervous but resolute. She brandished the

Colt awkwardly; her hands were unsteady. It was obvious that she'd never held a gun before. Her concern was that Evaline seemed to be having a difficult time undoing the knots that bound her father to the chair.

"If'n you was smart, you'd let loose the lawman," Ward suggested. He gestured with his eyes toward the second bedroom.

Janette kept her gaze steady on the two men.

Ward sucked a tooth. He maintained an indifferent demeanor.

"Keys are in my pocket," he said.

"Reach for 'em," Janette said. "But do it slow and toss 'em over here."

"I can't get these ropes untied," Evaline suddenly blurted out in frustration.

Janette turned her eyes to the girl. Just for an instant.

Just long enough for Ward Crawford to withdraw with a trained flourish the Colt from his holster.

The barrel of which was aimed at her by the time Janette returned her attention to the two outlaws.

The movement was so swift no one could have seen it coming—or reacted in time to prevent it. Janette Watson had only that one second to connect with her own mortality. For in the next moment Ward tugged on the trigger of the six-shooter and all in the room watched as Janette's eyes slid down towards the blood that blossomed between her breasts. She dropped to her knees and rolled onto her side, her eyes glazed as she died.

Evaline screamed. George Watson's eyes bugged from their sockets. Ward once again had taken charge, confirming his authority with outright murder. He surveyed the situation: Janette lying dead, Cora unconscious with a small trickle of blood forming at the corner of her slightly parted lips. And Ehron Lee was standing powerless to attempt another move against his armed partner.

"Reckon that's what yuh call a wasted effort," Ward said to everyone. He then addressed George Watson specifically.

"Your missus was a brave woman, Superintendent. But she shoulda had me drop my belt 'fore she played it like the cavalry."

Ehron Lee regarded Ward with a look of contempt.

"Tricksters," Ward said sourly. He cast his eyes down toward the motionless Cora. He gave her body a gentle kick with his boot heel. "Yeah, and you almost had me with your fancy talk."

"She meant what she said, Ward," Ehron Lee told him sturdily.

Ward spoke out the side of his mouth. "Sure. Sure she did. And look at her now, stretched out on the floor."

In the bedroom Buck and Melinda had listened to the struggle between Ward and Ehron Lee. Then they heard the gunshot. Melinda had cringed at the report and tensed upon hearing Evaline's piercing scream, and her face fell. Buck looked at her but didn't know what to say. Whatever had gone on in the front room did not sound encouraging. Someone had died, and whoever that person was, Buck was certain it was not Ward Crawford.

He didn't want for any of the hostages to be dead, but he desperately hoped that it wasn't Ehron Lee who'd caught the bullet. Although the odds were still stacked against them, with Ehron Lee dead, all bets were off.

Buck could read Melinda's expression. She feared it *had* been her husband who'd been killed. Buck did not want to consider that as the outcome . . . but he had to concede there was a strong likelihood. Two men had been fighting, followed by a gunshot. Some conversation had been heard by both but what was said and by whom could not be discerned by either behind the closed door of the bedroom. The talk had been muffled.

Ward ordered Ehron Lee to remove the gags from Harrison and Watson. Immediately Watson launched into a tirade against his wife's murderer. Ward looked pleased as Watson spit out curses, and swore to somehow get even. The brutal action had triggered a rage of emotion from the man who for many years Ward had perceived as a cruel if dispassionate tormentor.

Judge Harrison just looked numb. He barely acknowledged his daughter as she wrapped her arms around him in a tearful embrace.

Ehron Lee stood with them in the front room, though off to the side, where Ward, standing alone in the kitchen, could keep watch on them all. He wasn't about to lose his advantage a second time.

He spoke to Harrison. "So tell me, Judge, which one of yuh is it gonna be?"

Harrison swallowed past the lump in his throat. "You know the answer."

Evaline's eyes widened. She turned to Ward and pleaded, "Please, he's my daddy. Please don't kill him. *Please . . .*"

Ward's face took on a look of mocking sympathy as his eyes veered toward Ehron Lee.

"Touchin', ain't it, Burrows, the way she cares for her skunk of an old man," he said. "Too bad she couldn'ta been with us at Rockmound, huh?" Then he looked firmly at the girl and responded to her desperate plea with a slow shake of his head.

"Your *daddy* made his choice, little girl," Ward said in derision. "Now best you move yourself outta the way lessun you wanta join him in the hereafter."

But Evaline wouldn't budge. As she knelt before her father, she shielded his body with her own, hugging him as tightly as she could while she sobbed.

Harrison gazed down sorrowfully at the daughter he for so many years had neglected. He wished his hands were free so that he could touch her, take her hand in his—to finally, in some way, express to Evaline the affection she had yearned for. He felt despondent, regretful at never returning the love she had for him. A love she was now demonstrating by offering to give up her own life to protect him.

It was a love he had not earned. Nor a sacrifice that he deserved.

"Y-You do what he says, Evaline," Harrison urged gently. "Go on."

Ehron Lee spoke up. "Only a rat would shoot a girl in the back."

"You keep forgettin'—*amigo*—you ain't got no say in this anymore," Ward reminded him darkly.

Evaline still wouldn't move. Harrison looked desperate. He had no doubt Ward Crawford was crazed and determined enough to put a bullet in his daughter's back to get at him.

It was then, with a sudden surge of strength driven by adrenaline, that he thrust his body upward to a standing position, pulling the chair with him, thrusting Evaline aside as he did so . . . and he faced Ward defiantly.

"Do it!" Harrison demanded. "Now!"

"Daddy, no!" Evaline shrieked.

She averted her eyes at the last second for she knew there would be no mercy from the man called Ward. She heard the single shot, then the thud of the body and the crack of the wooden chair as both crashed to the floor.

Then silence, the wall clock ticking . . .

"Snake-bellied sonofabitch," Watson at last muttered.

Evaline became hysterical. She had a naturally pale complexion but now her coloring was white enough to remind Ehron Lee of his old cell mate Woody Milo. He watched as the girl crawled pathetically on her hands and knees to where her father lay.

"Look at him, Burrows," Ward said with a perverse delight. "Gotta make yuh feel good, after all these years, finally seein' the man that took away your life lyin' dead."

But Ehron Lee felt nothing. Absolutely nothing. No satisfaction, no sense of justice. With all that had happened in just these several minutes, the hatred that had corroded his body and soul for so many years ceased to exist. Yet neither could he truthfully say he felt compassion for the girl crying as she cradled her dead father's head. By witnessing these two senseless acts of violence, by his being instrumental in their happening . . . Ehron Lee had become little more than the shell of a human being.

Ward, however, was near giddy over his accomplishment. "Yeah, look at him now. Buzzard meat. How many lives did his decisions wipe away? And all it took was a single bullet to end his."

In the next room, the second gunshot prompted Buck to impulsively start to tug hard and repeatedly on the handcuffs that locked his wrist to the bedpost. It was a futile gesture and Buck knew his attempt at breaking loose was in vain, but he was both humiliated and frustrated in his helplessness and had to do something. He looked desperately at Melinda.

"I'd risk losin' my hand if'n it would get me free," he said.

It was heroic talk but Melinda knew his words weren't mere bravado. She noticed how his efforts had been so determined that his wrist had begun to bleed against the hard metal.

"That ain't gonna do any good," she scolded him, grabbing his forearm and attempting to brace his struggle. "You're just hurting yourself."

Buck ceased his effort and a flicker of embarrassment crossed his face, as if a man of his position should not surrender to such a frantic display of desperation. Melinda sympathized with his situation. She so understood that, in her own anxiety, had she the proper tool at her disposal, she believed she would have willingly cut off his hand to free him.

"I—I just can't sit here while people out there are bein' shot," Buck said through clenched teeth.

"There ain't nothin' you can do," Melinda said, forcing herself to speak reasonably.

She was right, of course, but her words provided Buck with scant consolation. He was a government-appointed lawman, and as each shot rang out, he felt he was failing in his duty.

Buck looked at Melinda remorsefully.

"Your son's already lost a father," he said. "Now because of me . . ." He couldn't finish.

Melinda understood. She lowered her eyes and took Buck's free hand in hers, massaging his wrist affectionately.

"I made the choice to come," she said softly. "Whatever happens . . . don't be blamin' yourself."

Buck managed an awkward smile. "Wish I could accept it that easy."

Melinda looked steadily at the marshal before she drew in and let loose a breath.

"Before he became what he is now, Ehron Lee was the best man I ever knew," she said. "But he changed and he ain't that man no more. Leastwise I suspect he ain't, not from what I seen of him. But you been a good, a decent man from the first time I met yuh, Buck Leighton. You meant good for us all 'round."

Buck appreciated Melinda saying those words. She spoke with sincerity though it did little to lessen the guilt he felt. He still believed that he had somehow acted carelessly, and that it was through negligence on his part that he had brought them both to this critical moment.

Buck sighed. "When that door opens, you might as well know that whoever's there won't be takin' no chance to release me."

Melinda didn't say anything. She realized that what he was saying was likely true.

"The killin's started and they won't be lettin' no lawman go," Buck concluded.

Melinda summoned her optimism and spoke with a forced confidence. "'Less it's Ehron Lee, and I can tell him . . . 'bout our son."

Buck hesitated. Telling white lines framed his lips, and he responded with a short nod. He could not bring himself to tell Melinda, though by now she probably understood, that with each passing moment their hope of surviving this ordeal was fading.

There followed an ominous quiet, and they both waited apprehensively.

* * *

"The stink that coyote wore when alive ain't gonna improve now that he's dead," Ward said as he coldly observed the body of the murdered judge. "Get that carcass outta here 'fore it starts a-molderin' and really smells up the place," he snarled at Ehron Lee, emphasizing his command with his revolver.

The young girl, Evaline, was tightly embracing her father's corpse, oblivious to Ward's cruel words. The eyelids were partly open, but though her fingertips gently touched them, she couldn't quite bring herself to shut her father's eyes, for that gesture meant forever and she was in denial of finality.

Ehron Lee kept his expression emotionless as he stepped over to Evaline and, at first, tried to gently urge the girl away from the body. She resisted, and in frustration, Ehron Lee finally took her with both hands by the shoulders and lifted her aside. She cried, screamed, and struggled, and even attempted to scramble back over once she was pulled free, but Ehron Lee met her with a threatening glare and she froze in position, recognizing the killer instinct reflected in his eyes. She timidly started to back away.

"Don't take him too far, Burrows," Ward said cautiously. "Just dump him out back. And get back in here quick."

With Ward's gun trained on him and the doubtless knowledge that another pull on the trigger meant nothing to the man, Ehron Lee proceeded to do as instructed, though he obeyed with neither a word nor a gesture of acknowledgment.

"Oh, and Burrows," Ward said, casting a squinting eye toward George Watson, then shifting his spiteful gaze to the body of the superintendent's wife. "When you come back, get rid of this, too." He spoke specifically to Watson. "The buzzards can have 'em both. We'll be long gone by then."

"I'll live to see you burn in hell, Crawford," Watson said irately, his voice tremulous with hate, no longer concealing his rage.

"Ain't expectin' nothin' less," Ward returned in an unruffled tone. "Only 'fore that time comes, Superintendent, it'll be *you* what's waitin' for me."

Desperately, Watson turned his focus and vented his fury on Ehron Lee.

"What are you doin' with this madman, Burrows?" he demanded. "You're not of his kind."

Ehron Lee halted. He twisted his head and looked at Watson contemplatively before his expression darkened, his head pumped full of blood. The reminder of why all this had to happen consumed him like the blaze of a fire reignited.

"No . . . I wasn't," he said, issuing his words with a series of heaving breaths. "Not until you . . . you and the judge here made me this way. And for however long you got left to live, you remember that. Carry it with you to your grave."

Ward looked pleased, if still somewhat uncertain, at his partner's apparent return to form. The man of prison-bred fury he had known and watched fester in his own private hell behind the walls of Rockmound.

"We followed rules, Burrows," Watson said, his voice reasonable, adopting his professional tone. "Rules set by law."

Ehron Lee's eyes widened and were glazed with contempt.

"Set by law!" he challenged. "You treated us like vermin, you sonofabitch. Beat us, starved us, worked us worse than dogs. Then yuh took away our privileges. Rules? Them was rules set by you. Your *own* law, *Superintendent* Watson."

"That's the talk, Burrows," Ward said with a vigorous nod of his head.

Ehron Lee's mounting rage was mirrored by the restlessness of his physical action. He appeared so overwhelmed by the heated words he spewed that, as if propelled by a force outside himself, he edged away from the door, near which he had dragged the judge's body, and inched closer toward Ward, who was observing and admiring his partner's vindictive tirade.

Ehron Lee spun around toward Ward.

"Gimme the gun, Ward," he implored. "After what that scum did to me, this one's mine. Gimme the gun!"

Ward eyed Ehron Lee uncertainly. He liked what he was witnessing, but his instincts were still in doubt as to Ehron Lee's sincerity. Then, at that moment—in that quick second when Ward was debating his trust in his partner—Ehron Lee made his own decision.

Positioned close to Ward, he seized his opportunity, taking advantage of Ward's weakening defenses. Ehron Lee swung around, drew back his fist, and delivered a swift, hard punch to Ward's jaw. Ward's legs buckled and he dropped to the floor, on his knees with his head bowed, dazed and semiconscious, and Ehron Lee swooped down and quickly grabbed the gun from the loosened fingers. Then he glanced up at the dumbstruck George Watson.

He spoke a stony reminder. "Don't think I didn't mean any of what I said."

Watson was stunned by Ehron Lee's sudden, decisive move and could not respond beyond offering a vacuous nod.

Ehron Lee knelt down and reached into Ward's pocket, searching for the keys to unlock the handcuffs confining Buck Leighton. Ward was moaning, still groggy and helpless. Ehron Lee took the keys and stepped quickly to the bedroom, where his wife and the marshal were held. He found himself pausing for a moment before he twisted the latch and pushed open the door. Once he did and was standing in the threshold, he allowed himself his first thorough look at Melinda, then he gazed into her startled, fearful, yet somewhat expectant eyes. The look they exchanged lasted only seconds and the connection was empty, seeming to forever solidify the separation that had come between them. Neither spoke; Ehron Lee just tossed the keys at her before he turned and walked back into the front room.

"Crawford's a mad dog, Burrows," Watson said. "He won't be taken in alive, will fight you every step of the way, and there's no point in you lettin' him do so."

"Talkin' your law ag'in, Watson?" Ehron Lee said acidly. "Y'still ain't got much to back it up with."

Watson regarded the bindings that kept him helpless.

"I have no call to make decisions for you," he conceded with a sigh.

Ehron Lee glared at him. "That's right. You don't."

Still, Watson responded to the moment and drew in a hopeful breath.

He said, "All I can say is this, if you're willin' to listen. I saw what went on here. I know you didn't kill anyone." He turned his head toward the stricken Evaline. "Know as well as this girl that you turned ag'in Crawford to help us. Make the right choice now and I'm willin' to stand by my word."

Ehron Lee discharged an ironic laugh. "That kinda guarantee means nothin' to me. 'Cause the way I see it, I got either prison or the hangman in my future."

"I'll back up his word, Burrows," Buck Leighton said. He was standing in the hallway, massaging his hurt and bloodied wrist. Gradually a tentative Melinda followed him out of the room.

Ehron Lee shook his head. "People are dead 'cause of me. I ain't gonna just walk away."

Melinda broke in sharply. "Then ride outta here, Ehron Lee."

His attention resting on his wife with eyes that were cold yet sad, Ehron Lee did not see the subtle maneuver of Ward, who, though feigning his posture, had regained his senses and whose hand was sliding toward his boot . . . withdrawing a small, sharp-edged knife, which, at the precise moment, he thrust into the back of Ehron Lee's leg, slicing into an artery and drawing downward.

Ehron Lee barely suppressed a cry of anguish, but he grimaced and blanched and his body jerked reflexively as the blade continued to dig deeper into his flesh and now twisted against bone.

A grinning, yellow-toothed Ward started to his feet. He moved with as much agility as he was able, but Ehron Lee, despite the searing pain and his starting to lose his balance, managed to twist his body around, gun still lifted, the barrel of which came within nearly an inch of Ward's head.

Their eyes locked and each displayed a different emotion: Ward's coal black eyes were wide and apprehensive, yet expressing a subtle doubt that his partner would actually carry through with his action; Ehron Lee's blue eyes were narrowed and, at that moment, confident . . . and it was Ehron Lee who made the only decision still left open to him.

He pulled the trigger.

Ward Crawford's skull exploded as the bullet penetrated at close range. The outlaw toppled backward, stone dead. His expression registered the same look of shock and disbelief that had appeared on the faces of many of the people he had killed.

Another killing. Evaline Watson screamed—before her expression seemed to grow dull.

After seconds had passed, Ehron Lee let the gun drop numbly to his side. Only then did he raise his eyes back to Melinda. At the same time Cora started to stir from her unconsciousness. Her eyelids fluttered, opened blearily, but she didn't immediately move from her supine position on the floor. Her tongue traced along her mouth and she instantly tasted blood. She raised an outstretched arm and wiped the back of her hand along the corner of her lips where the blood had started to congeal. When she recovered sufficiently, she half rose on an elbow, glanced over at Ehron Lee, who was down on one knee, and slid herself over toward him. Cora noticed the gaping wound at the back of his leg, which was spreading a pool of blood down from inside his trousers onto the floor.

She hastened to help, briefly halting when she caught sight of Ward's lifeless body lying not far from her. Her mouth moved without any words coming out. Ward was beyond help, and she pulled herself together and once more displayed an obvious and troubled concern for Ehron Lee's injury, which was immediately noticed by Melinda, who responded by unconsciously tightening her grip on Buck's forearm.

Ehron Lee tried to discourage Cora's attention by getting himself onto his feet.

"Don't worry none 'bout me," he said sternly. "Get some sheets from the bedroom and cover up them bodies."

Cora gazed numbly at the corpses of Janette Watson and Judge Harrison.

"Ward killed 'em," Ehron Lee told her. "Weren't nothin' I could do."

Cora felt sick to her stomach as her eyes shifted from the two bodies to a traumatized Evaline and a distressed-looking George Watson. Realizing that it was cruel to leave the bodies of their loved ones exposed as they were, she hastened to do as Ehron Lee instructed.

In the meantime Ehron Lee kept his gun leveled on Buck.

"Your call now, Burrows," Buck said, calm and unthreatened.

With a painful effort Ehron Lee took a few steps back, maintaining his advantage, before he focused on George Watson. His expression was intense and hinted gravely at what his next move might be. It was understood by all that Ehron Lee might want to close accounts and pay off the obligation he felt he still owed himself. Judge Harrison was dead. Watson was the last one left. What difference would it make to the situation if Ehron Lee wiped the slate clean? Debt paid in full. Nothing worse could happen to him.

Melinda stared at her husband with an expression of dread. She knew precisely what was going through his mind.

Ehron Lee's eyes slowly veered back and forth between Melinda and Watson. The ensuing seconds were tense and uncertain.

Finally, the severity stamped upon Ehron Lee's features dissolved into a look that suggested defeat. Although he still gripped the revolver aggressively, he popped a breath as he dropped himself onto a kitchen chair.

"What's the point," he muttered, punctuating his comment with another heavy exhale. With a jerk of his head, he gestured for either Buck or Melinda to release Superintendent Watson. It was Buck who complied.

Cora came back into the front room with coverings pulled from the beds. She had heard Ehron Lee's words, saw his expression, and her face flushed with relief. After she gingerly laid sheets over the bodies of the dead woman and the judge, she hastened to fetch some cloth with which to fashion a bandage for Ehron Lee's leg.

As Buck struggled with untying the rawhide ropes that bound Watson, he spoke to Ehron Lee.

"It ain't too late, Burrows," he said.

Ehron Lee focused on Melinda, a faint smile creeping over his lips. Melinda's own smile twisted into a look of concern as she noticed the amount of blood draining from his wound. She started to step forward to assist Cora.

"No, you keep back," Ehron Lee said quietly to her. Then he spoke to Cora. "It—it's better to leave it this way."

Cora responded abruptly and incredulously.

"You can't wanta die," she said as she knelt beside Ehron Lee and carefully prepared to bandage his leg. She grimaced as she examined the extent of his injury. The knife wound was long and deep and bleeding profusely; she didn't know how much she could do.

Ehron Lee smiled weakly. "Ain't my dyin' so much. Just don't wanta see Melinda dirtyin' her hands on my blood."

Melinda looked hurt and offended by Ehron Lee's remark. Yet in a strange way she understood—understood why she was held back while this girl Cora was allowed to do whatever she could to tend to Ehron Lee's wound.

Ehron Lee looked down at Cora while she worked on attempting to stanch the bleeding and said nothing.

It was then that Melinda finally spoke what she had avoided saying—words that, whatever their significance now, she could no longer withhold from him.

"You have a son, Ehron Lee. *We* have a son. A fine boy." Her voice became apologetic. "I—should have told you sooner."

Surprisingly, Ehron Lee didn't much react beyond a slight lowering of his head. And then, for just a moment, he weakened.

"A son," he murmured . . . before his hardness returned. "He never knew me. Better now if he doesn't."

Melinda looked pained, confused, at what she perceived as Ehron Lee's harsh attitude.

She quickly offered, "I named him Charlie. The name we planned if'n it was a boy."

"He's got a right to know his father, Burrows," Buck put in. "To know that whatever else went wrong, that you, his pa, risked your life to save ours."

"Damn heroics," Ehron Lee scoffed.

"You can't ignore what yuh done," Buck countered.

Ehron Lee didn't want to hear any sanctified justification for what he'd felt he had to do. The way he saw it, there was no bravery involved; he was as much concerned with saving his own skin.

Once he saw that George Watson was untied, he said hastily, "Go on. All of yuh, just git." Then he looked with compassion at Cora. "You, too, Cora. You was never really involved in this." Finally, he regarded Buck with a determined expression. "You hear me, Marshal? If you owe me anything, you promise me that Cora here won't be punished."

Buck hesitated and he responded with a frown. He was a lawman, took his job seriously, and had a duty to perform.

Ehron Lee noticed his reticence.

"I want your word," Ehron Lee demanded, once again raising his gun to amplify his point.

Buck ignored the threat; it was a hollow gesture and Ehron Lee knew it. Instead he briefly glanced at the girl and finally nodded. "You have my word."

Cora grabbed on to Ehron Lee's uninjured leg. "I ain't leavin' you."

Ehron Lee looked ready to scold her before he responded with a benign smile. "There ain't no sense in that," he said.

She shook her head determinedly. "I'm stayin'. If you're stayin' behind, so am I."

Ehron Lee hadn't the strength to argue. He felt himself growing weak, becoming light-headed and steadily losing his focus. But he did look across at Melinda, then struggled to release his eyes from her before he nodded in halfhearted acknowledgment of Cora's stubbornness.

"I told yuh all to get outta here!" he repeated emphatically to the others.

Watson rose stiffly from the chair, keeping a cautious eye on Ehron Lee. He helped escort Evaline to the door before he halted. Evaline could no longer respond to all that had happened; the shock of what she'd experienced had thrust her beyond all comprehension. She had gone into a stupor where she no longer could rationalize or place significance on her situation or surroundings, including the body of her father. Watson, however, had shed all remnants of his professional demeanor as he looked with grief upon the sheet covering the lifeless form of his wife.

"She was a fine woman," he muttered. "She . . . never . . . deserved this."

There was nothing Ehron Lee could say, other than, "There's horses out in the corral."

Melinda held herself back. And then she stepped directly over to her husband and, gently cupping her hand over his, gazed tenderly at him, perhaps remembering. Cora had turned her head aside at Melinda's approach but didn't interfere with what she understood had to be shared between them.

"Come with us," Melinda softly urged Ehron Lee.

Ehron Lee reluctantly met her gaze and, once he did, offered a small, sad smile.

"Melinda," he said, carefully measuring his words. "We both know things can't ever be as they was before. At the very least I'd be goin' back to prison and I couldn't go through that hell ag'in. Reckon if they hanged me, it would be for the best. But maybe . . . maybe if'n you'd like, just hold on to some of those better memories we once had."

He gave a wink, and as his eyelid dropped, a single tear was released.

"I always have," Melinda assured him, speaking over a lump in her throat and squeezing his hand as her own eyes glistened.

Ehron Lee sighed as he tried to regain his composure. "Reckon if anythin', I'm glad we had this chance to . . . well, for me to know the truth. Can't make up for what went on here, but least makes it easier for me. But you gotta go on makin' that life for you and . . . and for young Charlie that you been buildin' for yourselves." He turned to Buck with a strained look. "And that's one more favor you can do me, Marshal."

Upon hearing those words, Melinda pressed herself close to Ehron Lee and wrapped her arms around him. As their bodies connected, it generated shared warmth. At once a dozen memories were evoked, each of which Melinda absorbed: the feel of his muscles next to her, his smell, the sound of his breathing. She didn't want to let go.

Ehron Lee wanted to reciprocate but he resisted. Not to take her into his arms for one last embrace was almost too much for him to bear. But he also knew that if he gave in to that urge, he could never let her go.

Buck understood Ehron Lee's request as he did Melinda's need to spend those moments with her husband, and he nodded and spoke his promise. "I'll make sure they're looked after."

Ehron Lee glanced over Melinda's shoulder and gave an appreciative nod in return.

Melinda kept herself nestled beside Ehron Lee until she realized that he would not budge from his decision. He would stay behind. Tears rolled freely down her cheeks as she finally ended the embrace and gave his hand a final squeeze before lifting her small, slight body to kiss him. Ehron Lee rocked his head in acknowledgment. He tightened his grip on her delicate fingers, maintained it . . . and then he released her.

"Go on," he said wearily.

It was clear to all of them that Ehron Lee knew he was dying, and that he'd chosen to accept his fate in his own way. No one could truly dispute his decision.

The small group stepped outside into the bright morning daylight and halted abruptly—startled by what they had never expected to encounter.

Like shadows maneuvering in a practiced silence, the

Chiricahua had surrounded the frontage of the cabin. The way they were positioned on their horses left no doubt that they were prepared for aggressive action. They sat not upon saddles but on blankets of varying color and design. All were bare-chested, and around their necks they wore primitive string collars decorated with what appeared to be beads and small fragments of bone. The younger men among them had their faces etched with war paint and bore spears, which were held upright.

Melinda's eyes widened. Fearful and uncertain, she pressed her body close to Buck and he wrapped his arm around her protectively. Evaline just stared at the Indians with a numb, uncomprehending expression. She neither knew nor cared whether they had come in friendship or aggression. George Watson understood this. He observed the girl with concern and reached over to take her hand in a comforting gesture. She did not resist, nor did she offer any show of acknowledgment of his touch.

The chief, who sat at the forefront, presented an intimidating figure. Yet he was also an educated man. He both could understand and speak the language of the white man. While he did not dismount from his horse, which stood as tall and proud as its rider, it was the dark-skinned, granite-visaged chief himself who presented the demand of his people. In his hand he held a long, feathered staff.

"Let it be understood among you that we wish not to make war," he stated formally. "We have killed only the white man who has crossed the grounds beyond the northern ridge of the mountains. He who has left his footprint upon the land we hold sacred and beneath which we have buried our dead. We have chosen by our council to let others live in peace." He paused to allow the intent of his words to be understood by the group.

When the chief next spoke, his voice was darker, making clear his purpose.

"But a debt must be paid by the one among you who has taken the life of our brother," he said. "He who has slain the son of a respected elder. What we seek is for the one who committed this act to come forward, to confess his crime, and pay the debt owed to our people. If that is agreed upon, we will permit the others to go free. No further blood need be shed."

No one responded to the grim ultimatum, which, in fact, none understood.

The chief waited patiently. He did not display an outward acknowledgment of the silence other than a tightening of his lips.

"The one who has guilt upon him must be punished by the laws dictated by our people," the chief further added. "Chiricahua law is strict and has long been observed. We seek flesh for flesh, blood for blood. If this confession is not made, we have decreed that all of you must suffer."

Again, no one spoke.

"Young Jishnu, which among these men killed Dahana?" the chief said to one of his warriors, waving a finger among the people standing outside the cabin.

The Indian youth who had been with the brave killed by Jess Colfax studiously looked over the small group. His expression was grim and intense, his narrow eyes squinted deeper into slits. He could not identify the man who had killed his friend for he had not remained long enough to positively know. Still, he was of a fierce pride and possessed of warrior blood and demanded to see that death avenged, whether or not the man guilty of the crime was among those people.

There also was another consideration, one which he had not shared with his tribe. He had fled the site of his friend's murder. He had displayed cowardice. As long as the killer lived, he would have to live with his shame—unless Chiricahua justice was served.

Cora stood watching through the kitchen window. She turned to Ehron Lee, who was growing ever weaker and paler from the blood loss his bandage could not contain, and she finally uttered his name in a gasp.

Ehron Lee turned to her and saw the fear darkening her expression.

Cora took two deep breaths before she uttered, "Chiricahuas."

Ehron Lee's forehead creased in a frown. With effort, he pulled himself from the chair and stumbled toward the window. The look on his face was vacant as he viewed the assembled warriors.

"My God, what are we gonna do?" Cora exclaimed, her voice tremulous.

Ehron Lee had no answer. He stood leaning his body forward, maintaining his balance with both hands braced against the counter. He held himself that way for several moments before he turned to Cora. He offered an enigmatic nod, and summoned the strength to slowly, painfully, limp toward the front door. Cora hesitated, then she followed, tentatively.

Upon stepping outside and holding himself steady against the doorframe, Ehron Lee looked into the stern, stoic features of the mounted Chiricahua braves and their chief. Almost immediately the young Indian named Jishnu pierced Ehron Lee with his dark-eyed stare.

He raised his arm and pointed a stiff, accusing finger.

"He . . . it is he who is responsible for Dahana."

Ehron Lee looked back at the brave. He detected death in the young man's eyes. While he could not understand the accusation placed upon him, neither did he dispute it.

Once more, the chief expressed his demand. His voice was calm, controlled, but his words were serious with intent. He again stated that the one responsible for the killing of the young brave must pay the penalty that the Chiricahua demanded; otherwise he would give the command for his warriors to exact retribution upon them all. Given their number and the determination expressed by each, the vengeance enforced promised to be swift, and would result in a massacre.

The chief's eyes leveled upon Ehron Lee and held firm. He lifted the feathered staff in a subtle yet resolute gesture.

"You are the one Jishnu says is responsible," he said, his

voice as stern as the expression embedded on his countenance.

Although a quick, puzzled furrow creased Ehron Lee's brow, he did not respond. Instead he looked at each of the people with whom he was standing. All of them had suffered because of a plan he had initiated and with which he had forged forward. He determined that the killings must finally end and that somehow there must be restitution. A payment to the sad-faced girl, Evaline, whose father had been killed before her eyes; George Watson, whose wife had been shot in a courageous attempt to bring to an end this madness perpetrated by both himself and Ward. Buck Leighton . . . and most especially Melinda.

Yes, he resolved, there had to be an end, and while Ehron Lee could not comprehend the condemnation thrust upon him by the Chiricahua, in a strange, fragmentary way he recognized it as another form of justice.

Still, only briefly succumbing to a moment of physical weakness, did he consider that the vengeance he had sought could be completed if he—he alone—permitted it to be . . . if he simply denied the accusation made against him by the young Chiricahua.

The notion passed quickly. Another thought overtook him. The legacy left to his son. Not only could he not deny his child a mother, but he could not allow a selfish action to further taint the memory his boy might someday have of the father he never knew.

He realized that perhaps this could . . . *would* be his redemption. The redemption he only just now was aware he sought.

As Cora inched beside him and he responded to her closeness by wrapping his arm around her shoulders, Ehron Lee felt the confidence to do what was needed—to, at least in part, set things right.

"I'm the man you seek," he stated with emphasis.

The others reacted with shock and surprise. Melinda could not accept her husband's confession, nor could Cora, who impulsively broke away from Ehron Lee's embrace to gaze upon him with a look of astonishment. She knew without a doubt that he was innocent. She knew that if anyone was responsible for the killing of which he was accused, it had to be Jess Colfax. He was the one who had gone off into the hills. He was the only one who could have encountered an Indian. No one else had strayed from the cabin.

Ehron Lee could read into what she was thinking. It was probably true. But Colfax was dead. The Chiricahua would not accept that. They needed a live body upon which to exact their vengeance.

Ehron Lee glanced upon his companions with a nod and a smile that suggested contented resignation. He had nothing to say. Even if he'd had the words, he would not speak them, for he understood there could be no real comfort to either Cora or Melinda. They had to know that by admitting his guilt, the Chiricahua would inflict upon him the most terrible punishment. Death, when it finally came after hours, perhaps days, would be merciful.

Yet his sacrifice would not be entirely selfless. He was confident that long before they reached the Chiricahua camp, he would be spared whatever fate the tribe had planned for him. He recognized that Ward had done him a favor when he'd stuck that knife into his leg. He was bleeding to death; the makeshift bandage Cora had fashioned was not stanching the flow of crimson. Without proper medical care, the wound would prove fatal. Already he was weak and groggy, and he could feel his heartbeat weaken with the slow yet steady pumping of blood as it coursed from his body. Maybe a half hour. Probably less.

It really made no difference. Not now. Not anymore.

He stepped away from the others and limped toward the waiting Indians. Although his leg was weak, Ehron Lee strode with a determined purpose each of his companions recognized. A strong hand was put forward and Ehron Lee took it and was helped onto the back of a horse by one of the Chiricahua braves. Ehron Lee allowed himself a final look at those he was leaving behind, and through his own red-blurring haze, he noted the tears of both Melinda and

Cora. They wept freely, but neither tried to interfere with the decision he had made. They . . . all of them, would now be allowed to go. Each had realized their freedom through Ehron Lee's courage . . . both in his defiance of Ward Crawford, and now by his bravery in making this final sacrifice.

Yet no one moved immediately. They all stood quietly, watching as the Chiricahua slowly turned their horses and, in their own silence, now no longer acknowledging those standing outside the cabin, rode off toward the beckoning depths of Brimstone Canyon.

Buck kept his eyes forward on the departing Indians as he tightened his embrace on Melinda and said with emotion, "When the day comes, don't ever be ashamed to tell your boy 'bout what his pa done."

The sadness in Melinda's features turned to strength as she, too, kept her gaze focused straight ahead, her memories intact, the pride that overwhelmed her firm and permanent.

"No," she replied solidly. "His son will know. He will know the truth. He'll grow up to be a man proud of who his father was. Neither of us will ever be ashamed of Ehron Lee Burrows."